ENCHANTRESS AWAKENS
BOOK TWO

THROUGH A SOMBER SKY

KRISTEN R. MOORE

Through A Somber Sky
Copyright © 2024 Kristen R. Moore

Cover design by nox.benedicta.art

Elora and Sorin art by Anamaria Sandru

Interior Formatting by Book Savvy Services

Edited by Brit Corley

Kirsgard Mountains
The Wicked Woods
Wickersham
Davenport
Galdosa River
Copenspire
S. Trinity Forest

Valebridge
Ramshire
Holden Sea
N

"Let me tell you something about wolves, child. When the snows fall and the white winds blow, the lone wolf dies, but the pack survives."

— GEORGE R.R. MARTIN

CONTENT WARNINGS

*To those of you who picked up a book about a broken Enchantress
and saw themselves reflected in her fragmented pieces.
Who fell in love with a hidden village in the woods and moonlit
dances and a merry band of misfits.
If you're still stuck in the broken bits of life, I hope this story helps
piece you back together.*

A Summary

Before we begin, let's take one last journey Through the Wicked Wood

King Roman Rudhek has banned all magick outside the Kingdom of Valebridge. Any Enchantress caught using her magick should be brought to his Majesty immediately. Any that fail to comply will meet their death.

After losing her mother and fiancé, Cade, against the royal guards and hunters on Kirsgard Mountain, Elora has found solitude in the Trinity Forest near the Galdosa River. She spends her days hunting, forging, and keeping out of King Roman's sight.

On a fateful afternoon, Sorin Trednik conned his way to the top of another poker game. Only this time, luck wasn't completely on his side. After a mad dash through Copenspire, with little other options, he plunged in the river in hopes of retreat on the other side.

After staving off two guards and escaping unscathed from two massive wolves, Elora helped Sorin to her cabin where they struck an accord.

She will help him into Valebridge, and he will help her

locate the Awakening Stones, the only conduit for awakening magick from Mother Gaia.

One horse theft and several days later, Sorin and Elora arrived in Loxley. A hidden village protected by wards deep in the Trinity Forest. There Elora learned that she is not the only Enchantress outside of Valebridge. Agnes, Sorin's mother, and Samaria, Sorin's sister were also Mother-blessed.

Jarek, Galen, Sorin, and Elora formed a plan to retrieve the Stones from the mountain. With the Stones, Samaria would have a chance to awaken the magick she'd longed for since birth and Elora would be able to protect them from landing in the hands of the corrupt king.

Plan in place, the crew set off across Teravie. After a quick stop in Wickersham, Sorin decided it best to avoid the coast and town of Ramshire, where King Roman had the largest outpost of guards stationed. Wanting to protect Samaira and Elora from possible capture, the crew ventured through the wicked wood.

But not before Elora learned of her power.

As a Dyrsjel, she contains not one, but two powers. Elemental magick flowed in her veins, giving her the ability to change one element into another.

The other side of her magick, the Dyrsjel side, granted her the ability to wield the Awakening Stones, giving her the power to guide Enchantresses into their magick.

The revelation of her new magick and wolf companions left Elora stunned. She was only just getting familiar with the wolves when she learned the truth of Sorin's past.

He is the half-brother to the corrupt King Roman and true heir to the crown.

Caught between wanting to flee and wanting to find the Awakening Stones, Elora ultimately decided the latter is more important. She must find the Stones before King Roman does, otherwise he may be able to access all of Mother Gaia's magick for himself.

The Wicked Wood is no easy feat and when the crew

entered, they knew there was no going back. Sorin reveals his past bargain with the wraith, Grawgeth. To save Samaria in their youth, he sold the last ten years of his life to the nymph and in return she let them live.

As it goes with most evil and wicked things, Grawgeth was not pleased to let them pass through without payment. All the while, the nymph has taken a particular notice of Elora, the last Dyrsjel.

After a dizzying spell of twists and turns, Elora found herself trapped within the wood with the nymph masking herself as her mother. Elora dug deep within herself to find the strength to do what she needed to do, and when she is on the verge of ending Grawgeth's life, another deal is struck. A deal that will change her life forever.

After narrowly escaping the wood, Sorin and Elora discovered their lives were entangled in more ways than one. In a memory from Sorin, it's revealed their mothers were friends long ago and in the same memory, there was talk of the Fates.

Neither Sorin or Elora could decipher what the memory meant, but their connection to each other has grown tenfold. Something is forcing their lives to cross and while they aren't certain the purpose of their fates, they were determined to figure it out together.

After Elora's injuries from the wood had healed, the crew planned to trek up to Nevek Peak and retrieve the Stones. But before they can, an accident with Ruse tore them apart.

Trapped in a deep trench, the wolf's injuries impaired her ability to walk and communicate with Elora. With no other choice, Elora traversed down the ditch to help Ruse.

All the while; Sorin, Sam, Jarek, and Galen fought a battle of their own.

Dozens of royal guards and hunters flooded the area around the trench, trapping them. While their efforts were grand, the crew ultimately ended up in capture.

With no weapons and a dampening on her magick, she felt

hopeless as the man she used to love, Cade, revealed himself as the mastermind behind her mother's demise.

After striking a bargain with King Roman for an escape from the mountain, Cade set the attack against Elora's mother up, hoping for both of their capture to bring to the king.

Elora is then forced up Kirsgard Mountain to retrieve the Awakening Stones. After the Stones are lifted from their resting place, she and the crows fight off the guards, leaving her to flee down the mountain.

All the while, Sorin, Jarek, and Sam woke to find themselves captured by the enemy. Fret neigh, our roguish thief had been bound by his wrists a time or two and broke free just in time to end their captor's lives.

As Elora fled from the mountain, an injury to her leg slowed her down. Alaric met her at the bottom, his stamina also drained from fighting. Not wanting him to get hurt further or risk the lives of any of the crew, she passed Alaric the Stones and surrendered herself to Cade.

With Galen missing, Sorin, Sam, and Jarek reconnected with Alaric and despite their instinct to stay and fight, the crew decided it best to head back to Wickersham and recoup before forming a new plan to save their friends.

Once back at Valebridge, Elora was thrown into the dungeons. She waited for King Roman to show himself but when a visitor finally came, it wasn't who she expected.

Galen stepped forth, shattering everything Elora thought she knew. With Elora's magick nullified from Galen's tonics and her body safely away from him, he explained the longevity of his plans.

First, find the Dyrsjel. Then, find the Awakening Stones. Lastly, use the two together to harvest any and all magick Mother Gaia had to offer in order to bring power to he and his partner, King Roman, and to bring justice for the murder of his sister.

Galen will show no mercy and will stop at nothing to get what he wants.

It's only a matter of time.

Part one:

—Hope—

ELWYN

They say it's a funny thing, fate. What's worse is knowing what fate has destined for you. Knowing you can't avoid it because you're a piece of a puzzle in someone else's life.

The panic from the vision I had only moments ago vanishes when I glance down at the babe still sleeping soundly in my arms.

For her, I will gladly meet my fate with open arms.

The moment she landed on my chest, the vision came, swift and blinding. It took me a moment to realize what it was I was seeing. Having just given birth, my mind was both muddled and euphoric from what my body endured. But now the vision is clear. My fate has been predetermined long before she was here, and even if I had a way around it, I wouldn't stop it. Not if it means she will live.

I just wish it didn't mean my death.

A knock at the door has the baby stirring in her sleep.

"Come in," I whisper, trying my best not to disrupt her further.

The door creaks open, and a scuff of heavy boots gives away my visitor's identity.

I keep my eyes on the babe. Keep my thoughts trained on anything other than the man who is now standing next to my bedside. His hand wraps around my forearm, but still, I don't look. "You're not supposed to be here."

He gives my arm a squeeze. "I know, Elwyn. I just had to see her once."

I don't fight the tears as they come. They drop onto my cheeks and run down my chin and neck.

He bends low to kiss my head. "Just once."

It's unusual for an arranger to continue seeking his Enchantress after the conception of a child. Even though it's outlawed for Enchantresses to marry, he always stole little moments of my time. And I've always been glad for it.

Only now, I wish he wasn't here. Wish I didn't have to tell him what I Saw. Who our daughter really is.

His hand glides up my arm until it cups my chin. "Won't you even look at me?"

Turning, I meet his gaze and my stomach drops. There is much to say about the man I love, but his kind eyes have always been the driving force behind my madness for him.

He smiles, but it does little to hide the sorrow lined in those eyes I adore so much. As if he already knows the fate neither of us can avoid. "It's her, isn't it?"

He strokes away the dark curls hanging in my face. I've told him many times throughout my pregnancy the suspicions I had. The dreams and visions I Saw. Never once wanting to believe them. Never once trusting what I knew to be true.

"She's—"

"Don't say it." If he says it, then it's real. I don't want to hear it aloud. I want to savor this moment. With him and her.

But the questions beg to be asked.

Why my daughter?

Why me?

But there is no denying the Fates. No denying what she must do or who she is. And certainly no denying Mother Gaia.

He bends down, placing kisses on both of my tear-stained cheeks before turning to our daughter, still sleeping bundled in a wool blanket next to me.

His hands find their way to my shoulders, pressing gently into the knots forming there. "What have you named her?"

"Elora," I whisper and run my fingers through her fuzzy golden hair, smiling up at him. "She looks like you."

His handsome face greets me back, but it's lined with something more serious and my stomach clenches at what's coming.

"Come with me." His grip on my shoulders tightens. "The two of you will be safe, whatever happens with the Fates we can deal with it."

I bite my lip to stifle a cry. Or a laugh at his absurd proposition. It isn't the first time he's asked me to leave Valebridge, but I do believe it will be the last.

"I can't leave, you know that. I'll keep her safe." I rest my hand atop his, still placed on my shoulder. "You don't need to worry—"

"Of course, I need to worry." He backs away. "I worry for her." He glances at Elora, then back at me. "I worry for *you*."

He steps closer again and cups his hands on either side of my face. His kiss is gentle. Laced with so many promises neither of us can keep.

I pull reluctantly away from him. "We're the safest here, in Valebridge," I say. "This is where Enchantresses belong, and this is where we'll stay. Whatever happens that leads to..." I can't say it. I've Seen it, but I can't say it.

My death.

"Whatever happens, if we need to flee, we'll know where to find refuge. We know where to find you."

His eyes soften, but his mouth is a hard line. He doesn't want to leave without us, but there isn't any way for us to go. It's forbidden for Enchantresses to leave Valebridge and after Celia and her boy left, I never heard from her again. I have no idea where to find her and couldn't risk leaving with Elora so young. My only duty now is to keep her safe. Keep her *alive*. And staying in the place I know best is the only way to do just that.

"I understand." He bends down to place a gentle kiss on our daughter's head. "Do you know who will guide her?" He swallows, maybe hoping to hide the crack in his voice, but I hear it clear as day. He's scared.

I am too.

Smiling, I run my finger down her velvety, rosy cheek. "Wolves, I think."

He chuckles, his fingers lightly dancing over her forehead. "Our little susi." His use of the word lights a fire in me. Hearing him speak Scandavi has always been a reminder that he has no real ties to Teravie, but he stayed.

For me.

Then for her.

And now he's losing us both. Perhaps the heartbreak will be the final push to get him to return home. A silver lining, if I can call it that.

"Be well, Elwyn." He kisses me again, long and slow.

Heat rises to my cheeks, and I'm grateful for his lips against mine to stifle the cry that begs to be let out. As he pulls away, I swallow the lump in my throat.

"I'll think of you, *both* of you, every day." His whispered promise heats my skin, his forehead pressed against mine. "Every night." Another kiss. "You know where to find me."

My heart cracks, but still, I don't move. Don't scream at him to stay as he inches for the door. Don't cry as his back finally turns and the door clicks shut. My arms are unsteady, my body shakes and convulses, but as Elora coos from beside me, all worry for what my future holds is lost. I smile at her before scooping her back into my arms and placing her against my bare chest.

I don't know when my death will happen; all I know is that

it's imminent. That Elora and Celia's boy, Sorin, will find each other and what they'll need to do is a worry for another day.

As I hold my baby in my arms, knowing what she is, who she is, I'm overcome with nothing but pride.

Death can wait, for tonight is about rejoicing in the miracle of life.

ONE

ELORA

I DREAMT OF THE FOREST TONIGHT.

Of the lush pine trees and familiar birdsong. I dreamt of the dizzying crows cawing overhead. A sound I often took for granted, now I'm desperate to hear.

Every night is the same. The forest and the trees and the birds. An occasional nightmare and muddied images I can't quite place.

But no matter how hard I try, my mother's never there.

I haven't dreamt of her in weeks, and I'm scared I'm forgetting. Forgetting her voice. Forgetting her touch and the magick only a mother's comfort can provide. Squeezing my eyes shut, I try again.

Dark hair.

Silver eyes.

But that's all I have.

Descriptors I'm not entirely sure are true. I wish I could see her. I've even tried to dream of the Wicked Wood, of the moment I got that final, false glimpse of her. But no matter how many attempts I make, she doesn't come.

Rolling my shoulders, I move from my bed and slink onto the cold floor, stretching my legs out in front of me. I rub my shackled wrists together, desperate for a bit of reprieve from the iron.

A hint of wetness has gathered in the cracks between the stone walls. The rainy season must have started. I've been here already much too long. Sighing, I close my eyes.

"I should just tell Galen about the Stones," I say aloud.

No.

"But Loxley—" I bite my bottom lip to keep myself from screaming. Galen's threat to burn Loxley feels like a direct failure on my part. So many people are at stake and for what? It wouldn't be the first time I've failed to keep my loved ones safe.

It isn't over yet, Enchantress.

I sigh again, resting my head against the wall.

I refuse to think too deeply about the voices I hear now. I fought them for so long in the Trinity Forest, and now that I've accepted them as a part of me, I don't allow myself to debate how sane it is to have conversations with myself.

"How can it not be over? His men are near Loxley. If Alaric brought Sam the Stones—"

Unless he's bluffing.

I chew the inside of my cheek, careful not to bite so hard as to break skin. But fatigue outweighs my anxious thoughts, so I close my eyes and picture a face instead. One that has no resistance coming forth in my mind. His strong jaw. His dark hair and heavy lids after we've kissed.

I miss you, I want to say, but I don't get the chance before the door at the top of the stairs swings open, and two pairs of boots come bounding down.

"Wake up." Galen's voice cuts through the thick silence that fills the darkness.

I'm already awake, but I may as well have been sleeping. There's nothing else to do in this Mother-forsaken cell.

"This is your last chance, Elora." He unlocks the cell and steps just barely inside. "I'm sure those in Loxley will be disappointed to hear their lives could've been spared had you cooperated."

A feral growl releases from deep inside me, and if it weren't for the restraints around my wrists, I would've found comfort in wrapping my hands around the delicate skin of his throat.

You need to keep it together, Elora.

A deep chuckle gurgles up my throat as I stare into the empty vats of Galen's eyes. I force myself to stand, then hobble toward him. My knee, while mostly healed from the night on Kirsgaurd Mountain, hasn't quite been the same.

He winces at the sound of my laughter. It's slight, but it's there, and I ready myself to bite.

"What's wrong, Galen?" I grit through my teeth. "Guilt eating you up? You know where Loxley is. You don't need me to—"

The sting of his knuckles across my cheek is a nice distraction from the throbbing of my head.

"Do you think I haven't checked Loxley myself? Haven't had hunters stationed around its ward? The Stones aren't there." He glances over his shoulder and gives a gesture to the guard behind him.

My heart races as I spot the small vial placed between his fingers, one I've become all too familiar with.

"Make this easy on yourself this time." Galen exits, leaving only me and the guard and the poison that will null any bit of strength I may have left. As if the iron around my wrists isn't already doing a great job of that.

Coward.

The guard's hands shake as he reaches for me. I smile, wide and feral, at the indent my teeth made on his hand the last time he came.

The guard moves swiftly, capturing me and forcing my jaw open. The tasteless tonic slides down my throat and when I try to spit it out, he holds my jaw tightly until I'm forced to swallow.

"Good girl," Galen says from safely behind the bars. "Now let's go, no time to waste." He whistles a tune as he skips up the stairs. The guard drags me behind him, and my head lolls.

Do not give up, susi.

THE ROOM IS the same as it was before. Sterile and cold, despite the oil lanterns lining the white walls. There are several metal work benches pushed against the walls. Each one is filled with glass vials and liquids of all colors.

The guard straps me to the metal bed, the iron stinging against the exposed skin of my neck. Galen whistles the same tune as he mixes various liquids together, a pungent sting hits my nose.

My heart races as the guard leaves and it's only Galen and I. The straps around my wrist rub against the open wounds from the shackles.

Galen stands over me, his icy eyes calculating. "Ready to cooperate?"

"Do I have a choice?"

He smiles, and the sight of it makes my skin crawl. "There's always a choice."

He props himself onto the table, crossing his arms over his chest. "When my sister was sick, the Healer had a choice." He pulls the enchanted blade from the belt on his waist. "They chose not to help her. They chose to let her die because what good was she to them?" He wipes the blade on his shirt, polishing it only for it to get dirtied again.

"She had no magick," he says. "Not an Enchantress, just a girl with a faulty heart." His eyes meet mine and for a moment there's something there. A small flicker of emotion that reminds me that despite the cruelty of the last few weeks, he was a child before all of this. A person with a family and hopes of his own.

"I have said it before"—I keep my eyes locked on the blade —"I'm sorry for your sister. But perhaps there was noth—"

"Don't," he snaps. "Don't defend them to me." He shakes his head. "She was everything to me." He runs the tip of the blade up and down my arm, carving a small line into my skin.

"You know," he says, "Rose was the only good thing in my life until one of you took her away." The blade hovers over the wounds on my wrists.

"We had a deal, she and I." He sighs, closing his eyes for a moment. My heart races, my eyes watching the knife. "We were to run away together." His eyes snap open. "I was finally going to be free of my father. *We* were finally going to be free of him." He shakes his head again. "But of course, that didn't happen. And I spent years and years under his scrutiny and fists alone."

The blade slides against my skin without warning, digging deep into my flesh. I cry out in pain, blood spilling onto the table. "Galen, please!"

He digs the blade farther and the enchantment it's laced sets to work.

Its poisonous magick seeps into my blood. Rooting and searching. Looking for something to take with it. I scream again as he angles the blade up and under my skin.

The tonic he's given me has silenced my magick but under the pain and the potion, something slithers inside of me. It retracts further into my being with every push of the blade.

After a few more moments, a few more desperate pleas, the pain sears through me and I'm tumbling into a pit of nothingness as darkness overtakes my vision.

Two

Sorin

"We're here, girl." I give Amis a quick rub on the nose before tying her to a nearby tree. We rode straight through from Wickersham, only stopping for necessities. She more than deserves the rest.

Despite it being the first weeks of Autumn, the forest is alive today with sun and birdsong. The yellowing leaves littering the ground and the crisp air, the only reminder of how long it's been since Elora and Galen were taken.

Weeks.

Much too many.

The thought of the two of them sends my heart racing, nerves stretching taught on my insides. I brush my hair out of my face, willing my hands to steady themselves so I can get back to work.

I take a deep inhale, savoring the chill that fills my lungs before focusing on the task at hand.

The object I'm looking for is warded using forest witch magick, much like that of Letty and Eviey's, but there is a small tell hidden amongst the foliage. One that is so subtle, it would be easily missed by anyone not familiar with the forest.

Squinting, I locate what I'm looking for through a small

crack in the bed of vines. The gold glistens in the late afternoon light.

Just like I remember.

Stepping forward, I glance back at Amis just once to make sure she's okay. My heart pinches at the sight of her. The wolves disappeared a few days after we made it to Wickersham, as soon as Ruse was well enough to walk. It broke me losing that piece of Elora, but a small part of me still hopes they're waiting for her. Doing whatever they can to be ready for when she's free.

The final thread of my sanity snapped the moment I laid eyes on Amis. Charles brought her with him from Loxley and now she feels like the last tether I have to Elora. Something tangible. A solid reminder that the time spent with Elora was real.

Amis grazes peacefully on the lush forest floor and with her contentment, I return my focus to the gold medallion. It's cool as I brush my thumb against it, a gentle thrum reverberates from the metal.

I take a step back and the ivy shifts, bends, and parts down the middle revealing a worn golden gate beneath it.

"Clever." I smirk. Someone will be here to greet me at any moment. I remove my bow from my back and straighten out my tunic, attempting to look put together and not as if I've been half awake for the last several weeks.

"What is your purpose?" The guard's voice is low and gruff, his eyes narrowed as he draws an arrow from his quiver and places it against his bowstring. He wears dark leathers and a peculiar cloth covering the lower half of his face.

I square my shoulders. "I've come to speak to Lord Thaddeus."

"Everyone that comes to the Jade Guild wishes to speak to Lord Thaddeus." The strings on his bow pull taught. "So, again, I ask you what is *your* purpose?"

Sighing, I run a hand down my face. I knew I'd be met with a bit of reluctance, but I have not the patience for it. The Jade

Guild, despite having locked their doors four years ago, is responsible for overseeing all of the Trinity Forest. Just as the Onyx Guild is responsible for the residents in all of the Kirsgaurd Mountain range. The Bloodstone Guild in charge of the dwellers and taboo cities of the Montrock Caves. And of course, The Cerulean Guild, who surveys the coast of all of Teravie.

Not that any of them have done anything to help the towns that reside in their respective Guilds during the blight or during Roman's reign.

"My *purpose*," I say, drawing out the word, hoping my irritation shows in my tone, "is to speak to Lord Thaddeus. None of the rest is quite frankly your business. Now, go on." I gesture him away. "Tell him Sorin Rudhek is here."

The guard shifts, his leather boots squealing. His blue eyes go wide for a moment before he shakes his head and clears his throat. "I don't care what your name is." The tip of his arrow is pointed through the gate, aimed directly at my chest. "Leave, now."

"Let me be very clear." I step forward, wrapping my hands around the gate and dipping my head to meet his eyes. Ignoring the slight stab of his arrowhead to my chest, I drop my voice low. "Go tell Lord Thaddeus that Sorin Rudhek from Loxley is here, or I will use your own weapon against you then drag you with me as I search the Guild until I find him."

I shove my hands in my pockets and take a step backward.

"Rudhek," he says with a roll of his eyes. "Wait here."

Minutes tick as I pace back and forth in front of the gate. The stone that makes up most of the Keep is partially covered in green ivy. The single tower looms overhead with an arched window overlooking the forest. The guard stationed there doesn't lower his arrow, but his eyes dart between myself and the entry.

Ignoring him, I rub my hand over the back of my neck. My shoulders ache from the constant tension but knowing Sam stayed in Wickersham to wait for the others offers some semblance of peace. The last couple of weeks have been torturous, but Agnes and the others from Loxley should arrive in Wickersham any day now. Together, we'll pull every ally we have, and together, we'll get Elora and Galen back.

"He'll see you." I flinch at the guard's voice, so lost in my thoughts. "Follow me."

He guides me through the stone keep, his body rigid, eyes glancing over his shoulders every so often. Likely to ensure I haven't wandered off. I chuckle and shove my hands in my pockets.

I'm not sure what they expect from me, but having a last name like Rudhek is sure to earn some uncertainty from strangers.

The thick vines from outside continue inside as we weave through a labyrinth of hallways. Bright yellow wildflowers tangle with the greens making for a beautiful, natural tapestry. At the end of the enclosed hallway, a large rectangular window lets in a shock of bright sunlight on this particularly bright Autumn day.

Before we make it to the end, the guard makes an abrupt left turn. Skidding to a stop, I peel my eyes from the sun shining through and turn to the guard. He's stopped in front of yet another ivy-covered wall. A man in similar garb joins him, and the two whisper back and forth for a moment.

My attention drifts to the Jade Guild. To the stone walls and endless forest that pours around it. The last time I was here with William, my adoptive father, was in my thirteenth year. He had a meeting scheduled with Lord Thaddeus to discuss a slough of crimes happening within the forest, and because Sam was busy training with Ulric, I got to attend with my father, alone. And I cherished every moment.

My stomach turns thinking of him. Thinking of how disappointed he'd be if he knew the years I let waste by. The people I've let down. Shaking myself free of the thought, I run my fingers across a few of the green vines scattered over the walls.

"Is Lord Thaddeus a big fan of ivy?"

The guard turns over his shoulder, brows furrowing. "Turn around."

"I don't like the sound of that." I laugh, taking a step backward to do what he's asked of me.

The ground shifts, and the horrible noise of stone scraping against stone makes my ears ring. Despite the guard's instruction, I spin to face the wall. It slides slowly apart to reveal a small, hidden room.

"Lord Thaddeus will see you now," the guard says.

Casting him another smile, I breeze past him, biting my tongue so as to not upset my already surly guide.

The sunlight beams through several large windows, filling the hidden room with warmth. Vines and foliage scatter across the glass but not thick enough to keep out the light. A cool breeze sends a few of the fallen leaves across the floor.

A throat clearing draws my attention, and there on the dais sits a throne of woven branches with Lord Thaddeus, perched like royalty.

He's just as I remember him, albeit significantly aged. His graying hair is swept back, barely gracing the tops of his shoulders. He dons the Jade Guild colors, wearing a green tunic with gold lining and dark breeches. His light eyes scour my face, the lines etched into his fair skin much more pronounced than when I saw him last just after my father died.

My jaw ticks at the memory. The sleepless nights I spent traveling here from Loxley. Begging Lord Thaddeus to show me the way to Valebridge. To help me take the throne. To avenge my mother. But just as Agnes always had, he denied each request.

"You're bold to show your face here, Rudhek."

"Are you surprised, Lord Thaddeus?" I smile, pushing the discomfort I feel in his presence away. Taking a step closer to the dais, I place my hands back in my pockets. "Did you think you could stay locked away forever?"

He scoffs and stands from his throne of branches. He takes the two steps down to the ground, pointing to a pair of wooden chairs surrounding a small, oak table. "Sit."

Once seated around the table, a woman sweeps by, dropping off a kettle of tea and two chipped mugs. Without speaking, she fills our cups, the steam hitting my cheeks in an instant.

At first glance, the room we're in is grand. Stunning greens and dripping yellow light. White-washed stone and a throne made of earth. But as I wait for my tea, I realize just how broken everything looks. The deep crack running through the center of the dais appears as though it could snap in two any given moment. Even the chairs we sit in are worn on the arms. The dress the woman wears is fraying on the edges, her sallow skin at such odds to her shining hair.

"The last time I saw you, I told you you'd achieve greatness," Lord Thaddeus says before pausing to take a sip of tea. "But that mouth of yours would doom you."

The woman makes her exit and my eyes trail after her golden hair, barely recognizing the words Thaddeus has spoken. My skin prickles, and I finally turn to him.

He glances at my arm, where my black shirt has been pushed up to my elbows. "I see the rumors of William's reckless son aren't true. You bear no ink from the curse of the Wicked Wood."

Oh, the rumors were *very* true.

I take a small sip of tea, the bitter taste of pine needles coats my throat as I swallow it down. "My point in being here is brief, but unfortunately, the terms are severe." I place my mug on the worn tabletop.

Lord Thaddeus eyes me for a moment before setting his cup down as well and crossing his arms across his chest. "You have five minutes."

My eyes narrow at his command.

"You aren't the king, Sorin Rudhek," Thaddeus says, "so don't expect me to treat you as such."

"That is my point, exactly." I take another sip of my tea. "You're one of the few that know my heritage. My father—William trusted you. And for many Winters aided your Guild and your people when the first uprising happened."

"That was decades ago." Thaddeus huffs a laugh, throwing his hands in the air. "We haven't needed help from anyone in years. We're managing fine."

I nod, taking in his moth-eaten tunic, the shake of his hand as he reaches for his tea, the slight sag of his shoulders when he leans forward.

The Jade Guild is anything but fine.

"You have shut off communication with King Roman for the last four years." I watch him intently. "Why?"

His cup lingers at his mouth. "For reasons that are none of your business."

"But they are my business. Everything that happens here is my business." I shoot him another smile, knowing damn well it will only frustrate him further.

"And why is that?" The table rattles as he slams down his cup. "William was a good man, and he helped the Jade Guild when we were desperate. But that was long ago, I don't owe you anything, and you do not *rule* anything except for that village of outcasts."

Twisting my father's ring on my fore finger, I grit my teeth. "You don't owe me anything, but what of the people in your jurisdiction? Who live right here in the Trinity Forest? Or have you forgotten them in the years since you locked up?"

A muscle feathers in his jaw, and his eyes drift to his lap. "My duty is to Valebridge. To ensure law and civility is upheld in the Trinity Forest and all of its towns. My duty is not to you despite how highly you may think of yourself."

"And yet you've closed your doors to the king? Haven't attended an Autumn Moon Ball in four years." I whistle and place my hands behind my head. "Perhaps your duties have changed?"

"Get on with it," he says, his lip snarling. "Tell me why you're here."

"My point is, surely there will be benefits to aiding the rightful heir to the throne." I place my hands back in my lap.

His eyes narrow slightly before his face relaxes. "So, you think it's time to take the throne?" He laughs, low and deep, and my fingers dig into my palms. "How can you be so certain the council will accept you?"

"Because you're going to help me," I say bluntly before braving another sip of the tea. "And so are the other Guilds."

A crease forms between his brows, but his body is unflinching.

"Listen, I wouldn't ask for your participation if there was another way. I know you've denied me in the past, but this can't go on any longer. Your removal from events in Valebridge must cease." I square my shoulders, feigning the confidence I know I'll need to win him over. "I need you to pull the other Guilds together for the Autumn Moon."

"Giving demands already?" He shakes his head, but I can't stop now. Not when there's so much on the line.

Not when Elora and Galen's lives are on the line.

I lean onto my elbows, so my face is closer, and my body is taller. "I understand your lack of interest in going to Valebridge. No one wants to bear witness to the horrors done there to the Enchantresses." My mind drifts to my Enchantress and the possible horrors she has already faced. Swallowing down the rising panic in my throat, I continue, "But we can't sit back any longer. We've wasted years hiding away like cowards. It's time to take a stand and time for change. I am that change."

A few beats of silence pass before he lets out a long, ragged sigh. "What is her name?"

Baffled, my body recoils back. "I beg your pardon?"

Thaddeus smiles, his eyes crinkling as he does. "The girl you seek to save. What is her name?"

My stomach flips, but I don't let my panic show. "Elora Leigh."

Nodding, Thaddeus reclines in his chair. "So, it's true," he mumbles.

"What—"

"You know my nephew, Evren, is about your age. Was always difficult to keep him locked down." Thaddeus smiles. "But he's here now. He is to be my heir, since I have sired none. And his wife…" He leans back in his chair, the shake of his hand more prominent than before. "His wife, Tallulah, is an Enchantress. Such a lovely girl."

I force myself to keep my composure. How he has any idea about Elora, and why he chose to harbor an Enchantress for his nephew yet denied my efforts to go to Valebridge all those years, is perplexing, but I don't press him for answers right now. I can't.

"All the more reason to help me get the throne," I say, my confidence resuming. "I'll put a stop to this madness, Thaddeus. I should have—" A knot forms in my throat thinking of all the years I've let slip by pretending the problems in Valebridge weren't my own. All the lives I didn't bother to save because I only saw what was right in front of me. "I should have put a stop to this years ago. *We* should have stopped this."

He runs a hand down his face before his weary eyes meet mine again. I can see the battle behind them, wanting to help but wanting to stay safe. It's the same battle I've had with myself for years. Desperately wanting to keep Sam and Agnes protected. Keep Loxley protected.

"You don't know what you're talking about, Rudhek. It was never as easy as bringing you to Valebridge." His eyes roam my face, his fingers laced together on the tabletop. "I assume you have a plan? I won't risk Tallulah or Evren being put in harm's way. They've been through enough."

Nodding, I finish off the bitter tea despite my instinct to throw it in a fire. My mind is reeling with questions I know he won't answer but nonetheless, relief unclenches my shoulders. For whatever reason, he's decided to help me, and right now, I need all the help I can get.

"Get me into Valebridge. Get the other Guilds to agree to attend the Autumn Moon Ball and fortify my decree as the rightful heir. Together we can stop Roman and then you and your family will have nothing to worry about. They'll be free. Tallulah, Elor–" I choke on her name. "They'll all be free."

Thaddeus steeples his hands, watching me over the tips of his fingers. The same scraping sound from before echoes through the room and I turn my head to see not the reckless boy I remember from my childhood, but a man.

His dark auburn hair is pulled back low at his nape, a few rogue waves hang around his face, framing his green eyes and freckled skin.

Evren.

Next to him is who I assume to be Tallulah. She's lovely with silky, onyx hair bound in two braids. Her glowing, tanned skin is enhanced by her lavender dress and the brightness of her blue eyes catch my breath. She doesn't smile, but grabs Evren's hand, keeping her eyes pinned on me.

"We'll help you," Evren says, his eyes trained on his uncle. His grip on his wife's hand tightens, her eyes bouncing between Thaddeus and I.

My gaze drifts back to Thaddeus who simply nods. Slumping back into my chair, my shoulders deflate. I'm one step closer to the throne.

One step closer to her.

THREE

SAMARIA

THE COFFEE IN MAHAFFEY'S PUB TASTES LIKE SEWAGE.

Seeing as it's the only option I have, I choke it back and wait for the rush of energy to kick in. The past two weeks have dragged as we've waited for Agnes and the others to join us in Wickersham. They should have been here much sooner, and each day that passes with their absence is torturous.

Every waking minute we spend idle has me itching with anxiousness. The Stones I've kept hidden in my pack ignite the magick beneath my skin, the feeling much like soaking in a hot bath when you've been out in the cold all day. But without Elora, I have no way of knowing just *what* magick waits for me or how to awaken it. I should be used to this feeling, having lived my entire thirty years knowing it was unlikely my magick would be awakened at all. But now, with the Stones so close, it feels more possible than ever.

My stomach sours, and I shake my head clear of the selfish thought. Elora is enduring Mother knows what in Valebridge and all I can think about is what I'll gain if we free her.

When we free her.

Despite knowing better, my head lifts from the table with

each chime of the bell on the pub door, hoping by some miracle Agnes or Letty's face will appear. In my darkest moments, I sometimes imagine Elora or Galen will appear instead.

The last image I have of Galen replays in my mind. His eyes widened with horror before my vision went black. Sorin swears he saw him thrown onto the back of a horse, but my mind has drifted to darker places. What if he never made it off the mountain?

A lump forms in my throat just as another chime from the bell rings. And, like a dog trained for obedience, I glance up from my empty cup. I'm immediately disappointed when it's just another passerby looking for a quick bite and a break from the rain.

"Another cup?" Jarek's hands are warm as they massage the back of my neck. I lean into his embrace, encouraging him to keep working the knots forming there.

I push my empty cup away and take a deep inhale through my nose in an attempt to relax. "I'm not sure my stomach can handle much more of this."

"I don't blame you, there." His nose scrunches as he downs the rest of the sludge the barkeep, Park, calls coffee and sets the empty cup on the wooden table.

"It's been too long," I say quietly and angle my body sideways to face him.

His fingers slide from my neck and land on my hips before tugging me closer.

"I know, my queen. Agnes and the others are bound to be here any day." His hand runs up and down my spine, and I know I shouldn't be frustrated with him, but I am. Jarek is the other half of my being and my love for him is endless, but his ability to keep calm in any situation infuriates me for all the wrong reasons.

But mostly, it's envy.

"Aren't you worried? What if something has happened to them?" I regret the edge that's laced in my words, but I'm too tired. Jarek knows me well enough to know I don't mean the harshness that's there.

"Of course I'm worried, Sam." His lips brush my forehead, a reminder he's right here with me. "But what good does it do to dwell?"

I blow air through my nose loud enough for him to hear, and he responds with that perfect smile that won me over all those years ago. His blue eyes captivate me, even the fine lines starting to form around the edges aid in his beauty. I run a finger over his tattooed knuckles that are placed across my lap. His sandy blonde hair is up in a knot, the usually close shaven sides have started to grow out, concealing the tattoos that adorn either side.

"I suppose you're right, dwelling is getting me nowhere." Resting my head on his shoulders, I close my eyes and try to imagine what it would be like *not* to be in a constant state of worry. How it must feel to face each day with a clear mind and not one that plays each way a situation can go *wrong* before it lands on what could go *right*. That is, if it ever lands there at all.

Must be nice.

The chime on the door slams louder than usual, and because I can't help myself, I pop my eyes open.

Charles' black cloak drips onto the pub floor, leaving small puddles to form at his boots. He's one of Sorin's right hand men in Wickersham, his tall frame and shaved head make him distinguishable even through the dreary rain.

"They're almost here," Charles says, walking toward us.

I tear myself from Jarek's warmth and slide out the opposite side of the large booth.

"You're certain?" My voice is weary as I head to where my cloak hangs on the wall.

"Got word from the stablemaster just now, they're due to arrive any minute." Charles nods.

My heart races as I pull my tight curls into a low bun, then secure my hood over my head. Jarek joins me, donning his cloak as well.

They're here. My mother and the others are here, and we're one step closer to getting Elora and Galen back. My fingers itch as I pull my bag onto my shoulder, the Stones still securely inside, and head out the door.

The walk to the stables is miserable in the downpour. I've always respected each of The Mother's four seasons but the constant rain that comes with Autumn is one thing I could do without. I smile despite it. Elora would probably love this gloomy weather.

We step into the small barn, our boots squelching, and my heart stammers as I see my mother, Letty, and Eviey dismounting their horses.

I feel like a child as I dart towards Agnes, but I can't help the swell of emotions that seeing her brings. Relief that she's here.

Guilt that she's here.

Her limp is more prominent than ever as she meets me half-way, confirming the guilt sitting low in my gut.

I should have never made her come all this way.

Wrapping my arms around her, I take a deep inhale of her familiar scent—peppermint and pine. A sense of home washes over me, and the feeling leaves me relieved and nostalgic.

She pulls me back and pats both of my cheeks with her cold hands. Her silver coiled curls spring free as she draws back her hood, and her amber eyes drift behind me to where I know Charles and Jarek stand.

"Sorin?" Her voice is hushed, and a pang of jealousy hits me that she hasn't asked how I'm doing before she asks about him. I should be used to everyone being in Sorin's favor, but it still hurts to see myself pushed aside. I love my brother, but I'll be damned if it doesn't hurt to be cast in such a large shadow.

"He'll be back in a few days. He seeks aid from the Jade

Guild." I try my best to keep my voice light as I grab her hand again and give it a squeeze of reassurance.

The last thing my mother needs is more worry, so I pull her in tightly to my side, rubbing her arm.

She nods but remains silent as we make our way out of the stables and into the gray rain.

BACK AT THE SHERWOOD INN, the walls of our room are suffocating as the six of us shuffle in, cupping and rubbing our hands together to warm the dampness from our bones.

"How was the ride in?" I ask cautiously, setting down a tray of tea from the pub on the only table in the room. The walls of the Inn are thin, and you can never be too certain who might be listening. While Loxley isn't a secret to all, it's a secret to most, and I wouldn't want to give away too much information to wandering ears.

"It was just as you'd expect." Agnes purses her lips and stretches her long, thin fingers near the fireplace. The different runes permanently inked across her brown knuckles make me smile. My mother's words are vague, but I know she has the same intuition as I do.

Be cautious.

I nod, shooting a glance at Jarek. I hand him one of the cups of tea and the other to Agnes. Letty and Eviey help themselves, making small talk with Charles on the opposite side of the room.

My mother has always been a fighter. Fierce and powerful yet kind and just. The perfect leader for Loxley, even when my father, William, was still at the helm. The two of them were the ideal pair. Their love for each other and their children is almost fearsome to those not in it. But today, as she sits across from me, she looks tired. The typical amber glow to her eyes is more dull than when I saw her last. And her limp...

"Where are they?" Her voice is quiet as she cups her mug with a slight tremble in her hands, not yet bringing it to her mouth. "The Stones?"

Her eyes remain on the fire, but Jarek and I catch each other's gaze only for a moment. His brows pinch together, and I know he's having the same concerns about her health that I am.

"They're here, in my bag." I stand to fetch the pack from Jarek, but before I can cross the room, Agnes grips my arm. Her eyes are glazed and milky white. Her nails dig into my tunic, piercing the soft flesh underneath. A shudder runs through me as I recognize what is about to happen.

A vision.

I steady my breathing and focus on the rise and fall of my chest as my mother's face transforms before me.

"*Not all those you trust are worthy.*" Her voice becomes a low howl, and in an instant Jarek is at my side. His palm is heavy on the small of my back, but my eyes stay focused on my mother's face.

"*Those who once were, are no longer. And those who are, will rise.*"

If it wasn't for my gray linen shirt, I'm certain her nails would have broken the skin on my arm.

Like a wave crashing into the shore, Agnes' features soften. Her eyes return to their soft honey; her brows relax as her shoulders unclench. Her grip lessons on my arm, but her touch lingers.

A soft whoosh of air escapes my lips as her fingers slide from my arm. I open my mouth to speak but all the words lodge in my throat.

Not all those you trust are worthy.

"Clear the room," Agnes snaps, though no one moves.

"Shouldn't we discuss this plan together?" I gently place a hand on my mother's shoulder.

"No."

Stubborn dragon. I peer at Letty and Eviey, fully expecting them to argue, but instead, they're already following Charles out the door.

"Let's get you two a hot meal," he says to the twins as the door clicks shut.

Good man.

Jarek, however, stands rooted. His eyes meet mine, and I nod, assuring him it's okay to stay.

With only myself, Jarek, and Agnes left in the room, we unwrap the Stones. My mother and I gasp as the four Stones lay openly on the bed, their magick pulsing through the air. Panic claws at my chest thinking of possible hunters nearby.

My eyes dart between Agnes and the Stones. "Should we really be risking taking them out?"

"Relax, Samaria." Agnes beams down at the four crystals. "With no Dyrsjel present, their magick won't be emitted." She turns to me, a slight smile slanting across her lips. "We're safe."

Safe.

"All this fuss for a bit of rock?" Jarek moves to grab the ruby Stone; fire.

As quick as a whip, Agnes reaches out and slaps the back of his hand.

"Don't touch!" She traces her fingers over each of the crystals but doesn't pick them up. "I'm sure the Mother is not pleased with the Stones being shoved in a bag, let alone being touched by a *man*." She cuts Jarek a scowl, then me.

"How was I supposed to know he couldn't touch them?" I ask. "It's not like I've received many history lessons on Enchantresses or the Awakening Stones."

The words are softly spoken, but Agnes' eyes narrow anyway. The bitterness of my sheltered upbringing rising to the surface.

"Where else were we supposed to put them?" Jarek asks,

flopping himself onto the bed. "Besides, didn't you say they were a bit useless without a Dyrsjel?"

"*Useless*?" Agnes and I both say in unison.

I may not have had many history lessons, but just from being in the presence of the Stones and knowing their power, they are anything but *useless*.

"Maybe that wasn't the right word." Jarek sighs, scratching a hand along his jaw. "Would it be best to leave you two alone?" His eyes find mine, desperation lining them.

Shaking my head, I walk over and place a kiss on his mouth. "Go," I say, gesturing to the door. "I'll meet you at the pub when we're through here."

He lets out a long breath like I've just relieved him of work for the day. Rolling my eyes, I kick him in the arse as he heads toward the door.

After he's gone, I rejoin my mother at the table where she's arranged the Stones; fire, earth, water, air. She cups her tea in one hand and uses the other to run delicate fingers along each vibrant Stone.

"They're truly amazing, aren't they?" she whispers, her eyes never leaving the Stones. She gazes at them with such admiration. My stomach twists at each line around her eyes and mouth. The tremble in her hands and the silver of her hair.

How has so much time gone by? I remember days from my childhood like they were yesterday. Agnes and my father, doting on each other in the way they always did. Kissing and playing. Before he got sick. Before we lost him.

"Yes," I finally say, taking a slow sip of my tea that's now gone cold.

She runs her finger across the blue Stone. "I wish your brother were here."

"Well I'm here, Mother, or have you already forgotten?" *Shite*. I wince; the words are out of my mouth before I can bite my tongue.

My mother's eyes snap to mine, the glow beneath them is faint but her irises flare as she watches me.

Clutching my mug, I tip it to my lips and swallow down the rest and avoid her gaze for as long as I can. I hate that my jealousy rears its head as ugly as a sprite. I hate that she sees right through me, and I *hate* that no matter how old I get, I cannot help but feel this way.

"Sam," Agnes says, shaking her head lightly. "Your brother's destiny is far greater than—"

"Yes," I cut her off, my exhaustion getting the best of me. "I'm all too aware of how important Sorin is." The bitterness sticks to my tongue. I've been told every day of my life since I was seven years old just how important he is. How we must protect him. How he is the true king. And I know I shouldn't take my frustrations out on my mother, but sometimes the child inside of me takes charge and I'm no longer thirty. I am shrunk down to a seven year old whose life was turned upside down. "What I need is for you to help formulate a plan to help get Sorin into Valebridge safely."

"Sit down, Sam." It's only when my mother uses her most stern tone do I realize that I've stood from my chair and have been pacing.

I glance down, picking at my fingers before I rejoin her at the table.

Her eyes scan my face for a moment, before she sighs. "Don't think for one second, I have more love for Sorin than I do for you."

Her words jolt me. They hit me so heavily that my body physically pushes away until my back is pressed firmly against the wooden chair in which I sit.

"That wasn't what I meant," I whisper.

Damn that inner child.

"Yes it was." Her tone softens, but her gaze doesn't. "The reason I have a more..." I glance up as she closes her eyes, breathing in deeply through her nose. When she opens them, there is no spark lining her irises. She clutches tightly to her teacup. "The reason I have a more fierce protection over your brother is because of *who* he is, Sam."

I nod, unable to find anything else to say.

"Please stay for a while. It would be good to catch up with my only daughter, because despite what she thinks, I have missed her very much." She loosens her grip on my arm but her fingers stay atop it.

"Okay, mum." I sigh, pushing away my cold teacup. "I'll stay."

Four

Roman

I wake before dawn, darkness still lining every corner of my chamber and yet for the first time in weeks, I feel rested. Galen's breaths tickle the back of my neck, his slender arms and legs intertwined in mine. I'm not sure what time he came back to my chambers, I must've been asleep already. He's always slipping away, planning his next move.

Our next move.

I don't ask questions when he's away. I suppose that's cowardly, to not ask questions, but I've never pretended to be brave. Even as a king.

"Why are you awake," Galen grumbles from behind me. He's always had a keen sense about him, knowing things when maybe he shouldn't. Like that I'm awake, when I should be sleeping. Or how I'm feeling when I haven't offered a word. His intuition is one of the first things that drew me to him.

"No idea." I turn to face him. His eyes pop open, and I scoot forward so my nose brushes against his. "You were gone awhile."

He nods but says nothing.

I run my hand through his hair, pushing the blonde locks out of his face, then down the side of his cheek until it rests upon his shoulder. I twist the hair at the nape of his neck. "When do you leave again?"

"After the Autumn Moon." Galen runs his hand along my bare arm. I close my eyes at the softness in his touch. Savoring it. "If the Guild's come this time, I want to be here for it. Having their support will change everything. I need you to convince them this time. Make them see our vision."

Now it's my turn to stay silent.

I don't want to talk about what I need to do. How I must convince the Guilds that we need their support to show the people of Valebridge that what we've been working toward is dignified. They have denied my invitation to the Autumn Moon for the last four years, have denied their duties to report to Valebridge on the happenings of their respective Guilds. Have disrespected me as their king.

The thought of their rejection yet again makes my stomach clench with nerves.

Galen strokes a piece of hair from my forehead, bringing forth a contented sigh and washing away any thoughts of self doubt. Reading my emotions like a book he's studied his entire life.

I revel in our quiet moments. His body is secure and strong next to mine. A lifeline through so many painful moments in years past.

Though our time together has been few and far between these days, it's so easy to get lost in it. To forget what is happening just outside my door, to my people.

"The Enchantresses are not your people." Galen once told me.

Maybe they're not.

Maybe there would have been an uprising after all, and if we hadn't been proactive, more people could have died. Far more than the first uprising before my time as King. More people just like his sister, Rose.

Galen has written us in a way of saviors, and I'm a fool to have believed him.

Perhaps I'm still a fool. Blatantly ignoring the harm we've done. Especially now with the new prisoner to deal with.

"We need to discuss—"

"No," Galen says. "No more discussion tonight."

His hand makes its way to the back of my neck as he draws me in. His lips find mine in the darkness with ease. His mouth is warm, soft, and I part my lips even further as the intensity of his kiss grows. I run my fingers through his hair again, gripping the strands and pulling him on top of me. "I have missed you," he says, lighting a fire in my stomach.

I need him closer, because I know when this ends, he'll be gone again. And we'll slip into our roles. Galen as the quiet leader of our plans, and I as the corrupt king leading a country that despises me.

I chase the thought away and bury my fears into kissing him. His strong hands run over my bare chest, through my hair. Every touch ignites fire upon my skin. I moan against his lips, our tongues meeting briefly as his hand wanders down my body, memorizing the sculpted muscles of his arms and torso. My stomach flips as he pulls at the strings of my pants, but my heart breaks just as violently.

He's leaving again.

He's done it again.

Hurt someone.

I push the thoughts into the farthest, most shadowed recesses of my mind, and I kiss him and kiss him, until I'm drowning in the touch of his skin and the taste of his tongue.

Everything else can wait, everything else is secondary.

Right now, there is only this.

Only him.

The sun has risen to mid sky by the time I make it out of bed, Galen up long before me. With only a few weeks until the Autumn Moon, there's so much work to be done. Invitations to be sent. But if we're to convince the Guilds we need their support, we must break ground on the Dyrsjel magick. Without it, our promises of unlimited power and magick will be unfulfilled and we can't risk losing more of their trust.

"I think I'll question the new prisoner myself," I say when I emerge from the bathing chamber.

"Oh?" Galen shouts from behind the wall, still finishing up in the bath.

"Perhaps it's time for a fresh set of eyes." Harvesting magick hasn't always been smooth. It was messy, at first, using the enchanted blade of Galen's own crafting to expel the magick inside each Enchantress. But with the years we've had to practice, Galen has practically mastered it.

All but this Dyrsjel it would seem.

I run my fingers over the purple amulet that hangs from my neck. It pulses against my touch, full of magick that was never meant to be mine.

Ours.

Wet slaps sound from the bathing chamber as Galen plants his feet on the marble floor. It takes only a few seconds until he's in my main room, nothing but a cloth wrapped loosely around his waist.

"Do you not trust that I'm handling it?" He crosses his arms and leans against the doorframe. "And why do you care how long it takes? I said it would be done and it will."

Why do *I care?*

Maybe because for the last five years Galen has withheld so much from me. Maybe because even though the magick we have harvested together has proven successful, and we have been able to wield it, I don't quite understand how this Dyrsjel magick has taken so long to harvest. Or maybe I care because I don't want anyone else to get hurt. Maybe because deep down a part of me wishes to be the one with the upper hand.

"Of course, I trust you can handle it." I slip into my dark blue tunic and pants. "But this is different. There's a much more powerful magick at hand here and seeing as how it's been weeks of failed attempts, maybe it's time to change things up. You can't always be doing *everything*, let me help."

I cast him a smile but it's left unreturned.

"I don't need your help with this." He turns and dresses himself quickly.

Heat spreads over my cheeks and down the back of my neck at how quickly he dismisses me.

"We need to stay our course," he says, finishing up the ties on his black shirt. "The plan has always been to find the Dyrsjel, then the Stones. Your involvement isn't needed for either of those things. I can handle harvesting her magick on my own."

"I am still your king," I say, squaring my shoulders. I hate the words as soon as they leave my mouth. Galen has never been a subject to me. He's my partner. The root of my heart. But his blatant dismissal lights a fire in my veins. Mostly because he knows how often I am already dismissed by others. I can handle it, the way people look at me. The whispers of inadequacy. But from him, it strikes deep, leaving me tending to a wound that has worked so long to heal.

His glacial eyes snap to mine. Then, his features soften and once more returns the man I love. "Of course, little bird."

His nickname sends a shiver down my spine.

My little bird, always trapped in a cage. Let me be the one to set you free.

He crosses the room so that he stands just inches away. "All I'm saying is you haven't always been fond of the part that comes next. Because her magick is so much more stubborn, we'll have to break her walls—"

"You mean hurt her." I cross my arms across my chest. I'm tired of these games. The twist of tongue that's intended to make me feel better about what we're doing, as if I cannot handle the full truth.

Galen's eyes shift again, narrowing, showing that other side of him I know lives just beneath the surface. "If it comes to that, then yes. We'll hurt her if we need to. But it's a small sacrifice for what we've been working toward." He plants his hand around my forearm. "Her magick will give us the power to wield the Stones and after that, we'll have no need for Enchantresses anymore. This will all be over. Justice will be paid and you, little bird, will be a very powerful man." Leaning forward, he places a gentle kiss on my lips.

He says it in such a way that I always believe what we are doing is for the good of the people. Guilt washes over me for questioning his motives. I know he mourns the loss of his sister. Wishes to rectify her untimely death at the hands of an inexperienced Enchantress Healer, but how many innocent lives is worth the loss of one?

"And what will you have me do?" I wriggle free of his grip. "Simply let the Enchantresses go? They will never forgive us."

"They won't need to." Galen cuts me short, making his point vividly clear.

They won't need to forgive us because when we have control of the Stones, the Enchantresses will cease to exist.

"You're talking about murdering...hundreds of people, Galen." My stomach twists itself into a tight knot. It isn't as though our hands have been clean all these years. We've killed many in the process of learning to harvest magick. And once their magick has been drained... But to line them up for execution... I shudder. "An entire population—"

"You once told me your greatest wish was to rule without the shadow of your father looming over you." Galen's voice drops as he backs away, resting against the large post of my bed. "This grants you that, Ro. This will give you all the power Silas could never dream of having. Not just in Valebridge, but in the world."

He pushes off the bed and takes a few strides toward me, closing the gap between us again.

He runs his hand down my face, before tucking it under my chin. "No one will ever doubt you again," he whispers before leaning in and planting a kiss on my neck. "No one will hurt you or question you or belittle you." His tongue glides over the soft skin of my throat before he kisses me deeply.

My stomach swirls and I fight with myself not to drag him to my bed right now.

His hands land on my hips, pulling me flush to his body. "You will have the advantage. You will have the *power*."

That single word is enough to snap me back to reality. I grasp his arms to keep them from running over my body, my fingers digging slightly into his muscled forearms.

"Does it give me all the power, my love?" I whisper, our breaths still intertwined and heavy. "Or does it give *you* all the power?"

Snarling he backs up again, running his hand down his face. "What is it about this Enchantress that has you so distressed?" He pulls at his hair, pacing the room. "I didn't hear you fight for the countless others."

He isn't wrong. I've played the part of corrupt king so well; I've started to believe that is just who I am. But now, with how different Galen has become... How much more volatile and secretive... I run my hands down my jaw. Somehow simultaneously wishing for the heat of his touch to disappear from my skin and ignite me further.

"Maybe I'm just tired." I shrug, moving to the settee to slip into my boots. I smooth the wrinkles from my shirt. Perhaps I should change it altogether before the commoners add disheveled to my list of inadequacies.

"Tired." Galen laughs, his head tipping back. "Tired of what, Ro? Tired of a country that takes what we're doing for granted?"

I pause, laces still pinned between my fingers.

Tired of a Kingdom that *resents* me.

Tired of hurting people.

Tired of lying to myself.

Tired of Galen leaving.

"Tired of..." I run my hands through my hair, attempting to tame the curly locks. "I'm tired of everything." I sigh, slouching against the settee. "The people are at unrest. The Guilds have shut me out—"

"I just got word this morning that the Jade Guild will attend the Autumn Moon. I can't imagine the other's responses will be much longer now." Crossing his arms, his mouth tips upward at the sides. Clearly proud of this information and turn of events he decided to withhold from me.

"How? We haven't sent invitations."

Galen shrugs. "I sent a page the day I returned to Valebridge. I'm not sure what's changed, but it's an opportunity we can't pass up. This is our chance to win them over. Force them to see the good we're doing by ridding Valebridge of Enchantresses and putting the magick into our *own* hands. With the Guilds on our side, it'll be easy to convince Scandavi and Hofin. Their soldiers have been restless, not to mention the people of Valebridge have been questioning more and more."

My jaw clenches. Of course he's right. Valebridge has been anything but united the last few years and the violent outbursts and frustrations against us, *me*, have been more notable. I can hardly pass through the courtyard without some profanity shouted my way.

"If we are backed by them," Galen continues, "the rest of the country will have no choice but to aid in our favor. *We* control our fates, remember?"

It's me who finally raises my voice this time. "How can you be so indifferent about the lives and people we are hurting?"

Galen flinches, his eyes widening slightly.

He studies me long enough for the silence to thicken

between us, and that nagging self doubt to sprout up again in my stomach.

When I'm about to apologize for raising my voice he lets out a long breath. "I am indifferent, Roman"—I flinch at the use of my full name, it sounds so formal coming from his mouth—"because *no one* was ever there to save us. We saved ourselves from the hands of our fathers and ignorance of our mothers." He cups my face in both of his palms.

"So why should I waste my life saving anyone else?"

FIVE
ELORA

A SHARP PAIN PIERCES MY ABDOMEN SO I CURL ONTO my side, hoping the pressure will give me a sense of fullness. Since the last failed attempt to harvest my magick, the meals sent to me have been more and more sparse. I have no doubt this is intentional. Galen is doing his best to whittle me down to nothing so that I'm more cooperative for harvesting.

It infuriates me that it's working.

I have never felt more weak, even in my darkest days after my mother died. And with her voice gone from my head, the tether I've become reliant on, it feels as though there's nothing keeping me afloat.

This is it. This is the moment I break.

My head spins, so I close my eyes, pushing against my stomach as tightly as I can. My consciousness drifts in and out, images taking hold in the otherwise dark corners of my cell that make me less and less certain what is real and what is inside my head.

I don't fight my body this time and let sleep take over. My dizziness subsides as I close my eyes and drift to sleep.

There's nothing before me but inky black.

"I'm here with you," a voice whispers against the back of my neck.

Spinning around, I stretch my hand out. "Sorin?"

I reach and I reach, but I can't find him.

"I've missed you, love." His voice ghosts across my skin. His fingers are feather-light against my jaw and even in the impermeable dark, his touch is familiar and comforting. "When this is all over, I promise we'll go away. Just you and me. Somewhere quiet, just like you like." His lips find mine, and my knees go slack. "But right now, you need to do this."

"Do what?" I ask, savoring the warmth of his body next to mine, even if I can't see it.

"I have to go." He kisses the back of my hand before slipping away from my reach. "I'll see you after."

"Wait." I grapple for his shirt, anything to grab onto but my hands swat around nothing but the darkness. "Don't leave." I rub my eyes, trying desperately to see but it's no use. "What do I need to do?"

I bolt awake, sweat settling on the back of my neck and upper lip. My lungs push against my chest, my hands trembling at my sides.

I rub my chest until my heart slows to a healthier rhythm, taking a few deep breaths. "Just a dream."

There's a creak from the door at the top of the stairs.

"Great," I mumble as I wait for Galen to join me in my cell. Wait for him to fill me with that awful tonic and wait for the guards to haul me up the stairs. My mind drifts to my dream, of Sorin's touch and his words.

There's a pause on the stairs, boots coming to a heavy stop, so I tilt my head to get a better listen. It's amazing what the body can do. Without much light, my hearing has sharpened. Whereas before my capture, I wouldn't have noticed how many people descended the stairs, now I can easily identify that there is only *one* set of boots instead of two. Peculiar given Galen never visits without a guard, too cowardly to face me alone.

The steps resume as the oil lantern on the wall flicks on and into the light of the flame steps not Galen, not a guard, but…

Sorin?

My stomach somersaults, all thoughts of hunger lost. My head spins. A man with dark hair and a sharp jaw begins to take shape through the dim light. I fight the urge to grip my chest. To soothe the crack splintering through. Pulling myself to my feet, I brace my hand against the wall for support.

"Hello," he says.

My chest deflates.

Not Sorin, but King Roman.

He stands casually on the other side of my cell, dressed in a navy top and dark leather pants. No armor, no extravagant garb, which I would have expected from the king. It's been years since I've been in Valebridge, and while Roman and I never met directly, my chest tightens at all the familiarity. While the angle of his face is so similar to Sorin, it's in Roman's eyes that lies the biggest difference. Bright green shining beneath full, furrowed brows.

He watches me, his eyes roaming over my face then down to my shackled wrists. "Do you not bow for your king?"

Scoffing, I take an unsteady step forward. "I'll bow to my king when I see him next."

I inch my way to the bars of my cell, glancing upward at Roman. He's taller than Sorin, but slimmer. His shadow incases me like an insect under a boot, but I'm not afraid of this man who claims to be the ruler of Teravie.

"Where is your partner?" I ask through gritted teeth. The voices in my head thunder loudly, their disapproval dripping with every syllable.

The king doesn't flinch, but a small smile twitches at his lips.

His silence grates me, so I ask him another question. "What do you want?"

Several more moments of weighted silence fill the small space between us, my fingernails dig into my palms.

"You know my brother," he finally says, more of a statement than a question.

His words catch the breath in my lungs, freezing them there. He crosses his arms, that slight smile stretching across his lips. I struggle to regain my focus. My eyes find his again, and it's only now that I remember his age. That he and I are merely a year apart.

Nodding, I hold my gaze. "Yes, I know Sorin."

A muscle feathers in his jaw when I mention Sorin's name. But he's quick to regain indifference, smoothing a few wrinkles from his tunic.

"Again I ask what is it that you want?" My stomach aches from hunger, but I ignore it, not wanting to give him the satisfaction of sitting or backing down.

He cocks his head to the side, his dark curls catching in the dim light. The same dark brown as Sorin's, and my stomach churns. "I want to know where he is. Where he *could* be."

I take a step backward, my laughter causing more pain to my already screaming stomach. "You're the king, find him yourself." I curl my lip, eyes narrowing.

If they haven't found Sorin, he must not be in Loxley.

All the possibilities of where Sorin and the others could be race through my mind, but Roman's quiet laughter brings my attention back to him. Uncrossing his arms and stretching them above his head, he grips the bars.

"Well aren't you a pretty, feral little thing." He smirks and when a small dimple forms on his right cheek, bile rises in my throat. "Galen said you were a handful."

"Don't speak his name to me." The words are venom from my tongue, and I wish for a moment I had Ruse's teeth instead of my own. Bigger teeth, bigger bite. My legs gives out, and I drop to the floor to rest my back against the bars so that I face away from Roman. "He's a snake and you are no better."

Roman *hmmm's* from behind me, his fingers tapping rhythmically against the iron bars. "Maybe that's true," he says. "But what good is a snake if there isn't a mouse. And you, mouse, have something I need."

My heartbeat quickens and my breaths become short and painful.

My magick.

He's come for a try at harvesting my Dyrsjel magick. It's only a matter of time before one of them is successful with it; they'll control the Stones. And the wolves... I bite my lip to stifle a cry.

Ruse.

I don't even know if she's alive and that scares me more than anything. Glancing at the scar on my arm, I shudder remembering the painful incision from the enchanted blade I'll have to endure again.

"So, is it that you've come to learn about Sorin's whereabouts or you've come to take a turn at harvesting my magick?" Steadying myself, I turn to face him again. "Which is it?"

Roman peers down at me, his smile is shy but there. Kneeling down, he joins me on the ground.

My brows raise. Odd for a man of his power to sit so comfortably upon the floor. I'm stunned as I watch him stretch his legs out, resting his head against the wall across from my cell, as if it were put here just for him.

"It's quiet down here," he says through a sigh.

"Is this a game to you? A way to pass the time? Shouldn't the king have something better to do?"

Roman laughs, the sound bouncing off the empty cavernous room. His smile is wide, cheeks dimpling. "No games, Dyrsjel," he says. "I haven't come to take your magick. Yet." Our eyes lock and it sends a wave of uncertainty through me. "Tell me of this brother, where he may be or what you think he's planning, and perhaps I'll pay you a favor."

"No."

Roman smiles again, quick and closed lipped. "Fine. If you won't tell me where you think he is, at least tell me *something* about him that could be useful."

My eyes narrow, arms crossed across my chest. "Feeling sentimental?"

"Something like that." Roman's face grows serious, the playful smile tucked away, and the stern look of a ruler snapped in place. "I'll up the ante," he says, stretching his arms again. "A hot meal, daily, in exchange for any sliver of information you're willing to give."

I lick my lips then bite the inside of my cheek so as to not do it again. "No."

His green eyes widen, something wicked dancing in them before he nods and stands. "Suit yourself."

My stomach growls, the pain cutting through my entire abdomen. As Roman moves farther away, panic sets in.

I haven't eaten in days. If I could get a meal, perhaps I could regain some of my strength. Would have better chances fighting the guards again when they come for me. And more than that, I don't have to tell Roman anything truthful about Sorin. I could easily spin a web of lies and throw him off course.

Roman takes three steps up the stairs, before I'm pulling myself up by the iron bars.

"Wait!"

Roman stops, turning to face me again.

"A hot meal." My stomach rumbles again. Sharpness scrapes at my insides and for a moment my vision goes white. "I'll tell you whatever you want to know about Sorin," I pant out, desperate to lie down, "if you can ensure I get a hot meal *daily*."

He has no reason to believe I'll tell him anything truthful so either he is naïve and careless, or he sees right through me, and I have yet to discover his intentions.

"Deal."

Six

Sorin

Autumn and all her glory has set through the forest as I ride my way back to Wickersham the following morning. After a fitful sleep and a meager breakfast, my body and mind are fighting for who is more exhausted.

I blink away the fatigue to bask in the colors of the leaves and the setting sun. Rich oranges dance along bright yellows and greens. A blanket made of fallen leaves litters the ground, squelching under each press of Amis' hooves. Closing my eyes, I listen to the call of the birds. I envision the maples that line Loxley's streets. Their vibrant rust-colored leaves lighting up our small village. The buzz of some nearby sprites lulls me further into my daydream. The exhaustion pulses through me, and as Amis sways up and over the next hill, my grip on the reins loosens. How easy it would be to sleep. How needed it would be...

A howl cuts through the birdsong.

Jolting forward, my eyes spring open. "Heel." Amis does so instantly, the soft padding of her hooves now silent. Craning my ear, I wait.

Another howl.

Still distant, but absolutely a howl. Pressing my heels into

Amis' sides, I steer her in the direction of the sound. "Go Amis." I press my heel harder until we're flying through the trees. Wet branches whip against my cheeks, spilling dewdrops into my hair and soaking my clothes.

But I won't stop.

More and more howls echo through the darkening forest, and it isn't until I'm closer do I contemplate that the howls may not belong to Ruse or Alaric. They could very well belong to another pack of wolves.

And I have just ridden myself directly to them.

My stomach sloshes with nerves as Amis presses forward. I crane my ear again, chest tightening.

Silence.

The wind picks up, pulling my hood back and stinging my ears and cheeks.

Come on. Please be you, Alaric.

At the edge of the clearing, I halt Amis. I hop down and don't bother tying her off. If we've stumbled upon a wolf den, she'll need to be able to defend herself. My boots skid to a stop in the underbelly of the forest as another sound vibrates off the trees.

Not a howl this time, but canine no doubt.

A few more yips, and I'm running toward it, leaving all concern behind me.

Yip, yip, yip goes the sound and I'm running and running, until I'm falling straight down a hill. Sliding, unable to catch myself against the slippery leaves, I dig my fingers into the earth to slow my fall, lungs stinging as I attempt to catch my breath. The yipping has ceased and before I look down, the hair on the back of my neck raises. Swallowing my fear and cursing my stupidity, I brace myself as I slip further onto the other side of the hill and closer to what lies at the bottom.

A wolf's den.

Shite.

Landing directly on my arse, I throw my hands to my back,

reaching for my bow, the feathered ends of my arrows giving me a false sense of confidence when I'm stopped short by a rather large, wet tongue lapping against my cheek. Opening my eyes, one at a time, I burst into a fit of laughter as Alaric stands above me, his massive gray and white frame looming in the waning sunlight.

"Thank the Mother," I say through a laugh, ignoring the fact that it very easily could have not been Alaric I ran into tonight. Standing, I brush off the dirt and leaves from my pants before reaching up to give the wolf a scratch behind the ears. "Where have you been, mate?"

He nuzzles my hand, and a rush of emotions hits me all at once.

If he's this far from Valebridge, does that mean he's giving up trying to get to Elora? My stomach drops, wishing desperately I had her gift and could speak to him the way she does. His amber eyes meet mine, and within them, I can see all the things he wants to say but can't.

He's never going to give up.

Just as I will never give up.

So why are you here?

He whines before licking my cheek again.

"I miss her too." His coat is thick and smooth under my hand and when a low grumble sounds from behind Alaric, my heart warms. I know that grumble. Have heard it many times.

"Ruse!" I want to run to her, but I know better than that.

Her emerald eyes narrow, but she makes no effort to move. Another grumbling nose vibrates up her throat and at that, Alaric moves past me and toward the den. Dark and deep, it's quite large but also quite discreet. Branches and leaves adorn the top and bottom. The opening is only large enough for the bodies of the massive wolves to move in and out of, not an inch more.

Alaric disappears, and I brave a glance at Ruse to my right. She hasn't moved. Sitting perfectly still, her eyes trained on me.

Swallowing thickly, I count the minutes before Alaric returns and try my best to ignore the narrowed gaze of the massive wolf next to me. As I'm about to give up and make my way back to Amis, a yip sounds from inside the den. The same noise that I heard just before tumbling down the hill.

It couldn't be.

Could it?

As Alaric emerges from the den, my eyes widen and jaw goes slack as four wolf pups stumble out behind him. Two gray and white pups, matching Alaric almost identically. The third, a deep brown with specks of white on its snout. Then my eyes focus on the last pup, the smallest. Pure black. Just like Ruse.

My gaze darts between Alaric, the pups, and Ruse's stony face to my right. The pups growl and snip at each other. Tiny masses of fur roll about the ground, tails wagging and bodies wiggling.

"Puppies?" I laugh again. Turning to Alaric, I pat his side, my smile wide. "You two have gone off and had yourself a litter?"

I shake my head, watching as the puppies pounce on each other. Ruse's disappearance after we returned to Wickersham makes so much more sense. Her cold and distant demeanor even before that, perhaps a way of protecting herself and her unborn litter. She must have been already pregnant when we traveled through the Wicked Wood and perhaps her instincts drove her here the moment she was healed.

I breathe a sigh of relief, knowing how much more painful her loss would have been had she not survived the injury the night Elora was taken.

But she did survive.

And now, their pack has grown.

I smile again, watching the pups clumsily sniff and wrestle with each other. It feels good to smile but quickly my mind drifts. Settling again on Elora and how much I know she'd love to see this. I glance at Ruse, her eyes still locked on me.

"You're a mum, Ruse." I take a step toward her. She doesn't move or make a sound, so I continue on. Reaching out, I let her sniff my palms, before I stroke her inky black fur. Her body tenses under my touch, but she doesn't run or turn away.

I stand at her side, watching as Alaric and the four pups tumble about. "Well done, girl."

AFTER A FEW FAILED attempts to communicate with the wolves, I conceded and left them with their litter in their den. The more distance that's placed between the wolves and me, the panic I've tried so hard to keep down creeps farther up my throat. Alaric and Ruse are a part of Elora, and leaving them behind feels like a betrayal. It feels like abandonment.

Stopping at the stables on the outskirts of Wickersham, I leave Amis for the night. She could use a long day of rest, and I could certainly stand for a bath after riding straight through. My boots slosh through various puddles as I head toward Mahaffey's.

The bell on the door chimes as I stride in, shaking the raindrops from my hair before peering around for my sister and mother. To my surprise, the pub is almost empty save for a few local patrons I've come to know over the years. Park catches my eye, giving me a quick nod as he finishes polishing the bartop. I slink into one of the wooden stools at the end of the bar and without a command, he slides me a tankard full of ale.

"Sam?" I ask before taking a long drink.

Park grunts, throwing his cleaning rag over his shoulder. "She's at the inn." He leans against the bartop. Park's a tall man, closer to Jarek's height than my own. His thick, blonde beard is trimmed shorter than usual, matching his neatly cropped hair. Strands of silver woven throughout, more prominent at his temples. "Your mother," he continues, and my head perks up, "Letty, Eviey, they're all here. They're all safe."

I let out a long breath before I take another drink. The ale isn't quite what I expected. Notes of cinnamon burst on my tongue, settling warm in my belly. "Any news or movement from Valebridge?" I drop my voice so only Park can hear.

He doesn't turn, keeping his attention focused on the task at hand, polishing the tankards.

"No," he whispers. "Everything has been—" He shrugs before setting the tankard down. "Normal." I nod then take another sip. "I imagine it went well enough with Thaddeus then?"

I polish off the rest of the delicious ale. It's sweet, a bit tarte. Is it apple? Either way, I know Elora would love it, and the thought turns my stomach sideways. "Thaddeus came around." I slide my empty tankard to Park. "I need to find Sam and Agnes. Keep your eyes open and your ear to the ground. As soon as you hear something—"

"I know, Sor," he says, reaching out to shake my hand.

My shoulders relax as I slide my hand from his firm grip. Park's been a friend and ally for years. He and his sister Jeanette have been vital in our illegal trades that keep Loxley afloat. I haven't given him enough credit. A pattern I seem to be repeating lately. Never appreciating those who do so much.

I open my mouth to tell him but before I can he takes a step backward. "Steal from the rich."

Smiling, I back up as well, inching closer to the door. "Even more from the richer."

SEVEN

SAMARIA

"AND SO, YOU'RE SAYING YOU KNEW CELIA WAS SICK when she arrived in Loxley with Sorin?"

Agnes nods, refilling our teacups for the dozenth time. We've been here for well over an hour, chatting, catching up. A rarity for the two of us to have so much time alone. At first I wasn't sure we'd have anything to talk about, but then, of course, the conversation drifted to Sorin and here we are.

"Yes," she says. "Celia was doomed the moment she left Valebridge, I'm afraid. But somehow the forest called to her. Loxley called to her. Or perhaps it was something grander than all of that, that allowed her to find us hidden in the woods."

My brows pinch, thinking of a tiny Sorin being dragged through the woods with a mother whose life was withering away before his eyes.

"Can I come in?" Whipping my head, I turn to the door where Sorin lingers. Water drips from his hair, his clothes just as damp. "Are you well?" he asks as he strides across the room. He bends down, giving Agnes a kiss on her cheek.

"I'm better now," she whispers, perhaps thinking I cannot hear her. As if sensing my thoughts, Sorin faces me with furrowed brows then back to Agnes.

"Is something wrong?" he asks, long and drawn out.

"Just tired, dear," Agnes says before I get the chance to answer.

"Same." I shrug. "I'm going to turn in, let's reconvene in the morning."

Before I can make it to the door, Sorin's hand grips my arm. "Don't you want to know how it went with Thaddeus?"

I pull my arm away. "I imagine things went well and that's why you're back so soon?"

Sorin says nothing as he watches me. Curiosity and perhaps a bit of frustration inked into all the sharp features of his face. I've never been one to be so distant, especially from him. He's my best friend. The brother I never thought I'd have. But the older I grow, the more I've come to realize just how much of my life—my childhood—was spent around his secret.

Around whom he is. The true heir to Valebridge.

"The Jade Guild will help us." Sorin's shoulders relax slightly. "I haven't a clue what made him change his mind." He moves to the bed, sitting down to pull off his boots. "All those years I begged for his help and now..." He runs a hand through his damp hair before glancing up at me. "Are you sure there's nothing wrong?"

"Nothing is wrong." Other than the fact that he can read me plainly. "Let's talk tomorrow." I shoot him a small smile, before I head down the hall to mine and Jarek's shared room.

I don't make it far, however, before he finds me. "Oh," I say through a laugh, bumping into Jarek. "I was just coming to look for you."

"Likewise." He grabs my hand, kissing the back of it. His blonde hair is tied up, his dark shirt tight against his broad chest and shoulders. "Long chat?"

He draws back and his eyes tell me he knows something's bothering me. But my relationship with Agnes has never been something I easily talk about. Fear of sounding like a petulant child cutting me short, so I bury down my resentment at being her other, less impressive child and smile at Jarek despite the falsity in it.

"Yes."

"Let's go." He takes my hand and drags me toward our room.

"What about the pub?"

"Forget the pub." Once we're inside, he latches the door. "What are you thinking about, my queen?" Jarek asks, helping me peel my clothes off, then his own. He tosses his shirt aside before scooping me up and carrying me to bed. A tiny spark ignites in my stomach.

"I'm thinking that I'm not that tired anymore." Propping myself up on my elbow, I kiss his cheek. Then his neck. He grumbles something in Scandavi before turning and kissing me deeply.

"You are a terrible liar, Samaria," he says before kissing me again.

I've never been able to hide my feelings from Jarek. He has a way of knowing me better than I know myself.

"Just usual mother daughter frustrations." My fingers trace the bumps and curves of his muscled arm. "She has a powerful way of making me feel insignificant."

Jarek grasps my hand, locking our fingers together. "You are anything but insignificant, Sam."

There goes that tiny spark again, growing much more rapidly now. I move to sit in Jarek's lap, my legs straddling either side of his hips. "Tell me again all the ways you love me."

He chuckles, running his fingers down my spine. His strong hands push the silky fabric of my camisole against my skin, causing delicious friction. "Will you believe me this time when I do?"

"No." I sigh, leaning forward so my head rests on his shoulder. I bite down slightly before placing a kiss there. "But tell me again anyway."

His hands trace lines down my back, his beard softly

scraping against the bare skin of my shoulder. "Do you remember when we first met?" he asks. I nod, closing my eyes, letting Jarek take control. It isn't an easy thing for me to give up; control. But Jarek is my safest place and with him I never feel any need to battle for authority. "I was running so fast I knocked your brother right on his arse." Jarek laughs, his entire body shaking as he does. But his grip around my waist tightens. "You helped Sorin up then looked right at me and said—"

"If the Mother blessed you with eyesight, I recommend you start using it." I smile, drawing idle circles with my fingertip across his shoulder blade. I'll never forget that moment. How frustrated I was to be running behind, how captivating this large man with eyes like the ocean was.

"Aye," Jarek mumbles against my neck before placing a kiss there. "But before you and Sorin turned away, you helped me up. You stuck out your hand and pulled me to my feet." He pulls me back so we're face to face. "I knew it then you were someone I needed to know. Not just wanted to know, but *needed*. And by the grace of the Mother, you told me to hurry on and follow you. That if I was in such a rush, I must be desperate for work." He smiles before placing a kiss on my lips. "It wasn't long after that I fell in love with you Sam. In *all* the ways that make you, you."

"Even the temper?"

"*Especially* the temper." He brushes a kiss to my bare shoulder. "I love the fire that makes up your soul." A shudder runs through me as his hands trail across my arms with feather-lite touch, causing the hair on my skin to raise until his hands settle on my hips again, pulling me closer to him.

"I love the way your body fits perfectly to mine." His hand slides across the curve of my hip and lands on the inside of my thigh, digging his fingers gently into my skin. The thin cloth of my undergarments is barely noticeable against his rough fingertips as he moves his hands closer to where I want them. My body takes over as my hips push forward in response to his touch.

"Most importantly"—he takes his free hand and uses it to cup under my chin, so I'm forced to look at him—"I love your fearless, beautiful heart, Samaria."

Tilting my head, he takes a deep kiss, parting my mouth with his own, biting slightly on my lower lip as he pulls away. All while his hand rubs firmly where it's anchored between my legs. "You wield your empathy like a weapon," he continues, flipping me on my back and settling over me. "You look into the darkness of others and instead of running from it, you question *why* it's there in the first place."

His fingers push away the small fabric of my undergarments, finding my center. A soft moan leaves me as I tilt my hips forward.

"You are soft and kind," Jarek continues, his fingers circling right where I need them to, "strong and compassionate."

Gripping his shoulders, my nails dig into his inked flesh.

"And there is *no one* in this world that is deserving of your full attention." His lips brush against my ear, his beard scratching against my cheek, and my breath hitches as he finally pushes into me. "Not even me, my queen."

My body heats from his touch, from his fingers working rhythmically inside of me, from the words I've made him repeat on numerous occasions for my comfort.

Maybe it's selfish to have him tell me again all the reasons he loves me, but his truth is the only one I care for. So often my mind plays tricks on me. Convincing me that the love others have for me isn't real. That I'm alone in this world, despite the reassurance I'm given that I'm not.

"I love you," I pant out, before he slides off the bed and onto his knees. He drags me forward by the back of my calves so I'm on the edge of the mattress before positioning his face between my legs. I prop myself on my elbows, biting my lip to stifle a moan as Jarek leaves a trail of kisses on either side of my inner thigh. I've seen many beautiful things in my life, but none quite measured to the sight of Jarek on his knees.

He swipes his tongue, his fingers and mouth working together, and it's enough to push me over the edge until I'm seeing stars. Once he's sure I've met my release, he crawls back up, cradling my body between his arms.

"I love you too, Samaria." He kisses me, and this time, the role reverses. It's me who takes control. I push him into the mattress and climb on top of him, placing kisses along his neck and shoulders. He moans my name and it's the last bit of encouragement I need before I join our bodies together. How could I ever doubt his love for me when I feel it in every part of his body. In every inch of his soul and in mine.

We are the same, he and I, and I am a silly girl to forget it.

EIGHT

ROMAN

"I NEED TO REST, GALEN." I KISS HIS DAMP FOREHEAD before rolling onto my back. My breaths are short and hot, but when his hand slides across me again, I lose all hope of going to sleep.

"No, you don't," he says before dragging me back on top of him. We are slick with sweat but it doesn't stop him from force-fully pulling me down for another kiss. I can't help the moan that's coaxed out of me, muffled between his mouth and mine.

I should tell him.

Tell him I have not been as loyal as he always says I am. That in my own way, I have defied the very thing we've been working toward. Galen's hands are strong as they draw lines down my back and through my hair.

I should tell him I made a deal with the Dyrsjel that will surely foil his plan of starving her into submission. But the moment the truth comes out, he'll be angry. Livid. It isn't as though he's never been angry with me before, it's something I've come to expect. But even still, the thought paralyzes me.

Tell him.

Tell him.

Curse this conscience of mine.

"Wait." I pull myself from him and roll onto my back.

"What is it?" he asks gently. So tender and still a bit breathless from our kiss. That spark of need coils again in my abdomen. Only for me is he soft in this way, and something about that shoots straight through me. For a moment, I debate abandoning my conscience altogether. Who needs morals with a man like Galen in your bed.

But, alas, no matter how many times I've worn the mask of the corrupt king, it always seems to fall.

"I need to tell you something." I run an unsteady hand through my hair.

Galen props himself on his elbow, his blonde hair a mess as well. "Surely it can wait." He leans over to kiss my neck.

"I gave the Dyrsjel food." I spit out the words quickly, not allowing myself another moment to change my mind. Galen's mouth pauses against my skin.

"And why would you do that?" His voice has switched again. Not a drop of tenderness. His blue eyes find mine, and there's no curiosity there. Only anger.

"She was starving, Galen. How do you expect to pull her magick if she's dead?"

His nostrils flare, but he says nothing before ripping the blanket back and hopping out of bed. "So, you undermined me? Went against what I ordered? What have I done to lose your trust?" There's genuine hurt in his tone and it makes my stomach sour. I have trusted Galen with everything the last six years. My life. My future. My heart. While the things he's done are not always things I agree with, he's done them for me.

For us.

I shoot from the bed and tug on his arm, forcing him to turn and face me. "I trust you, always."

His eyes narrow. He doesn't believe me. Why should he? Ever since the Dyrsjel arrived, I've made poor decision after poor decision. I can't even properly explain why. She's nothing to me. Sorin's nothing to me. Galen is all I have, so why am I so determined to ruin it? At the end of the day, what is the point of any of this if he is not by my side?

"Come back to bed," I whisper, running my hand down his cheek. I lean in for a kiss, but he pulls away.

The sharp lines of his body are prominent in the moonlight, his brows still pushed together. He remains silent as he begins dressing himself, my heart sinking with each layer of clothing he dons.

"Where are you going?"

"To fix this problem you've caused." Before I can argue, he storms out of the room.

Fucking conscience.

"YOU NEED TO WAKE UP." I tap on the iron bars before stepping back to rest against the stone walls of the dungeon. The Dyrsjel flinches, her gold eyes illuminating the dark corners of her cell. I wasn't sure if I'd find myself back here again, not after how angry Galen was that I gave her food, but after he stormed off last night, the fate of this Dyrsjel has gnawed at me.

The air in the dungeons is stagnant yet damp, making for the most peculiar and unpleasant odor. I'd hold my breath if I didn't have things to say.

"What do you want," she grumbles, not standing from her bed. I lit a second lantern this time, and the extra warmth it gives illuminates the bruises on the side of her face.

He certainly didn't go easy on her.

I look down to get away from the purple and red splotches, but when I do, my gaze lands on her wrists.

Red and bubbled from the iron shackles.

Swallowing thickly, I take a step forward. "I brought you this." I raise the small loaf of bread and canteen of water so she can get a proper look. I'll admit at first I wasn't sure requesting such items from the kitchen would work, but the handmaids brought it without question. Their conversation, minimal as it typically is.

Her eyes widen. Then, quickly, they snap shut. "Go away."

Sighing, I slide the loaf and canteen through the bars, making sure the cloth wrapped around the bread stays put. If Galen knew I was here again, I'm not sure what he'd do.

To her or to me.

But I knew what he was going to do last night. I knew, and didn't stop it, because if there's anything about me that's certain, it's that I'm a coward.

"I'm sorry about that." I point to her face though she still has her eyes closed. Silence presses down around us. I have only a few minutes to spare before my meeting with the council, so I make my next point brief. "I shouldn't have told him about our deal. But he's out for the day, he won't know I've been here."

I have no idea why I'm telling her this, but my shoulders unclench at my admission.

Her eyes open and she glances at me, then down to the food before sliding her gaze to me again.

"I've never been great at keeping secrets." I attempt to lighten the mood, but she doesn't flinch. Doesn't smile. She only watches me with those golden eyes. "I'll let you rest, enjoy the bread."

"You look like him." Her voice is so soft, I almost miss it.

My heartbeat races and fingers clench around the bars. She must notice my sudden nerves because she smiles. Not an affectionate smile, but one of hunger. One of a predator. "Your hair is the same color." She points to my head, and I absently run a hand through my dark tresses. "Your jawline is as sharp as a blade just like his." She joins me at the cell door, pushing the bread and canteen aside with her foot before gripping the bars.

My eyes fixate on the loaf until her shackles make a terrible clanging noise against the iron bars. She scours my face, and naturally, I want to shrink back. To hide in the shadows from which I came, but I hold my ground. I return her scrutinizing gaze just as intensely, making sure she remembers whose presence she's in.

Corrupt King.

"But there are differences about you." She tilts her head to the side. "You're taller." That earns her a smile which she doesn't return. "Your eyes are green and Sorin's are—" She stops to close her eyes. "Dark as night."

Her eyes snap back open, and I'm not sure if it's the flames from the lanterns or something else, but they flicker for a moment. Something otherworldly swirls in her irises, making my heart race. "You may be the king for now, Roman Rudhek," she whispers, leaning into the bars so her face is pressed against them, "but you will *never* be the man he is."

She smiles, a wolfish grin that has the hairs on my arms raising before she backs away. "Is there anything else you wish to know, my king?"

My words lodge in my throat. Embarrassed at how intimidated this Enchantress has made me feel. Angry that I've let her get under my skin. I don't answer her, I simply back away and head up the stairs. Her menacing laughter echoes throughout the chamber, and I have to hold my chest to steady myself.

Immediately, I'm no longer the King of Teravie. I am transported back to the helpless boy in my father's study.

Get out of here, Roman.

My steps increase, taking two stairs at a time as clouds of dark press into my peripherals. Bursting through the door at the top of the stairs, I slam it shut. I don't bother checking the lock before sprinting down the hallway and back to my chambers.

I shouldn't have asked to know about Sorin.

I should have kept my mouth shut and let Galen take care of things his way, just as he always has.

NINE

ELORA

ROMAN HASN'T BEEN BACK SINCE OUR LAST encounter nearly a week ago and to my surprise, neither has Galen. The food, however, hasn't stopped coming.

I run my fingers along the tip of the knife's blade one more time before shoving it under my pillow. I have no idea if Roman left it wrapped in the loaf of bread intentionally, or if it was a mishap. Either way, I hold it close every night. Waiting for the right moment to use it.

I swallow down the rest of my meal before I begin my exercise. I know they're only feeding me to keep me alive until they can find a way to harvest my magick, but I don't care. The food has given me a false sense of hope and now that I've gone so long without, I leave nothing to waste.

With the dizziness of starvation gone, I begin to use my endless amount of time alone to think of a way to get out of this cell. I work on stretching and moving my body. Rebuilding strength in my knee where it was injured and making sure my bones aren't too stiff.

Little by little pieces of my broken self start to come together. I don't have any way of looking at myself, but for the first time in a long time I know I'd be proud of my reflection. I have been burned to bits, and instead of remaining as rubble, I have taken the opportunity to grow. They say the Phoenix rises from the ashes...but they make no mention of how badly it burns along the way. Is this my moment to rise? To fight through the pain of the flames in the hopes I'll sprout wings? But what if the fire hasn't gifted me wings. What if, instead, I have grown claws and teeth.

So sharpen my teeth, I will.

After how long it's been, trying to reach out to Alaric seems futile. But seeing as how I've nothing better to do while I wait to be dragged back to that room, I try anyway.

Breathless from my exercise, I slide down until I'm sitting on the stone floor with my back pressed against the wall. The lantern flickers as I close my eyes and reach out for Alaric. The iron rubs against my wrists, a reminder that this *won't* work.

And yet, I try anyway.

Can you hear me?

Alaric?

After a few more unsuccessful attempts, my shoulders sag as my eyes pop open.

"Curse these damn shackles."

Be patient.

"No!" I scream and despite the soreness in my legs I stand and begin to pace. The vision of the knife under my pillow flashes in my mind.

No.

What I thought was left as a weapon to defend myself, I now realize is perhaps more of a test of will. I shake my head to rid it from the thought. Of the sharp point of the knife meeting the softest flesh of my wrist. I think of Roman and the satisfaction it would give.

"I need out of here!"

My voice echoes back to me, making me cringe as it hits my ears.

"I need air." I claw at the shackles around my wrists,

desperate for a reprieve but all it does is sting the areas that have already been ripped open.

My breaths come and go so quickly it's hardly as if I'm breathing at all. A sharp pain in my chest forms and with it, the darkness I've held off for so long creeps into the edges of my vision. My throat tightens and hands tremble.

I rip the knife from under my pillow and throw it across the cell. It hits the bars with a loud *clang*.

Shoving the pillow over my head, I welcome the darkness this time. I embrace the sweep of shadows as I close my eyes and lose myself to sleep.

"Can you see it, love?" Sorin's voice pulls my attention, and when I turn to him, he smiles, his white teeth flashing against his dark stubble. "Right there." He points just past my shoulder. I follow his finger until I see it.

A tiny yellow bird is perched on a low branch of a nearby pine.

A smile spreads over my face. "What is it?"

The bird sings, high chirps drifting through the woods. Its bright yellow and dark feathers are prominent in the otherwise gray and green surroundings.

"It's beautiful." I take a step closer, but heavy raindrops hit the branch. The bird flies away.

"A goldfinch." Sorin wraps his arms around my middle and kisses the side of my neck. "They are meant to bring good fortune."

I cast him a smile over my shoulder. "You believe that superstition?"

"Of course." He smiles, cheek dimpling just as the rain increases, soaking our hair and clothes. Laughing, he grabs my hand as we sprint through the forest.

"Some good fortune!" I yell over the rising storm.

"I never said good weather!" He laughs, his hand still clasped in mine.

Dark clouds roll in, blocking any light from beyond the pines. A gall of wind splits between us, breaking our hands apart.

"Sorin!" I stumble, tripping over an exposed root. "Sorin!"

The wind whips around me again, pulling at my hair, sending twigs and branches through the air. They bite and cut against my skin. I scream Sorin's name again, but through the storm and the darkness, he never answers.

TEN
SORIN

"I am not staying behind," Agnes says across the table from Sam, Jarek, and myself at Mahaffey's. She crosses her arms, her honey eyes piercing like daggers.

To avoid her gaze, I focus on the pub. Only a few patrons are here this early in the day. The constant rain from outside pounds on the door and slams against the windows. The blight is even more severe now that the colder weather has hit, but Jeanette was able to round up a few bowls of porridge to hold us over. I stir the creamy oats but don't take a bite, before I glance back at my mother.

Her eyes are still narrowed, her lips pursed.

"Mother," I say with a sigh. Stubborn dragon as always. A part of me wishes Ulric was here, I know he'd be on my side in this. "You're not staying *behind,* you're staying to make sure Park has all the help he needs. The people here look up to you. They know what you and William have done for them, you're an asset, and I need you here."

Sam mumbles something. I can't hear what she says, but still it grates my nerves.

"If you have something to say, Sam, by all means the floor is yours."

Her brows pinch together so, naturally, I cast her my best grin.

"You should stay here, Mum. Just as Sorin says." She looks to our mother before returning to her food.

I finish off the last of my bland porridge, a plan beginning to form. "Agnes, Letty, and Eviey will stay here to help Park rally those who are with us if the need for their help arises in Valebridge. Sam—" I turn to her, but she doesn't look up from her bowl, so I readjust and focus on Jarek. "You two will come back with me to the Jade Guild. There we'll work with Thaddeus and Evren to form a plan to get me into the castle for the Autumn Moon."

Sam pushes her empty bowl to the middle of the table. "You're awfully confident the council and Guilds will be willing to verify you as the rightful heir."

"And is my confidence a bad thing?"

"No." She looks me in the eye. "But it could be a dangerous thing. What if you go there, show them this piece of parchment, and they simply decide *not* to believe you. What then?"

My stomach knots. Of course that's a very real risk. It will be mine and Thaddeus' word, and our word only. But seeing as how distant the other Guilds have been since Roman has taken the throne, something tells me they'll be more than willing to listen. "That's a possibility. But verifying my birthright isn't the only reason we're going."

"Of course, I know that," she snaps.

"The horses are ready," Jeanette says, interrupting the rising tension around the table.

"Thank you," Jarek offers, his gaze darting between Sam and me.

"I will stay," Agnes says but not without a large huff of air first. "I'll help Park in whatever way I can. Ulric is manning Loxley and the three of you—" She makes a point to look each of us in the eye. "Go to the Jade Guild as quickly as the horses can carry you. A storm is coming, and you shouldn't be caught in it. Once there, form your plan. Send word using one of their men. We'll be ready should trouble arise."

I glance at Sam briefly, her brows are still pinched together but she nods.

"Okay, Mum," she says. Reserving her softness just for Agnes I see. "Be safe. I'm going to pack." She kisses our mother on the cheek before sliding out from the booth leaving Jarek, Agnes, and I at the table.

Before Sam can make it two steps toward the door, it flies open and in walks three men.

Sam freezes, her fists immediately clenched at her sides. She's never bothered to mask her brilliant fiery eyes while in Wickersham before, and now I can't recall if she had today. My chest squeezes when the strangers cross in front of her. Sam doesn't move as the men sit down at the bar, slinging their cloaks across the backs of their chairs. Three snarling grizzlies are stitched into the fabric.

Hunters for King Roman.

My heart races, my mind dizzying as to why they've decided to come to Wickersham of all places. They couldn't be here for Sam. She has no magick as of yet. Jarek shuffles next to me, drawing my attention. His hand rests upon the small blade on his hip. I slide my gaze to Agnes whose eyes are no longer the warm honey I'm so used to, but instead a milky white.

Shite.

A vision.

Magick.

"Mum." I slide into the spot beside Agnes. Shaking her shoulders, her eyes don't flutter. Don't change. I know there's no stopping this but with the hunters here...

Glancing up, I spot the three of them talking amongst each other at the bar. Park pours ale into large tankards. His eyes meet mine briefly, but he continues pouring. Chatting to them about the weather, distracting the men while Agnes has her vision.

"She has risen before, and she will rise again." Agnes' voice is loud. Much, much too loud. I hate myself for what I'm about to do, but what other choice do I have? *"The—"* I slam my hand across her mouth before she can say another word, turning her so she faces as far away from the hunters as possible. Her mouth moves behind my hand but the words are muffled and indecipherable. After a few excruciating seconds, her milky eyes begin to change, returning back to her warm tone. Bewildered, I forget to remove my hand before she swats me away. "Child, you best remove—"

"Hunters," I whisper, releasing my grip from her shoulders.

Her eyes go wide, but she remains quiet. Sam has returned to the table, the worry visible in the shake of her hands.

"Everyone relax and act normal. We'll wait another minute and then head for the door, *calmly*."

Agnes and Sam nod. Jarek, to my right, doesn't but I know he's with me. His eyes trained on the door.

"Now," I mouth.

One by one, each of us rises from the table. I smile at Park, bidding him good day. The hunters don't turn, too focused on their ale and talk of their travels.

Three steps to the door.

Sam trips behind me, stubbing the toe of her boot on a knot in the floor.

My stomach drops.

"Easy lass," one of the hunters says. I look over my shoulder, foam from his ale trapped in his long, red beard and the way he stares at Sam makes my fists clench. The other two chuckle before returning to their drinks. Jarek's face reddens, but he stays quiet as he helps Sam from the floor.

Two steps to the door.

"Ladies first." I gesture for Sam and Agnes to take the lead to get them out of here as quickly as possible. Agnes passes in front of me, but Sam remains between Jarek and I.

One step to the door.

Agnes reaches the door first, but before she can push it open, the cold metal of a blade presses against my throat.

"Did you really think we wouldn't know what she was?" the hunter behind me says.

My skin heats as my mother turns, her eyes blown wide. The blade digs against my throat as I turn to face the hunter, a few drops of blood trickling down onto my shirt. From my peripherals, Sam is in the same predicament. A blade tucked under her chin. And behind her, Jarek as well.

Shite. Shite. Shite.

"Let's all just calm down," Park says from behind the counter.

"Stay out of this, barkeep," the hunter holding Sam barks. "This Enchantress is the one breaking the law." He removes his blade from Sam's throat and points it at Agnes. "You are under arrest for the use of magick and to be handed over to—"

A loud guttural sound releases from Jarek as he flings his head backward, colliding it into the hutner's nose. Blood spews, coating the ground and the hunter's face. Screams erupt from inside the pub as patrons flee for the back door.

Here we go, then.

I follow suit, elbowing the hunter holding me in his gut. As he doubles over, the blade slips enough from my throat for me to maneuver away.

Park is up and over the counter before I can scream his name. His wooden club smashes into the back of the hunter who still holds Sam. She spins, now free from the hunter's grip, as her boot lands in the man's chest. He topples to the ground, and she kicks him again until his eyes roll to the back of his head. She goes to kick him again, but I take a step forward and grab her arm.

"Enough, Sam." Her eyes flare, fire igniting. Hatred and whatever pent up anger she has is letting loose on this man who dignifies hunting innocent Enchantresses. I share her rage, but now is not the time to linger. Jarek's fist collides with the last hunter's jaw, the final blow landing him face down on the floor.

"Jarek," Sam gasps, running to his side. Blood spills from his nose, but otherwise he seems to be okay.

"Drop your weapons."

My stomach curdles. I spin around, and my heart slams against my chest, the ache ricocheting deep into my bones.

"I said drop them." The third hunter, the one that was holding me, stands shakily with a dagger to Agnes' neck.

One by one, our weapons clatter to the floor. The two disabled hunters groan from the floor. Their faces and bodies, bloodied and bruised by the hands of my family.

But I didn't do my part.

I let this man stand and now he holds a blade to my mother's throat.

"It's my job to take this woman to the king. Anyone who stands in my way will be arrested for treason," the hunter says, his blade pressing deeper into my mother's skin.

Treason.

As if what Roman has been doing isn't treason itself.

"Arrested by who?" Jarek says from behind me. "Looks like you're out of men."

The hunter's lips turn up in a smile, and as if on cue, the door swings open and in comes not one, but five more hunters.

ELEVEN

SAMARIA

Everything in life seems to happen either very quickly, or very slowly. And at this moment, everything happens so very, very quickly.

One minute, I grasp Jarek in a hug, thankful he is alive; the next, I'm gripping my chest, terrified that I'm about to witness my mother be taken from me.

"This can be easy," the hunter holding Agnes says. The five other hunters now surround us completely. "Let us take the Enchantresses, and you men are free to go."

Jarek tenses behind me, his grip firm upon my shoulders, but the hunters have their weapons drawn. I glance at our weapons on the floor, but they're just out of reach.

Think, Sam. How do we get out of this?

"What's your name, hunter?" Sorin asks casually.

"Don't speak." The man's hand tightens around Agnes' mouth. "Hand over the other Enchantress and be on your way, or my men will—"

"We'll do no such thing." Sorin crosses his arms as though he's conversing with an old friend. "I have a better plan." He snaps his fingers, and I don't need to see him to know he's smiling. Cocky bastard. "You unhand my mother before I bury that blade of yours deep in your belly."

The hunter laughs, and it's then I know we're in for a very long fight. Jarek bristles behind me. Two hunters to our rear. Two to our left. One to our right, plus the one holding Agnes.

We've had worse odds.

"Kill them all." The hunter dips his chin before pushing open the door and slipping out with Agnes in tow.

"No!" I lunge forward, but a fist to my jaw has me stumbling backward before falling to the ground. My teeth clash together as blood pools in my mouth. Jarek shouts something from behind me that I can't decipher, then everything goes red.

Jarek scoops his ax from the ground, and before I can properly right myself, it's in the air. Swinging, he clips the leg of one of the hunters to our left. Screaming, the hunter falls but, in an instant, the rest surround Jarek. Their weapons drawn.

I pull myself up, shaking off the stars still dancing behind my eyes from the punch. The hunters have Jarek surrounded, but I don't have my bow.

Wickersham has always been our safe haven. A place I never needed to mask my eyes. Never had to worry about hunters. But now, they've found us.

My stomach churns. How long until they find Loxley?

Park grunts next to me as he and one of the hunters battles over his club.

I have seconds to scan the room to find any semblance of a weapon. Then, there it is. Sorin has one hunter pinned to a wall, his hands around the man's throat.

Typical.

But I use it to my advantage. Sprinting across the room, I pull the dagger I know is hidden in my brother's belt. Jarek shouts again, blood falling in pools to the ground. Is it his? Panic makes me question my ability, but it doesn't last long before adrenaline replaces it.

Lining the dagger up, I take a deep inhale before releasing the blade.

Time slows.

Sounds cease.

My eyes trail the dagger, hoping to the Mother I don't miss. Because if I miss, it'll hit Jarek instead. Sucking in a sharp breath, I sprint back across the room right as the blade lands in the side of the hunter's neck who had Jarek pinned.

He falls, and before he can get back up, I pull the blade out. The hunter holds his hand to his wound, but his life is over before he can muster a cry.

With one man standing, Sorin joins my side, caging me between Jarek and himself. Scuffling sounds behind me, but when I hear Park shout to Jeanette, my stomach unclenches.

No more surprises.

The hunter standing before us, merely a boy, looks around at the carnage brought forth by the three of us. He opens his mouth to speak, but nothing comes out.

"Go," Sorin barks, his dark eyes flaring under the pub's lanterns. The hunter drops his sword to the ground. His hands shake as he opens the door, but he waits until his boots hit dirt before he's running.

Sorin sighs, glancing around at the four dead men. "We need to hurry." He rolls his shoulders, his eyes darker than I've seen them before. "If they make it out of Wickersham, it'll be more difficult to find Agnes."

My mother's name snaps me back to reality and the guilt I have for killing that hunter quickly dissipates.

"Let's move. Now." It isn't often I see this side of Sorin. A natural born leader who isn't afraid to shed some blood.

"You got it, boss." Jarek wraps the wound on his arm with a rag from behind the bar. Nodding, I meet Sorin's eye.

We rush out of the pub, and I follow Sorin's lead. The entire incident lasted maybe minutes, but as I scan the quaint town of Wickersham, there's no Agnes in sight. No caravan. No horses.

"Sorin…"

"Stop." His voice is low, his predatory side fully inhabiting him now. Gone is my cheeky, pain in the arse brother. Straightening, I force my breathing to slow.

She's fine.

Agnes will be fine.

"There." Sorin points toward an alley pressed between the Sherwood Inn and another decaying brick building. Sorin takes off in a sprint across the muddy streets, his feet carrying him with grace. My jaw aches and blood still pools in my mouth from the brute who hit me, but I spit it out and follow him.

Jarek is close behind, his ax glued to his hand. My heart twists, realizing we've left those men for Park to clean up. And I know he will. His allegiance to my father and then to Sorin has always been strong. He respects them. Respects what they've done for villages like Loxley and Wickersham.

Steal from the rich, even more from the richer.

He's too good a man, Park Mahaffey, and I make a mental note to repay him somehow later.

Sorin disappears into the alley, it's dark from the rain but there at the end of it—

"If you take another step, I won't save her for the king. I'll kill her here and now."

As we get closer, I pull the bloodied dagger from my pocket. Jarek raises his ax, taking the time to give my shoulder a quick squeeze.

The hunter who took Agnes has a blade tucked under her chin, his back facing the opposite exit of the alley. Sorin already has his blade ready, I can't see his face, but I can tell from his energy that he isn't afraid to get his hands dirty for a second time today.

"Let her go," Sorin says, his voice breaking. Something in

his tone reminds me of defeat, and for a moment, I'm terrified. If Sorin feels defeated, we most certainly are.

Then I remember who my brother is.

The first rule of poker, Sam, is to play your opponent, not the cards.

It's a bluff.

Perhaps he's trying to fool the guard into thinking he's won.

Sorin drops his weapon, making a show by kicking it dramatically to the guards feet. Agnes meets my eye. There's no fear on her face. Only eerie calm. She even smiles, like she knows just what Sorin is doing as well.

"And your friends." The hunter gestures to Jarek and I. We drop our weapons onto the ground, splashes of mud flying into the air and landing on my boots.

"You've been spared your life," Sorin says, his voice cracking, as if he's torn apart by the situation and not raging mad. He truly is the best player. "Now please, spare my mother's." I can't see his face again, but I'd bet his smirk is replaced by false tears.

Anything to win.

The hunter's eyes are wide as his gaze bounces between our faces. I dare another glance at Agnes, and it's then I realize what Sorin has done. He's kicked his dagger hard enough to not just land at the hunter's feet, but my mother's feet.

Slowly, her foot digs into the muddy ground. Angled just enough under the blade that all she has to do is kick her foot up and it would spring in the air.

Clever bastard.

Sorin takes a step toward the hunter and Agnes but because he's unarmed, the hunter doesn't balk away as he did before. He doesn't move.

"This Enchantress is under arrest." There's a sense of unease in his tone now, his eyes darting between us.

All these men who have been fed falsehoods the last five years still believe what they're doing is for the good of the country. I refrain from scoffing, not daring to move another inch. Sorin hangs his head, his shoulders drop in false defeat.

"I know, I'm sorry," Sorin whispers. The hunter's grip on Agnes loosens slightly, distracted by his win. Pride is a devilish thing.

Play your opponent, not the cards.

Sorin looks up abruptly, his shoulders no longer hunched. My skin raises again, knowing just what he has planned. "I really am sorry." This time, he nods and Agnes takes her cue.

She kicks her boot, the dagger balanced on top of it flies into the air. Before the hunter can make sense of what's happening, Sorin catches it and takes the final step forward to the man that holds my mother. The hunter drops Agnes in desperation, as if hoping to defend himself, but he's too late. Before Agnes falls to her knees, Sorin has the blade embedded in the man's belly, digging it into him until he's pinned against the brick wall.

Just as he promised.

Rushing to Agnes' side, I pull her up into my arms and lead her out of the alley, leaving Sorin and Jarek to do what needs to be done.

TWELVE
ROMAN

WITH ONLY TWO WEEKS UNTIL THE AUTUMN MOON, there are no shortages of preparations that need to be handled. Galen has been distant since our last fight, and for the first time in our relationship, I haven't sought him out.

The amulet around my neck stings my skin as I wait for the council to arrive. My stomach turns remembering how many failed harvesting attempts it took to finally have a successful one. I wrap my fingers around the stone. The purple stone, held secure by gold hooks, slides easily up and down the delicate chain it's attached to.

The first time Galen *successfully* harvested magic into the amulet, I thought I might pass out from the rush of power alone. The necklace had been Galen's idea. Then again, so much of our plans have been his idea..

As soon as Galen wrapped the necklace around my neck, the Enchantress magick of Sight coursed through me. Visions of the past and future blurring together. It was impossible to decipher. Now that I have had years to practice, the visions are less diluted. The other magick we have stored inside the stone is still volatile, but useful when I can rein it in.

"Your Highness," a voice interrupts my thoughts. Glancing

up, I tuck the amulet under my shirt as my handmaid pulls the door back. "Can I bring you tea?"

I run my fingers through my hair and debate her seemingly innocent question. I should stay in the study. Have tea. Ready myself for a meeting with the council where they, again, will question how long we can expend our resources of hunters and guards in search for the Stones. But instead...

"No thank you." I wave a hand through the air. "I'll be going for a walk." She smiles before she leaves. I toy with the amulet again as I exit the study and head straight for the dungeons.

"WHY ARE YOU HERE?" the Dyrsjel asks as I settle onto the ground near her cell.

"I'm not entirely sure," I admit. She turns, the iron from her shackles clanking as she positions herself opposite me. "You look better than when I saw you last. Not as repugnant with all that bruising."

The crease between her brows deepens. "Is that a compliment?"

"Sure." I shrug. "Take the compliment."

"Charming," she mumbles. "Thank you for the bread." My stomach dips at the mention of the food I brought her last. The gift I left her. If Galen ever found out about it, he'd certainly go mad. Perhaps that's why I did it. My way of showing him I still have some control. Of proving to him that I am powerful on my own.

Maybe I'm trying to prove it to myself.

"You're welcome," I say, keeping my eyes on her hands. Making a note to not lean too close to her cell.

"I suppose you're really here to learn about Sorin." Her icy facade cracks when she says his name, her eyes casting down. "What do you want to know?"

The amulet around my chest pulses and burns against my skin, so I pull it and rub it between my fingers. "How did you meet him?"

She startles, jumping back slightly. "That is what you wish to know?"

"Yes." I smile at her, but she looks away too quickly to see it.

"We met on the river," she says, her eyes drifting shut. A quiet smile playing on her lips. "He was running from a fool's game of poker, and I happened to be where he ended up."

"Ah," I say. "So just by chance then?" Her eyes snap to mine but then she must notice the amulet because they drift to my chest.

"Yes, just by chance."

"And where might he be now?"

Her eyes narrow, the gold in them illuminated by the flickering light of the lanterns. "No idea, Your Majesty."

I tilt my head to the side, watching her for any signs or tells she might be lying. Restless fingers, wandering eyes. But her body is still, her eyes focused and clear. "My partner has told me a lot about the two of you." It's slight, but I don't miss the curl of her lip. "He says you two got to know each other fairly well in the few weeks before you arrived here."

"What is your point, Your Majesty."

I grip the bars, putting my face closer to hers. "My point is that he wouldn't lie to me. Which means you know Sorin well enough to know where he could be hiding. Maybe even know where the Stones are. I've helped you." I nod to the discarded cloth that once housed the bread. "Now you help me."

Her lips purse, her eyes still narrowed, but she says nothing else. I wait another few minutes in excruciating silence before I sigh and turn for the stairs.

"Roman." Caught off guard by such a casual title, I spin to look at her. "Sorin is smart, maybe not in the way that Galen is, but smart nonetheless. He'll never make it easy for you to find him. Or the Stones, if he has them." She bites her bottom lip, showing the only sign of worry since I arrived.

Nodding, I turn to leave again—

"The man that brought me in," she says, grabbing my attention. "Is he still alive?"

I pause on the steps to think for a moment, trying to remember who it was that eventually brought her to me. Then it hits me.

Cade. My guard long before he was an officer. His allegiance I've been meaning to thank, come to think of it.

I glance at her over my shoulder. "Yes."

She smiles, her hands sliding from the bars. "Good."

ELWYN

The merriment of the castle is infectious as the preparations begin for the Autumn Moon.

I'd be lying if I said I didn't house a certain excitement in my step as well. The Autumn Moon is the only celebration in Valebridge where outsiders attend, which means tonight, I'll see him. We've kept our encounters brief the last few years. Keeping to our usual hallways and hidden corners of the castle. But this year is different. I feel it in my heart.

In the five years since Elora was born, I've questioned my decision to stay in Valebridge almost every day. But never once has a premonition told me it wasn't safe here, and so here is where we've stayed.

And in all honesty, it's brought me so much joy watching Elora learn and grow alongside others just like her. Albeit, the lessons of which she's learning have been altered for her safety, she's learning all the same.

Lining up the tapered candles along the long dining tables, my heart pinches at the thought of Elora never knowing about her Dyrsjel lineage. Never knowing that it's the wolves outside the Valebridge walls calling to her every night, putting her to sleep. I've done my best to keep her magick hidden from King

Silas, and I'll continue to, if that means keeping her alive for whatever the Fates have planned for her.

As I put the last of the candles in place, I glance around the room. Navy and ivory ribbons hang from the grand chandeliers. The flickering light of the candles cast shadows along the marble walls. Smiling, I head toward the exit, and as I do, a handmaid rushes in with a dozen black roses.

You know where to find me.

My skin prickles thinking of him. Maybe I should have left with him all those years ago, but I had just birthed Elora. Had just Seen the vision of my fate. Had learned who our daughter was. I was terrified. Frozen in place. But it's been five years and nothing unusual has happened. Nothing grim. So tonight, I will tell my love the words he's wished to hear.

We're coming with you.

Eagerness and anticipation lead my steps. Tonight, the moon will be full and so will my heart.

"I WANT TO GO WITH YOU!" Elora shouts, her lip snarling up on one side.

Little wolf, indeed. Chuckling, I finish braiding her hair.

"It isn't a party for children, Elora. You'll stay here with Margerie. Come morning, I'll tell you all about it in so much detail it'll be as if you were there yourself."

She frowns again before reluctantly climbing into our shared bed. "Will you tell me my favorite story before you go?" Her golden eyes are wide, her bottom lip stuck out.

Laughing, I pull the covers up to her chin. "Only once this time, *susi.*" I point my finger at her and she nods with a sleepy grin. I know my daughter though, and it'll be at least three times before I'm able to slip down to the party.

Once she has settled onto her pillow, her breathing slowing,

I begin the story she admires so much. "It always begins the same. A storm, a crown, and a bargain made—"

"But how does it end, mama?" She yawns before rubbing her eyes.

"That *susi*, is a story yet to be told." I stroke her hair as she settles deeper into her pillow. "Now, once upon a time, there was an Enchantress who loved a little girl very much..."

With Elora snug in our bed, I slip out of the room and check the hallway mirror once more. I smile at my reflection. My silver eyes match the moon's full light. My beaded, navy gown swishes as I make my way to the grand hall, and my matching mask sits snugly across my nose and around my eyes.

The music fills the foyer and as the hall doors open, I'm hit with a symphony of sounds. Beautiful strings and high voices fill my ears. Dozens and dozens of people dance and sway under the firelit chandeliers.

My senses are immediately overwhelmed, but nothing could deter me from finding him. There, in the back corner, he stands alone. Donned all in black, including his satin mask. His hair, a familiar shade of gold, matches the hair lining his upper lip and over his chin.

My stomach swirls at the sight of him. I push past the revelers, my heart racing. He chats with someone I don't recognize, sipping from a heavy glass chalice. As I get closer, my stomach dips again. He finally sees me.

His eyes, the eyes that steal each of my dreams at night, find mine, and I'm lost. Lost in hope. In joy. In love.

We're coming with you.

I've rehearsed the words all year. Have repeated them over and over again until they no longer made sense. Words I should've said five years ago, but I was too afraid. Too uncertain of what the future held for Elora and myself.

Tonight an unwavering confidence fuels my every step. I'm ready to leave. To be a family. Ready to no longer fear repercussions should I leave Valebridge. His lips part, as I inch closer. I push my way past the final dancer before I'm directly before him.

"Elwyn," he whispers.

I wish to cry. Not of sadness but of happiness, just by hearing his voice. I have missed him every day. Every second. And I know he's missed me. I know he's missed Elora. Excitement makes my voice come out much higher than usual, but I don't care because tonight everything changes.

"We're—"

"Darling?" a woman's voice from behind me freezes the words on my tongue.

His eyes widen and replacing the admiration I saw only moments ago is fear. Shame?

"Darling, shall we dance?"

I don't turn to look at her. I can't.

He nods, looking past my shoulder and smiles. "Of course, just a moment, dear."

My skin heats, hands shaking at my sides, and as much as I wish to run away, I am rooted in place. Anger and jealousy and all the things I have no right to feel swarm in my belly. Tears sting my eyes, but I refuse to let them fall. This is what I asked for, isn't it? I told him to go. I refused to leave with him. Did I expect him to wait forever?

The music speeds and the noises of the dancers behind me gets raucous.

I need to leave.

Quickly.

As he walks by me to join the woman on the dance floor, his hand grazes mine. "I'm sorry."

Heat blooms with his touch and my body shivers. I don't let him speak another word. I head for the farthest exit of the grand hall. Avoiding the dance floor at all costs.

He has chosen someone else. Has started a new life. And I am here. Stuck inside these walls with a child I'll never see fully grow up.

After stopping and having a ridiculously long cry in the handmaid's restroom, I find the courage to brave the hallway to my chambers. As I round the final corner, what I see before me stops me in my place.

It's him. He's at our door.

No. No, no, no.

I sprint down the hall, ready to shove him out of the way when he clicks the door shut himself.

I pull his arm away from the door. "What are you doing?"

"El." He reaches for my hair, but I release my hold on his arm and slap his hand away.

"You need to leave." His eyes turn down. I've hurt him. Not tonight, but all those years ago. But what choice did I have, then? He doesn't know what I Saw. Doesn't know the fate I must live with. I was trying to *save* him from it while keeping Elora safe at the same time.

"I wanted to see her," he says, straightening himself. "Wanted to see you."

My eyes burn, but I force them to look at his hand. I need to know what I fear is true. And there it is. On his left finger, a black ring confirms what I suspected, bringing a weakness to my knees and a brick of lead to my stomach.

"You really should go." I turn my back, desperate to be out of this gown and done with this night, but a strong hand on my arm stops me.

"I wanted you to leave with me, Elwyn. I wanted this life only with you, do you not remember my pleas? Five years ago, and every year after, I begged you to come with me. Have dreamt of nothing else." His whispers tickle the back of my neck. I fight the urge to lean into his body. To encase myself in his warmth and scent. But I don't. "It's only ever been you."

"Except it hasn't," I say, swallowing down my own self pity. I continue to face the door. I don't want to see his face. Don't want to see every memory of us etched into it. "I have Elora to look after. Go before your wife starts to worry."

He releases his grip, but his fingers linger on my skin. He says nothing as he backs away, the warmth I was so desperate for immediately gone and out of reach.

I wait several moments before I turn to face where he'd been. Hoping by some sliver of insanity that he'll still be there. That I'll still be able to whisper those words to him I've dreamt about since the last Autumn Moon.

We're coming with you.

But he isn't there. He is long gone, and with him, my last bit of hope.

THIRTEEN
SORIN

THE ECHOING THUDS OF MY BOOTS ARE A REMINDER that I truly have lost my mind.

"Sorin?" Park says as I pass him in the hall.

I don't acknowledge him, don't stop, until I get to my room.

Slamming the door shut behind me, I finally glance down at the blood coating my hands. The sticky liquid is still hot and a wave of nausea hits me. Sprinting, I push open the bathroom door and thank the Mother there's water in the basin. I shiver as it splashes against my skin, but I don't stop rubbing until the entire basin is stained red and my hands and face are mostly clear.

I slump to the floor and rest my head on the back of the tub. It's been a long time since I killed a man with such brutality. The men on the mountain the night we lost Elora were one thing, the hunter in the alley just now... Likely a man just trying to feed his family.

Just like me.

Nausea hits me again, but I force it back with a few deep breaths.

"Can I come in?" Sam asks as she joins me in the bathing chamber, not waiting for an invitation.

"By all means," I groan. Even my voice sounds different. Tired. Drained.

Sam's brows bunch together, and I can only imagine how dreadful I must appear to earn that look.

"That bad?" I chuckle, pulling myself up from the floor.

She steps aside, making room for me to exit the washroom and slink into one of the chairs by the fireplace.

"Mum okay?" I shoot her a glance.

"She's fine." Sam joins me near the fire in the chair next to mine. "A little shaken up, but she's with the twins."

"Jarek?"

This breaks Sam's haze, her eyes light up. "He's helping Park clean up."

Fuck. I really am an arse.

"I should go—" I stand and turn for the door.

"No." Sam grabs my arm, pulling me back down. "They've got it, Sor I want to talk to you about the plan."

"The plan?" Laughing, I kick my feet out, so my legs are fully stretched. "We can save it until morning, Sam. Our mother was almost just taken. *You* could have been taken."

"We don't have time to wait until morning," she snaps. Her eyes pierce the side of my face, and I'm truly worried that if I look at her, a dagger will come shooting out and land between my eyes. "We need to leave tonight. More hunters will come, they always do."

"I don't disagree. I just thought you all could use the rest."

"Would you stop it?" She kicks me in the calf. "Stop acting like we're children in need of constant care. We've fought just as many battles as you, even Agnes."

"What have I done to deserve such bitterness, Sam? Since I returned yesterday it's been as though there's a viper in the room and I'm backed in a corner."

She snorts, the arrogant smirk we share playing on her lips.

"Nothing." She shrugs. "I want to leave in an hour before the sun fully sets."

"Giving orders, now?"

"Someone needs to." Before her words can fully sink in, she's headed out the door.

MY STOMACH TWISTS as I pull Amis to a stop about thirty minutes to the Jade Guild keep.

"Something wrong?" Jarek asks, my mother tucked in safely behind him. He pulls his horse to a stop next to mine. Sam joins us next, then Letty and Eviey on their shared horse.

"I need to check on something." I steer Amis off the trail, nudging her slightly to the grassy hillside to my left. "Agnes knows the way, I'll catch up."

"We should stick together," Jarek says. "It's getting dark and who knows how many hunters are patrolling."

"All the more reason for you to go. Get Sam and mum to the Jade Guild, I'll be there soon."

Amis chomps her bit, filling the silence stretching between us. The others pass glances at each other as if they're able to communicate without words. Sam leans forward, whispering something in Jarek's ear. I open my mouth to snap at them to move, but Jarek nods and leads the twins toward the Jade Guild. Sam, on the other hand, watches me with the viper-like gaze I've been avoiding since yesterday.

"What are you doing?"

"What are *you* doing?" she asks as she leads her black mare closer to me. "What are you going to look for?"

Rolling my eyes, I wish just for once that my sister isn't as stubborn as I am. "Fine," I say over my shoulder. "Try to keep up."

Her scoff is audible as I lead us right for the wolves.

The moment we crest the hill, yips and howls fill the air. Sam watches me as I slide off Amis and gesture to the hill. "Let's go."

She dismounts her mare then crosses her arms. "Is that what I think it is?" Her gaze has softened and now she looks reminiscent of the sister I'm so used to. The kind, soft, bright woman I admire so much. Smiling, I nod before sliding down the hill. Sam follows close behind, laughing as she topples to the ground.

Instantly, the pups are on us.

"Oh!" Sam laughs as one of the pups licks the entirety of her face. "Hello." Then all four pups scramble on top of her, making her laugh harder. She picks up the twin gray ones for a kiss. "Where did they come from?"

"From them." I catch the wild black pup before it can scurry away. It licks my hands and face with vigor, and I feel a laugh bubbling in my chest. Before I can let it out, I glance at the den. Alaric and Ruse emerge, their coats shining and eyes bright. Alaric yips, running to Sam and licking her face. Ruse, as always, keeps her composure. Keeping a watchful eye on the four pups still running about.

"This is incredible," Sam says, her voice breaking at the end. My attention shifts from Ruse to my sister, a few tears falling down her cheeks. For the first time in weeks, I think they're tears of happiness and a tiny fraction of the weight on my shoulders lessens.

The pups eventually leave us, retreating to the den with Ruse to feed. Sam and I sit with our backs perched against the grassy hill we slid down.

"Will they know where to find us if we leave them?" Sam asks, picking at a long piece of grass.

I rest my hands behind my head as Alaric nestles into my side. "I'm going to ask you something and I need you to truly consider it before you give me your answer." Sam's body tenses in my peripheral, but I keep my eyes on the den before us. "I want you to stay at the Jade Guild and look after the pups. I don't know how I'll do it, but I need to convince Alaric and Ruse to join me in Valebridge which means leaving the puppies behind."

I let out a long breath thinking of the miles and hurdles ahead of us until we get Elora and Galen back. "I need you to stay and help look after mum and the twins. Help look after them." I gesture to the wolf den where several snores begin to rise.

Sam is quiet for a few moments, so I glance at her. She's picked up a bundle of grass and is tearing the blades into small pieces. "Maybe this once you're right."

"Did I hear that correctly?"

She rolls her eyes before tossing the grass at me. It barely misses my face.

"There's nothing more I want than to get Elora and Galen out of there," she whispers. "But maybe it would be wise for Jarek and me to stay. Keep the Jade Guild protected in case anyone gets suspicious of their sudden appearance at the Autumn Moon. I'll do whatever I can do to keep the puppies safe."

"I know you will." I slide closer to take her hand. "And whatever it is I did—"

"Stop." She grips my hand tighter. "You didn't *do* anything. I think the entire situation has just been weighing on me. A good night's rest should help." Her smile is weak but it's there.

There are many reasons I am determined to take the throne, but seeing my sister no longer afraid to live freely is one of the biggest ones. There isn't anyone I trust more than Samaria Trednik, and tonight, I make a vow to myself, whatever happens, she will never live in fear again.

Fourteen

Samaria

"WE'RE STAYING BEHIND TO LOOK AFTER SOME fucking puppies?" Jarek slinks into our small bed at the Jade Guild. Tallulah, a fellow Enchantress I was surprised to meet, was kind enough to show us the way. She insisted we take the larger of the three spare rooms but even as the largest, it's tiny. Jarek's body takes up most of the space, but I can't say I mind having a room with walls detached from my mother and Sorin. A bit more privacy than we've had in a long time.

"Only for a little while," I say through a laugh. "We'll meet up with them at the Onyx Guild after the Autumn Moon."

Jarek grumbles something, running a hand through his beard.

"Besides, they're not just any puppies." I join him on the bed and tangle my arms around his. "Wolf puppies. Alaric and *Ruse's* puppies."

The rigid corners of his face go slack. He has a soft spot for Ruse after we helped her heal, and I knew he wouldn't be able to deny helping her again.

"Sorin's worried that if the royal guard catches wind of the wolves being near Valebridge, they'll try and trap them again and use them against Elora, so to be as discreet as possible, the puppies will need to stay."

Jarek leans back on the bed and the mattress gives way with a loud squeak. Sighing, I discard any hope of being together tonight without waking the entire Keep. Jarek may be the most gentle-natured man I've ever met, but he sure as hell doesn't make love like it.

"And he thinks Ruse is going to willingly leave her litter?" He shakes his head. "Your brother really is a cocky bastard."

Shrugging, I gesture for him to lay back farther. When he does, I curl into his side and rest my head on his chest. He's not wrong about Sorin, but despite his arrogance, he has a gift. He could talk his way out of any corner.

"If there's anyone to convince two wolves to follow him, it's Sorin." Yawning, I reach across him and twist his long, blonde locks through my fingers as we drift off to sleep. "We'll find a way. We always do."

THE IVY that covers the walls of the Jade Guild brushes against my arm as I walk the hall to the main room where we're meeting the rest of the crew.

I run my hand along the wall, letting the leaves tickle my fingers. The small round window at the end gives away how gray it is outside today. Not unusual for this time of year, but the dreary clouds and thick droplets of rain against the window-pane signal just how much time has passed since Elora and Galen were taken.

"Ready for this?" Jarek asks, taking my hand.

I stare at the window a bit longer, a part of me wistful and dreaming about just a few weeks ago when the forest was soaked in sunlight. When we were all together. Jarek squeezes my hand, so I peel my eyes from the window and look at him.

"Ready."

Voices compete with each other as Jarek and I enter the meeting room. The walls here are covered in ivy as well, but not as dense as the halls, leaving tiny splinters of the limestone underneath.

"This is a terrible plan," Agnes says, her hands held firmly on her hips.

Sorin's face is just as stern as our mother's. "Well, it's the only one we have."

"What are we walking into?" Jarek whispers.

I disregard his question and head straight into the chaos. Even though Agnes and Sorin are not blood, they've always argued as such, and I, as the oldest sister, have grown quite accustomed to playing mediator.

"Fighting already?" I pour myself a cup of hot tea, I settle into a wooden chair and watch as the two of them glare at each other.

"Mum thinks me sneaking into Valebridge is a terrible plan." Sorin turns to me, clearly looking for some sort of sibling comradery. Typically, I'd be more than happy to side with him. That's what siblings do. Look after each other. But sometimes it's too tempting to ruffle his perfect feathers every once in a while.

"Perhaps she isn't wrong." I take a slow sip of tea as the rising anger reaches Sorin's face, tinting it red.

Hit my target.

Jarek pulls up a chair across from me, kicking me lightly under the table.

"Really, Sam?" Sorin mumbles, pushing past me toward the table with tea and a few meager platters of bread and fruit. I laugh, taking another sip of tea.

"All I'm suggesting is you don't go alone," Agnes says.

"He won't be." The four of us turn to find Thaddeus, Evren, and Tallulah at the entrance of the main room. "I'll be going, Agnes," Thaddeus says.

The three of them join us at the table. "Good morning," Tallulah says quietly enough that only I respond with a smile. Her dark hair is braided, a few wisps brushing her defined cheekbones.

"Of course, Thaddeus." Agnes' voice and eyes soften, but her hands grip tightly to her skirts. "You understand a mother's need to protect her son."

My eyes drift back and forth between Agnes and Thaddeus. He nods, making his understanding clear.

"We leave in two days," Thaddeus says. The seven of us cram around the small table, sipping tea and pretending like our plan isn't absolutely impossible. "After the Autumn Moon, we'll head to the Onyx Guild. You all may meet us there if you'd like. I have business with the Lord there and it will give us time to form yet another plan. "

Agnes crosses her arms, nodding slightly.

"And which plan is that?" Evren asks, his voice is low and gravelly. The pinch between his brow lessens only when Tallulah takes his hand.

"The plan to get that imposter off the throne." Thaddeus scoffs. "The Lord of the Onyx Guild is a trusted ally whose political views align with our own. He's been informed of our arrival and looks forward to meeting the true heir." He shoots Sorin a grin, and I bite the inside of my cheek to stop myself from making a snide remark.

"The Autumn Moon is quite the spectacle in Valebridge," Thaddeus continues. "But because our presence has been lacking the last four years"—he cuts a glance to Tallulah who smiles—"it will be extremely important to get our story straight. I don't know King Roman as well as I knew Silas, but from what I've heard, he can be a bit temperamental."

Before I can think better of it, the chuckle is out of my mouth.

"Something funny, Sam?" Sorin asks, his eyes like daggers. Still bitter about earlier, I see. Perhaps it's time to cut him some slack. Shaking my head, I fake a cough before reaching for my tea.

What's funny, of course, is how similar Roman and Sorin truly sound.

"How can you be certain you can trust the Lord of the Onyx Guild?" I pour another cup of tea. I take a small sip, hiding my curling lip behind my cup. Mother, I wish we had some coffee.

"Well." Thaddeus stretches his long, thin fingers. "When he heard of the mistreatment of Enchantresses in Valebridge, he locked up his doors just as we did."

"Technically," Evren interjects, "you waited an entire year before locking up."

"And so, you pride yourself on hiding here safely?" I glance between Evren and Thaddeus. Heat rising to my cheeks and the tips of my ears. "Locking your doors and turning an eye to what's been happening in Valebridge seemed like the best thing to do?"

The men before me share a glance, their eyes casting downward.

"And what is it that you've done?" Tallulah sets her cup on the table a bit harshly; it rattles against the wood top. "Have you been to Valebridge to fight against these injustices?"

I bite my tongue, the anger flooding my cheeks quickly turning to shame.

"I didn't think so." Her voice softens, but her stare is hardened as she keeps her sapphire eyes on Sorin and I. She pushes her dark braid over her shoulder. "Maybe it was cowardly for us to lock up, but when you've been beaten and shackled like an animal, you tend to have some reservations about taking a stand."

"Tallulah, I'm sorry—"

"We're on the same side, Sam." She cuts me off, but I don't mind because she's right. I did nothing to stop this because I kept my eyes on what was right in front of me. Loxley. "And it seems like we share the same regrets of not helping sooner."

I glance at Sorin, his chin resting on his knuckles. He's watching her but his eyes are so distant.

"Let's not turn on one another now," Tallulah says. "Not when we finally have found the courage to do something important." She grabs Evren's hand. "Everyone had difficult choices to make when King Silas died. What matters now is that we are all in agreement on making the right choice."

"The right choice," Sorin mimics, his eyes completely glazed over. Is he even awake? I nudge him under the table, and he shoots me a scowl which I return with vigor.

"Sorin will pose as Evren," Thaddeus continues. Oblivious to mine and my brother's silent, ridiculous war. "As long as we don't run into any Royal Hunters as the ball—"

"You shouldn't," Evren says. "Hunters aren't allowed at the balls. Only Lords and Ladies and specifically chosen guards. Besides, you'll be in a mask." His green eyes meet mine for a moment.

"A mask?" Jarek asks, his hand clasped tightly to mine.

Evren nods. "Everyone will be. It's traditionally a masquerade. A way to contain anonymity during the night's debauchery."

"And how do you know so much about this event, Evren?" Agnes asks, her amber eyes scouring his face.

"I was a guard," Evren says, his voice lowering. "And after that, a hunter."

Tallulah tucks a piece of fallen hair behind his ear, and as she begins to pull her hand away, he catches it. Placing a delicate kiss to her knuckles. "Clearly, much has changed." His smile is faint and no one else speaks on the subject for the rest of the morning.

"Cora!" Jarek screams, waking me from my sleep. His eyes are still pressed tight, fingers clenching around our sheets.

"Cora!" he screams again, this time bolting upright.

"Shh," I whisper, running my fingers down his arms. "It was only a nightmare, Jarek." I sit up behind him, wrapping my arms around his chest. His breathing is strained, skin damp with sweat. "Only a nightmare, my love."

His breathing begins to steady, his shaking body slowly calming. It's been a long time since he's been plagued by nightmares of his home, but I run light kisses down his back until I feel his muscles relax.

"Thank you," he says, as we both lay back down. He rests his head on my chest, his arm draped around my middle.

I stroke his blonde hair, not missing the slight tremble of his shoulders. "Do you want to tell me about it?"

"The same as the last," he says against my skin. "Cora and Helen and Ma, their bodies and blood and—" He presses his face deeper into my chest.

"It's all right," I say. "I'm here. It was only a nightmare." But the truth of the matter is, there's no way of knowing just what waits for Jarek in Scandavi. When he was forced upon a ship four years ago, his family was alive.

But we know all too well how quickly things can change.

His breathing becomes heavy, his arm still tucked around my middle, pinning me in place. I relax my shoulders but my mind is racing. Too occupied thinking of this man who has wandered so far from home. Who has been forced to stay in Teravie during the blight. The seas overturned with storms, too deadly to sail.

He has so many unanswered questions about his family and the fate of his home. Just how long will he stay before he goes searching for answers?

FIFTEEN
ROMAN

THE WHIP CRACKS AGAINST MY SKIN A SECOND TIME, but I don't flinch. If I do, it'll only drive my father to raise it again. So, I stay perfectly still, tears stinging the sides of my eyes, jaw clenched.

"Get up," he says, voice flat and unbothered.

Swallowing the lump in my throat, I stand on uncertain legs. I bite my tongue to keep from wincing, the pain shooting across my back as I turn to face him.

He places the whip back in its holder on the wall. "What did you learn?"

My lip snarls as he flexes his hand, as though he's in pain from the work he's done on me. My gaze lingers a little too long and before I can correct it, his eyes snap to mine.

"I asked you a question, Roman." He takes a few strides toward me. I suck in a breath at his abrupt closeness, fighting the urge to shrink into the corner.

"I-I..." My tongue trips over itself as my father looms over me. He doesn't even have to speak for my body to react to him.

Fight or flight, Roman.

Much to my father's despair, it's never been fight for me. I wish I could run, right now. Straight through the doors and never *look back, because no matter how I pretend, I'll never be the son King Silas Rudhek expects me to be.*

Preferring books over weapons and art over bloodshed. It's the same damn foolery that's ended me up here today. Squaring my shoulders, I tilt my chin, so we're eye level. "I'll never miss training again," I say with much more conviction than I feel.

His dark eyes narrow. He doesn't believe me. I don't even believe me, but what else can I say? Certainly not the truth. That I'll always choose the library over the sparring ring, just as I had earlier today.

He wasn't supposed to be in Valebridge and so I took my chances, running from training and straight into the welcoming arms of a thousand tomes. But much to my disappointment, his trip to Scandavi was cut short, and he arrived back in Valebridge just in time to hear word from my mentor that I'd skipped yet another session.

I open my mouth to defend myself, but before I can speak a word, his knuckles connect with my cheek in the lightest of touches. Brief and warm and harmless, he runs his fingers down my face.

"Good," he whispers before smiling. "I only want the best for you son." His fingers linger, cupping me just under my chin.

My heart races, cracking my ribs with its incessant vigor.

"Now get cleaned up." His fingers slide away as he turns for the door. "We have scholars coming this afternoon for a visit. The last thing I need is for you to embarrass me further."

The oak doors slam as he exits the study, leaving me broken and bleeding and alone. But the pain in my back is nothing next to the phantom burning of his hand brushing my cheek.

It's amazing all touch is capable of. When you've spent so much of your life starving for it, the smallest gesture holds the most significant meaning.

And my father knows it. I have no doubt he uses it against me and always has. Deprived me of all physical touch. Hugging, shaking hands, anything remotely resembling affection since my mother died when I was just barely two. He took it all away so that in moments like this, moments I am beaten down and vulnerable, all he must do is offer me the faintest touch. The smallest silver lining that maybe he does care for me, and all my woes against him are forgotten.

And because I'm as weak as he claims, I fall for it every time.

I run my fingers over the spot he grazed, savoring the memory and pocketing it for later. Adding to the collection of pathetic touches and hugs I've gathered from him over the years. Always ignoring the fact that they've all been given after the searing pain of a whip to my back.

The rational part of my mind knows it's manipulation. Knows he's doing this to keep me under his thumb. His disappointing heir with the soft heart and brittle spirit. The most twisted parts of my mind, however, accepts his behavior for love. And I'm more inclined to believe that part, anyway.

With a deep inhale, I make my way out of the study and back to my room to ready myself for another day as King Silas Rudhek's broken, delusional son.

The memory leaves me gasping. Every night since the Dyrsjel and I first spoke, the nightmare has been the same. My father and the study and all the ways he used to make me feel small.

Just as she had the other day.

I take a few large breaths, the sudden inhale of oxygen burning my lungs. Sweat covers my forehead, and when I roll to ensure I haven't woken Galen, my breathing falters.

He isn't there.

Sitting upright, I let my eyes adjust to the darkness before scanning the room. No lamps are lit, meaning he isn't in the bathing chambers or reading in one of the chairs like I so often find him. It's not unusual for Galen to stay up much later than I do, but after the nightmare I just had, his touch is the only thing I know will calm me down. I pull on my robe and head straight for the study.

The castle at night is just as lovely as during the day. The arched, open windows allow the moon's light to shine through. White lanterns line each hallway, their flames flickering as I walk with haste. I pass a few handmaids on my way to the study, and after several declines for drinks or service, they finally leave me alone.

Just as I suspected, orange light spills from under the study door. Smiling, I quicken my pace so I can find some assurance in Galen's arms. But as I get closer, several hushed voices seep from the door's cracks. My mind races. Who would he be meeting with at this hour? And why didn't he tell me?

Pressing my body against the door, I hold my breath so I can get a better listen.

"That wasn't the first time Roman's been down there, sir. A few of the other guards have seen him conversing with the prisoner on two separate occasions. Not to mention the food is still being delivered." My stomach drops. The audacity this guard has to speak of me so informally. I lean closer, waiting for Galen's reprimand for not using my proper title.

"I want an extra rotation outside the dungeon. It isn't to be left unattended; do you understand?" There's a beat of silence, and I assume the guard has nodded because Galen continues, "If anyone so much as sees Roman heading in that direction, inform me immediately."

"Yes, sir," the guard says.

"Another thing," Galen says. "Gather a group, tell them it's time to make good on our promise. I've waited long enough."

"Shouldn't we wait until after the Autumn Moon? Wouldn't want to send too many guards away with all of the extra—"

"Are you questioning me, Deidrick?" Galen snaps followed by a few minutes of silence. I swallow; a knot in my throat makes it painful to do so. I move from the door, finding a shadowed corner to tuck myself into.

"Of course not, sir." The guard, Deidrick, exits a few moments later, hastily making his way down the hall in which I just came. I keep perfectly still until he rounds the corner and is out of sight.

Minutes pass without another guard so I move from the corner. The door to the study remains open, but other than the crackling fire, there's no more talking. No more movement. Heat licks up my spine, filling my lungs with anger I'm ready to spew.

How dare you send guards without my consent.

How dare you let them speak my name.

Anger rises in my throat and a million curses threaten to spill from my tongue. After I hear no one else leave the study, I stomp forward with every intention to tell Galen exactly what he deserves to hear. But as I enter the study, a scream ready in my lungs, I pause.

Galen's heavy breathing isn't loud enough to be heard from the hall. He's asleep in the chair, a book still open in his lap. His face is so soft when he sleeps, as if it's the only time he feels peace.

The anger subsides and before I can think better of it, I cover him with a blanket and leave.

Sixteen

Elora

"It's time." The guard just outside my cell rattles the keys.

I don't move from my bed. If they're going to take me back to that room, they can drag me. I've contemplated this moment for the last several nights. Knew it would be sooner rather than later that they would try to take my magick again, and while at first the knife Roman left me seemed tempting against my flesh, I've formed another idea.

"Did you hear me, Enchantress?"

Still, I don't speak. Don't move. I wait for that terrible screech of the iron door to open. I wait for the clinking noise of the ring of keys on his hips to sound just by my ear. I wait until his hand is on my arm.

"I said get up!" His grip tightens, thick fingers digging into my flesh.

That's when I strike.

I spin to face him, using my free arm to attempt to claw at his face. My abruptness must catch him off guard, because he fumbles back a step. I use his surprise to my advantage. His hand drops from my arm, and just as he's going for the chains of my shackles, I jump from my bed and leap forward, scratching and biting any bit of skin I can sink my teeth into.

"Get off me!" He yanks my hair back and I stifle a cry. Slamming me to the floor, he then presses his boot against my chest so hard something cracks.

I wince and let myself crumble. Let him believe me weak. It isn't difficult, considering all the years I've believed it myself.

He scoffs, kicking me out of his way to grab the sheet from my cot to wipe at his face. "You'll pay for this, witch."

I bite my tongue as I pull the knife that Roman left from under my shirt, then place it behind my back and wait.

He tosses the bloodied sheet back onto the cot, his dark eyes narrowed when he turns to me again. He takes a step forward. Then another.

Breathe.

Breathe.

When his hand lands around my arm again, I put all the strength I have left into the blade, jump to my feet, and ram it straight into his eye.

He recoils back, but before he can scream, I rip the pillow from my bed and shove it tightly against his mouth. His nails claw into my flesh, his scream muffled by the fabric. I continue to push against his mouth, even as he rips at my hair.

Biting my tongue, I don't let myself scream. I can't risk anyone else hearing. I dig the knife deeper into his eye, twisting as I do and the pressure and pain must be more intense, because he lets go of my hair to grab my arm.

That's when I make my second strike.

I yank the knife from his eye and make a clean precision along his neck. He screams behind the pillow but then his sounds turn wet and ragged. I push and push as hard as I can with shackled wrists, until his reddened face pales and his body no longer struggles.

The knife drops to the floor, my hands shakily roaming the

guard's chest and sides until my fingers enclose around cool metal.

Keys.

I find the smallest one on the ring, the one I've seen used a dozen times, and as quietly as possible remove the shackles from my wrists. A broken cry leaves me, the loss of the iron around my skin an instant relief. I quickly press my hands to my mouth, so I don't make any more sound. The pain in my wrists is searing, but I ignore it before carefully grabbing the key ring and hooking it through a loop on my tarnished breeches.

Cautiously, I take a step out of the cell. Holding my breath, I watch the door at the top of the stairs. Waiting for another guard, or Roman, or possibly even Galen to appear.

Not even a pin drop of noise, so I take another step toward the stairs.

Then another.

And another.

My foot hits the first step and all I can see is the wolves. Sorin and Sam. Jarek and Loxley.

I'm almost there.

I take another two steps before my heart sinks.

"Help us," a small voice says behind me. Frozen, wood from the banister splinters under my nails. I glance over my shoulder. Was that in my head?

"Please don't leave us," another voice says.

My body stiffens

No. Those are not the voices of my demons. Turning fully, I see only my cell. My cell and the dead guard and nothing but darkness. Scanning the dungeon, I can't make out where the voices are coming from, so I grab the torch from the wall and against every instinct, I head back down.

Turning to the right of my cell first, I pat the keys attached to my hip as a reminder that I am no longer caged.

As I round the corner, the torch slips from my hand. I

stumble backward into the wall. Gasping, I cover my mouth and use my free hand to shakily pick up the torch.

After a few deep breaths, I step closer to the voices and angle the torch to illuminate not one, but six other cells identical to mine. And within each of them, an Enchantress.

SEVENTEEN

SORIN

"Would you stop fidgeting?" Sam slaps my hand then pushes down forcefully on my shoulders until I'm planted back in the chair.

"I'm sorry," I mumble, "but I hate this."

She laughs from behind me, her fingers working the ties of my mask again, pulling it tight against my slicked back hair. The clothes from Evren fit, but they're stifling. The green and black fabric of the structured pants and shirt have my skin crawling.

"It's either you wear this mask or you're thrown in a cell, which do you prefer?" she asks, pointedly.

I roll my eyes, only because she can't see them.

"It's only practice, you'll need to be able to do this on your own for the Autumn Moon so just sit still for another minute."

"Fine." I hate when she's right. Which is always.

"Besides"—she steps in front of me—"you look annoyingly handsome in a mask."

"Oh my." I throw my hands in the air. "So, does my sister still care for me?" I don't expect her boot to collide with my shin so forcefully, but when it does, I give out an embarrassing shriek.

"I always care about you."

"Yes, but lately you can't tell me something hasn't been off."

Her posture tenses and her eyes avert mine.

"See." I stand from the chair, already hot from the mask and garb I've been forced to try on. "So just tell me what it is."

"It's everything. I worry about Elora and Galen. I worry about Mum." She pushes my shoulder lightly. "I worry about *you*. Sometimes I don't know what to do with all of this worry and it builds up and turns to frustration." She sighs, brushing my shoulders and straightening the lapels of my black jacket. "Anyway. I think this is it." She nods to the mirror.

I turn over my shoulder and glance at my reflection.

The mask Sam chose is black, with intricate carvings. I run my fingers along the delicate outlines of the sculpted fur and whiskers. Evren mentioned he has met the king on one or two occasions when he was a captain in his guard, which makes me even less confident this mask will be enough to conceal me. But, Evren also made it clear the king often does not attend the party for long, so there's a chance I won't even run into him.

I sigh, the pressure of the next few days pushing down on me.

The wolves outside the keep howl, a reminder that the time for us to leave is drawing near.

Ruse and Alaric were hesitant to join the Jade Guild, but something in them must have snapped because they've been with us for several days now.

It's as if they sensed a change. As if they understood me when I said I was going to get her back.

"Just remember what Evren told you," Sam says. "You answer by his name, you were a hunter, but you came to the Jade Guild to assist Thaddeus in his old age."

"Right." I nod, but my mind has drifted. Panic begins to gnaw its way through my gut.

Everything hinges on the Autumn Moon.

On the trust that hangs between Lord Thaddeus and I. He's promised to aid us, promised that the other members of the Guilds will be in attendance. If this plan doesn't work, if we don't get Elora—

No.

I won't let myself think that far. We *will* get her out. We have to.

My heart constricts as I look at the mask again, smirking under it for my sister's cleverness.

"You've outdone yourself." I say to her over my shoulder. She smiles, leaning against the doorway.

"You'd better get a move on, Thaddeus will be waiting for you."

"I'll see you at the Onyx Guild in a week, Sam. Be careful." I fight the urge to scratch at the mask around my eyes. "Take care of the pups."

She laughs. "Please, Jarek has already named them. That man couldn't resist a puppy if he tried. I love you, brother," Sam says, giving me her biggest shite-eating grin. "Be safe."

"I love you, too."

With Sam gone, I take one more glance in the mirror before changing and meeting Thaddeus. A smile dances over my lips as I trace my fingers over the black mask.

The Autumn Moon is a party for sheep, and my sister has dressed me as a wolf.

THE CARAVAN CREAKS and wobbles as it makes its way down the cobbled streets into Valebridge.

My fingers are restless, tempted to draw back the curtains and get a peek at the royal city, the very one I grew up in. The one I've dreamt about returning to often as a boy. But I remain in my seat, eyes focused on Lord Thaddeus across from me. He hasn't stopped talking since we left Ramshire and on the second hour of travel, I tuned him out completely.

Is this what people mean when they say I talk too much? I'll have to reconsider my entire personality after this trip.

"Did you hear me, Sorin?"

Shaking back to reality, I blink a few times to disperse the glaze that's taken over my eyes.

"Sorry, Lord, I'm a bit distracted." I can't see much of Thaddeus's face behind his mask made of ivy and golden branches, but I imagine it's the same look of annoyance he's so fond of giving me.

"I said the heads of the Guilds will meet us in the grand hall."

I nod, half listening.

"They've agreed to review your decree of birth. Once they've deemed it suitable, they will hold a meeting with the council. If the council verifies it to be true, there will be a trial to remove Roman from the throne. Once he's dethroned, a coronation will take place in a few weeks. We'll return—"

"You forgetting an important piece of the plan, Thaddeus?" My knee bounces in time with the caravan as we hit another stretch of cobbled bumps.

Thaddeus pushes up his mask so it rests on his forehead. His eyes narrow before softening at his realization. "Right," he says. "The girl. Of course. How could I forget—"

The caravan comes to an abrupt halt, and he topples forward. I barely catch him in time before his knees hit the floor.

"Thank you," he gruffs, settling back into his seat for a moment. His yellowing teeth glint in the moonlight that's fought its way in through the musky curtains.

The door swings open and a cacophony of sounds hits me from outside.

Varied string instruments play over one another. Songbirds and bards compete to have the highest voice. If the circumstances weren't so vile, I may have even enjoyed the mixture of sounds and revelry. The musicians set forth with another upbeat tempo, setting the mood for a night full of undeserved revelry. Steadying my breaths, I wait for Thaddeus to finish chatting with the caravan driver.

Rain coats the cobblestones and lamp posts lit with an ever glowing flame line the road, leading up to the ivory castle. Spires shoot toward the sky like weapons. Large arched windows carved from marble surround all sides of the castle, each adorned with rich Autumn colors. Orange and red and yellow leaves piled together in elegant bouquets. Swallowing thickly, I return my gaze to the path before me. Hundreds of white pumpkins, carved with the bear crest, a candle lighting them from the inside out, line the path to the castle.

Thaddeus pats my back. "Ready, Evren."

It takes me a moment to remember that's the name I'm to be called tonight. Nodding, I follow him and dozens of other partygoers away from the caravans and into Valebridge.

Inside the ballroom of the Valebridge castle my jaw drops in awe as we're greeted by rich swatches of navy and gold. Grizzly bears made of sculpted ice are centered in the large ballroom, surrounded by tables and tables overflowing with delicacies. I bite my tongue, thinking of the townsfolk in Wickersham and even Loxley. Tighter rations have begun now that the cold has started and even more so since the blight, yet here in Valebridge, it's as if there is an oversupply.

I follow Lord Thaddeus, stopping every so often to greet and shake hands with his acquaintances. I can't keep focused long enough to remember their names.

My heart races as I scour the room in search of the exits. One on the left, a large archway draped in deep navy where the handmaids seem to be coming and going. Trailing the crowded room, I spot a second, smaller exit. A few servers in masks have come donning trays of various deep liquors. But other than the handful, it's much less bustling than the other exit.

That's my escape.

With only Elora in mind, I take a step forward, before I'm tugged back.

"Not yet," Thaddeus mouths. He has me pulled so close; I can see his eyes searching the room as well. Perhaps for the other Lords and Ladies.

My heart slams before glancing again at the now empty archway. My chance to slip out unnoticed is dwindling and if I don't—

"Lord Thaddeus, what a pleasure," a voice sounds from behind us.

Thaddeus drops his grip from my arm as we turn in unison to the man at our backs. His dark curly hair is wild and unkept. His green eyes blazing and bright even through his navy mask. Black leaves outline the bottom half above his cheekbones, the sides extending to sharp points.

"Your Majesty," Lord Thaddeus says, confirming that it is King Roman who stands before me.

My half-brother. My stomach twists as the king glances between Thaddeus and I.

Thaddeus bows, tugging at my black shirt as he does. Following suit, I'm grateful for my mask to conceal my disgust. My rage. As we straighten, my jaw remains clenched to keep from saying something. From lunging forward and using that spiked mask against him.

"Allow me to introduce you to my nephew, Evren, heir to the Jade Guild."

"It's an honor to be here, Your Majesty," I manage to say through gritted teeth. I meet Roman's eye, and beneath his mask, there's amusement there. A smirk twitching at the corners of his mouth.

"The pleasure's all mine, Evren," he says, perfectly cordial. He brings his chalice to his lips, eyeing me over the cup. "Evren," he repeats. "Familiar. Have you been to Valebridge before?"

My stomach clenches, my mind racing through all of the details Evren told me of his life before we care.

Guard.

Captain.

Hunter.

Does Roman recognize that I'm not Evren?

Thaddeus bumps my arm, soft enough it goes unnoticed by Roman who continues to study me.

"Briefly," I say. "But I'm afraid it was so long ago I don't recall much of it."

His eyes narrow, as if they're searching for something.

A memory perhaps.

"I'm honored to be here tonight, Your Majesty." This softens his gaze, and my stomach settles. "It's a wonder to experience the beauty of a Valebridge ball firsthand."

"Happy to have you." He raises his glass before turning his attention to Thaddeus.

They talk as old friends, catching up over the change of the seasons. The blight. But it isn't until I hear one word that my mind clears and my focus sharpens.

"Yes, the Dyrsjel is here," Roman says casually, holding his chalice of wine between his first two fingers. I hone in on his movements. The slight sway on his feet, the smirk he's unabashedly wearing now. The hint of pink across his cheeks.

My little brother is more of a lightweight than I am.

He leans in closer to Thaddeus and I. Sour wine invades the space as Roman grips Thaddeus' arm. "Now that we have your allegiance, you'll be amazed to see all we can do with her magick—"

"What am I interrupting, Your Majesty?"

Time stops. My pulse thunders in my chest and the music around me becomes muddled and unclear. The rage that quickly blinded me earlier is displaced with confusion. A man steps forward, his mask an identical match to King Roman's.

But his hair. Icy and perfectly polished. His eyes. Sharp and blue.

My fists clench, and my heart rate spikes.

"Hope you haven't had too much fun without me," the man says. "Lord Thaddeus, correct?"

Thaddeus dips his head as the man slips his fingers into Roman's. I track the movement, my stomach swirling.

Maybe it isn't him. Maybe I'm wrong.

"And you are?" the man asks, his eyes even more vibrant under his dark mask. My voice lodges in my throat. Thaddeus bumps my arm with his elbow but still, I can't move. Can't speak.

"Forgive my nephew," Thaddeus says through a chuckle. "It's been a trying year. Kind sir, this is Evren Fletcher, heir to the Jade Guild."

The man turns to me, his mouth forming a smile, but his eyes narrow as they meet mine again.

"Pleasure," he says, a bit forcefully. I manage to dip my chin in a quick bow, but still, my words are lost.

"Now pardon us, Lady Mordona of the Bloodstone Guild has just arrived," the man says. "We have much to discuss before the night ends. Cheers, gentlemen." The man backs away, leading a tipsy Roman through the crowded ballroom, his hand pressed to the small of his back.

Before they make it three steps, Roman bends down and kisses the man deeply. The kind of kiss that suggests it isn't the first. No, it's the kind of kiss of lovers who have kissed many, many times.

My stomach churns, knees weakening as I watch the two of them mingle and chat and look perfectly comfortable with each other.

It wasn't Galen.

But even as I lie to myself, a warning sounds inside of my head and now nothing before me appears to be real.

The dancers blur, the music fades.

It can't be real.

"Get it together," Thaddeus says, pulling me out of my stupor.

I follow him to a table piled high with desserts. My head spins again, knees threatening to buckle beneath me. So, I focus on what's directly in front of me. On the ridiculous amount of food Roman's flaunted for this Mother-forsaken party. Tiny square pastries overflowing with custard and fruit. Pumpkin tarts topped with cinnamon and nutmeg. An enormous tiered platter stuffed to the brim with almond cakes dusted with powdery white sugar.

"You'll get us thrown to the gallows before we can even meet with the Guild members if you keep acting a fool!"

Snapping my attention to Thaddeus, I still can't find it in me to address what it is I just saw.

Who it is that betrayed me.

Betrayed her.

I must be mistaken. There's isn't any way—

"Have you fallen ill, *nephew*?" Thaddeus grabs my arm.

Shaking my head, my eyes scan the room. "I need to relieve myself," I grumble, honing in on a blonde haired man in an elegant black cape attached much too closely to our lush king.

Rage boasts my chest as I abandon my place near the dessert table, but before I make it two steps, Thaddeus grips my arm again.

"Careful," he whispers. "Remember *why* you are here." Turning, I meet his eyes. He glances toward the foyer just to the right of the ballroom. To where I am to meet with the other Guild members shortly. As his grip lessens, I clasp his shoulder.

"I'll be back." But not without her.

Then I'm off, weaving through a sea of masked royalty and nobles. Skirting my way around the pompous show of wealth being flaunted at every corner. Chandeliers swaying from the ceilings, dipped in gold. Huge swatches of navy fabric adorn the walls in elegant swooping patterns. The crescendo of music rises, as does my heart rate as I lose sight of the king and his escort.

Hoards of partygoers flock to the dancefloor, clogging my path.

"A dance, handsome?" Startled, I turn to see a woman glancing up at me. Her creamy white skin stands out against her vibrant red hair, and I flinch as her hand wraps around mine, pulling me to the center of the room.

Pulling me away from Galen.

I turn again, his back is to me now, but over his shoulder he looks. Just once. Those blue eyes I'd know anywhere meet mine, and my heart stops all over again. His lips pull to a tight line, but his eyes remain locked on me.

He knows.

I open my mouth to shout, but before I can, the music quickens again and with it, the crowd of revelers erupts into a frenzy. The red-haired woman pulls me around the dance floor like a ragdoll, I'm too lost in my own mind to bother what my body is doing. Too focused on my best friend standing merely feet away and yet, there may as well be an ocean between us.

Galen is the reason she is locked up.

Galen is the reason she is gone.

But why?

Small hands slide up my back, and it's that contact that finally breaks me. Whipping my head downward, the woman casts me a smile. Her eyes widen and lust quickly fills them under her golden cat mask.

"Sorry," I mumble, pulling her hands away from me. She scoffs but quickly recovers as another gentleman in a simple emerald mask swoops by and pulls her in for a dance. The two of them spin widely, heads thrown back in laughter. Dozens of couples swarm me.

I'm stuck. Frozen in place. Nausea roils in my stomach as I watch these people dance and gorge themselves knowing what's happening right beneath us. Knowing the starvation in the villages and storms that curse the seas right outside the Vale-bridge walls.

My stomach twists again, my arms searching for anything to grab onto. I push my way out of the crowd, desperate for air.

I find my way to the exit I spotted earlier. Only Galen is no longer there. Frantic, I scan the room again. Surely, the king would be easy to spot.

No luck.

Sighing, I reach up and rub at the very real pain starting to form in my chest. Whether it be panic or heartbreak, it's all the same at this moment.

Thaddeus spots me from across the room, his ivy mask glaring brightly against the gold candelabras mounted to the wall. I should stay. I should do what I came to do. Seek the Guild members. Fortify my decree of birth. My hand begins to travel to my jacket pocket where I know the single piece of paper that will change everything sits, but I stop.

There isn't any more time to waste. Thaddeus shakes his head from across the room but it's too late.

My mind is made.

I slip silently in the dark doorway, away from the party, away from the Guild members surely waiting for me in the opposite direction. I follow a narrow path that leads out of the ballroom, but before I can make it to the end, someone stumbles down the hall.

Eighteen
Samaria

THE PUPPIES HAVE GROWN SIGNIFICANTLY IN THE last few days. They tumble about, entangling themselves; it's difficult to tell which body ends and another begins.

Ruse and Alaric have left for Valebridge with Sorin, how he got them to understand him I'll never know. So now it's on Jarek and I to watch over the raucous pups. Keeping them indoors was certainly an argument with Lord Thaddeus, but Sorin convinced him it was for the best considering they haven't quite learned the art of being inconspicuous. Their growls and yips from the greenhouse proving his point.

"They grow fast, don't they?" Tallulah steps to my side. I hadn't realized anyone else was in here, but I suppose a Florecas like herself would probably be fond of the greenhouse, given their ability to grow and conjure plants.

"They do." I offer her a smile which she returns. Her eyes, more blue than I've ever seen, are radiant under the gray light that filters through the windows of the room. "The Stones?" I let my question linger in the air.

"With your mother," Tallulah says. Relief settles in my chest so I prop myself against a workbench and try to trick myself into relaxing. "She's been resting, but I've ensured she has plenty of tea to keep her company."

Warmth blooms in my chest. The Stones are safe and my mother's been cared for. Her health has been worrisome to Sorin and I for the last several years, but stubborn as she is, she's never seen a Healer.

"She plans to travel back to Loxley as soon as she feels well enough."

"Good." I nod, biting into my bottom lip. Ulric is more than capable of managing Loxley in our absence, but having my mother home, where I know she's safe, will surely help the weight on my shoulders. Changing the subject, I rub the exhaustion from my eyes. "Have you and Evren been together long?"

Her smile broadens, intensifying her beauty. "A little over four years," she says, gesturing to me to follow her.

We find a small gardening table and a few chairs near the back of the greenhouse. I dust the chair quickly to free it of dirt and sit down across from her.

"We met out of pure luck," Tallulah continues. "Or perhaps the Mother had something to do with it. She works in mysterious ways, after all." She chuckles, and I smile.

"And he said he was a hunter?" Relaxing into my chair, I glance around the small greenhouse. Windows line two walls while one is attached to the Jade Guild. White-washed stones make up the ground and not to mention the rows and rows of beautiful green plants and flowers. The puppies bump into a tower of stacked pots, nearly tipping them over.

"He was," Tallulah says. I tear my eyes away from the pups to glance at her. She pulls a pile of long grass into her lap and begins weaving them, creating a tapestry of green, her fingers quick and nimble, as if they've done the task a hundred times before. "It feels like a lifetime ago."

"Will you tell me about it?" I ask. "I could use the distraction, my nerves have been on edge these last few weeks as I'm sure you could imagine." She smiles as she continues her weaving. "Besides, I must know the story of how you managed to make such a surly man bend his knee to you."

Tallulah tips her head back and laughs, the sound bright. "It wasn't love at first sight or anything like that." She places the half-woven leaves onto the small table and faces me. "There was a lot of pain and fear between us. So much misunderstanding." She frowns but only for a moment before her features relax again. "But somewhere in those weeks together, the fear of each other morphed into wondering instead."

"What kind of wondering?" I pick at a loose hem on my shirt.

Tallulah sighs as she leans back into her chair. "The kind that sweeps you away. Wondering all the different alternatives in life. Like—" She bites her lip. "Like what if magick was never outlawed and hunted? It's a terrible thing to be glad for, but would I have ever met Evren? What if I had never been forced to endure those horrible things, would I have found this love I thought only reserved for storybooks?" She laughs, shaking her head before picking up her leaves again. "I'm getting sentimental, forgive me."

"Nothing to be sorry for," I say. "Your story is beautiful, just as this greenhouse is." I gesture to the vibrant green plants and bright pink flowers proudly on display.

"Evren built it." Her eyes scan the space. "It was his wedding gift to me, though I think it's unfair because we never said we were exchanging gifts. I still owe him one."

"You know, Sam," she says, lowering her voice and leaning across the table, "it's only a matter of time before you access that magick of yours. I know how painful it must be. How it must feel to have such a large part of yourself blocked off." My throat tightens but I nod, allowing myself to be vulnerable with this stranger. Just as Elora had been with me. "But when the Dyrsjel arrives, the Ceremony will happen for you. And when it does, we'll all be here to help you find your way."

"Thank yo—"

"Lu!" Evren shouts, bounding into the greenhouse with a lead foot.

Tallulah and I both turn, the same wide eyed expression plastered on our faces.

"You and Sam need to get underground, *now*."

It isn't two seconds later and Evren is gone and Tallulah is grabbing my arm, leading me out of the greenhouse.

"Underground?"

"Yes," she says. "Someone must be at the gate."

"What of the puppies?" I glance over my shoulder at the four pups still wrestling with each other.

"Evren will see that they remain locked in the greenhouse." Tallulah pulls me through a maze of tunnels. Twists and turns, up a flight of stairs and then back down again. My head dizzies, but before long, we've reached what I presume is the last level. An arched cellar door covered in vines opens easily and we slip inside.

My eyes struggle to adjust to the darkness of the space, my hands gripping the walls on either side of me for reassurance. Tallulah leaves my side and a few moments later, the room is filled with soft, warm light from a small oil lantern. Shuffled boots sound above us, some faint shouts in the distance.

Jarek.

I start for the door but Tallulah grasps my arm tightly. I turn to look at her.

"My mother!"

"She'll be okay," she says, reaching for me. "There is another safe room, just above us. I'm certain Evren showed her the way."

My shoulders deflate.

"It isn't often we get visitors, but Evren and Thaddeus insist I hide when we do." She shrugs. "Just in case."

Her words do nothing to soothe me. My mind replays the caravan. Losing Elora and Galen. I can't lose my mother too.

The Stones. It's all so much, the cramped space of the room closes in on me and—

"Come sit." Tallulah turns and leads us to a pair of chairs. Books are piled high onto a small table and a knit blanket is folded neatly on the ground. How many times has she visited this space? And for how long? She grabs a few of the books before taking a seat.

I join her at the table. She hands me a book with a smile. I take it but my eyes keep drifting to the door. Above us has quieted, no more shouts or boots scurrying back and forth so my shoulders relax. Must be nothing, just as she said.

I thumb through the pages of the book, the words all bleeding together. Giving up, I place it back on the table and stretch my arms and legs. I try not to think about my mother being cramped into a similar room, the Stones now placed in her protection when they should be with me. I try not to think about being underground. I try not to focus on how little air there is down here or how dark it is even with the small lantern.

Breathe, Sam.

Before my mind can shift to a dark place, more shouts erupt above us. Louder and more intense than last time. Tallulah jumps to her feet and her abruptness has my heart racing.

Not just an ordinary visitor, then.

"We need to help." I head for the door without waiting for her to answer. "Jarek and my mother are up there and if something is wrong—"

Tallulah grabs my arm again.

"It's not safe." Her eyes are wide, and I've forgotten, for a moment, that she isn't like me. She wasn't raised in a protected village with parents who cared for her. She wasn't afforded the freedoms I had until the uprising. Perhaps was never taught how to fight or defend herself. Taking her quickly in my arms, I clasp her shoulders.

"You can wait here if you want." I give her a quick hug

before heading back to the door. It pushes open silently, the dark, winding staircase looming before me.

Hope I don't get lost.

I take a tentative step out. The voices above me are louder now, the scuffling is quicker. My heart races as I take another. The dagger placed on my hip is the only thing giving me any sort of peace. It's not my bow, but it'll do.

As I take a third step up the stairs, the door behind me shuts. Glancing over my shoulder, I see Tallulah just as she joins me on the staircase.

"I'm coming." She takes a steadying breath. As if she needs the extra oxygen to fuel her steps. "I'm not always brave, but if the last few years have taught me anything, it's that I'm capable of more than I think."

Tallulah guides us through the labyrinth of staircases and hallways. Each level we go up, the voices and shouting rises.

Who could be here?

And why?

The pups. Dread coils in my stomach. If they got out or escaped somehow... If a hunter or guard found them...

My palms sweat as we round the last corner. Tallulah covers her ears as noise reverberates off the stone walls. Through all the chaos, a distinct Scandavi voice travels through.

Jarek.

"Set up in there!"

Pushing past Tallulah, I stumble and squint against the abrasive sunlight. But as my eyes adjust, my mouth falls open. I expected navy blue and grizzlies. Royal hunters or guards. Fighting and steel. But, instead, before me are men and women dressed just like the people of Loxley. Simple clothes and colors. All shuffling about. It takes a moment, disbelief and fear still pulsing through me, to realize they are not just dressed like the people of Loxley.

They *are* the people of Loxley.

All here, inside the Jade Guild.

"What is happening?" I step toward the line of people still filtering down the hall.

My hands tremble.

"What is happening?" I ask again, but no one hears me.

Evren is somewhere I can't see, but I hear him shout orders. Something about filtering to the second level.

"What is—"

"Sam." My chest constricts at the sound. Turning, Ulric is before me. His face and hands are covered in ash. His ruddy cheeks and nose are lined with scratches and knicks.

"What happened?" I pull him into a hug. His arms wrap around me and smoke fills my nose.

As we separate, his eyes glaze over. Dozens of people continue to filter past us. Listening to the orders of Evren and Jarek that I've completely tuned out.

"They burned it." Ulric runs a soot covered hand over his bald head. "They burned Loxley."

NINETEEN
ROMAN

"You're drunk," Galen says, pulling me through the crowded ballroom.

"Well, it is a party." I gesture to the dancers behind me. "We haven't celebrated in ages, why are you so uptight?" I plant my feet as firmly as I can to the ground so he can no longer pull me.

His eyes cut like ice through his dark mask that matches my own. His gaze wanders past me, so I follow it. He's locked eyes with that Lord's nephew. Evan or something close.

"See something you like?" I snicker, taking the last sip of my wine.

"What?"

"You haven't peeled your eyes from that man since he arrived." My words slur, the wine going straight to my head. I've never been one to handle alcohol particularly well but considering the tensions the last few weeks, why not indulge?

Several moments pass by and I realize Galen hasn't responded to me. His eyes still locked on the Lord's nephew. "Truly, Galen. Could you be any more obvious? At least wait until I'm not in the room before you make a pass at someone else."

His grip tightens around my forearm. "You need to go to bed before you say something that you'll regret."

"This is my party." I wriggle away from him. "*You* go to bed if I'm bothering you so much." Before he has a chance to say anything else, I turn and disappear back into the crowd of dancers.

"A dance, Your Majesty?" The voice startles me, and I almost drop my empty wine glass. I glance down, and she looks up at me with big, brown eyes. Her blonde hair piled high in dozens of ringlet curls. The golden color reflects off the lamplight, and suddenly, I'm sick. She looks so similar to the woman we have in chains downstairs. The woman Galen has beaten and starved.

The wine in my stomach threatens to spill onto the floor.

"I must decline." I push past her and weave in and out of the crowd, only stopping when I reach the dark hallway meant for the castle servants. Exhaling, I take a moment to ground myself and lean against the wall of the hallway, letting the wine resettle in my belly.

The hallway is barely lit, not unusual for this time of night. But what strikes me as odd, however, is that there are no servants coming or going.

Shouldn't they be refilling drinks and filling food trays?

I suppose it's no matter. Better they don't see their king drunk out of his mind. The thought makes me chuckle. How high and mighty I have forced myself to look. How cruel and unjust. If only the people really knew—

"Your Majesty?" The Lord of the Jade Guilds nephew appears before me as if from thin air.

"Oh." Clearing my throat, I pull my mask off. "Sorry, Evan is it?"

"Evren," he says. The dark lines of his wolf mask are sharp and angular and they catch the light as he straightens from a bow. "My apologies, Your Majesty. It seems I got turned around looking for the washroom."

I cast him a smile, but with his mask, I can't tell if it's unreturned.

"Please, remove your mask, Evren. No need for them outside of the party, and I would be pleased to meet the next heir of the Jade Guild face to face."

I want to see you.

I want to see who has caught Galen's eye over mine.

Evren's hand reaches for his mask but stops before dropping back to his sides.

"I should be getting back to my uncle." He steps forward, but I stick my arm out to block his path.

"Now, now." He takes a step backward, and his dark eyes find mine through his mask. There's something familiar in them that makes the hair on my arms raise. "It would be rude to disobey a direct command from your king, wouldn't it *Evren*? Remove your mask."

The air in the hallway seems to be running out as my lungs work tirelessly to catch up with the erratic beating of my heart. Why are his eyes so familiar?

Evren says nothing before slowly unclipping the back of his mask, letting it slide off completely and hang at his sides.

"Your Majesty." He bows, concealing his face.

"You may stand."

He keeps his face to the ground, his grip tightening around the mask clutched in his hand. When I'm about to ask again, he lifts his head. My breath catches. His dark hair matches his eyes. The same tone I'd know anywhere. His defined jaw is lined in dark scruff. Just like *his*. Just as that Enchantress described.

"Remind me," I say through a labored breath. "You are Lord Thaddeus'...nephew?"

His eyes cast down a moment, and I don't know why but it is the last bit of proof I need.

"That's correct, Your Majesty."

Heat rises to my cheeks, and before I can stamp the temper down, my hand is around his throat.

His body slams against the wall. And even though he must be strong enough to fight back, he doesn't.

"I do not like being lied to," I whisper. "Tell me your real name, and I'll let you live." My fingers tighten, but still, he doesn't fight back. Our faces are inches apart, and when he opens his mouth, I already know.

"Sorin," he says. "And if you're going to kill me, you'd better decide quickly before I kill you first, brother."

The sharp prick of a blade pierces my side. Glancing down, I see the steel is lodged between my ribs.

"Don't call me that." I take a stumbling step away from him until my back is pressed against the stone wall opposite him. "I should lock you up right now."

"Tell me where Elora is." He holds his hands up, as if he means peace, his brows furrowed. "Please tell me where she is and I'll go."

"And why would I tell you?" My eyes dart between his blade and his face. But his face... It's too similar. Too close to Silas'. To our shared father's. I glance away, toward the end of the hall where the party is growing more raucous, sounds of revelry floating down the hallway.

"If Galen—" Biting my tongue, I don't let the rest of the words slip free. That if Galen knew I helped him, helped *her*, there would be no telling what he'd do.

Sorin takes another step forward, dropping the blade completely this time.

"Whatever it is you're planning, Roman, stop this now. There's still time to rectify—"

The way he says my name sends a ripple of anger through me. As if he has any idea who I actually am. "Do not speak to me that way," I growl, pushing myself off the wall.

"My king," he says with a bow, "and my brother... Make the right choice and end this now. Tell me where she is and we'll leave and never return. The kingdom is yours to do with what you please, but she..." He runs a hand down his face, and it's only now that I see just how broken he actually looks.

His hands tremble, purple lines the underside of his eyes. There are at least five years between us, but it may as well be a lifetime. "We will leave the country. Tonight if you wish. Just let her go."

His rich brown eyes hold mine and the wine in my stomach sloshes again.

He looks more like our father than I do, and perhaps it's that very fact that has me questioning whether or not to kill him. I envy him. Not only for the looks he shares with Silas, but knowing he didn't grow up under his constant scrutiny. His judgments. His cruelty.

"She hasn't done anything to deserve this," he whispers. "You can make one right choice. I promise, the throne is yours."

One right choice.

All I have to do is tell him which corridor to take. Which passage to follow. No one would ever know we spoke. And yet, I hesitate. Do I even want the throne?

The thought catches me off guard. For so long, it was all I hoped for.

"The throne is the beacon of power. No one can hurt you there, Roman. And only those foolish enough would try." Galen's words stroke against my mind. He's right. As long as I am in charge, no one can hurt me. No one can hurt him.

"Your Majesty!" a guard shouts from the end of the hall, pulling my attention. His weapons are drawn, his face red and cheeks puffed. "Your Majesty, come quickly!"

Nodding, I wave my hand to dismiss him before turning back to Sorin, but when I do, he's vanished. Like a phantom in the wind, the only proof he was ever here is the small dagger left at my feet.

TWENTY
ELORA

"You must move quickly," one of the Enchantresses says. "Another guard will be down soon."

"How?" The keys rattle in my shaking hands as I approach the first cell. "How are you here and I haven't heard you all this time?" I didn't think a heart could break so many times. But over and over my heart shatters as I glance at each woman locked in chains.

"It's the keys," the Enchantress before me says. Her eyes like molten, blue flames; her cropped dark hair shining under the low light. "Only the bearer of those keys can hear us and we them. It's some sort of spell. Crafted by evil, I'm sure." Her eyes meet mine. Pain and anger are laced there, but not fear.

She gestures for the padlock on the iron door. "Now quickly."

As the key slips in, it's as if my mind has left my body. As if I'm watching from above like a spirit. The final twist and the cell opens with a loud click. We both freeze, our eyes wandering slowly to the staircase where I'm sure another guard will come rushing down.

Another minute passes.

No guard.

The door before me swings open, and the Enchantress takes a tentative step out. My eyes go directly to her wrists. Not raw, but scarred and raised. I unshackle her and catch them before they have a chance to fall onto the ground.

"Give me the keys," she whispers. Without thought, I do as she says. One by one, she unlocks each door. My mouth hangs open as each Enchantress steps out of their cells. They've been here the whole time. A few paces from me. These women...

"Let's go," the dark-haired woman says, tossing the keys back to me.

"Wait!" She and the other five Enchantresses turn in unison. They all share the same scarring around their wrists. The same look of determination across their faces. "You can't just..." I gesture to the stairs.

We'll get caught.

The dark-haired woman smiles, but there's nothing warm in her expression. "You can wait here if you want, Enchantress. But we—" She turns, glancing at each of the other women by her side. "We have had enough. We're going." She quickly bolts for the stairs, and one by one the rest of the Enchantresses follow.

They're not afraid.

No. Because they no longer have anything to lose.

Not giving myself any time to think twice, I pocket the keys and follow them up the stairs.

The Enchantresses ahead of me take their time, tip toeing on bare feet down the narrow hallway. String instruments sound around us, stopping and starting again, never playing a full melody or chorus. Almost as if they're rehearsing. My stomach grumbles as wafts of sugary baked goods fill the hall.

The Autumn Moon.

My breath hitches. Can it be the Autumn Moon already? Have I been here that long? The thought instantly guilts me as I glance to the six women ahead of me. They've been here much longer given their emaciated state and scarred skin.

Coming to a stop, the dark-haired Enchantress gestures for me to join them. "What's your magick?" she asks, her back flush against the wall.

"Elemental. But I'm not sure—"

"We've been mostly drained." Her eyes peer around me, toward the end of the hallway. Any moment someone could round the corner. My heart races as I watch her.

"We don't have much left," she continues, "but with your help maybe we won't be completely defenseless." She smirks, but as she tucks a wisp of hair behind her ear, her hand trembles.

"I haven't been able to access it." My stomach drops at the admission. While Galen hasn't had success harvesting my magick, it's as if it's been buried away, tucked tightly inside of myself, hiding from the threat of being stolen. "But I'll try." I offer her a quick smile which she returns.

"Someone's coming!" another Enchantress whispers from behind us. Sure enough, over the loud string instruments, boots shuffle around the corner. Clattering trays and chatter accompany it.

With all seven of us, there's no way to hide. So, instead, we form a line across the hall. The way we came only leads back to the dungeon, so with our backs to the door, we wait for whoever rounds the corner. I raise my hands, as do all the Enchantresses next to me. The lump in my throat makes it impossible to swallow.

The magick is in you, susi.

I wish it was my mother's voice whispering inside of my head, knowing she's the final thread of power I need. But I remind myself of her words, anyway.

The magick is in you.

"One guard," the dark-haired Enchantress says. "Two more in the adjacent room."

My mouth gapes. How could she know such a thing?

A guard rounds the corner. His armor clangs and the tune he whistles comes to an abrupt stop, his eyes going wide.

"What are you—"

Without another thought, I raise my trembling hands. There's a weightlessness in my fingertips as I stretch them, no longer bound with iron and it brings a surge of hope in my chest.

The man's face reddens, his cheeks puffing out as he pulls his sword from his side. In two strides, he's halfway to me.

"Now, Enchantress!"

My body aches, my head spins, but I dig down as far as I can, reaching that well of magick I know is trapped inside of me.

Come on. I know you're there.

The metal on the guard's armor grates against the string instruments, the heat from his body closes in on me, and when I'm about to scurry away, something uncoils inside of me.

That tiny spark of magick, buried in me like a seed in the soil, springs to life, twisting and twining through my palms.

The guard gives no indication that he feels my magick; his sword extended, the tip of cool metal brushing under my chin. Two of the Enchantresses break the line and flee back toward the dungeon. But I don't move. It takes less than a second to reach into his lungs and find the element I'm looking for.

Air.

His eyes bulge, the sword under my chin drops to the ground with a loud clatter, but I don't move until every last bit of air from his lungs turns to earth. Thorny brambles break free from his chest, long vines pushing out through his eyes and nose. His body twitches as branches and thorns encompass him, and when his mouth parts, nothing but dirt falls from it.

"We need to move." The women beside me flinch as I step around the guard, but they don't follow me. "Now."

The dark-haired Enchantress snaps her eyes to mine, wide

and silver lined. She says nothing, but she steps forward and the others follow her.

All except...

"You two." I point to the Enchantresses that fled back toward the dungeon. "Come on, we don't have much time."

Their bodies are trembling, clasping onto each other. They're not much older than I am. Both blondes. Both with eyes the color of night.

"We can't." The taller of the two shakes her head, cradling the shorter one against her chest.

"If you stay here, you'll die." I bite my tongue for how direct my words are. But we're running out of time. They don't budge from the doorway. I shrug. "Suit yourselves."

I turn to leave, but the dark haired Enchantress stands in my way.

"They're afraid," she says. "And probably in shock to be with each other again." She peers around me and smiles at the two women. "Sisters who have been separated for years, find it in yourself to have some empathy."

My heart and shoulders drop, but I do not forget her lack of empathy or patience for me in the dungeons. I square my shoulders before glancing back at the sisters. They cradle each other, fingers clasped tightly together. I imagine if it were Sam I was reunited with, I wouldn't let her go either.

But I also wouldn't risk another moment in that cell.

"They're going to get us caught," I say, forcing myself to keep the cold wall I've crafted so well around myself. I hate it, this cold indifference I've tricked myself into believing was who I really am, but right now there isn't any time to spare. "They can stay if they want, just like you said before."

Her eyes burn through me, and I know mine are shining right back. We stand there a moment, nothing but the string instruments sounding between us, before I turn and head for the other end of the hall. It's faint, but the scuffle of four sets of feet sound behind me.

Peering around the corner, I hold my breath as I watch the band continue their rehearsal. We're near the grand ballroom. My mind tries to pull me in, memories of my childhood in Valebridge swiftly floating to the surface.

Oftentimes, I push these memories away. All but the ones of my mother. Every other memory crafted from my childhood in Valebridge seems wasted.

Painful.

But right now, I open myself up and let them come. Ballrooms and luncheons. My mother and her classes. My heart constricts, but I push myself hard, searching my brain for the memory I need most.

A particular memory of this very room.

A memory of a door.

Pushing my back flush against the wall, I hold my breath as a server walks by so busy whistling a tune he doesn't notice five very large flies on the wall.

"Aside from the musicians," the dark-haired Enchantress whispers, "there are two guards in the next hall over."

The hall that leads to the back door. Nodding, I shake my hands at my sides. My energy is waning from using my magick on that guard. I'm not sure how much more I have to give.

"What's your magick?" I whisper to the Enchantresses. As they explain, my heart sinks further. A Seer and a Healer. The dark-haired Enchantress explains she's an Intuitive, able to read bodies and energies which explains how she knew how many guards were where.

"And you?" I ask the red headed woman.

"An Empath." Her pink, full lips curl up.

My head snaps to the Empath, her magick mingling with mine. Observing. Reading me. She smiles but my stomach lurches.

Each of the women's gifts are powerful, in their own right. But I send a silent plea to the Mother that they can also fight because without it, I'm not sure we stand a chance.

"We need to keep moving," the dark haired Enchantress says. Her blue eyes flicker as she holds her hands up. "The hall is clear. Are you sure it's that way?"

My stomach knots, but the memory is there. A sunny afternoon after my lessons with my mother. Eager and excited, I bolted through the door and headed straight for the woods, my mother calling after me not to spoil my dress before lunch.

I glance at the Enchantress and nod. "We need to round the corner, avoid the musicians, and head to the narrow hall. There's a small door that will lead out to the castle gardens and beyond that, the forest." My hands tremble and wrists ache as I push my hair out of my face. "Once we're outside, make your way through the gardens until you find the outerwall of trees. Stay quiet."

I meet each Enchantress in the eyes. They nod and when I glance behind them, to where the two sisters stood before, they're gone.

"Let's go."

We tip-toe our way around the corner. One of the musician's catches my eye, but with the low light of the room, he doesn't balk or raise a brow. The string instruments begin again, the sharp notes pulsating off the stone walls. Their music stirs something in my chest this time. The slow crescendo, the rise and fall of the strings. A memory forms, of a ball just like this one. Perhaps another lost moment of my childhood seizing the opportunity to arise.

Hazy images of dances and gowns. Of blue and gold. A man with dark hair and a woman—

I stub my toe and tumble to the ground. I hiss as my knees hit the marble floor, but I right myself quickly before any of the musicians on the small stage notices. Their music doesn't stop, doesn't falter, so I press forward until we've made it through the ballroom and to the small hallway.

It's darker than the others, used mostly by servants and handmaids if I remember. As the four women filter in behind me, something like hope blooms in my chest. It's difficult to see in the low light, but a rounded shape comes into view as my vision adjusts.

The door.

"Run!" I don't look behind me to see if they follow before I'm sprinting to the door.

Please be unlocked, please be unlocked.

With as much force as I can muster, I push it open and stumble into the falling rain. Wet, fat drops soak my hair and cheeks. A cry breaks from my lips as my feet and hands hit the dirt. My eyes drift to the sky as rain pelts over my skin, stinging my wrists. Another cry slips from me as I close my eyes. My magick stirs in my chest, a low pur of approval as my fingers sink into the damp soil.

Earth.

Over my shoulder, the other Enchantress stumble out of the small door behind me. Their eyes as wide as mine, their smiles beaming through the darkness.

Then, we're running through the sopping wet, castle grounds. Carried by our bare feet and broken bodies. We're running as if our life depends on it, because it does. The slap of rain against my cheeks sends a rush of adrenaline through me.

Rounding around a few neatly groomed hedges and thorny rose bushes, I can taste freedom on the tip of my tongue. Sweet and full of promise. We're almost through the gardens.

"Come on!" I don't look back to ensure the other women are keeping pace. All I can envision is Ruse and Alaric. Sam and Sorin and Jarek. My head spins as a distant howl echoes from beyond the trees.

Alaric?

He doesn't respond but the howling increases and with it, my steps.

We're almost there.

My heart stammers, my feet digging into the muddied ground as a scream pierces the air. I squint against the rain, and through the darkness, I see the red haired Enchantress. Her body flails, her screams shrill as a guard pulls her back toward the castle by her hair.

"No!" I lunge in her direction. I don't make it far before I'm tugged forcefully backward. Screaming, I claw at my attacker, but their hold is too firm. My arms are pressed tightly to my body. I can't move.

Another howl.

Then another.

I'm here! Ruse, I'm here!

Then, I'm pulled further away and the freedom on my tongue turns sour. The other Enchantresses disappear from my view and the hope that propelled me earlier vanishes.

I wiggle my body, working hard to get my wrists free. I bite down on the hand wrapped around my chest, digging my canines into flesh.

"Stop, Elora, you'll cause more of a scene." His deep voice raises the hair on my neck.

My body stills, a fresh chill clawing at my spine. My back is pressed to the man's chest, so I can't see his face.

I'll be taken again.

Dragged back to that dungeon.

My chest tightens and breathing becomes shallow.

I can't go back.

Can't be put in that cage.

I attempt to bite him again so he'll drop my wrists, but his body is like steel around mine.

Unmovable.

So close. We were so close.

Just as my heart splinters, the man turns, dragging me with him and the lanterns from the castle begin to fade from my view.

He pulls me to a wooded area, the pine trees moan and sway with the rising wind. I tumble to the ground as he lets me go. None of the other Enchantresses are within eyeshot, no more howls echoing through the wind. All I see is the castle and a few servants lighting the white pumpkins that line the bridge, the faint string of music sounding from within.

Turning my attention to the man, his gray hair is cropped short on the sides and only slightly longer on top. His facial hair is the same shade of gray, trimmed neatly. His dark attire, black from collar to boot, sends a memory straight to my mind, but it's muddied and faint. He takes a step away from me. He cradles his hand, the one I've bitten, to his chest.

"Who are you?" I scurry backward but don't stand. My legs trembling from the sprint from the castle.

"My name is Calix," he says and takes a deep breath. "I'm here to help you."

Part two: Retribution

TWENTY-ONE

SORIN

THE GUARD ROUNDS THE CORNER, DRAWING ROMAN'S attention. I take the opportunity to slip from his hold and sprint down the hallway.

Deep and piercing pains thrum across my chest. I rub my hand against my heart over and over until the pain begins to fade.

Slow down.

Breathe.

Shuffles echo down the hallway, so I dart through an open door. Lucky for me, it's a supply closet. Broom handles clank together as I squeeze myself in, but because the space is so small, I'm forced to leave the door open a crack.

Roman steps into view, now with a guard following closely behind. Roman pulls his hands through his hair, his mossy eyes frantically searching the shadows.

"They're gone, Your Majesty." The guard's voice trembles. His red face is damp and sweaty. As if he's been running all evening.

"Who?" Roman grabs the guard by the collar of his shirt. "I haven't the patience for riddles." Roman sighs, dropping the man's shirt and pinching the bridge of his nose. "Explain yourself plainly before you find out why they call me the corrupt king."

He hasn't placed his mask back on, and I finally have a chance to really look at him. I didn't know our father well. Only broken memories, most of which I've chosen to suppress. But his dark hair and jawline are those of a Rudhek. My stomach turns, and I'm regretting the drink I indulged in earlier.

"The..." The guard peers over his shoulder. "The prisoners, Your Majesty. They're all gone."

The air in my lungs freezes.

Roman pulls his curly locks through his fingers again. Something like relief flashes across his face, the crease between his brows smoothing. Then in the blink of an eye, his face contorts. He lunges for the guard again, but this time refrains from touching him. Instead, he runs his hands down the front of his shirt. "Why weren't there extra guards on patrol?"

"They're all here, Your Majesty. For the ball. And anyone not here is on assignment, from Sir Galen."

Galen.

The last bit of hope I had that what I saw was a mistake, shreds. I cradle my head in my hands, breathing slowing through my nose.

"No one else hears about this, do you understand?"

"What about Sir Galen—"

"*No one.*" I glance through the crack in the door. Roman's brows are furrowed, a muscle in his jaw flexes. "Send any and every guard you see outside. I want a man stationed at every corner. Do what you need to with the others, but make sure the Dyrsjel is returned or you're *all* on the line."

The guard dips his head, and before I can let out a breath, he scurries out of sight.

Once the guard is gone, Roman runs a hand down his face. He backs himself up so he's propped against a wall. His mask hangs loosely at his side, and it's the first time I remember just how young he is. His eyes snap to the doorway, so I slink back, attempting to use the shadows to my advantage.

Footsteps inch closer.

Closer.

I hold my breath.

"Ro?" Galen's voice is distant, but my traitorous heart warms at the sound of it. I want to run to him. To tell him there's still time to make this right. Whatever this is, perhaps a misunderstanding.

"Coming, sweetheart," Roman says, his voice so close it's as if he's in the closet as well. My lungs sting from the pent up air, and just as I'm about to exhale, the door pushes shut from the outside.

Slinking to the floor, I allow myself an extra minute to catch my breath.

All of my rage should be aimed at Roman. For so long it has been. The son my father chose over me. Deeming him more fit to rule just because his mother was that of noble blood. His treatment of Enchantresses only deepened my anger the last few years, but as my fingernails dig into my palms, it isn't Roman's face I picture.

It's Galen's.

My stomach twists. I need out of this closet. Out of this castle. But if there's a chance Elora escaped tonight, I'll be damned if I leave without her.

Despite the tension in the hallway, the party has continued uninterrupted. Dancers still crowd the space as the musicians up their tempo and vigor.

I keep myself tucked into the wall of the room, nerves sloshing in my stomach, until I reach the entryway where we arrived. My shoulders unclench when I realize Thaddeus is there with the members of the Guilds.

They haven't given up on you yet, Sorin.

"It's about time," Thaddeus whispers, pulling my arm.

"In the drawing room," a woman says. Her scarlet, silk dress hugs all of her curves. Her dark hair, piled onto her head with crimson lips to match her dress. Small flecks of gold glitter against her ebony skin.

Lady Mordona of the Bloodstone Guild.

"Almost lost your chance." A woman with hair and skin as pale as snow brushes my shoulder as she passes by. Her beaded, turquoise gown swishes in time with the music as she walks.

Lady Oletta of the Cerulean Guild.

Thaddeus pushes me forward, but I shrug out of his grip. I can't read his expression as he turns to face the room across from us. "Thaddeus we must leave—"

"Don't be foolish!" He grabs onto my arm again. "We've made it all this way, we will not leave without a meeting." He pats my arm, offering a quick smile before heading into the drawing room.

My feet pull me forward, my legs uncertain, my heart even more so.

I have to get to her. I have to—

"Sit." Lady Mordona snaps her fingers before pointing to a chair at the end of the table.

Despite the gnawing instinct in my gut to leave, I do as she says. Once seated, everyone pulls off their masks, and I truly get a look at the ladies. Oletta looks similar to Agnes in age. Lines creasing around her mouth and eyes, especially when she smiles. Mordona is much younger, but something in her dark eyes tells me she could outsmart any one of us.

"Come on, boy. Let us see this so-called decree before the king himself waltzes in here." Lady Mordona's stare sends a chill down my spine. She watches me as she sips casually from a crystal glass filled with light pink, bubbly liquid.

I smile, but she looks away. With shaky hands, I pull the sacred paper from my pocket. Thaddeus reaches for it. My hand tenses around it.

"It's all right," Thaddeus says.

My hand trembles again as I let go of the parchment. My eyes don't leave it as he passes it straight to Lady Mordona and Lady Oletta. The two of them read for what feels like ages. Whispering back and forth to each other.

Placing my hands in my lap, I twist my father's ring until the skin beneath the cool metal begins to sting.

"Well it certainly looks legitimate," Oletta says.

"Not to mention he could be Silas' twin." Mordona laughs, the sound grating on the last bit of patience I have to be here.

A few tense moments of silence fill the space when the door to the drawing room bursts open. My chair tips backward as I stand abruptly, hands going instinctually to the blade on my hip. Only I remember, it isn't there. I dropped it in the hallway.

Fuck.

"Lord Calix," Thaddeus says with a long sigh. "We were beginning to worry."

Calix's eyes are frantic as he glances around the table.

Then, they meet mine. His face contorts, softening his expression.

"Sorin Rudhek," he says. Not a question, but an understanding. I nod. His eyes direct to Thaddeus, then to Mordona and Oletta. "The boy is who he says. I'm sure of it."

Nerves erupt in my stomach. How is this man so sure? I glance at Thaddeus but he's focused on Calix. His smile looks victorious, as if he's won in some way.

"It isn't that simple, Cal," Mordona says. She finishes her drink before setting it down on the oak table. "It isn't just our vote. It's the council as well."

"But with each of you backing me, backing this"—I point to the paper still in Mordona's hands—"there must be a fair chance."

She smiles, all teeth, and it reminds me so much of Ruse's that my knees shake as she stands and joins my side. "You have a fair chance. But don't think we offer our aid without a price." She leans in, her breath tickling against my ear. "Nothing is ever free."

The hair on my arms raises. What could she mean—

"That's a conversation for a different night," Lord Calix says.

I turn to him, and it's then I realize his pristine black boots have been smeared with mud. Not to mention his lapel completely disheveled.

He cradles his right hand to his chest, his soft eyes narrowed. "Sorin, Thaddeus, I think it's time we leave."

"What's the rush?" Oletta chimes in. She swirls her finger in her drink before popping it into her mouth. "Thaddeus?" She points to him. "You insisted we come to this dreadful event. Don't tell me you're leaving so early."

Thaddeus chuckles, but it's nervous and stifled. He glances again at Calix, who nods.

"We'll reconvene in a week," Thaddeus says. He stands from the table, smoothing the lines from his green suit. "One week, ladies, at the Onyx Guild."

Lady Mordona backs away, her dark skin shining with that iridescent, gold powder. "One week, Rudhek. And my price will be set." She smiles and as she waltzes out of the room, the red bloodstones hanging from her ears catching the light.

I follow Thaddeus to the door, but Calix's hand lands on my back, pushing me further. "Quickly," he whispers.

"You're pushing your luck with those two," Thaddeus says to Calix. "It was difficult enough to get them to come and now we're leaving just barely before we've spoken."

"I have my reasons," Calix says.

Outside the castle the rain falls in sheets. I place my mask back on just in case we run into anyone on our way to the caravan. Calix pushes ahead, practically jogging through the mud.

"I'm an old man, Calix Winterborn! What is the rush!" Thaddeus shouts, hobbling behind me.

Calix turns, his eyes finding mine. He hangs his head a moment before he takes a few steps forward so we're face to face.

"She's with us," he whispers. "Elora's with us."

TWENTY-TWO

SAMARIA

IT'S BEEN A DAY SINCE THE PEOPLE OF LOXLEY arrived, and while Agnes and Ulric do their best to settle them, Jarek and Evren take it upon themselves to begin inventory of the Jade Guild. Food, weapons, medicines.

"Let me at least help with something," I insist.

"We have it under control, Sam," Jarek says as he glances up from the bags of flour he's stacking. "Go be with them."

Them.

The people of Loxley. Nerves flutter in my stomach. I've yet to truly talk to anyone other than Ulric and maybe it's because a part of me is ashamed.

Ashamed I let this happen to our village.

Ashamed I left them to fend for themselves.

"Any and all supplies must be cataloged so we can ensure we're not over using," Evren says to Jarek, the two of them cramped together in the Jade Guilds small larder.

"I wish I could sketch this right now," Tallulah says through a laugh. "Two giant men hunched over some flour and sugar."

She laughs again when Evren grumbles something incoherent.

"I have to be going," she says, a smile still on her lips. "I'll be in the greenhouse, if you'd like to chat later." She squeezes my arm before leaving, the bag of herbs on her hip swaying from side to side.

Leaving Jarek and Evren to topple over each other in the larder, I sit in the meeting room, feeling more useless than ever. My palms itch, the magick I know is stored beneath me begging to rise to the surface.

"In time," I whisper to it. Not quite believing myself.

Lead sits on my shoulders and my mind races as I weave about the Jade Guild, thinking of all we must endure the next few days.

Weeks.

Months.

However long it takes to rebuild Loxley.

My home is gone.

The bustle has calmed, but the overflow of extra people inside the Guild is apparent. With the shortages of rooms and space, people are camped down every passage and corner.

I wander through the halls, stopping to say hello to all the familiar faces whenever I can. A few children have set up a game of dice on the stone floor. Their cheeks still ruddy from ash and soot, but they smile wide as they play round after round.

"Sam!" they call, their smiles beaming. "Come play with us!" My chest tightens. I kneel down and kiss each of their heads.

"Maybe in a little while." Their smiles fade but only briefly before they start up a new game.

My stomach clenches as I make my way past a mother and her two children, napping on the ground, a bed of ivy under their heads like pillows.

Turning the corner, I peer into the greenhouse. Cots have been lined up inside so Tallulah can work on those most injured in her own space. I watch through the window as she chats with Agnes while tenderly treating an older woman who I quickly realize is Marian. Her white hair is stained gray from ash. Her hands are red and blistered, but when Tallulah brushes a strand of hair from her face, she smiles. As if Tallulah's touch and presence alone has eased her pain.

I make round after round, stopping to chat with those who are not resting. With each recount of the Loxley fires, my guilt grows heavier and a pain forms behind my eyes.

I worry that the lead in my shoulders has become permanent as I sit with Thomas, one of Sorin's right hand men from Loxley.

"It was a normal day, Sam." He wipes his hands with a cloth, attempting to free them from the soot still stained from yesterday. It's still smeared on his cheeks, across his lightly freckled nose. Even his light auburn hair has a coating of ash. "Goats and chickens had been fed. Wards had been checked. We were just about to begin preparations for the full moon when we first smelled the smoke."

"Where did it start?" I readjust my position on the ground, crossing my legs.

Thomas tosses the cloth down before leaning against the stone wall.

I shouldn't make him recall this so soon. Sorin would—

"It started at your house." His eyes find mine. "By the time Ulric and I made it, the house was completely engulfed. We couldn't save anything."

My throat tightens further. I fold my hands together in my lap to conceal their shaking.

"Then," Thomas continues, "that's when we saw the arrows."

"Arrows?"

He closes his eyes. "Arrows tipped in fire rained down from every direction, Sam." His gaze meets mine again. His blue eyes, glassy with tears. "Dozens and dozens at a time. I've never seen anything like it. They burned your home first. Then hit every roof in the village. Every larder. The barns. The stables." He shudders, pinching the bridge of his nose. "There's nothing left but stone and rubble, Sam. And my parents—" He shakes his head again.

The pain in my throat intensifies as I attempt to swallow past the lump forming there. "I'm so sorry, Thomas."

He turns away, trying desperately to wipe his eyes unnoticed.

"Ulric told me you helped get people out. Helped get them here." I grab his hand, giving it a gentle squeeze. "I owe you everything."

A tear slips down his cheek, but he brushes it away quickly. As if he hopes I wouldn't see.

"Who could have done this?" His voice shakes as he presses the heel of his palm to his eyes. Thomas is close to Elora's age, perhaps only twenty three, but I often forget given how mature he's always held himself. Until right now, with the shake of his voice and the tears staining his cheeks. The loss of his home and parents settling into the faint creases of his face.

My heart constricts knowing the burden he'll wear, thinking there was something more he could have done. He shouldn't have been there to care for Loxley alone.

It should have been me.

"They knew right where the break in the wards were," Thomas says. "They waltzed right in as if they had been there before."

My stomach turns in on itself.

Not all those you trust are worthy.

"Get some rest, Thomas." I brush a piece of his hair from his forehead and wait until he's asleep to leave.

Before heading to bed, Evren called me for a meeting with Tallulah and Jarek. I sit silently, my eyes bouncing between the three others around me.

My home is gone and there is nothing I can do about it.

Anger pools in my stomach, sharp and acidic, begging for a release. Yet what use is it? It won't bring Loxley back. It won't change the fact that Sorin and I were not there when our people needed us most. In a way, I'm grateful for the rage. It takes up so much space, it hardly leaves room for anything else.

Especially sorrow. For that, I have no time. Not yet anyway. Not when so many around me have been through so much worse. I sigh, rubbing my fingers along my temples to soothe the ache. In every story told to me today, it all started the same.

They knew just where to get in.

"They can't all stay here," Evren says, snapping me from my haze. "We counted the rations and then we counted them again." Evren sighs, glancing up at the ceiling.

"Evren." Tallulah grabs his forearm but he shakes his head anyway.

"The amount of food it will take to feed everyone..." Evren rubs the heel of his palms over his eyes. I hadn't considered what these last few days must be like for him. All of us invading his home. Threatening the peace he fought so hard for.

"The folk of Loxley are no strangers to working hard," Jarek says. His hand finds mine under the table, giving it a squeeze, but it does nothing to stop the pain coursing through me, settling into each one of my veins.

"That won't make the crops grow any better." Evren lets out a long sigh. "Won't make more provisions suddenly appear. More animals to hunt." His weariness shows in his green eyes as he settles back in his chair. "We haven't been unaffected by this blight. We barely grow enough to feed those who live here and as we head into the cold months..." He scratches at his bearded jaw.

"We can hunt," I say. Tallulah and Evren glance at me. Jarek's hand tightens around mine, so I tighten back. "We can garden. Sew. Forge. Heal." Nerves flutter in my stomach as everyone's attention remains locked on me. But I swallow the feeling down and do what I know Sorin would do.

Talk.

"The people of Loxley have made a life for themselves out of nothing. Do you think Agnes or my father had assistance when they fled Valebridge?"

Evren's jaw tightens but his mouth remains shut.

"They built our village from the ground up," I say. "Those who found them, the people you are now harboring, are some of the most loyal and hardworking people I have the privilege of knowing."

Tallulah's smile catches my eye, but it's Evren's frown that pushes me forward.

Make him understand, Sam.

"I'm not saying it will be easy and I can't imagine the pressure you must feel with the blight." I release Jarek's hand, placing both of mine upon the table. "But we have just lost *everything.*" Thomas' face replays in my mind. His shattered voice and broken spirit fuel my confidence.

He lost his *parents,* for Mother's-sake, I want to scream.

"Our livestock. Our larders. Our homes and even some of our *people* lay in rubble. At the end of the day, are we not fighting for the same justice? Against the king? We'll pull our weight. We'll ration whatever food we can. My people will be eternally grateful. *I* will be eternally grateful. And when this is all over, my brother will repay you tenfold. You can mark my words."

Evren's eyes shift to Tallulah's. She nods, their words unspoken but seemingly understood.

"Spoken like a true leader." Evren's voice is so quiet I almost miss his words. My skin prickles. I am anything but a leader, I wish to say but bite my tongue instead. "But if the plan in Valebridge goes awry and King Roman finds out it is the Jade Guild who has harbored you—"

"Then we will be ready." Jarek stands. "You're not alone in this fight." He extends his hand to Evren who takes it. Then, to Tallulah. I do the same, wiping the sweat from my palms before grasping each of theirs.

"All right, then." Evren pulls Tallulah into his side.

"We're in this together, now," she says, not knowing the impact that one little word has on us.

THE SMELL of baked bread wafts through the halls as I pass by Eviey and Letty in the kitchen on my way back to mine and Jarek's room. Flour is dusted on the counters and over their wrinkled hands.

"You are a menace," Letty says, throwing her hands in the air.

"It's only a bit of honey." Eviey laughs. "A little extra sweet might do everyone some good around here." Smiling at the familiarity of the forest witches and the baked bread, I leave them to it for the night.

The growing darkness is sprawled across our small room, and as I collapse onto the bed, the cry I held so tightly before breaks free.

The weight on the bed shifts and Jarek is there, his eyes trained on me.

"Hey." I sit up, wiping my face with the sleeve of my shirt. "I didn't know you'd be in here so soon."

"You don't have to hide," he says, rolling to face me. "Sit with your tears, Sam." I lay back down and roll onto my side so we're face to face. He leans forward and kisses my wet cheeks but his body is rigid. His eyes finding focus just past me.

"Something ails you." I trace a finger down the center of his nose. He closes his eyes, a sigh leaving his lips.

"After seeing everyone today, seeing how broken they are..." His eyes open, their piercing blue color bright even in the dim light. "I could only think of one thing. In each broken face, through each cry and wail, I could only see them. Cora and Helen and Ma."

My heart freezes in time with my breathing.

"When this is all over, when it's safe to finally cross the Holden Sea I have to go back, Sam. I have to go home."

I worry my bottom lip, pressing my eyes shut so tightly little stars of white dance behind them. In the deepest corners of my mind, I knew this day would come. The day Jarek would travel home, back to his country.

Back to his family.

But leaving like this, when everything is so uncertain, I can't imagine it.

"Say something." His whispered words ghost my skin, leaving gooseflesh in their wake.

"What can I say?" I wipe a tear from my cheek.

Jarek's brows pinch together. His hand finds mine, pulling me closer into him. "Your people need you here," he whispers against my hair. A truth I'm desperately trying to avoid.

"It's Sorin they need." My defensive walls click into place, my body going stiff under his touch and words. I have never been the one that's needed and the fight in my chest is ready to burst forth.

"No, Sam. Sorin will rule Teravie if all goes as planned, but the people of Loxley will look to you for guidance. They'll need your strength to rebuild if that is what they choose."

My body begins to tremble, so I slide away from him.

Jarek's hands cup my face, scooting closer to me, closing the gap I just created. His forehead meets mine, and the part of me forged together by the two of us, snaps in half.

"Leaving without you by my side," he whispers, "will change the rhythm of my heart, Sam. I think it's forgotten how to beat on its own, without you. I won't ask you to leave your people, not when they need you most." The burning in my throat intensifies as Jarek looks me in the eye. "But I want to make it clear, this is the hardest decision I've ever made and it's not one I take lightly."

"Then don't make this decision."

Don't leave me.

Pulling back, his hands slip from my face. "What would you do if you were me? If it were Agnes and Sorin?"

Anger ignites in my chest, blooming through my lungs and burning up my throat. Not at Jarek but at *myself* for not seeing sooner how he longs to be home. How could he not? He was stolen from his sisters and mother. Did I expect him to be complacent never knowing their fate? "I've been selfish for keeping you here."

"You are anything but selfish, my queen." He kisses my knuckles before sliding away from me. My head spins as he stands from the bed.

"What if I wanted to come with you? What if that was my choice?"

When he turns, his face tells me what we both already know. I could never leave the people of Loxley like this. Couldn't fathom leaving Agnes in her current health or leaving Sorin to undertake all he's about to on his own. The tightness in my throat eases against my will, making room for a sob to rise in its place.

Jarek returns to the bed and pulls me into him. "My love for you won't cease just because there's an ocean between us." He kisses my forehead, then my lips. "We'll find a way, Sam." He kisses me deeper, his hands gripping my back so tight, my lungs strain under the pressure. "I promise we'll find a way."

I claw at his shirt, guiding him back onto the bed. His lips find mine, his hands roaming my body. Piece by piece, our clothes shed. His rough hands glide up my legs and then between them. My back arches into his touch, but when I close my eyes, all I see is him leaving.

Boarding a ship and sailing an ocean away.

I break apart our kiss and roll onto my side before he can see the tears as they slip from my eyes. He doesn't question why I've stopped. Instead, he lays next to me, so I bury myself into his chest. His breathing grows heavy, and only when I know he's truly asleep, do I allow the rest of my tears to shed.

Twenty-Three
Roman

Galen guides me through the ballroom; his hand on the small of my back like I'm a prize he fears to lose.

Once we've made it through the crowded room, his hand slips away leaving the spot cold. He hasn't said a word, and neither have I. My head dizzies from the alcohol and more so from the news of the prisoners.

Not to mention Sorin.

"Shall we retire?" Galen's voice is flat. Unamused. Like he's rehearsing a line not speaking to his lover. He doesn't turn to me as he speaks, his boots continuing their clacking against the stone floor. The hallway to our chambers is never ending tonight. When I don't answer he glances over his shoulder. "Ro? Are you all right?"

A lantern on the wall flickers from the breeze of his abrupt stop.

"That man," I say, steadying myself against the wall. "That wasn't Evren of the Jade Guild, was it? It was Sorin. That's why you couldn't stop staring at him." Galen's face doesn't flinch, but the hand that was once on my back flexes.

"Enough." Galen steps forward, caging me against the wall.

"Your obsession with the Dyrsjel and Sorin has gone too far. I should have never told you about him."

"Wh—"

"Do you think I don't know about your little visits, Ro?"

I push off the wall and brush him aside. "What I do with my prisoners is my choice." Guilt swirls in my stomach and a sharp pain forms behind my right eye, making me squint.

I really shouldn't drink.

Galen laughs, a sound I often crave yet so rarely hear. But this time it has my skin crawling. When I turn, our noses nearly brush. He smiles.

He runs a thumb across my cheek. Leaning forward, his lips brush mine. "You're keeping something from me."

I close my eyes to steady myself, wishing I was still propped against the wall. "Just like you're keeping things from me," I snap. "I heard you whispering to my guards the other night. Telling them to keep an eye on me." His pupils flare, a smirk toying on the corners of his mouth.

"My little bird, always so afraid to fly. So afraid to accept that he has wings to do with as he pleases." His breath is hot and sweet, like honey mead. "Is it the height you fear?" He kisses my lips again. "Or the freedom?"

My stomach twists into knots.

For most of my life I lived under my father's dictation. I did what he asked because when I didn't, there were consequences. Severe, brutal, unimaginable consequences. Galen's father wasn't much different and so we understood each other.

We saw each other.

And when my father died, I thought myself *free*. I was rid of the burden of constant perfection or at least the illusion of it. Rid of the abuse and the pain and the never-ending fear that came along with his company.

It was Galen who took that burden from me. Who *freed* me.

And I should owe him eternally. Should love him whole-heartedly.

But sometimes, even if I hate myself for the thought, I wonder if removing one monster from my life, merely replaced him with another.

"I have promised you everything, Ro. Freedom from your father, power over an entire country. And yet, every chance you've gotten the last month, you've fought me." He cocks his head to the side, studying me. My lungs burn and breathing staggers when he runs his thumb over my bottom lip. "So, tell me what it is I need to do for us to go back to the way we were."

I open my mouth but nothing comes out. His gentle touches and sweet scent dizzy my head further.

"Forgive me," he says, "whatever has gotten under your skin the last few weeks, let me mend it. Let me remind you that we do this as a team, or not at all. I'm sorry, is that what you want to hear?"

I lean in close, my lips brushing against his. "Beg me," I say. His brows dart up as I recline away from him. "Beg me for it." His eyes dart to my lips, then back at me. "For my forgiveness, for you sneaking around. Excluding me. Not trusting *me* to be a part of your plans." His throat works hard to swallow, his eyes still glued to mine. "Beg."

"I already told you I'm sorry."

I fist his shirt in my hands, pulling him closer. "I know, I heard you the first time, but I want to hear it again. This time from your knees."

His eyes narrow as he takes a step backward. This push and pull of power between us now palpable and stretched taut.

"Yes, Your Majesty," he says. He drops to his knees, one at a time. I glance down at him, his eyes meet mine, heavy with lust and I hate that this is what makes me feel that I have the upper hand. Hate that he's only doing it to appease me, but I don't stop him. I let myself believe for a few moments that I *am* in charge here. His fingers fumble with my buttons, his breath hot against my pants—

"Sir?" a guard asks.

I clear my throat and Galen stands, smoothing the front of his shirt as he does. "We are not done here," he whispers. I glance around him and that's when I realize the guard, my royal guard, isn't addressing *me*.

"What is it?" Galen runs his fingers through his hair, smoothing it back to practiced perfection.

"All of the prisoners are gone, sir." The guard's voice shakes. I clench my fists at my sides, venom pooling in my mouth. I was specific in my terms to not tell a soul and yet here is my own guard, betraying my orders. "I...I was told to tell you at once."

"What did you say?" Galen steps toward the man, leaving me breathless behind him.

The guard swallows. His eyes trail past Galen for a moment, landing on me, so I right my shirt, smoothing the wrinkles.

"We found a dead guard in the Dyrsjel's cell. Bloodied his eye real good—"

"Bloodied his eye how?" Galen glances at me briefly over his shoulder, but I don't flinch. I keep my eyes on the guard, though my stomach drops and the drinks from earlier threaten to spill out of me.

"We found this." The guard steps forward and hands Galen a soiled knife. Galen's shoulders tense, his knuckles whitening at his sides as he presses his hands into tight balls. My eyes track to the knife and a tiny spark of amusement rises in my chest.

I don't know why I gave Elora the kitchen knife. I suppose I wanted to see what she'd do. If she was brave enough to fight for herself.

To see if she was braver than me.

"I want every available man on this," Galen says. I don't have time to react that he is giving the same orders I have already issued before he continues. "If they are not found in the next hour, there will be consequences."

The guard doesn't hesitate, doesn't seek my approval before he gives Galen a quick nod and rushes down the hall.

A few moments of silence pass between Galen and I. His back remains turned, the blade still in his grasp. I open my mouth only to snap it closed. What is it that I can even say? I caused this mess and he knows it. But as he turns to me, his gaze narrowed, I realize that while I can admit what I did was reckless, I'm not sorry for it.

"This was your doing," Galen says as he steps toward me. He runs the blade down my arm before pressing the hilt of it into my palm. "Why?"

"What makes you so sure I knew about this?"

Galen grins at my response. He leans closer until his forehead touches mine, and I suck in a sharp breath. Anger and violence, I expected. I've had many years of Galen's outbursts to know what sets him off. But the gentleness of his touch puts me on edge.

"You can't hide from me, Roman."

Before retiring to my chambers, I sit half drunk in the study, replaying Galen's words over and over again.

You can't hide from me, Roman.

I rub at my temples, nursing the soreness beginning to form there. Why is it that I am merely a puppet in my life? Controlled by the men around me, whether I've chosen them or not.

"You wanted to see me?"

Straightening myself, I run a hand through my hair, though it's no use with the curls.

Cade joins me in the study. He's dressed in his usual guard attire aside from the heavy chain that's normally across his chest. Dark pants and a thick, navy top. He tugs at his leather vest as he takes the chair across from me.

"Tea?" I ask, snapping my fingers for the handmaid I'm sure is lurking just outside the door. A moment later, just as I could've guessed, she's at my side, pouring my cup for me. I glance at Cade who holds a hand up.

"No thank you," he says.

"I promise not to keep you from the ball for too long."

"It's no worry, Your Majesty." He crosses his legs, then uncrosses them. "I'm not one for dancing."

I drop a cube of sugar into my cup, watching it dissolve completely before taking a sip. The minty notes hit me first, my sour stomach settling slightly. "I haven't had a chance to thank you for securing the Dyrsjel."

Cade waves a hand through the air and looks anywhere but at me. "Just doing my job, Your Majesty."

There's a bite in his tone, but I decide to ignore it. Sighing, I recline back. It's not unusual for people to avoid my gaze. So many don't believe in the vision Galen and I have for Teravie. For the future of our people. Ridding magick from those we don't believe deserve it.

Why should Enchantresses be the only ones who are Mother-blessed? Does Mother Gaia not see all of her children as equals? This is the tale Galen has spun to me over and over again, a tale I've spun to myself. It was a way to defy my father, even after his death.

"Something bothering you?" I take another sip of my tea, letting the liquid cool on my tongue before swallowing it down.

"Of course not, Your Majesty," he says, finally glancing at me. His hazel eyes are cloudy, the lines around them deeper than they should be for a man of his age.

"Are you lying to me, Cade?" I place my tea cup down on the small table to my right before propping my elbows on my knees. "You didn't show any remorse when you hauled the Dyrsjel in?

When you signed a contract to find her, so what's changed?" A smile turns up my lips as his knee begins to twitch. His nervousness is obvious and for whatever reason it relaxes me. For so long, I was always the weakest person in the room. I forget how wondrous it can be to be on the other side of that threshold. To be the one who holds all the control instead. "I asked you a question, Cade."

"Sorry—" He takes a steadying breath, rolling his shoulders back to look me in the eye. "No concern, Your Majesty, it's just that I've repaid my debt. I brought you the Dyrsjel and—"

"Except that you haven't done your job," I say. "How is it that for a third time the Dyrsjel has escaped your watch?"

His face blanches.

Reaching inside my vest pocket, I pull out the formal paperwork to release Cade from my guard. I dangle the parchment, his freedom, in the air like a bated line for a fish. "Do you know what this is, Cade?"

He shakes his head, his eyes going wide.

"It's your ticket to freedom. A pardon from Valebridge, relieving you of your indenture to me." I toss the paper on the table before reclining in my chair again, threading my fingers together in my lap. "But only until you've completed one more task for me."

"One more task," he repeats, his voice going up at the end like a question. "But I thought—"

"Thought what?" I challenge him, sticking the parchment back into my breast pocket. "Thought you'd come here and argue with the king?"

He flinches, his once pale cheeks now tinted red. "No, Your Majesty. Please, tell me of this task, and I'll ensure it's done."

I thrum my fingers against the tabletop.

"I need you to find someone else for me. Someone with just as much value to me as the Dyrsjel. I have an army of men looking for her, but I need your sole focus on this. Can you do this for me, Cade?"

"Yes, Your Majesty." His eyes are trained on his lap, his jaw clenching and unclenching. He thought I brought him here to free him.

Pity.

"I need you to find a man called Sorin Trednik." Cade's eyes widen as he meets my gaze. "Oh, yes. You already know of him." Smiling, I take another sip of tea. "Find him. Bring him to me, and only me, and your debt is repaid. You'll be a free man, I swear on my father's grave."

Cade seems to weigh my offer, even though I believe he knows he doesn't have any choice in the matter. After an excruciating awkward silence, he stands and bows. "Sir Galen has already sent a search team for the Enchantresses that managed to escape, surely they'll be looking for Sorin—"

"I didn't ask for your opinion on the matter. In fact, I didn't ask you a question at all." Standing from my chair, I push my fingers into the wood of the table and lean forward. "You will go, alone, in search for Trednik, and you will not speak to me again until he is found. Otherwise this"—I gesture to the parchment—"will be as if it never existed, just as the delusion of your freedom."

Cade chews the inside of his cheek before dipping his chin. "I won't let you down again, Your Majesty."

"I should hope for your sake, you don't." My hand cuts through the air, dismissing him at last.

Faint music from the ballroom ghosts the room as Cade exits the study. It'll be hours before the party is over, and yet I can't bring myself to go back down. Even the task of entertaining the Guild leaders has been pushed aside.

I let out a long sigh, basking in the powerful feeling of controlling someone's fate. Even if that someone is just an officer in my guard and even if his fate means sending him on a search for a brother I shouldn't bother to recognize.

I reach for my tea, annoyed it's already gone cold. "What are you doing, Roman," I whisper to myself before snapping my fingers again and demanding a fresh kettle.

Twenty-Four

Elora

"The other women?" I ask the driver.

He says nothing, keeping his face forward.

The rise and fall of my chest hasn't slowed since Calix shoved me into the back of this caravan. But it's been too long and his departing words repeat over and over in my mind.

"Don't make any sounds. Any movements."

Don't let them take you.

I tug at my earlobe before glancing out the small, curtained window. The caravan is still parked near the bridge but now more guards have filtered out. They shout amongst each other; the glint of their blades makes my stomach lurch.

Looking for you. Time to run, susi.

Run. Yes. That I'm good at. I tighten my shirt around myself and place my hand on the door—

"We need to search this caravan by order of the king."

I freeze, my hand still gripping the handle.

"No need," the driver says, suddenly finding his voice. "Lord Calix will be back any moment then we'll be out of your hair."

"You didn't hear me," the guard says. "We've been

instructed to search every caravan, no matter who it belongs to."

"Suit yourself." The weight in the front shifts as the driver steps down. My heart sets a bruising pace as I eye the door. The men are on the opposite side. No way out.

I'm in a cage.

I slide my hand from the door and bite my tongue to keep from crying. My throat is too tight, my body too weak. The door pushes open—

A loud crack sounds outside.

The guard shouts, but I can't make out any words. Metal hits metal and I take it as my opportunity to run. I push the door open, and when I land, my bare feet hit something sticky and wet. Crimson pools beneath me. Darkness rushes my vision. My lungs squeeze and the images I fight every night come cascading down.

Snow.

Crimson.

Steel.

"Elora."

I'm snapped out of my panic by a voice. I don't look up from the ground as the darkness washes from my vision. I don't trust that it isn't in my head for so many of the voices are.

"Elora." A hand brushes mine, and I don't need to look to know but it's the touch that my body remembers. Recognizes even in the storm of panic. I'd know it anywhere. In any shadowed corner of the earth. His thumb tucks under my chin and lifts upward.

"Sorin." My voice cracks.

He pulls off his mask, and his dark eyes find mine. Every wall I've built around myself the last few weeks shatters. The lump in my throat grows painful as I fall into his chest. His clothes are wet and bloodied, I'm sure from the guard, but I don't let it stop me from wrapping my arms around him. As his fingers snake through my hair and his lips brush my forehead.

"I have you," he whispers against my skin. His hands hold tightly against my back. "I have you, love."

He came for me all the while I was coming for him. I've always wondered if the darkness yearns for the sun each night. If it wishes to have only a taste of its golden warmth and light. But now I know it to be true. Because he is here. Good and light and warm and safe. And despite all of my darkness, he is the sun I crave.

"We need to hurry." Calix steps forward, clasping a hand on Sorin's shoulder.

Sorin pulls away but doesn't let go of my hand as he guides me back into the caravan.

Once inside, my hearing is muffled by the sound of my heart overworking in my chest. But through the constant thrumming comes a noise loud enough to make me jump.

A howl.

"Ruse." I rip open the curtain of the caravan just in time to get a glimpse of a set of emerald eyes in the distant woods. My heart beats faster but this time for an entirely different reason.

She's alive.

"Ruse," I say again, my voice breaking at the end.

Sorin wraps his arm around my middle, his chin resting in the crook between my shoulder and jaw. "She's okay," he whispers in my ear. "Alaric, too. They know the way. They'll be right behind us."

My shoulders unclench as Ruse's green eyes fade into the darkness, another faint howl creeping in through the cracks of the caravan.

I pay no mind to the two men beside us as I turn to Sorin, running my fingers along his jaw. He closes his eyes and takes a shuddering breath as I trace the outline of his lips. Sorin grabs my hand, careful to avoid my wrists, and kisses my knuckles before wrapping me into his arms.

"Elora," he whispers; the sound is both broken and whole. That piece inside of us that's only made for each other rights itself, and despite everything, I'd endure it again if it meant finding him alive and safe.

"You'll stay at the Onyx Guild," Calix says, but I can't focus on anything other than Sorin. His warmth. The erratic rhythm of his heart. "My healers can help you."

This draws my attention and I turn to him. He gestures to my wrists and on instinct I pull my shirt down to cover them up.

"Healers? Enchantresses?" I ask.

Calix shakes his head, finally meeting my gaze. "Just medicine, I'm afraid. Not Mother-blessed," he says through a smile.

It's with his words my memories from tonight slam into me. He must read by expression because before I can ask him, he's reaching for my hand. I flinch at his touch, but his fingers clasp around mine and I'm surprised to find comfort, not fear.

"My men found two of them just before the king sent the guards, but any others..." He pulls his hand away and glances down. "I'm sorry."

I let out a long sigh, tears burning in my eyes as I recline into Sorin's chest.

"We've got a few hours," the other, older man says. "Let's all get some shut eye. Dawn will bring a new world of problems for us and Mother knows we haven't any solutions."

I wake with a start.

Sitting up, my hair is stuck to my neck, my breathing shallow and painful. Dim, gray light trickles in from a window, barely lighting the space, but there's a *window*. My breathing slows as I slump backward against a wood headboard.

Not in a cage.

I reach around and trace the ink on the back of my neck. It no longer burns, but the weight of it is enough to cause an ache.

The bed moves, and I remember I'm not alone. Now that I'm unshackled, I can mask the ink, so I do, still not ready to discuss the bargain I made with Grawgeth in Sorin's stead.

Sorin sleeps beside me. His dark hair is ruffled, the scruff lining his jaw barely there. I don't wish to wake him, but my fingers find their way to his face. Just as they had last night. A way of reminding myself he's truly here. Gently, I trace his lips. Then his nose and his jaw. I slide back down into bed, keeping myself facing him. He must sense me, because he yawns, stretching his hands above his head.

"How did you sleep, love?" A smile twitches at his lips, and my body naturally curls into his. His skin is warm and smooth, and I have a thought to pinch him or myself to make sure this is real.

"I slept well, actually," I say, and his arms wrap tighter around me. "We're at the Onyx Guild?"

"Yes." He kisses the top of my head, and my stomach flutters. "The others will meet us here in a week."

"Sam and Jarek?" I ask as Sorin runs his fingers up and down my arms. I savor the touch, but my mind snags on the night prior. "Are the other Enchantresses well?"

"Sam and Jarek will be here." Sorin's fingers run through my hair, and I realize that while I've been changed into a simple, cotton shift, I haven't bathed. In weeks. I cringe and pull myself away from him. "And as for the Enchantresses, I assumed we would talk to them together."

"I'd like that." I grimace as I bring my hands up. My nails are broken at different lengths, dirt caked beneath them. "We have many things to talk about, I'm afraid." I glance at him, but he's moved to his back, staring at the ceiling.

"That we do," he says. He sighs, his chest deflating. "Galen —" He presses his palms into his eyes, and my heart squeezes.

"Sorin—"

"We don't have to speak of it now," he says. "Unless you want to." He glances at me with an attempt at a smile. "Anything you want, Elora." He props himself on his elbow. "I just—"

"Later." I lean forward to brush a kiss to his forehead. Galen's betrayal is one that I've had weeks to sit with and while it stung, it's nothing I imagine to what Sorin is feeling.

His best friend.

A brother in arms.

"Later," he mimics, wrapping me in his arms again. My body relaxes into his as I examine my wrists. The wounds around them are still open but not painful. I tilt my head as I study them.

"One of the healers applied some cream." Sorin gestures to my wrists. "You fell asleep in the caravan. I carried you inside and didn't want to wake you. She left extra on the bedside table."

I glance over my shoulder to see a small tub wrapped in parchment and topped with lavender.

"The wolves?" I sit forward with a start, closing my eyes and focusing on pushing a message through our bond. Sorin says something but I don't hear him as I concentrate.

You're okay, Ruse?

Yes.

It's barely there, a vague whisper, but as the message hits me I muffle a cry in relief.

Without the iron around my wrists, my magick stirs, itching at my skin. Smiling, I glance at Sorin again. He's propped on an elbow, staring at me. I lean forward to kiss him but stop myself as I catch sight of my filthy hands and nails again. "Is there somewhere I can bathe?"

"There's a bathing chamber attached to our room. I'll call for some warm water and towels." He leans forward and lays a quick kiss to my cheek. "I'll see you after your bath at breakfast."

"You're not joining me?"

His eyes widen, a faint blush spreading over his cheeks. "Is that what you wish, love?"

I glare at him, not willing to repeat myself.

He smiles, then laughs, and a tiny piece of my broken self stitches back together. "I'll get the water and the towels, wait here."

Once alone, I study the room more closely. Just as expected for the Onyx Guild, the walls and floor are black stone. The room is simple, a four-post bed and a bathing chamber just as Sorin said. Peeking through the dark curtains, a splash of dull light hits me and just over the horizon I can make out the Kirsgard Mountains. My hands tremble as I pull the curtains tightly shut.

Sorin returns a few moments later with two handmaids. Their long, black dresses sway against the floor as they fill the basin. They drop a few towels on the bed and leave without a word.

My stomach clenches as I join Sorin in the bathing chamber. Like the bedroom, it's mostly black apart from the porcelain tub. Onyx stones dangle from the ceiling on invisible strings, light from the small window hitting them and making the room sparkle.

"Ladies first," he says and just before he touches my night dress, he stops. His hands retreat behind his back and his eyes land on the wall past me.

He's afraid to touch me.

I grab his arm, guiding his hand to my dress, encouraging him. He hesitates a moment before sliding the dress from my body. Under the morning light, the black and purple bruises are painted like a tapestry upon my skin. I don't take my eyes off of him as he slips my camisole over my head. His face reddens, his jaw clenched tight. When he goes to my undergarments, his hands tremble against them so I place my hand atop his.

"I'm all right, Sorin."

His eyes flick to mine. There's a fire in them I haven't seen before. A rage that is so unlike his normal self that I almost flinch.

"I'm all right." I reassure him again and though he doesn't look to believe me, he continues undressing me until I'm bare. I step into the water, relishing in the sting it leaves against my bruised skin.

Sorin slides in behind me, his long legs wrapping around my body. His hands are gentle as he glides lavender soap over my arms and chest.

"Tip your head back," he says and I do.

Water prickles my scalp, the soapy bubbles fill the small room with their lavender and chamomile aroma. After my hair is rinsed and my body clean, we sit in contented silence. The window is cracked open but not even a caw from a crow comes wafting through. My back to his chest, my head on his heart.

"I missed you every day." His confession echoes throughout the room. I grip his arms and so he tightens them around me. "Every second." He kisses my head then his lips brush against my neck. "I couldn't sleep. Couldn't eat." Another kiss. I press farther into him, tipping my head up so I can see his face. "I won't let it happen again."

"You are not to blame for what happened." He silences me with a pass of his thumb over my lips.

"Of course I am," he whispers. "If I had come forward as the heir sooner, Roman wouldn't have—"

"You can't think that way." I sit forward and spin so that my body faces him. My legs wrap around his waist as I scoot forward and sit in his lap. His breath hitches as our bodies become flush with one another. "We're here now and that's all that matters."

His eyes train on my mouth and my breaths remain stuck in my lungs. His fingers dig into my sides, that electrifying touch I've been desperate for the past few weeks buzzes against my bare skin.

He won't kiss me first, I know that. Not with the damage

done to my body. But the bruises will fade. The memories, perhaps not as quickly, but I pay that no mind at this moment. I shift my weight again so I'm more firmly planted in his lap. Sorin's eyes close at the contact. Tracing my fingers up his chest, I watch as tiny droplets of water tickle along our skin.

"Elora..."

I grab his face, our lips meet not with a tenderness, but with a fierce longing. With familiarity and passion. Sparks of lightning, as Sorin once described it, ignite over my skin, and the more he kisses me, the more I crave it. I moan against his mouth as he pulls me tighter into him. Our kiss grows frenzied. Sorin's hands are in my hair, his teeth and tongue against my neck. Water sloshes out of the tub, hitting the marble floors.

Breaking away, I cradle his face between my hands again. We're both breathless as we stare at each other. He kisses me once more, gently on the lips. My body aches to be closer. But the voices begin to rise in my head, and I know it won't be long before I can't ignore them.

He must sense my change because his breathing begins to even out. His grip, a little lighter around my waist.

"Later?" I ask, adding to our long to do list.

He smiles. Bright and beaming, and I unabashedly place a kiss right on his dimple.

"Later," he promises back.

TWENTY-FIVE
SORIN

THE TWO ENCHANTRESSES THAT ESCAPED WITH Elora sit side by side around a dark marble table in the Onyx meeting room. Pitchers of water and kettles of tea line the center of the table along with a few plates of dried meat and assorted nuts that no one seems to care for.

Elora's nails tap against her teacup, her eyes darting between the two women before us.

"We cannot stay here long." The dark-haired Enchantress speaks first, her skin pale and eyes a stormy blue. She cups her mug of tea between her hands. "Hunters will sense any magick we have—"

"Only if you use it," Elora says. Both of the Enchantress' eyes fall to her. She tugs her earlobe but straightens herself. "If you don't use your magick, the hunters can't sense you. I lived for years that way—"

"Must have been lovely," the other Enchantress adds. She has deep, red hair that billows down to her shoulders. Despite the chill of the mountains, her sleeves are pushed up, revealing scars around her wrists, bubbled and pink against her dark skin. "Living a life in peace while the rest of us were mutilated. Murdered."

Elora flinches, her shoulders sagging.

"That isn't necessary," I say, my hand finding Elora's leg under the table. "While Elora and a few others managed to escape Valebridge, I assure you their lives were anything but easy."

I have you.

The Enchantress with the shorter hair glances at me. Her eyes narrow further, and a chill runs down my spine.

"And you are the heir of Valebridge correct?" She smiles when my body goes rigid. "Rumors travel quickly through Valebridge, heir. Even in the dungeons." She pours herself another cup of tea. The steam muddies her features a moment before it settles and her eyes are on me again. "So gracious of you to finally step up and help."

"Enough of this." Lord Calix enters the room with a sea of handmaids and guards behind him. Each one dressed in all black. Calix's fur lined cloak is laced tightly, a faint crest of mountains stitched across the front. Calix glances quickly at Elora and even quicker away. "We're happy to have you stay as long as you're comfortable, Enchantresses."

He redirects his attention to me. "Sorin, as well as all of us, have made mistakes and bear many regrets these last five years. But know this, we will stop at nothing until there is justice and peace for the Enchantresses. You have my word."

The Enchantress looks to the woman next to her and when she nods, she focuses back on Calix. "Whatever we can do to help," she says. "Please let it be known."

"Let's start with your names." Calix gestures toward the Enchantress while taking a long sip of tea with his other hand.

The women share a glance with each other.

"You're guests in this house," Calix says. "So please, your names?"

The redhead Enchantress pushes her hair behind her shoulders. "I'm Brigid."

Calix nods, his smile warm and inviting. So, unlike what I

presumed the Lord of Onyx Guild to be. Given the elevation and constant cold, I assumed a bit more of a bite.

The dark-haired Enchantress watches Elora as she draws a ring around the edge of her teacup. Her lip curls when my hand wraps around Elora's shoulders. "I'm Sera," the woman finally says. "Now"—she breaks her gaze from Elora and looks to Calix —"I'm afraid Brigid and I don't have much to offer. Most of our magick was harvested and what's left is unreliable. I managed to get us out of the castle—" Elora scoffs, crossing her arms. "But I'm not sure what use I'll be to you, Lord."

Calix holds his hands up, shaking his head. "I would never ask you to use your magick against your will." His gaze slides to Elora who is unsurprisingly silent by my side, I can practically hear her teeth grinding from here. "What I do ask is for your help mapping out the castle." Sera relaxes into her chair, a smile dancing on her lips. "Passageways, dungeons. Anything that may make infiltrating smoother."

"I have also lived in Valebridge, Calix," Elora says, her voice barely registering in the room. "It was my home, too."

Sera smiles, bringing her teacup to her lips. "And yet you fled."

My stomach boils, nails digging into the marble top—

"There isn't any need for hostility." Calix steals my moment to speak. "What has happened to you—" He glances at each of the women at the table, Elora included. "*All* of you, is unfathomable. Without working together, we'll have no chance at rectifying this mess the king has made." He lets out a sigh, rubbing his palm to his eyes. "Are you all with me?"

ELORA PACES throughout our small room. Back and forth she goes, between the chest of drawers and the black four post bed. She bites at her nails a few times before placing her hands behind her back, biting her lip insead. Her hair, a mess of waves from our earlier bath, is down and unkept. The dark pants that Calix provided fit more snugly than her normal breeches. The dark, long sleeve, wool-lined top is laced up in the front, and she pulls on the strings as she moves back and forth.

"Are you going to do that all day?" I say through a laugh.

She stops to frown at me before turning toward the bathing chamber, her back facing me. Her shoulders stoop and between both of our breaths, she sniffles.

"They were not kind to you."

"They weren't wrong about me," she says. Elora doesn't turn but her head straightens. "My mother and I fled Valebridge and never looked back. We lived in peace on the mountain while they were tortured and—" She hangs her head again. "I don't even know why I'm here. Perhaps I should have just stayed in Valebridge." My stomach twists. "I'm so tired of being in pain, Sorin."

I step toward her, making sure my boots are heavy against the ground so as to not surprise her. She stiffens when my hands brace her shoulders, but a moment later, her muscles relax.

"Where does it hurt, love?"

She says nothing, keeping her back turned.

"Does it hurt here?" I slide my hands gently over her back. Careful not to touch her bruises too deeply.

Her breath hitches, but still she's quiet.

"How about here?" I kiss her temple, and she lets out a sigh. "Yes, this must be what ails you." I kiss her temple again before turning her around so she faces me. Her lips twitch, as if she can't decide to smile or cry.

I drag her to the bed.

She sits down, and I take my time unlacing her boots then unfastening her cloak and pulling it off of her. I kick off my boots before climbing into bed. She curls onto her side, her back to my chest. There isn't much solace I can offer her, but maybe a momentary distraction will be enough for tonight.

My fingers trail along her leg, up the curve of her hips, until they skim underneath her tunic. "I know everything feels like shite right now," I say, "but I can't hear you say you'd wish to still be in Valebridge because if you were still there, it means you wouldn't be here and I don't think I can handle the thought."

She lets out a deep sigh, her hands propped under her cheek like a pillow.

"Now, does this feel okay?" My lips graze her neck as I whisper against her skin, fingers tracing tentatively across her hip. "I asked you a question, love."

"Yes," she whispers. "That feels okay."

I hold my breath, still unsure she's ready for any kind of intimacy, but I trust her enough to tell me when I've gone too far, so I continue. "What about this?" I glide my fingers under her shirt, tracing soft lines over her ribs, then her breasts. "Does that feel good or bad?"

She arches into me, and my eyes roll shut as I trace her breasts again.

I missed you so badly, I want to say. But this isn't about me, so I remain quiet. I kiss her neck, letting my lips drag against her skin before nipping slightly just at the bottom of her ear. "Answer my question, Elora."

"Good," she says, between heavy breaths. "That feels good."

"Good." I slide my hand lower over her bare skin, down her abdomen, until I'm at the laces of her breeches and that's where I stop. Doubt gnaws at my mind, making my fingers retreat before I can push this further.

As I slide my hand away, Elora grabs it, guiding it back down. Her hair slides away from her neck as she dips her head forward, revealing a glimpse at something dark marked on her skin. But as she moans again, my body heats, distracting me from what I think I saw.

I wrap my other arm under her, holding her body tight against mine. She tilts her head back so it rests in the crook between my jaw and shoulder. I continue my movement, running my palm over and over until she's wriggling beneath me.

"Good or bad?" I whisper, my breath coming out just as ragged as hers.

"Good, Sorin."

I remove my hand for a moment, and she glances over her shoulder at me, a frown forming between her brows.

"I don't think you have any idea what that does to me, love." I kiss her pulse. "My name on your lips is enough to undo me right now."

Her face softens as I unlace her breeches, painstakingly slow. I'd rather rip them off, but she needs to be outside of her mind for a moment so I take my time.

I kiss her neck, her shoulder. Elora turns to face me, so I move on top of her and kiss her deeply, my fingers tangling in her hair. My lips on her neck and her chest and her mouth.

"Good?" My voice is low, and now she doesn't answer me. Just a breathy moan that has my heart racing. My body is ignited just by kissing her. Touching her. Being close to her. I kiss her again and again, the memory of losing her teeming at the edge of my mind.

"Sorin." She pulls away, her chest heaving under mine. Running her fingers through my hair, she then drags them down my neck and across my chest. Her eyes meet mine, and I'm brought back to our first night together after the wicked wood. She opens her mouth, perhaps to say something, but I don't give her the chance before I brush my thumb to her lips and speak first.

"When you feel yourself retreating to all the shadowy places in your mind, just tell me." I swipe across her body lip again. "Just tell me, and I'll meet you there. And in the shadows, we'll face the demons together. I'll hold your hand until you're ready to climb back out, no matter how long it takes."

A tear slips from her eye, wetting my arm that's tucked beneath her.

"I told you before that the darkest parts of you will never be enough to scare me away. I meant it and now it's time you start believing it."

It's only when Elora is soundly asleep against my chest that I push her hair to the side and discover what I thought I saw earlier. I lightly trace my fingers along the ink on the back of her neck. The same black, circled pattern I received from Grawgeth all those years ago. My stomach sinks.

I should have seen this sooner.

A knock at the door draws my attention. I tip-toe across the room, pulling on my clothes as I do.

Lord Thaddeus waits on the other side. His clothes rumpled, as if he, too, dressed in the dark.

I step into the hall and shut the door behind me. "What is it?"

"It's the Jade Guild," he says. There's panic in his tone, the words rushing out all at once.

"Is my sister not on her way?"

He paces the small space outside our door, his hands fraying the edge of his tunic. "We must abandon the Onyx Guild and return immediately." My stomach clenches. "Evren sent word with a raven, it arrived only moments ago." He glances toward the ground. His hands tremble as they rake through his gray hair. "Loxley has been destroyed."

THE CARAVAN RATTLES as we make our way to the Jade Guild the following morning. Elora's grip on me is airtight, not letting a moment pass without our hands clasped together. She's nervous and it's understandable. The last time we were in a caravan, I was covered in blood and her wrists were still raw.

"Be there soon," I whisper against her ear. Her eyes are closed but the smile on her lips tells me she's not sleeping.

Thaddeus, however, has dozed off, his heavy snores keeping me and Calix awake. The Lord of the Onyx Guild insisted on traveling with us to aid in any way he can. Though I find his dedication odd, he's practically a stranger, I appreciate any effort to try and bring comfort to my people.

My people.

Bile rises up my throat. So many faces and memories of home pushing their way to the surface.

I distract myself by peeking outside the window. The forest has barely woken up, daybreak promised by faint songbirds and a blooming sky.

Loxley has been destroyed.

Thaddeus' words echo in my mind.

Loxley has been destroyed.

I have tried to imagine it. Tried to picture all he told me that happened to my home, but my mind refuses. Like it won't be true until I see Sam and she can confirm it. I close the curtains and brace my elbows on my knees.

Loxley has been destroyed.

Our village has been warded for decades. Protected. Sacred to those in need. It isn't lost on me that it's been infiltrated now by the kingdom. Especially when someone who knows Loxley as well as I do stands at the king's side.

I bite the inside of my cheek and close my eyes. There is so much anger brewing inside of me, I feel as though I'll come undone. Burst right out of my clothes. My jaw clenches and that's when I hear it.

A howl.

Elora bolts up, her eyes wide. "The wolves," she says, grappling for the curtains. "They said someone's out here." She bites her bottom lip, pulling the curtain shut.

"And who might it be?" Thaddeus' eyes are barely open as he asks, his gray hair sticking every which way.

"Hunters." Elora's knee bounces, so I place my hand on it.

"We'll pull off and take care of this," I say. She grabs my arm as I lean forward toward the driver. If it had been my way, we'd have taken horses, giving us more discretion. "I won't leave you, love." I kiss her forehead as the caravan comes to a stop.

"I'll join you," Calix says, eyeing Elora for a moment.

"The wolves can handle it," she says. I glance at her over my shoulder. "Ruse says not to go."

"Does she now?" I chuckle, kissing Elora again. "We'll be right back."

"I'm going too then," she says.

"Elora—"

"I'm going if you're going." I open my mouth to argue, but I know it won't matter so I shut it.

We take a timid step out, the breeze nipping at my ears, swollen droplets of rain landing on our cloaks. There's rustling behind me, leaves crunching. I turn just as a mass of black fills my peripherals.

Ruse.

Her lip curls over her teeth, and Calix flinches next to me. "Mother above," he says, his voice dropping low.

"She's harmless," I say. Not quite the truth, not quite a lie.

Elora wraps her arms around Ruse, the massive wolf's head dipping low to rest atop Elora's. Alaric joins them next and Elora wraps her other arm around his neck. They sit like that for a moment, the moaning of tree branches the only sound between us.

"Where? "Elora asks, pulling back, wiping at her face.

Ruse trots ahead, Alaric at her rear and as we crest over a small hill, a dozen hunters sit around a fire.

"Good girl," Elora whispers, running her fingers along her shiny, black coat.

The hunters sit with their backs facing us, their fire crackling, sending plumes of heat into the waking forest. Grizzly badges and vials litter the ground, as if they've been here awhile.

Camping out.

Waiting.

"What's the plan?" Calix asks, his eyes glancing at Ruse and Alaric. His throat bobs as Ruse shows her teeth again.

My fingers twitch, the anticipation of a fight getting the better of me. "My plan is to treat them as well as they've treated my girl."

I catch Elora's smile out of the corner of my eye, before I pull my bow and nock an arrow. I've never been a fan of killing, but I've always done what I had to do to keep my people safe. And *she* is my person. I'll be damned if I let anyone who thinks causing her or Enchantresses pain live a moment longer.

"Do it," Elora says and that's all it takes. The first arrow lands, hitting a hunter in the side of the neck and then it's nothing but chaos.

The rest of the hunters are on their feet, weapons drawn as the wolves sprint forward. Ruse meets the first hunter teeth first, then Alaric does the same. Calix falls backward, and I'm beginning to wonder why he came at all. Elora pushes past me as I let another arrow fly, hitting the farthest hunter square in the chest.

The men shout, only about a half dozen left when the forest shifts. My heart slams against my ribs as Elora lifts her hands, and pulls the weight of the falling rain down across the camp, engulfing the men that remain in a giant orb. She holds the water steady until the men floundering inside of it begin to still and only when there is no movement whatsoever, she lets the orb fall. It crashes to the ground in a thunderous wave, wetting everything in its path.

The limp bodies of the hunters flow through the forest, one landing close to my boot. I take a step back, but Elora remains rooted in place. Her boots and pants soaked as water rushes past, looking for an escape. The wolves flank her and she leans into Alaric, resting her head on his side.

"Is she all right?" Calix asks, his voice shaking.

"No," I say, turning to him. Of course she's not all right.

Elora glances at me over her shoulder, her eyes bright and

glowing. The wolves follow after her as she makes her way around the bodies of the hunters.

You are so strong, I want to say. To remind her that even though life has given her nothing but pain, she still has found a way to rise.

"She most certainly is not all right," I repeat to Calix, whose gaze is fixed on the sopping wet ground. "But she will be."

Twenty-Six
Samaria

I pace and pick at my nails as Jarek, Agnes, and I wait in the meeting room.

"Sit down, Samaria, you're making me dizzy." My mother pulls out the chair next to her and gestures for me to sit.

I shake my head and continue to pace. How can everyone be so calm?

The last few days have been torturous waiting for them to arrive. The moment we got word Elora was safe, my mind has been an endless spiral. So many plans to be made. So many questions to be asked.

A moment later, the doors open with a creak and my heart stops.

My brother joins us, his face unshaven and his eyes are warm, but the purple under them gives me an indication of how the trip here went. He grasps my mother in a hug as she meets him across the room.

"I'm fine," he whispers. He glances at me but I look past him. To the doorway.

To Elora.

She meets my eye and a smile creeps over her lips. "Sam," she says, and my heart very nearly bursts. Her hair is in its usual braid, her body looks strong despite everything, but it's her wrists that have me swallowing my tears. Disfigured scars line them where she's been shackled. The redness indicates how fresh the pain is, and when I glance at her again, her face is stony but her eyes are wet.

You don't have to be strong here, I want to say. To remind her that when she's with us, she doesn't have to pretend. But I say nothing, because I know better than anyone how to choose which face to put on.

Behind her is who I assume to be Lord Calix, dressed in black pants, shirt, and fur lined cloak. His graying hair is full and cropped short, a matching beard lining his jaw. He and Thaddeus join us first, Sorin and Elora trailing closely behind. My eyes stay fixed on the door, waiting.

"Where is Galen?" My question goes unanswered as every one filters in the room.

"Samaria, this is Lord Calix of the Onyx Guild." Thaddeus extends the introduction, and I take Calix's hand, giving it a firm shake, thoughts of Galen still racing in my mind. Why isn't he here?

The worst begins to sink in.

He's gone.

I glance at Sorin, but he's occupied with Agnes, their whispers low and private.

"It's a pleasure." Lord Calix's voice is rough and low, a slight accent lining his words. His eyes draw past me for a moment to where Jarek stands. Dropping my hand, his eyes go wide and the accent I thought I heard before is confirmed as he begins speaking to Jarek in Scandavi. Words and phrases I can't understand except for one.

"Jeg ser deg," Calix says, grasping Jarek in a hug.

My face twists and a lump forms in my throat. I can't make out the rest of what they're saying but the one phrase I'd decipher anywhere. The only Scandavi I've bothered to learn and only because Jarek has said it to me so many times.

Jeg ser deg.

I see you.

Jarek says something else, his laugh bellowing through the room. I make a note as I follow Jarek to the table to make him teach me more Scandavi. Before sitting, Elora slips her hand in mind.

"You," she says and it's barely there, but she smiles. "It's *you* I've been missing." She squeezes my hand then wraps me in a hug.

"You're okay?" I ask as we pull away from each other.

"Getting there," she says quietly before joining Sorin on the other side of the table.

I slide into a chair next to Jarek. "An old friend?" I nod toward Lord Calix.

"Something like that, my queen." He kisses my temple but offers no other explanation for their strange encounter.

Now that everyone is seated, I rap my knuckles against the tabletop. "Why has no one answered my question," I demand. "Where is Galen?"

"We have much to discuss," Sorin says, drawing my attention. He gestures to the kettle. "We might be here awhile."

"I can't believe this." I cradle my face in my palms as Sorin and Elora recount their time in Valebridge. My head spins and I wish it were from too much wine and not what I'm hearing.

It was Galen who hurt her.

Who trapped Ruse that night. Who plotted against us. His friends. His family.

And without a doubt in my mind, it was he who destroyed Loxley.

Not all those you trust are worthy.

"It's pretty unbelievable." Sorin nudges my arm so I look up. His face is so much paler than when I saw him last, his eyes that much darker. "I saw Galen at the Autumn Moon and Elora has confirmed it. He is the one responsible for this."

Jarek mumbles something in Scandavi, his fists clenched into tight balls atop the table. Calix gruffs an agreement, shaking his head.

"He really did this to you?" I grasp Elora's hand. She nods. "I'm so sorry." My lip quivers and sour, vile creeps up my throat. "Why? Why would he do this?"

"He believes he's protecting Teravie from Enchantresses," Elora says. Her voice is hoarse and quiet. Like she's spent the last few weeks screaming and is only now realizing how to speak again. "His sister died at the hands of an Enchantress Healer and so he thinks the only way to get justice is to take magick into his own hands." She rubs her fingers over her eyes before tugging on her ear.

"Did you know about this sister?" I ask Sorin, regretting the accusatory tone in my voice.

"I knew she died when he was young, I didn't know the extent." He sighs. "I certainly would have never guessed *this*."

"He wasn't able to pull my magick," Elora continues. "Though it didn't stop him from trying." I wince as she guides her finger over the long scar down her forearm "He wouldn't stop, even when my magick refused to come forth, and he won't stop until he has the Awakening Stones. Won't stop until he has *me* to control them."

"The Stones are safe, susi," Jarek says. "They've been under constant supervision. Either by Agnes, Sam, or Tallulah."

Calix tenses for a moment before his eyes meet mine and he busies himself with another cup of tea.

"And you are also safe. He'll never hurt you again," Jarek says.

Elora attempts to smile but it's quickly washed away when Evren joins us.

"I'm sorry to interrupt," he says. "But this has gotten out of hand, Sam. They're in the larder for Mothers-sake!" I bite my bottom lip and pull Elora to her feet.

"What's going on?" She frowns as I stand from the table.

"Where are Ruse and Alaric?" I ask.

"Hunting." Elora's brows worry together further. "Why?"

"There's a lot we need to unpack and discuss," I say. Holding out my hand, she takes it. "But I need you to come with me."

She follows me through the narrow hallway, stopping occasionally to run her fingers along the vibrant ivy.

"There are a few new faces I'd like you to meet," I say, a bit of excitement thrumming through me.

"Sam, I'm too tired—"

The larder door swings open and four pairs of canine eyes fall on us. Flour coats Hati's dark fur making her look more like a ghost than a puppy. Instantly, Elora drops to her knees. She hasn't spoken, but the pups run to her, licking her face and fighting for a place in her lap.

"This," I say, kneeling beside Elora, "is Hati." The black, flour-coated wolf pup perks up at her name. "And this"—the brown pup growls as he's pushed to the back of the line, farthest from Elora—"is Skoll." Elora's face beams as the identical gray pups kiss her face. "And these two are Rook and Grey, the troublemakers."

"Hati, Skoll, Rook, and Grey," Elora whispers. "Alaric and Ruse did tell me last night, but they are so much more magnificent than I could have imagined." Elora glances at me, but for the first time since I've seen her today, there's light in her eyes. "Ruse and Alaric are mates apparently." She chuckles, running a finger down Rook's nose. "They're allowed to have secrets of their own, I suppose."

Skoll has made his way back to Elora's lap, licking up her neck and chin and when she laughs I do too.

She takes a deep inhale. "There is so much hurt," she says.

"So much pain and darkness and some days I wonder if any of this is all worth it."

Three of the four pups have made themselves at home on her lap, Hati sticking close to my side. "But they bring me hope." She scoops the three pups up and nuzzles into them.

Sighing, I plop myself on the floor next to her.

She bumps my shoulder with her own. "*You* bring me hope."

"I can stay here all night," I say. "Tell me everything or tell me nothing. I'm just happy to be by your side."

Elwyn

"Do you think he'll like it?" Rosy pink creeps over Elora's cheeks and freckled nose. She's chosen my beaded navy gown to attend her first ball. A lump forms in my throat.

She hands me her mask made of navy satin and tiny beads, and I take my time tying it gently around her. "He would be a fool not to."

Her grin widens as she spins around, one she so rarely gives, and I wish to bottle it up.

"Go on." I gesture to the door where Cade is waiting on the other side. I take an extra moment to fluff her curls and pinch her cheeks. "No need to sneak around tonight." I wink, and she rolls her eyes, but it's all of these tiny moments that make up who we are together. She kisses my cheek and lets out a long breath before opening the door.

I catch a glimpse of Cade as Elora walks out. His eyes are wide and his face now matches the color of her lip paint. She grabs his arm as he leads her down the hallway, to her first Autumn Moon. There's no promise Cade will become Elora's arranger, but the two of them have been inseparable all their lives. It only seemed right to have him escort her tonight.

I lean against the doorway, clutching a hand to my heart.

My daughter, nearly eighteen, is growing into a woman before my eyes.

Not much time left.

"I know," I whisper to myself. "I know."

Before Elora and Cade disappear completely, she turns one last time and smiles. That wide smile again, and this time, I commit it to memory, not letting myself forget it for a second.

An hour later, I sit with Cade's mother, Alice, around her small table drinking wine and eating leftover biscuits when shouting erupts from the castle.

"What was that?" Alice stands and pulls the small curtain from the window near her door. "Did you hear it?"

"I did," I say. I squeeze beside her and glance out as well.

More shouting erupts and Alice jumps back a ways.

"Must be a rambunctious party," Alice says, but I'm frozen against the window. My eyesight blurs, my hands shake, and everything is lost to a fog of white before my vision comes.

Three men around a fire.

King Silas. Prince Roman and... I can't identify the third man.

"Long live the king," the stranger sneers.

Silas downs his drink and then he's clutching his heart. His skin breaks out into a sweat but neither man moves to help him. Not his son. Not the stranger. The two of them sit side by side as Silas crumples forward. He gasps and claws for Roman's boot, but the stranger steps in front of the prince, shielding him from his father. He whispers something, something I can't hear and then—

"Elwyn!"

I come to with a gasp of air. Alice is holding onto my forearms, her light brows cinched together. "A vision?"

I nod, unease swirling deep in my stomach.

"We need to go find Cade and Elora." Alice's frown deepens, but she doesn't argue as I begin to put on my cloak.

The squall of snow makes it difficult to see as we trek to the castle but the shouting from earlier intensifies.

Something is wrong.

The frigid air burns my lungs as I begin to sprint, each step a promise that I'm that much closer to getting my daughter. I make it up the main staircase and weave around the guards with ease. I'm almost to the ballroom when a heavy hand wraps around my arm.

"You are the Head Enchantress?" a guard asks, his voice deep.

"Yes." My skin prickles as I glance quickly at Alice. She watches, her blonde hair tucked under her knit cap as she cocks her head to the side. The guard's grip tightens around my arm.

"I've been instructed to take you to the prince." He pulls me from the ballroom doorway.

"And where is the king?" Alice calls from a distance but the guard remains silent.

But he doesn't need to tell me where the king is because I already know.

The king is dead.

Inside the castle is pure chaos. Women are crying, men are shouting.

"It was a setup!"

"Long live, King Silas!"

My nerves get the best of me as I enter a small meeting room where I'm instructed to wait. My knee bounces thinking of Elora. But I relax a little knowing she's with Cade.

She's safe.

"Lady Elwyn."

I stand as Prince Roman enters the room.

"I'm so sorry for your loss, Your Highness." I drop to a low curtsey but the energy in the room thickens, making me fear what I'll see when I straighten myself. "I only just heard—"

"Please sit," Roman says.

I take a deep breath and face the prince.

Only, he's not alone.

The man from my vision stands at his side. His snowy hair and piercing blue gaze stirs something in me.

Don't trust him, Corbin says. I'm startled by his abrupt appearance in my mind, but I push him away. He knows better than to use our bond now, after all these years of keeping my Dyrsjel lineage a secret from Elora. But his urgency has my hackles raised.

"Lady Elwyn, you have been my father's Head Enchantress for all my life," Roman says. His hands tremble as they reach for a pitcher of water. "But it's time I let you go."

My eyes widen and fear plummets in my stomach. "I beg your pardon? Silas would never—"

"Well, he's dead," the blonde man says cooly. "And Prince Roman will be named King, so I'd think it wise if you listen to what he has to say."

I glance between the two men, my stomach somersaulting.

"Starting immediately, Enchantresses will no longer sit on the council." Roman's voice is hollow, rehearsed.

My nails dig into the wood tabletop, splintering the tender flesh under them.

"No Enchantress may use her magick, unless specifically requested by me. If anyone, Seer or Healer or Plague decides to go against this new law, the punishment will be the most extreme." Roman's voice wavers as he speaks his last words. His green eyes meet mine. "Do you understand?"

"Yes, Your Highness." I nod, sliding my fingers into my lap.

Roman dismisses me and it's not a moment too soon. The air in my lungs has seemingly run out, my head beginning to spin.

Almost to the door, I gather my skirts in my hands, when the blonde man steps into my way. He can't be more than a few years older than Roman, but his narrowed eyes look not at me, but through me.

"One more thing, Enchantress," he says, dropping his voice

so it's a whisper between us. "I'll need you to bring me the Awakening Stones."

The hair on the back of my neck stands, but I nod anyway, making him believe I will do just that. His lips curl into a smile that has Corbin, my crow, screaming in my head.

Get out!

Get out, Elwyn!

No man has ever touched the Awakening Stones. Has ever dared taken them from a Dyrsjel as only we have the power to control them. They are the tether between this world and the next. Between Enchantresses and Mother Gaia.

What could they possibly need them for?

"You're dismissed," the man says, as if he has some kind of authority over me.

I breeze past him and don't stop until I'm bursting through the ballroom doors. Elora and Cade are in a corner talking to Alice. My shoulders relax but the fear in my heart does not.

I watch Elora and Cade again, their hands wrapped around each other.

I think of her fate. Of who she was born to be.

I think of my own fate. Who I was born to be. What I was born to do.

There is no other option but the one that keeps Elora the most safe. We have to leave as soon as possible.

We have to flee.

Twenty-Seven

Roman

The pungent scent of smoke circles around us as we walk the horses down the road of the small village. Stone framed cottages line the street, their roofs destroyed and burnt to ash. Deep, black scars mark the trees on either side of us. The semblance of a town lies etched into the forest, its buildings crumpled and scorched. I cover my mouth as we move past remnants of people, buried in the rubble.

Dozens of hunters and guards filter through the town behind us, caravans squeaking and horses chomping on their bits, interrupting the chirping birds and swaying branches.

"What are we doing here, Galen?"

He glances quickly over his shoulder but doesn't stop his horse until we get to the end of the street. I catch a small glimpse of his amulet under his shirt, the purple hue radiant in the pale light of morning.

"The men will get restless if we don't break soon." It's been a nonstop trek since Valebridge and I'm getting tired with this continuous pursuit.

Burnt bones of a wood cabin sit in a smoldering pile just at the end of what once was a road. I grimace at the smell. Sour and rotted. Galen gets off his horse, his fingers going to the chain around his neck.

"Galen?" I slide off my horse and don't bother tying her off as I join Galen's side.

I wave the rest of the men off, none of them argue with being told to take a break. Galen's always been a difficult person to read, but after the prisoners escaped, he's become so cold I wonder how his blood still runs through him.

My spine straightens. I'm the cause of this mess yet again. I gave her the knife. Silently daring her to use it. It's been days of near silence between us and my patience is beginning to wear. "Are you going to tell me what we're doing here?"

"We're making sure the message was sent." Galen turns to me, his hands in his pockets. The hood of his cloak, drawn over his head far enough that only his lips and chin peek from under it. "It seems as though I can't trust anyone anymore, so I needed to see for myself the job was done. The Stones were not here and Sorin was not here, either. Which means he knows exactly where they are." He nods to the crumbled building before us. "He could have stopped this. *She* could have stopped this, but they didn't. I am not to blame for their lack of cooperation."

I glance again to the burnt down homes and shops of this quaint village. My head spins, and I wish I'd stayed on my horse so I'd at least have something to hold onto. "But the people that didn't make it out—"

"Like I said." Galen holds up his hand. "I gave Elora many chances to tell me where the Stones might be. She knew the consequences."

"But what good is it!" I push forward so that I'm by his side. My eyes snag on broken limbs half buried under a fallen tree before glancing back to Galen.

He shrugs as if he's not seeing the same destruction I am.

"This accomplishes nothing." I gesture to the rubble. The ash and soot and lives and hopes that have all been squashed by this madness.

Galen grips my hand, his nails biting slightly into my skin. "There are only so many places for them to hide, Roman. Only so many places to run." He looks back to the rubble. "All I've done is eliminate one possible place." He drops my hand, my stomach sinking along with it. "One by one, Roman, I'll burn all of the Trinity Forest until I find them."

WICKERSHAM IS JUST as unimpressive as the previous town we passed on our travels here. Small and dainty, the only good thing it has going for it is the pub.

And even that is grim.

Galen orders us a round of drinks as I settle into a booth in the corner. The seat is worn, the tabletop not much better. My fingers land in something sticky and I cringe.

I've kept my hood on, attempting to conceal most of my face. I dismissed the guards for the night, not sensing a threat in this decrepit little town.

Galen joins me with two bowls and two tankards of ale. He sets the bowl in front of me, and I'm thankful for the hood to hide my grimace. The soup is thin and briny, the vegetables meager, and I doubt there's even any meat. Maybe that's a good thing.

Nothing like our meals in Valebridge.

My stomach rumbles just thinking about home.

"You just going to stare at it?" I glance at Galen as he takes a slow sip of his drink. His face puckers, and it's almost enough to make me smile. Almost enough to make me remember the man I fell in love with. The man who loves books and mathematics and art. The man who hates ale and crowds and too many days of sun in a row. "Eat your meal, my heart, it's been a long day." He casts me a rare smile and I let it be enough for now. A quiet olive branch cast my way.

"Can you call this a meal?" I nudge his side and he smiles again, wide enough to cast a shadow over all the moments leading up to tonight that I've been angry about.

"I can fetch you some bread if you'd like?" A woman approaches our table, her hair is the color of rust. Her face, round and soft. She's lovely and my cheeks warm under her vibrant, attentive gaze.

"I know it isn't much." She gestures to my bowl. "But with the blight, we're on strict rations from the king." She lingers a moment, and my skin begins to crawl.

Does she recognize me?

Galen clears his throat, his boot nudging mine under the table. It's then I remember she asked me a question. "Yes, on the bread. Thank you."

A moment later she sets down a plate of hard bread, but I don't make any more complaints before diving in.

The blight hasn't been unnoticed in Valebridge, our crops drying up or some not growing at all. But at the woman's mention of it, I scan the pub and notice how emaciated the patrons look. How pale and pallid their skin is. How loosely their clothes fit.

They're starving while I've feasted.

"You haven't spoken to Sorin, have you?" The woman's question makes me choke on my dry bread. I hadn't realized she was still standing here. I cough several times before downing a few gulps of the bitter ale.

"Afraid not," Galen says in a tone as smooth as butter.

The woman's face falls. Her bright eyes casting down as she bites her bottom lip.

"Something troubling you, Jeanette?" I'm perplexed when Galen addresses this woman by her name then am immediately reminded of how he lived a life outside of Valebridge. A life so very different from my own.

She glances over either shoulder before leaning in close. Her dusty pink dress and brown vest fit snugly over her chest, and out of instinct, I recline backward as she gets closer. "It's just that we haven't heard from him since he killed that hunter the last time he was here. He scared us half to death actin' that way. Was so unlike him." She shakes her head. "Nothing's been quite the same around here since. Hunters and guards stopping by. I mean just look." She glances around the pub full of my men.

My stomach knots.

"Just be safe, Galen. And your companion too." She smiles at me, and I fight the urge to pull my hood tighter. She tilts her head and squints. "I didn't catch your name."

"Thank you for the meal, Jeanette," Galen says. "Hurry now, darling. You heard the lady. Best if we call it a night."

Galen leaves his barely touched ale at the table and leads me outside to the inn across the street. Neither of us speak of Jeannette or Sorin as we tumble into our bedroom. It's just as humble as I'd expect from a town of this stature. After several nights sleeping outdoors, I welcome the creaky bed and old curtains with open arms.

SHOUTING from the hallway wakes me.

Rubbing at my eyes, they take their time adjusting to the dark. My hand runs over Galen's side, and I tense when I'm greeted with nothing but cold sheets.

More shouting erupts and it's loud enough to pull me from the bed. I quickly dress in my loose pants and black shirt and head for the door. Orange light from the lanterns on the walls pools at my feet as I crack the door open.

"I already told you, I've been given specific orders from the king."

"I don't give a damn what you've been given." I recognize Galen's voice. The angry lilts a testament to his rising temper. "I didn't let you go, and it was *me* who made you that deal in the first place. The deal you fucked up."

"I repaid my debt. I brought you the Dyrsjel and now King Roman—"

"Years later and not without my help," Galen snaps, and I realize now who he's run into.

Cade.

I step into the hallway. Both men's gaze land on me, so I straighten my dark tunic and rake my fingers through my hair. "Perhaps the hallway isn't the best place to have this conversation?"

Galen frowns and shakes his head. My head tilts to the side as I study the scene before me more closely. It's the middle of the night and the two of them are arguing in the hall. Cade, in common clothes, looks as though he's just come from the pub.

But why is Galen fully dressed when I know for a fact he wasn't wearing any clothes a mere hour ago?

What are you hiding from me?

"You let him go," Galen snarls. "His penance for his mistakes haven't been paid."

"I didn't let him go," I whisper. "I put him on another proposition." The hallway remains empty but anyone could occupy the rooms here and I'm not comfortable speaking much louder.

"What proposition?" Galen's eyes flash, a muscle in his jaw flexing.

"Come back inside and we'll discuss—"

"No." Galen takes a step closer to Cade, turning his back to me. "The king may have given you orders but as the handler of your fate, don't forget it is me who you obey." Galen moves forward and grips Cade's collar tightly around his fingers. "Now get out of my sight."

Cade glances at me quickly and I nod. It's not worth fighting Galen on this. Not now, when he's so angry. Cade disappears down the hall, and Galen and I return to our room.

The silence is deafening as we climb into bed. My heart continues to hammer against the walls of my chest.

Galen's body is rigid next to mine, so I turn away, his breathing audible through his nose. I can feel it in the way he turns toward me that he wishes to talk. Likely wants to know what I put Cade up to, but I'm not prepared to speak anymore tonight. "Tomorrow." I promise him. "I'll tell you everything tomorrow, but tonight can we please just rest."

The bed creaks as he rolls away from me, a cold draft pooling between us.

"I love you, Roman." I suck in a sharp breath, his words hitting me in the chest. "If it's something I'm doing the last few weeks to make you forget, I'm sorry." He rolls again, wrapping his arm around my middle. My stomach tenses as he kisses my cheek. "Get some sleep, we'll talk tomorrow."

As Galen's breathing turns heavy, I have never felt more awake.

I think of the bruises on the Dyrsjel's body, directly from his hand. I think of the women before her and the bloodied marks around their wrists where we shackled them.

Where *I* shackled them.

I think of the village we visited today and the smoldering buildings of a town that once was. At the people who lost their lives merely because he was trying to prove a point.

I think of the starving people in the pub and the meager food I was given despite their rations. The generosity in the woman's face and the pain when she spoke of Sorin.

All of this affliction and suffering at my hand. At *our* hand.

Galen shifts behind me, and my stomach clenches again.

Please don't wake up.

It's the first time I've ever had that thought. For so many years, all I've needed was him beside me. More and more and more of his time because the moments we had together were never enough.

When I realize he's just rolled over again, my shoulders

relax. I spent my entire childhood seeking approval and affection from people who never had any intention of giving it to me. So when Galen offered me a chance at freedom from the burden of constantly begging for love, how could I not take it? I was only eighteen years old.

And yet, here I am, five years later and still stuck in my ways. Still seeking approval and affection in the wrong places and people. Still remaining small when I was born to take up space. I bite my bottom lip and close my eyes.

What would I give to make this right?

Better yet, what wouldn't I.

Would I give back mine and Galen's time together? Would I take back my father's life in replace of Galen's?

No.

Because for all the bad Galen has done, it doesn't right the wrongs of my father.

And the same goes for the opposite. Maybe Silas wasn't as spiteful as Galen, but he had his many flaws. I wince, thinking of the scars lining my back. The lash of his whip, fresh in my mind like it was yesterday.

I roll onto my back and stare at the ceiling. The wallpaper is crumbling and cracked, much like how I feel at this very moment. But through the decay it reveals something extraordinary. A tiny glimpse of the foundation that holds up the space. Beneath the tattered paper and crumbling ceiling lies another layer of paint. Completely untouched and smooth, the blue is vibrant against the rest of the dull room.

Why would someone cover up such beauty?

I look at the crumpled edges of the wallpaper again, worn down to almost nothing. Slivers of something, someone, just underneath the mask plastered on by others.

Is a person more than the things they've done? What about the things they could have stopped but didn't? Perhaps we are merely a collection of our actions and inactions. Rights and wrongs.

Perhaps the most powerful thing one can do is to look at the darkest parts of themself and acknowledge them.

See them for what they are, and live despite them.

I rise from the bed and tiptoe to where my clothes are folded upon the dresser. Piece by piece, layer by layer, I dress myself in the dark.

Too soft to be a king.

Too weak.

Echoes of my childhood, words that caused such infliction, now steeling my spine.

A small, ornate mirror hangs just by the front door, and while the room is dark, I swear when I squint I can see all the mistakes I've made etched into my face. But now, instead of hiding from them, maybe I'll welcome them. I run a finger over my dark brows, down the sharp line of my nose. All of those years I spent chasing this man away; myself. Hiding and becoming someone else's version of me. I don my cloak, the final layer, and gently open the door. My hand shakes on the knob as I twist it shut, a flicker of doubt swirling in my gut, remembering all the mistakes in the mirror.

But it's those mistakes that have brought me here. To the precipice of change.

The hallway is quiet now that Cade's gone, and with every step toward the door, my confidence in my choice grows stronger and stronger. I hit the bottom stair on the outside of the inn and point my chin to the night sky. The air is fresh and crisp, burning my lungs, but I accept it.

I take a final glance at the inn behind me, a small piece of my heart breaks knowing who I'm leaving behind. But my feet press forward anyway, straight to the pub where I know my guards will be playing poker or drinking.

It's time to take a stand, Roman. I smile despite the battle I'm about to face. Because maybe it isn't the hero that can save the world, after all. Maybe, this time, it's the villain.

TWENTY-EIGHT

ELORA

THE WOLF PUPS BUMP INTO A SIDE TABLE, A FEW yelps drifting over to where Sorin and I lay beside each other in our shared bed. I attempt to count the leaves on the ivy that dance along the walls, hoping the monotony of the task will lull me to sleep, but when it doesn't, I give up and roll onto my side.

Sorin's chest rises and falls evenly. His brows furrowed and bottom lip stuck out. I chuckle softly and trace my finger along his lip.

Must be some dream.

For someone who found out their best friend betrayed them, Sorin has taken the news unusually well. We've hardly spoken of Galen and what he's done. Hardly spoken of the fact that Loxley is now destroyed. I don't want to push him, and I know he doesn't wish to push me. It feels as though we're stuck. Our vulnerability hangs on a thread between us and neither one of us has had the courage to take a step forward and test the thread's strength.

One of the pups yelps, so I sit up.

Go to bed.

Hati glances back at me and tilts her head. I haven't used my bond with the pups often, but by the confusion on Hati's face, I'm sure she's heard me.

All of you, I say to the others. The four pups watch me, their dark eyes gleaming with mischief before one by one they move to the bathing chamber where we've arranged beds for them. Ruse and Alaric have been back, mostly so Ruse can feed the puppies. But they insist on keeping watch, sleeping outside the Jade Guild.

"That was impressive," Sorin says.

I lay back down and curl into his side. "You're awake?"

"Trying my best not to be, but your puppies were making that rather difficult."

"They're not my puppies."

"Aren't they?" His lips brush the top of my head.

The fire crackles and soon the yips and grumbles of the pups in the other room fade. I pull myself up so that Sorin and I are facing each other. He stares at me, his eyes dipping to my lips. The slivers of moonlight cast shadows over his face, sharpening his features.

"What is it?" I ask.

"Twenty-six." He kisses my forehead.

"What?"

He brushes the hair from my shoulders. "You have twenty-six freckles across your nose."

My stomach flips and mouth drops open. "You counted?" I laugh as I push his chest. "When?"

He shrugs. "Haven't been sleeping well." He grabs my hand and draws me closer to him. "Too distracted." His lips brush against mine, settling that ball of nerves bouncing around inside of me. He guides me back down so I'm resting against his chest again.

"We haven't talked about Galen," I say, keeping my voice low. Deciding to test that thread after all.

Sorin's breathing falters under me for a moment before his hands graze my back. "That's because, like Sam, I still can't believe it." His arms tighten around me. "Maybe I don't want to believe it." His heartbeat quickens, pressed against me. "So many times he looked me in the eye over the years, promising the same vengeance I sought from Silas."

He takes a long breath, his arms loosening. "When Silas died, and I swore off my hope of going to Valebridge, Galen and my friendship only grew stronger. And now maybe I know why."

I stroke a piece of hair off of his forehead.

"Maybe because it was then he didn't see me as a threat to his hidden plans. He knew I had no intention of returning to Valebridge." He kisses my forehead. "Until I met you, and you reminded me..." He sighs. "You reminded me that there's so much more than what's right in front of me."

I prop myself up on an elbow to look at him. "You reminded me of that, too. Made me see past my own selfishness."

He smiles, but it's half hearted. Tired.

"I really am sorry, Sorin. About all of it. Galen, Loxley."

He swallows but says nothing and I know that feeling all too well. When the truth is more painful than the wound.

"I've been betrayed before," he says. "My father didn't want me the moment I was born, but eventually you learn to live with the fact that your first breaths were filled with the disappointment of others." He smiles again, but there's nothing happy about it. Shadows dance across his tan skin from the fireplace. "My mother's love was more than enough, then Agnes and William took me in without question, and *their* love was so overwhelming I forgot what it was like for a long time to be the disgraced bastard son of the king."

"There is nothing disgraceful about you." I kiss his lips.

"There is," he says. "And I'm coming to accept those parts of myself. But Galen—" He closes his eyes. "I can't stop thinking... not about what he did to me, but what he did to *you*."

My stomach clenches, phantom aches pinging my sides where the bruising has healed.

"I think I could live with his betrayal," he continues, "but I'll never forgive him for hurting you. For hurting Loxley."

I lean down and kiss him again. "You're allowed to feel hurt, too. Emotional hurt is just as damning as physical."

"Maybe that's true," he says, tracing my bare shoulders with his finger. "Come here." He pulls me into his mouth and moans softly as I kiss him. He parts his lips, so I kiss him deeply, cupping his face in either of my hands.

"Wait," he says as I pull back. I move on top of him, straddling his hips as his hands land on the back of my thighs. "Is there anything you want to tell me?

"What do you mean?" I run my fingers down his bare chest.

He shrugs, but I can see a question hiding in his eyes that he refuses to ask. The ink on the back of my neck burns beneath the mask I've placed over it.

Tell him.

"There's nothing more to say tonight." I kiss him again as he pushes my nightgown up, his fingers gliding over my bare skin.

"We don't have to, if you're not ready." A bit of color has flushed over his cheeks, and for the first time since he came for me, he looks happy. He looks like *him*. All of the betrayal and the pain and the impossible work we still have ahead of us can wait one more night.

Our mouths collide. I run my hands through his hair as his teeth snag on my bottom lip, his fingers firmly planted on my hips. Sitting up, I peel my nightgown over my head. Drunk on the taste of him, I flinch as the cold air bites my skin, and before I can think of hiding the remaining bruises, Sorin sits up and slides me off of him so I'm laying on my back.

"Each kiss," he says as his lips pepper kisses along my skin, "is a promise." He kisses the bruises on my stomach. Then my shoulder. "A promise to never let you get hurt again."

He gently rolls me on my side and his lips make their way down my back, then up again. "A promise that so long as I live, I'll be by your side." He lays back down and pulls me on top of him. "As your partner and as your friend."

Sorin closes his eyes for a moment, and my stomach swirls. "As much as I am devastated and hurt, having you here has begun to heal me already. I can live with the betrayal, but I'm not sure I can live without you. At least, I don't want to."

He frowns and it looks so unnatural on him that I bend down and kiss the crease between his brows. "There's something here"—he rubs a circle over his heart, then mine—"between us. I felt it after the Wicked Wood, and I feel it now, even stronger than before." His hands drag lightly down my back before landing on my hips. "Whatever burdens you carry, just know that you'll never carry them alone. Not again."

I don't give him the chance to speak again before my lips crash into his. I roll my hips forward as Sorin's hands grip the back of my thighs. My body heats with every breath and touch of his tongue against mine. His hand dips between my legs as I lean forward and scrape his shoulder with my teeth.

"Elora," he groans as I move away to pull off his breeches. I kiss down his bare chest before I slide my tongue across his length. He moans and clutches the sheets, so I do it again before taking him in my mouth. His hand finds the back of my head, guiding me. His hips begin to move quicker and so I match his pace with my mouth. He groans again, and that's when I move from between his legs, situating myself back on top of him. His dark eyes are heavy as he watches me slide onto him.

Our moans and breaths come together as I begin to rock my hips forward. He places one hand gently on my hip and the other at the apex of my thighs, his thumb swirling just in the right spot.

My head rolls back as my pleasure begins to build. "I missed you." The words are short and breathy and not nearly as much as I want to say.

I thought of only you in my darkest moments.
Your touch.
Your heart.

There's so much I want to say but "I miss you" is all I'm able to manage. But it's as though Sorin hears those unspoken words because he pulls me closer and kisses me deeper. Our hips continue to move in time with each other, working as one, and as I roll my hips again, he hits something deep inside of me and I gasp aloud.

"There?" Sorin whispers against my mouth, his hands planting firmly at my hips.

"Yes."

He moves, hitting that same spot again and again until my vision is gone and pleasure shoots through my body. My fingers rake against his chest as I come down from the pleasurable high, and Sorin chases his own release. I continue to roll my hips and kiss his neck and throat until he joins me on the other side, panting and whispering my name.

The fire continues to crackle and burn as Sorin and I drift off to sleep. When I close my eyes, the nightmares that I have become so used to shift.

Instead, I dream of Sorin and wolves and an endless forest.

THE JADE GUILD is similar to the Onyx Guild in that it's made up of dozens of small mazes. As we wind through the halls, I run my fingers over the exposed stone walls painted with ivy and bursting with tiny, yellow flowers. Unusual given the time of year. The rainy season is perpetually gray, but the Jade Guild has somehow found a way to bring life into space.

Sam and I round another small hallway that leads to the exterior wall, but attached to that wall, is a tiny greenhouse. The large rectangular windows offer some light to the space. Though it's gray and muted the plants still shine.

"Tallulah will be in soon," Sam says. The greenhouse has been overthrown with makeshift cots and beds for those wounded in the Loxley fires but only Sam and I occupy the room at the moment.

"You said Tallulah was a Florecas? An Enchantress who can grow and conjure plants?" I sit down on one of the cots. My fists clench and unclench about a half dozen times before Sam grabs them.

"She is, but she's so much more than that. Even this"—she gestures to the plants and vegetables growing despite the blight —"she has managed on her own, without magick."

I gape at the abundance of green, an impossible task given the lack of sun we see this time of year.

Sam squeezes my hand before cupping my cheeks. Her glowing, amber eyes are full of equal parts warmth and worry. "I was worried sick about you."

She slides her hands from my face, and I ask, "How have *you* been dealing with everything?"

Sam shrugs with a smile. "Everything will get sorted, it always does."

"You don't have to do that," I say.

She tilts her head, brows stitching together.

Sighing, I brush her tightly coiled curls off of her shoulder. "You and I"—I point to her then back at myself—"we're way far past casual pleasantries."

She wipes her eyes with her free hand. "How is it that you're giving me the pep talk this time?"

"Oh how the times have changed," I say through a laugh.

Sam grasps me in a hug and my shoulders slump when she pulls away. "Galen hurt you." Her words come out so quietly, I think for a moment I imagined them.

"He did," I say. "He hurt all of us—"

"No." Sam shakes her head. "Don't minimize your pain,

Elora. He hurt you and the longer you suppress what happened, the worse it will be."

My lungs burn, tears stinging my eyes but my words fail me. There are so many horrible moments in Valebridge I haven't faced, mostly because I fear to. Facing them means they truly happened and if they truly happened, I'm not sure I'll ever recover.

"Heal up," Sam says. "You can trust Tallulah. I think you'll like her."

I nod and when she closes the door, I let out an overdue breath.

"Elora?" A woman stands in the doorway a moment later. I recognize her as an Enchantress immediately. Her dark hair is woven into an intricate braid, her blue eyes sparkling. "Can I come in?"

"Of course." I wave her forward.

"I'm Tallulah." The Enchantress holds out her hand and I take it, giving her a quick shake. "Welcome to the Jade Guild. Though I'm sorry for the circumstances of your arrival."

I smile at her, unsure of what to say. My mind drifts to Loxley and my brief time there.

"I just wanted to check on those." Tallulah points to my wrists, interrupting me from my thoughts. I rub them absently, my mind still fogged with memories.

Valebridge and Loxley and Galen. I shut my eyes and focus on the noises around me. The slight ping of rain hitting the greenhouse windows. Tallulah's boots scuffing against the stone ground.

"Lord Calix says a healer saw to you at the Onyx Guild." I open my eyes and find Tallulah staring at me. "I wanted to see for myself you've been taken care of properly." She smiles and there's something about it that puts my anxious thoughts at ease. "Not that I'm a Healer or anything." She shrugs, twisting her fingers through the bottom of her braid. "But I also wanted to make sure there's nothing else troubling you."

I hold out my wrists and fight to hide the wince as Tallulah begins inspecting my wounds. "Nothing else is troubling me."

Nothing she can help me with anyway.

She applies some healing cream before moving to clip a few leaves from various plants. "They'll scar," she says over her shoulder. "But otherwise, they seem to be healing nicely. Do you have any other pain?"

I bite the inside of my cheek. "No."

She pauses, glances at me for a moment, the light from the greenhouse ceiling catching on her tanned skin and blue eyes. Tallulah joins me at the cot again and hands me a small satchel of herbs. "I want you to take this, drink it as needed."

"It's really not necessary, the pain is minimal." I hand her the satchel back, but she closes her hand around mine and the herbs.

"It's not for physical pain," Tallulah says. "When you feel that tightness, here." She places her hand delicately on my chest, and I flinch. "Or darkness here." Her hand moves to my temple in a feather-light touch. "This will only help calm you." My breathing increases as she hands me back the satchel of herbs. "There isn't any shame in needing a bit of extra help." She smiles and my chest tightens.

"How did you know?" My cheeks redden, heat creeping down my chest. "That I..." My words seize on my tongue so I tap my temple.

Tallulah takes my hand again. The light gray tunic she wears hangs loosely from her body and the leather bag on her waist bumps me as she moves closer. "My husband, Evren, has the same trouble sometimes. Worrisome thoughts. Nervousness. It's nothing to be ashamed of, Elora." She smiles again, gesturing to my tightly clenched fists.

I relax them under her gaze, sweeping a strand of hair from my face, pretending as if I haven't been on edge since I woke up this morning.

"The tea will only help relax you," she says. "I encourage

you to try it." Her hands slip from mine as she turns for the door.

"Thank you." I grip the satchel tighter and bring it to my nose, inhaling the sweet tang of jasmine and soothing chamomile.

"Oh, before I forget." She turns, facing me again. "Sorin wanted me to tell you that they're conferring in the meeting room, they're waiting to start discussions until you arrive."

My heart constricts, and as soon as the door closes, I clutch the satchel in my hands like a lifeline.

TWENTY-NINE
SORIN

THE LONGER WE STAY AT THE JADE GUILD, THE MORE I realize just how small the rooms are. The six of us fight for space around the small table in the conference room. The same room I met Thaddeus in just a couple of weeks ago where I once marveled at the beauty of the greenery and openness, only now it feels stifling.

"We can't stay here long," Agnes says. "*None* of us." She nods to Evren and Thaddeus across the table.

"You're asking us to leave the Jade Guild?" Evren's brows furrow. He and Thaddeus exchange a glance.

"If what Elora and Sorin say is true, Galen will know where Sorin is hiding," Agnes says. "He knows of mine and William's ties to the Jade Guild. He's a smart boy despite this cruelty." Agnes closes her eyes and takes a long breath. "It's only a matter of time before the guards are at your doorstep, Thaddeus. Look at what he's done to my home." Her voice shakes on the last word, and I'm grateful for my sister who takes her hand, giving it a squeeze.

Agnes clears her throat and sips her tea. "He's cornering us," she says. "He knew burning Loxley would drive us out. Would drive us *here*."

I run a hand across my stubbled jaw. I'm so used to taking the lead, I've almost forgotten where I've learned it from. Agnes glances at me across the table. "My mother is right," I say. "He didn't find what he needed in Loxley, so he'll know where to look next. I'd be surprised if we have more than a few days."

Thaddeus shakes his head, his gray eyes focusing on his lap. "We've been safe here—"

"We've been hiding," Evren says, sharp enough that his uncle's gaze snaps to him. Their silent exchange sends a pulse of energy around the table.

Elora and Calix flank my sides and I can practically feel them tense.

"When Sorin showed up at the Jade Guild," Evren continues, "we promised we'd make a change. Didn't we?" Thaddeus remains silent but he nods. "The last thing I want to do is leave, but what other choice do we have, Uncle? Do we hold our ground and risk the lives of those we harbor? Do we fight, knowing the odds are stacked against us?"

Thaddeus sighs as he rubs his eyes. "We'll do no such thing. Not without resources, anyway."

"And where will we find these resources?" Elora asks. I slide my gaze to her, admiring the look of determination set in the sharp features of her face. "I'm not opposed to a fight." This earns her a smile but she's so focused on Thaddeus it goes unnoticed, so I brush the back of her hand with my knuckles under the table.

"You can stay at the Onyx Guild." All eyes turn to Lord Calix. He straightens his shoulders, puffing out his chest. "We had planned for some of you to arrive anyway, we can certainly make accommodations for more." He looks at me, perhaps waiting for approval, but I remain silent. The idea of moving everyone from the Jade Guild, including those from Loxley, all the way across the Trinity Forest and up the Kirsguard Mountains feels impossible. But I know my mother is right, there's no other choice but to leave. "It will at least buy us more time,"

Calix says. "If this Galen person is as determined as you claim—"

"He is," Elora says. "He won't stop until he gets exactly what he wants, which is the Awakening Stones and me." She bites her bottom lip, and I can see the thoughts swarming in her eyes. She sacrificed herself once before to save the Stones, I'll be damned if I let her do it again.

I take her hand under the table and give it a squeeze which seems to snap her out of her thoughts momentarily.

She mouths "thank you" and it takes a great deal of strength not to lean over and kiss her.

"So, we're all in agreement then?" Thaddeus asks, glancing at each of us around the table and one by one, we nod. "Then we shall head to the Onyx Guild in waves. Starting with the children and elders tonight. I don't want to waste any more time." Thaddeus runs a hand through his thin, gray hair. It trembles as he places it back on the table.

"We have failed you," he says, pointing his attention to Elora and Sam. "We closed our doors to protect one but turned a cold shoulder to so many. This ends now. Our people will fight."

"As will ours," Agnes says.

Elora took the wolves out for a quick walk around the Jade Guild with Tallulah. Her presence has seemed to ease Elora and she insists she's fine but my mind keeps replaying the bruises on her skin from our first night at the Onyx Guild. Yellow and purple marks made from him.

From Galen. My fist clench at my sides as I pace back and forth. Sam and Jarek enter the room without a knock or a hello.

"Why is it that you're always pacing?" Sam asks with a chuckle as she takes a seat on the foot of the bed.

"Why is it that you're always barging into my room?" I shoot her a glare and continue my steps.

"What is your problem?" She sighs, her gaze darting between me and Jarek. "Are you upset about the meeting?"

"No." I sigh. "It was fine." I collapse into one of the chairs near the fireplace. "I just can't stop thinking about him. About what he did to her. About Loxley."

Jarek joins Sam on the bed and the two of them pass a glance between each other. "Me too," she says. "We've all lost so much, the thought of starting over is unbearable."

Starting over.

"When Roman is off the throne, Valebridge will change. There won't be any need for secret villages in the woods."

Sam huffs loud enough to draw my attention. Her brows are furrowed and nostrils flared. "Loxley was more than a hidden place in the woods, Sorin. I thought you knew better than that. Maybe our people won't want to live in Valebridge." She throws her hands in the air, a deep blush creeping over her cheeks with her rising anger. "Maybe what they want is exactly what they already had." Jarek moves his hand to grasp hers but she pulls it away.

"Maybe they won't get a say," I grumble and immediately regret my words.

Sam scoffs, rising from the bed. "So that's how it will be? You're on the throne and suddenly you forget where you came from?"

"Sam..." Jarek starts but with a swift look from Sam, he tightens his lips.

"Except I didn't come from Loxley." My voice raises along with my temper, and before I realize what I'm doing, I'm out of my chair and in front of Sam.

"You're right," she whispers, the crease between her brows now gone, a look of hurt replacing it. "You *didn't.*" She brushes by me, bumping my shoulder as she goes.

My chest caves in on itself, knuckles whitening at my sides.

"That was uncalled for," Jarek says once Sam is out of the room.

I spin on my heels and he's already there. Behind me. Arms crossed and rage brewing.

"You're angry." He shakes his head. "You have every right to be angry, Sorin, we all do. But you don't get to take it out on your sister. She's been through enough."

Taking a step backward, I pull my fingers through my hair. Of course I shouldn't snap at Sam, she's done nothing. She has lost everything, just as I have. "I..." I shut my eyes.

And if the people of Loxley choose to rebuild, why would I stop them? But the rational part of my brain stopped working the moment Elora fell into my arms, and now all I'm left with is this pent up anger, this betrayal from a man who was my best friend. The loss of my *home*.

"I feel as if I'm going to explode," I admit, meeting Jarek's gaze again. "How could he..." I refocus my gaze to the ground. My hands shake at my sides. Sharp pains thread through my chest where my heart has been cracked open.

My mind, a carousel of images I can't shake.

Galen at the ball.

Roman in the hallway.

Elora's bruises.

The scars around her wrists and the ink along her neck.

The ink she *still* refuses to tell me about.

"He betrayed all of us," Jarek says softly, the frustration he had with me already diminishing. "All of that anger... All of that rage...needs to be let go." He takes a step closer, his massive frame casting a shadow over me. "Hit me."

"What?" Stepping back, I scoff up at him. "Don't be absurd." Though, the idea of hitting something feels rather tempting.

"I'm not." Jarek shrugs. "You need to release those emotions, Sor, or they'll eat you alive." He pushes my chest, not strong enough that I budge but not light enough that it doesn't send some primal fighting instinct straight to my brain. "Now come on, I can take it. Hit me."

"I won't," I grumble, attempting to push past him. But before I make it far, his hand wraps tightly around my arm, shoving me back against the wall.

"Coward," he sneers.

"Move." I grind my teeth.

Jarek smirks. "Make me."

A few seconds go by before I attempt to move around him again, but I'm unsuccessful as his arm blocks me. "There's no escaping this, Sor. Let out that anger before it kills you or gets someone else killed." With that, he leans into me further, the full weight of his body pressed against my chest. "Think of Elora. Think of the hurt she's feeling. Your best fucking friend lied to you. *Used* you. You're telling me you're not angry?"

I tilt my head to the side, attempting to put as much distance between myself and his words.

The truth.

My best friend betrayed me. He betrayed *her* after she trusted him. He hurt her. Hurt Loxley.

My lip snarls, recalling the day he helped Elora with her magick. The day he led us right into a trap.

I think of Ruse and how we nearly lost her.

I think of the puppies and how broken Alaric would have been.

Heat rises to my cheeks and trickles down my neck, my hands beginning to pain from how tightly I'm clenching them.

"You know," Jarek whispers, his palm still holding me steady against the wall. "Elora wouldn't have been taken if it weren't for you." My body tenses. "Had you not convinced her to leave, she would still be at her cabin in the woods, living the quiet life just as she wanted."

I know what he's doing. He's trying to get me to snap, and Mother-be-damned, did that just work.

"I'll ask you again to step aside," I say, clenching my jaw.

He's right. Galen betrayed me, but I brought her into this. I used her just as much as Galen used me.

I had a strong intuition that she was a Dyrsjel the day we met on the river. And I knew that if it were true, if she really was, only she could control the Stones and get Sam's magick. Knew she had to have been from Valebridge. Knew she would be able to get me in unnoticed. I knew all of those things, and I fucking convinced her to come with me without a thought of how it might effect *her* life.

And I hate myself for it.

Jarek offers no reply, the pressure on my chest where his palm rests increasing slightly.

"Fucking *move*, Jarek." The line between anger and violence is paper thin and when Jarek doesn't budge, it withers as if it were never there.

Unclenching my fists, I shove him backward with as much force as I can muster. He stumbles, freeing me from my position against the wall.

"Do it, Sorin," he says. "Let it out."

I shake my hands at my sides and ball them into fists. All I see is Galen.

Before I can think any further, my fist connects with Jareks jaw with a loud crunch. He does nothing to deflect my punch, though I know he's more than capable. Slowly, his head turns toward me. He runs a hand over his jaw before giving me a feral smile.

"Again," he commands.

And this time, I listen.

Another punch to the opposite side of his jaw.

One to the stomach.

Another to his kidneys.

He stands like a statue, solid and unmoving as he takes hit after hit.

With each strike, that rage burning inside me lessens. Each strike, I envision Galen. I see the man who betrayed me. Who hurt me. Who hurt her, and I can't stop. In one sick moment, the face I picture morphs again and I imagine I'm hitting myself for all the pain I've caused. All the years wasted and lives lost because of it.

Over and over, I throw my fists at Jarek, and over and over, he takes it. My body is drenched as I finally drop to my knees, attempting to catch my breath. Shakily, I bring my hands to my face, inspecting the blood and bruises littered across my knuckles.

I snap my head up to Jarek who waivers on his feet but remains standing. His face is bloodied, his right eye beginning to swell. Deep purple starting to set across his pale skin. A line across his lip where my ring cut into is thick and swollen as blood runs down into his beard.

"Fuck," I whisper, pulling myself to my feet. "Jarek I'm so sorry." My breathing is heavy, the exhaustion from the day settling upon my shoulders.

Jarek laughs, that deep bellowed laugh, as he grabs my shoulders, shaking me slightly. "You needed this," he says. "The anger and rage would have been a distraction, we need our bastard leader back and this was the only way."

Nodding, I scan his face again. No hint of anger lies there, but perhaps there's a bit of pride shining through his blackened eyes.

"Let's get you cleaned up." I wrap my arm around his shoulder, ushering him out of the room. Though, we hardly make it out of the door before Elora appears.

"What—" Her face twists before her eyes narrow. She passes a glance between myself and Jarek, pausing on my bloodied knuckles. She lets out a long sigh and pinches the bridge of her nose, closing her eyes.

"Why are men such *idiots*," she mumbles. "Come on, let's get you to Tallulah."

THIRTY

SAMARIA

"You couldn't help yourself, could you?" I apply a bit more of the salve that Tallulah made onto Jarek's cheekbone and across his nose. He has a split down his lip, but with the yarrow paste, it's already beginning to heal.

"He needed an outlet." Jarek shrugs, but there's a million more questions dancing in his eyes. "You need one too." He attempts to wink, but with his swollen eye, it looks more like a bug has flown into it.

Laughing, I place the cream onto the small bedside table. "Now? Really?"

Jarek laughs then groans as he coddles his bruised stomach.

"Nothing stops you does it?"

"Nothing," he says through another chuckle. He readjusts, moving onto his side and gestures for me to join him. "Since we can't do *that*, keep me company instead? Talk to me."

"About which thing?" I hesitate. We haven't talked about him leaving or what that means for us, and every time I look at him it's a reminder. A reminder that he'll be gone and I'll be here.

"Sorin, Galen," Jarek says. "Us." He reaches for my hand, but I move it to my lap. "Take your pick."

"No, I don't want to discuss any of that." For so long I've been the bright and cheery Samaria. Keeping her anxious thoughts and worries locked tightly in a box so as to not burden others with it. I've always been better at delving out advice than I have been taking it and so, no. I don't want to talk to Jarek about any of it. "I need to meet with Elora soon. She thinks she's ready for the Ceremony."

Jarek's non-swollen eye goes wide, but when he goes to sit up, he winces.

"Rest, you silly man." I lean over and kiss him lightly on the forehead. "The next time I see you, perhaps I'll be a changed woman."

"I hope that's not true." Jarek says behind me. "I love you just the way you are, Sam."

My throat constricts and as much as I want to, I say nothing as I leave the room.

ELORA, Agnes, and Tallulah are all waiting for me in the greenhouse. My stomach flips and hands refuse to steady as I sit down at the small, wooden table.

"Are you sure the hunters won't sense us?" Tallulah looks nervous but she busies herself with a few rose bushes needing pruning.

"No." Elora shrugs, as if the thought of hunters no longer terrifies her. "There's a good chance they will. But the first wave of people have already left, and seeing as how we're the next group to go, it's now or never." She glances at me, and I nod my approval.

"We have men stationed around the Guild," Agnes says, her hands clasping the tops of my shoulders. "The wolves are with them and they're in constant communication with Elora." She squeezes my shoulders and bends so her lips are closer to my ear. "It's time, Samaria."

I take a steadying breath. "Let's do it then."

Agnes hands Elora the small pack that contains the Stones. As Elora opens the bag, a glimmer of gold light spirals out, cascading up her arms and what appears to be through her body. She gasps but the line between her brows softens as she picks up the first stone.

The dark red stone glows as she places it before me.

"Fire," she says.

The next, white. Its crystal hue shimmers against the gray light of the room.

"Air."

A blue stone is placed in line, smaller than the others. The gold that shimmers around it makes my stomach clench.

Puffing my cheeks, I let out a long breath.

This is really happening.

"Water."

She pulls the last stone; a pale, shimmering green. She holds it longer than the others, closing her eyes and tilting her head. As if it's speaking to her. Smiling, she places the fourth Awakening Stone before me.

"Earth."

Agnes keeps her hands on my shoulders, and I realize now Tallulah is also close by, her hand resting on my forearm. Elora kneels before me. "Are you ready, Sam?"

"What if she doesn't answer?" My voice comes out pinched and tight. Like I've just gotten in trouble and I'm working my way around a lie.

Elora frowns, her mouth dropping open.

"There has been so much pain the last few years," I say, my bottom lip trembling. "What if the Mother doesn't answer?"

Elora smiles and grasps my hands. "She's never failed us before. You have to believe."

Her hand slips from mine, and the three of them take hands and form a circle around me and the Stones.

"Place your hands upon the Stones," Agnes says.

I glance to Elora for approval. She nods, so I place my hands on top of the Stones. At first they don't seem any different than when I briefly examined them back in Wickersham. But the longer my hands are on them, the more I realize how peculiar they truly are. They're not just warm to the touch, but they seem to be radiating from within. My fingertips buzz as I trace each Stone, their static energy traveling up my arms.

"This is my first Ceremony," Elora says, her cheeks flushing, bringing out the freckles across her nose. "But with Agnes and Tallulah's help, I think we're ready."

She takes a large breath, before she begins the Enchantress prayer. "We call upon you, our Mother Gaia, who has given us all. Provided life and magick and healing. To our ever-fruitful country of Teravie." Elora's breath hitches, and I know she's thinking the same thing I am. The blight and the injustices making it less than fruitful the last few years.

"We thank you and we honor you. May our gifts be a reflection of your power. May our kindness be an ode to your heart. May our lives be a dedication to your sacrifice and all you have given to Teravie."

Chills rake up and down my arms and my fingers begin to tremble.

"Grab the Stones, Sam."

I listen to Elora and pick up the Stones, palming two in each hand.

"Samaria Trednik sits before you, an Enchantress of the rightful age, ready to be guided into her magick. Ready to do her part in protecting this country, just as King Bastian and Queen Soleil intended."

My stomach somersaults at the mention of the first king and queen. It was their deal that brought magick to us. It was them who made all of this possible.

"Bless her Mother Gaia with the magick of your choosing just as you have with every Enchantress before her and every Enchantress after."

Several tense moments pass by, and nothing happens. Nothing but the buzzing from the Stones in my palms and the breathing of the women around me. My heart sinks, the fear I've held for so long begins to come true.

I'm too late.

Before I can think another thought, blinding light encompasses my hands, bursting from within my grip, seeping through the cracks between my fingers. I close my eyes and remain as still as possible, though my body immediately goes into flight, my legs twitching to run away.

I pop my eyes open as static energy travels up my arms. It's the same white light, moving and swirling around me. It's both hot and cold all at once. When the light reaches my lips, out of instinct, I open my mouth and close my eyes again. Otherworldly energy fills my heart and lungs and I try to gasp for air but there's no air to be had.

All time is lost.

I'm floating in an in-between realm where it is both light and dark, cold and hot, soft and hard. I see myself in the greenhouse. Tallulah, Agnes, and Elora still gathered around. I open my mouth to scream but all that filters out is more and more of that bright light.

As quick as it arrived, the light snuffs out. Snapping my mouth shut, I drop the Stones onto the table while taking several gulps of much needed air. The women around me begin to chatter but their words are lost on me. Nothing but buzzing and wind flows between my ears. My vision blurs, and when I begin to stand, I'm met with weak knees.

"Sit, Sam," Elora says. "Give it a minute."

I've waited over thirty years for this moment. Thirty years for this magick that's been clawing at my skin since I was born, and when it doesn't show itself right away, every doubtful thought I've had comes crashing into me. That I have waited too long for my Ceremony. That I have been deemed unworthy of magick.

I want to cry.

Scream.

Be angry.

But before I can do any of those things, I *feel* it.

Like a warm breeze, tickling along my skin in the Summer, it flows through my hands, down to my feet. My mouth drops open as I flex my fingers, tears wetting my cheeks.

"Sam," Tallulah says. She kneels beside me and takes my hand into her own. "Are you all right?"

I glance up at my mother, who wears the same etch of worry between her brows as Tallulah. "I don't feel any different."

"It takes time," Tallulah says as she stands. She squeezes my shoulders and it's only when she steps out of the way do I notice something moving out of the corner of my eye.

At first, I question myself. But as I stare at the space for a moment longer, a figure steps into view and there isn't any doubt at who is staring back at me.

He isn't as he once was. His eyes are not as bright. His dark hair more muted and dull. But as he smiles at me, I'm *certain* and it's the strength of my certainty that makes my voice break.

"Father?" I stand and push past the three very confused women around me. "Father," I say, this time not a question. The figure nods and waves me over. My cheeks are cold from my earlier tears and they sting as fresh, hot tears begin to fall. I reach the figure that appears to be my father and a whirlwind of emotions hits me all at once.

Joy and relief and grief and fear.

Reaching my hand out, I attempt to grasp his, but it goes right through him and lands in a rose bush on the other side. His body shakes, his grin splitting.

He's laughing.

My smile broadens as well, and when he places his fist to his chest and bows, I choke on a sob. My throat constricts, and as much as I want to ask the million questions running through my mind, I'm unable. As I bring my hands to my mouth, my palms sting. That itching, fiery sensation erupting over every surface.

Magick.

Taking a steadying breath, I focus on the apparition of my father before me, ignoring Agnes, Elora, and Tallulah who have now joined my sides.

I hold out my palms and flick my wrists upward and there it is. My vision wanes but only for a moment before the figure before me sharpens. His face, no longer muddied. His smile is radiant, splitting across his aged but handsome face. My fingers tremble with the weight of my magick, but my heart thumps with adrenaline.

The bridge between the living world and the next lies within my grasp.

"How is it that I can see you?"

I steady my hands in the air as my father smiles again, his round cheeks amplified. He reaches out and brushes his knuckles softly against my cheek.

"Because you, Sammy, are a Spiritwalker."

Magick thrums in my chest at his words, a deep pulsing rhythm that is so new and yet, it brings me so much comfort. This missing piece, just as Tallulah said, finally finding its place within me.

"I don't have much time, Sammy, the veil is thin for us without magick in our veins. I've waited so long for this. So long to speak with you one last time." His face flickers, as if he's made of dust and wind and my heart races.

"Don't go yet, please. Stay." I reach my hand out again, and his fingers thread around mine. So real and tangible. So firm and steady.

This is dangerous, I think. How easily I could lose myself in this moment. This magick that allows my father to be here. To hold my hand and wipe my tears.

"I love you, Sammy." Another tear slips down my cheek. *"It's time for me to rest now. Tell your mum and your brother. Tell them that I love them too."*

"I will, I'll tell them."

His fingers squeeze around mine one last time, and when I blink again, he's gone. I suck in a sharp breath at the empty space before me. Throat burning, I clasp my hands to my chest.

Elora places her hand on my shoulder. "Sam?"

Reluctantly, I turn. Elora and Tallulah share a puzzled look with each other.

My mother steps forward and grasps me in a tight hug. "Samaria Trednik," she whispers against my hair. "Tell me what I believe to be true, you're a Spiritwalker?" She giggles, swaying my body against hers in a dance-like hug.

Tallulah gasps, covering her mouth with her hands.

Agnes pulls away from me but keeps her arm around my shoulder. Her smile is bright and beaming. The most proud I've ever seen her. It stings. Seeing how proud she is at this moment and not for any of the other achievements in my life.

"I think I might be," I admit. My mind is still cloudy, replaying the image of my father's face. The feel of his hands on mine.

"A Spiritwalker?" Elora crosses her arms. "What does that mean?"

"She can communicate with the spirits who have not yet passed on to join Mother Gaia on the other side," Agnes says. She claps her hands and my stomach turns. "My daughter, a Spiritwalker!"

"Your eyes turned white," Elora says. "Like Agnes' and my mother's. I thought you may be a Seer."

I shake my head, fighting to hide the tremble in my lip. "This was certainly not..." I bite my lip.

"Did you see someone, then?" Tallulah asks, drawing me from my wandering thoughts.

Clearing my throat, I take my mother's hand. "It was my father, William." Agnes' smile falters for a moment but it quickly returns.

"He said to tell you he loves you," I say, and she grips my hand. I wish she wouldn't, because it reminds me of his, and I want so badly to open that portal again. To risk the hunters.

Instead, I turn to Elora. "He wanted to make sure Sorin knew as well. That he loves him."

Elora smiles, but there's uncertainty in it as her gaze drifts between Agnes and I. As if she can read my frustrations with my mother. I suppose she probably can read my emotions. Even having known each other for such a short time, we've seen each other at our deepest levels. I want to ask more about being a Spiritwalker but my question lodges in my throat as another apparition appears directly behind Elora.

Her skin, unlike my father's, is glowing. While his was more gray and nearly transparent, this woman's is ivory and glowing. As if she is made of the purest crystal. Her face doesn't waver as my father's did. Her long, dark hair pools down her back and she looks strong. Solid. And then I remember my father's words.

The veil is thin for us without *magick in our veins.*

She must be an Enchantress. She must be...

"Sam?" Elora cocks her head to the side, and when I meet her with widened eyes, her brows relax and her face contorts.

The apparition runs her hand through Elora's loose waves but Elora doesn't flinch. She has no idea that her mother is by her side. I raise my palms, magick needling along my fingertips. That momentary loss of time washes over me until I feel the portal open, thrumming against my skin.

"You're Elwyn, correct?"

Her silver eyes ignite as she dips her chin. A small smile

creeps over her lips as she continues to stroke Elora's hair. *"Can you give her a message for me, Enchantress?"*

My hands shake, still suspended in the air. Elora's golden eyes burn into me. *"Yes, of course."*

"Tell her I'm always with her. She was never alone. Not really. Tell her—"

My mind is racing, my body heating as I meet Elora's gaze. *"Wait, please. Let me pass one message along first."*

"Elora," I start, but she holds up her hand to stop me. Her bottom lip quivers, and she must know because she takes a step backward.

"Don't." She tucks her hair behind her ear, shaking her head. "Whatever you're about to say, don't Sam." She looks away for a moment, biting her bottom lip. "Not right now I just —" she rubs her forehead with the tips of her fingers. "Please, just don't tell me."

She exits through the greenhouse door without another word. I turn back to Elwyn. Her silver eyes cast down, but she says nothing before dissipating completely, fading into the air as if she was never here at all.

"We must tell the others!" Agnes beams.

My eyes blur. The longer I stand here, the more nauseous I become. I take a step forward and stumble slightly.

Agnes pays no mind, walking ahead of me rambling on about the rarity of a Spiritwalker.

"Perhaps it's best if you rest?" Tallulah grabs my arm. Her energy relaxes mine and I lean into her side as we leave the greenhouse together.

THIRTY-ONE
ROMAN

RAUCOUS POKER GAMES AND PROFANITIES RACKET the air of the pub but the woman from earlier, Jeannette, doesn't seem to mind as she drifts from table to table. She carries on her business with a smile on her face, stopping every once in a while to speak with the man behind the bar. When she notices my gaze, her eyes brighten before heading in my direction.

"You again." Her smile broadens, the warmth of the light making her fiery hair even more beautiful.

My words catch on my tongue. It's not often someone smiles at me the way she does, as if I'm not a monster hidden in plain sight. But then again, it's not often I'm around anyone outside of Valebridge. I tug my hood down, making sure most of my face is hidden.

Jeanette's brows pinch for a moment but her face softens. "There's a booth in the back—" She points to the corner where a wooden booth is mostly concealed with shadows. "Take it, I'll bring you a drink." She winks and squeezes my arm.

I flinch away from the touch, making her jump as well.

"I'm sorry," I mumble, gripping my arm.

"Not a problem." She smiles again, and my heart twitches at how genuine it seems.

Why are you here, Roman?

As if reading my thoughts, the guards shout and holler over another round of cards ending.

Oh, right. To gather my men and leave.

I spot one of my closer guards, Stefan, in the crowd. He looks weary as I gesture him over.

"Your Majesty." Stefan dips his head briefly. "I'm surprised to see you here." He glances around to the herds of guards and locals. "So many people for your taste." He smiles, placing his hands behind his back.

Jeanette sets a drink before me and leaves, swiftly attending to another booth with empty tankards. I take a sip despite not having enjoyed it earlier. "I think it's time we leave, Stefan."

He cocks his head to the side, a dark brow raising. "Oh? Has Galen given the order—"

"No." I slam my tankard onto the table. "But I have, and it'd suit you well not to question me again."

On goes the mask of the corrupt king.

My eyes bore into Stefan and it doesn't take long until he's glancing at his feet, his shoulders slumping forward. "Yes, Your Majesty. I'll tell the others to prepare to leave by morning's light."

"Tonight," I say. Stefan snaps his gaze to me, his brows pinched tightly together again. "We'll leave tonight."

Stefan doesn't ask anymore questions before he heads to the largest table of guards, whispering into their ears. The men mumble and curse but slowly, they pay their tabs and ready themselves to leave. A few pocket their shillings and don their cloaks.

I take a final sip of the sour ale and leave a generous pile of coin for Jeannete before joining them outside. The men huddle together, about two dozen of them, chattering and grumbling, waiting for direction.

"Gentleman," I say.

Their voices begin to quiet, and for a brief moment, I doubt what I'm doing. Doubt what I'm about to say. Doubt that I am in fact the King of Teravie and these are *my* men, not Galen's.

I've never stood alone before them. Never given directions that were purely my own but then I remember the blue paint and the layers and layers of peeling wallpaper, of lies placed on top of it. Squaring my shoulders, I clear my throat.

"I want to thank you for your efforts the last few weeks while we attempted to locate the Dyrsjel." I scan the crowd, watching their faces under the light of the moon. Most of the men seem unphased, a few certainly are drunk. But the majority look disinterested. "While she is an important part of the plan to harvest magick organically, I'm afraid we can no longer spare the resources. Our search ends tonight."

The men immediately erupt into a soft chatter. Leaning into each other. Their voices carried by the wind that flows through the emptied streets of Wickersham.

"Corrupt was never right for him," one of the men snickers.

"Soft is more like it," says another. This earns a round of laughter from the men.

A thrumming erupts in my chest. Not a steady rhythm, but something low and dangerous slams against my ribs.

"Is something funny?" I step to the closest guard to me and his smile quickly fades.

"No, Your Majesty." He dips his head but it isn't enough.

Make them respect you.

I run my fingers over the amulet that hangs around my neck. It flickers to life, a soft purple hue glowing from its center. The men go quiet. The only sound between us now is the soft pad of rain hitting the cobbled streets and the light whoosh of wind.

I take the man's chin in my grip, keeping the fingers of my other hand pressed to the amulet. "Does anyone have a problem with this new plan?"

I squeeze the man's chin tighter, pulling a thread of magick from the necklace. It spills over my arms in inky tendrils. Swirling and dancing, it continues down my arm until it forces itself into the man's nostrils and eyes. He squirms under my touch, gasping for air.

"Speak now." My grip on the man loosens as his life leeches from his body until eventually he falls to the ground. I use the toe of my boot to shove him off my feet, his body shriveled and pale. But because I'm not as monstrous as I've been made to seem, I do the courteous thing and leave him enough air to breathe and enough will to live.

For now.

The men remain quiet as I tuck the amulet back into my shirt, the magick I used still stinging against my arms.

"That was an impressive show." My face drains as well as my confidence as Galen steps to my side. His hair messily combed back, as if he ran straight here from our bed. Beads of rain form on his dark brows and upper lip, a few falling loose as he casts the men a rare smile. "You may go, gentleman."

Without a single hesitation the men head straight back to the pub, chattering and laughing amongst themselves.

My jaw clenches as one by one the bodies of the men before me fade to just one. Only the man on the ground remains. Their dismissal of me is the final straw. The absolute break in my armor.

"Come back to bed, little bird. We'll discuss this in the morning." Galen grabs my arm but I yank it away.

"No." I take a step backward. And then another.

The rain has increased but I can see his fury through the storm. His flared nostrils and the way his shoulders tense as he takes a step forward.

"Come back here, Ro," he demands again. He closes the gap between us, and when he pushes my damp hair from my face, I don't flinch.

"No." I push his chest and he stumbles backward. His eyes widen, his jaw flexes and I know there's no going back after this.

No going back to the man I've loved my entire adult life.

No going back to Valebridge as the corrupt king.

No going back to hurting people that do not deserve it.

"They won't follow you, Roman," Galen shouts through the now pouring rain. "They know what I'm doing is the right thing, and I think deep down you know it is too. Whatever idea has gotten into your head the last few weeks, it's the wrong one."

It's me who closes the gap now. I want him to feel my anger. Want him to hear the severity in my voice. I get close enough to him that he has to glance up at me, our chests nearly touching with each breath.

"When I return to Valebridge, the law will change. Enchantresses will no longer be hunted, but cherished. As they once were."

His eyes widen slightly before they narrow. He opens his mouth, and I already know what he's going to say so I say it first. "They couldn't save her, Galen. They couldn't save Rose but that doesn't make them evil. It doesn't give us the right to take and take and take."

He glances away and it could be the rain, but I watch as lines of water run down his cheeks and land upon his perfect mouth. "So, you'll have killed all of these women for nothing, Roman?" He shakes his head then runs a hand through his hair. "All of this, for nothing?"

"You don't get to do that." I fist his cloak and pull him into me, his chest colliding with mine. "You don't get to make me the villain when it was you who handed me the blade." I shove him away. "No amount of magick will ever bring her back, Galen. Nothing will change Rose's fate." A flicker of hurt flashes across his face but I turn before I can think twice.

"Roman!" he shouts again and again but still, I don't stop until his shouts fade to nothing, drowned out by the rising rain.

The innkeeper greets me with a scowl as I hurry inside. My boots squelch against the stone floor, my hands tingling from the damp cold. "I need someone to ready my horse."

He looks up and recognition dons on him when he glances at the grizzly bear crest on my cloak.

"Of course," he says hastily.

"I also need directions." My cheeks heat but I push past my embarrassment. That I have been king for five years, have lived here my entire life, and know very little of my own country.

"Where to, Your Majesty?"

Taking a deep breath, I begin to wring out my cloak, letting the water pool on the floor at my feet. "To the Jade Guild."

THIRTY-TWO

ELORA

SLOUCHING ON THE BED, I LEAN OVER TO UNLACE MY boots. My body is on fire after performing Sam's Ceremony, but my mind is restless, caught on a loop.

The way she looked not at me, but just to my side. The way her eyes widened and welled with tears. The way she spoke my name, as if she were about to speak a truth I'm not certain I'm ready to hear.

Sighing, I cradle my head in my hands. For so many nights I've wished nothing more than to hear from my mother, and yet when the opportunity presented itself, I froze.

"Typical," I mutter but before I can beat myself up further, my attention draws to the door as it opens with a high-pitched squeak.

Sorin pokes his head in. "Can I come in?"

Smiling, I kick off my boots. "You don't need to ask, it's your room too," I remind him. I'll admit being at the Jade Guild has been anything but easy. Comfortable, but getting readjusted after so long in Valebridge has been difficult.

He steps in all the way, closing the door behind him. "Right." He joins me on the bed. "I keep forgetting that."

Sorin brushes a soft kiss to my forehead before untying his boots as well.

"Those feeling any better?" I ask, noting the weariness lining his eyes and bruises lining his knuckles.

He sighs, but doesn't answer as he pulls off his boots.

My eyes linger on the curve of his back, the muscles there more defined with his shirt pulled taut. His hand finds mine, as it always does and some piece of me begins to settle and soothe under his touch. His scent of pine and tobacco, intoxicating. So many nights I dreamt of him. So many nights, I wondered if I'd ever be close with him again. I kiss his red knuckles lightly, smiling at the absurdity of his and Jarek's fight.

"There's something I've been meaning to ask you." Sorin leans further back and takes his hand with him, putting just enough space between us to make me question why he's here in the first place. Puzzled, I busy my hands with the hem of my shirt.

"What is it?" My defensive walls click into place before I can remind myself that this is Sorin and he is on my side. Always.

Sorin shrugs before spinning the ring on his finger round and round. He's nervous. Why is he nervous? Slumping forward, he rests his elbows on the tops of his thighs, looking straight ahead and not at me.

My stomach drops, my gnawing anxiety beginning its feast.

"When we were at the Onyx Guild, I noticed something interesting. Something I hadn't noticed before we were separated," Sorin says, his knee beginning to bounce.

The anxiety spreads, turning my insides out and my outsides prickling. It feels like ages before Sorin turns to me, the weariness I noticed before in his eyes I realize now is actually anger.

"Ink, permanently marked upon your skin."

Swallowing thickly, I say nothing.

"I think I would have seen the mark before, considering how little we typically wear in each other's company." He doesn't smirk, doesn't laugh as he usually ends most conversations.

My skin heats, fire spreads across my chest and to the tips of my ears. For weeks in Valebridge there was no need to, no *way* for me to mask the ink on my neck. Not with the iron around my wrists and with how exhausted I was at the Onyx Guild, I must have let the mask slip.

He knows.

He knows.

He knows.

"So tell me," he whispers, his knee stilling. "Why have I failed to notice this mark and *why* is it there at all?"

"I..." Biting my bottom lip, I swallow the lump forming in my throat. I shake my head and look away from him. I can't see the pain that's there. The anger. Not after everything he risked to come for me. Everything he's risked to keep me safe.

"So, it's true." Sorin's hand brushes mine. "Look at me."

Reluctantly, I do. "It's true," I admit.

Closing his eyes, he brings his palms to his face, rubbing at his jaw and forehead. He glances at me briefly before returning his gaze to the wall. "You took my debt from Grawgeth."

"Yes," I whisper

"And why is it that I never noticed?" Again, his knee begins to bounce as he spins his fathers ring around his forefinger.

"After the Wicked Wood everything happened so quickly. I didn't expect for us to..." Flashes of memory of Sorin and I in our shared tent makes my skin heat further. "I didn't want to upset you, so I masked it," I admit, a wash of embarrassment sweeping across my skin. "When I realized that you came for me in Valebridge, I couldn't..." I bring my hand to my chest to steady my heart and catch my breath. "There was so much going on with Galen and then Loxley and I couldn't put another burden upon your shoulders."

He closes his eyes, resting his chin on his folded hands.

"I couldn't stand the thought of you being upset."

"And what were your terms?" Sorin turns to face me. Our bodies, so close and yet he may as well be across the room. "What were your terms with the nymph, Elora?" His words are clipped, his face a stone wall.

Letting out a ragged breath, I grip the quilt in either hand, giving myself something tangible to grab onto. A reminder of where I am. That I am safe.

"Why does it matter?"

"What do you mean?" he snaps, standing from the bed. "Why wouldn't it matter?"

I stand to join him, a flicker of annoyance breaking through the panic. "All that matters is that you're safe."

Hurt flashes across Sorin's features. His face reddens, but his eyes show what he doesn't want me to see.

He's afraid.

"And what about you?" he asks smoothly, taking a step toward me. "What about *your* fate, Elora? If your soul is tied to the Wicked Wood, there will be no chance at an after life. No chance at living beyond the veil with Mother Gaia."

"I was trying to save you." I groan, scratching at my scalp. "The Wicked Woods play tricks on you. It messes with your mind, and if you hadn't already noticed, my mind is already a mess. I did what I thought best at the moment."

"Damning yourself isn't saving me," he says. "Am I just supposed to sit back and let you take my place in the Wicked Wood? And you purposely hid this from me?"

"What you're angry about is the *exact* same thing you withheld. You didn't tell me of your bargain until it was too late." I cross my arms if only to stop my fingers from picking at each other. "Don't for one second mistake my choice. Saving you wasn't and will never be a mistake."

His shoulders slump, the statement landing just as I intended. He takes another step toward me, so close now that the heat from his chest slams into me. "It was still reckless."

"Well, you would know. You are the definition of reckless,

Sorin." Shaking my head, I give in and pick at my nails, finding focus on anything other than this conversation. "Trust me, I've had enough time in the dark to sit with my decision and how it affects the man I love, whether he's an idiot or not."

"What did you just say?" His words are a whisper. An unsure question transcending between us.

"That you're an idiot." Scoffing, I resume my place on the foot of the bed. "Of course, you'd find a way to make that flattering."

"Not that part." His voice is low and it sends the hairs on the back of my neck straight up. "Tell me again. What did you say?"

Tipping my chin with his thumb, our eyes lock. My stomach swirls again and this time, it isn't the anxiety or the nerves. "I said," I whisper, my gaze never leaving him, his hand never leaving my chin, "that I love you. I know it's absurd considering—"

"It isn't." He closes his eyes and the weight of my words settles between us. I don't regret them, but I hadn't thought of how it might change things. We haven't known each other for long and yet... My skin prickles as Sorin reaches behind me and runs his fingers across the ink on the back of my neck.

"You love me."

"Unfortunately," I say, a smile breaking across my face. I have felt it for weeks, but at this moment, I'm certain I've loved him for many lifetimes. How else could I explain the dizziness he causes or the electric feel of his touch? The comfort and familiarity I feel in his arms, not to mention the countless times he has proven to me that I am enough, just as I am.

How could it be possible *not* to love someone like Sorin with his unwavering devotion and passion and—

He smiles, his cheek dimpling, and my heart stutters. His smiles have been so few and far between these last few days, I bask in the warmth it brings me, proving every point I've just made to myself.

Sorin places a gentle kiss on my lips, and it's the softness of it that makes my stomach dip. So much care in that delicate touch. Such finesse.

"I love you too, you impulsive, infuriating, perfect woman," he whispers against my mouth, before his lips are on mine again, this time with much more fever. Parting my lips, I let him in, his tongue sweeping against mine coaxing a moan.

As he pulls me into him, his hands are everywhere. In my hair, on my hips. Stumbling forward, Sorin fiddles with the laces on my pants, and we both fail to see the desk before I'm crashing into it. Our kiss breaks for a moment, and before I can suggest moving to the bed, Sorin scoops me up and plants me firmly atop the desk. Then, his lips devour mine. Hands freeing my laces, he breaks away to shove my breeches off completely. Fisting the fabric of his shirt, I draw him into me.

He keeps his eyes on me as he slowly undoes the laces of his pants. Sweeping my tongue across my bottom lip, I watch as he pulls his shirt over his head and tosses it to the floor.

Sorin says nothing as he lifts my shirt off of me, then my camisole. His hands land firmly on my hips, tugging me forward until I'm at the edge of the desk. I spread my legs and wrap them around him. He presses his length against my center, and my back arches on instinct but he makes no other move.

"I want to hear every sound." His teeth scrape against my shoulder. "Every moan." His tongue drags down my neck as his hands glide to the inside of my thighs, hovering just about where I want them. "And when you come for me," he says, sliding his hand between my legs, his thumb rolling between my thighs. Moaning, I roll my head back but he's quick to grab my chin, forcing my eyes to meet his. "When you come for me, I want to watch every second of it."

His kiss is deep, claiming as I moan against his mouth. His hand slides back right where I need it between my legs, and I moan again, attempting to push my hips further to encourage his movements. He circles his thumb before his fingers find me.

Biting my bottom lip, I keep my eyes on him, just as he prefers, as he works my body in the way only he knows how. My stomach clenches, knots of pleasure forming deep in my center, before his mouth crashes into mine and I'm rolling over the edge. I don't attempt to stifle my moan as I chase my release. My hips roll forward but with how I'm angled on the desk, it's not much help.

Before I can catch my breath, Sorin removes his hand to grip the back of my neck. His other hand finds purchase around my waist, scooting me closer still, until finally, he slides into me.

Gripping fistfuls of his hair, needing him closer, I run my teeth and tongue over his neck. His body heats against mine as he thrusts into me, over and over again.

"*Fuck*," he groans.

My eyes roll closed, savoring every inch of his skin that sears into mine. Every movement of his body, every muscled curve of his back. The desk rattles beneath me, the contents toppling off the side as Sorin's thrusts grow more rapid.

I grip his shoulders, letting my nails rake against his skin. My need, growing stronger with each movement. I'm spiraling and not just from this physical connection we have but from something much deeper rooted. Something I can't explain, and at this point, I don't care to try because for whatever reason, we found each other. And maybe that's enough. Love doesn't need to be accompanied by a grand gesture for it to be significant. It doesn't need to be loud or bold or dangerous.

It can be quiet. It can be comfort. It can be finding your home in another person and that can be enough. And it certainly doesn't need to be years old to mean something. Even if this love between Sorin and I is new and fresh, it is still *everything*.

My body clenches, and Sorin must sense my shift, because before I can unravel, he pulls my hair back so my face is inches from his. "Let go."

His words snap the last thread holding me together and my

body shivers as my pleasure pulses through me. I cry out his name, making sure he can see my face as I do. Giving him just what he needs to find his own release. He's close behind, a few more thrusts until we've both exhausted ourselves.

Bodies shaking, both of us hot from our movements, but neither of us dares to move. He dips his head until it meets mine, sticky with sweat and all. "My love for you is a desperate, maddening thing, Elora."

Something in my chest stirs at his confession. Something both foreign and familiar. It thrums against my ribs, matching my heart beat for beat.

I push the hair back from his forehead and lean forward to kiss his mouth, soft and slow, just as he always does to me. We take our time kissing each other, the rush and surge of passion sated, allowing us the pleasure of basking in one anothers acceptances of each other.

But as Sorin kisses me, as his hands hold protectively against my back, I open my eyes and the room around us, before so foreign and new, suddenly feels as though we've been here for so much longer. I close my eyes again and a haze crosses my mind, foggy and mist-like.

Images of Sorin and I wane in and out, just as the dreams I had of him in the cells. Moments I don't recall living but that *thing* deep inside of me remembers.

Or perhaps it's hope that I'm feeling.

Hope for a future that feels so far from here.

Sorin and I in the forest, a looming storm overhead. A flash of yellow feathers followed by laughter.

Then, a room I don't recognize is filled with riches and grandeur. Fur rugs and duvets piled high.

My breathing hitches as the visions slam into me over and over, like tastes of our future. A teasing, happily ever after that's just out of reach.

Sorin's grip tightens around my waist and I'm snapped from the visions.

"I'm not done with you yet, love," he whispers in my ear, scooping me up before walking and gently setting me on the bed.

My stomach flips with anticipation.

"And I'm still angry." He bites my earlobe before pulling away. His body glistens under the light of the oil lamps as he towers over me, and I have a hard time focusing on where to look. Every inch of him is beautiful. And every inch of him is mine.

"But we will find a way to get out of your bargain," he whispers, running his fingers down the tops of my bare legs. His fingers still, wrapping around my ankles lightly. "I promise."

"And how will you have me now?" I ask in a whisper, propping myself up on my elbows and forcing myself to forget whatever just happened in my mind only moments ago.

Leaning down so his arms bracket either side of me, Sorin's lips brush mine but he doesn't kiss them before he whispers, "Turn around."

ELWYN

It's been two years on this Mother-forsaken mountain. Two years of ice and wind and snow. Two years of knowing we'll never truly be safe again. Two years of avoiding the inevitable.

I run my hands along Nevek Peak; the frosted stone burns my fingertips. The Awakening Stones rest inside, their shimmering light shining through the growing darkness.

Corbin caws above me. He's been visiting far too often, but I'd be lying if I said his presence wasn't a welcome one.

Especially tonight.

Because tonight is Elora's birthday. The night she's been waiting for her entire life. The night of her Awakening Ceremony. There were only so many excuses I could use to postpone, and being that she's as strong willed as I am, it was a useless argument.

Corbin lands on Nevek Peak, his black feathers rustling. He caws several times before I run my fingers over his back.

"How can I convince her it's not safe?"

His head cocks to the side, his eyes watching mine intently. *You know your destiny, Elwyn.*

My stomach sinks.

Of course, I know my role in this life. In any mother's life, really. To keep her child safe.

But tonight is different, and though my visions have been less and less fruitful lately, something wrong lies within the wind. Flakes fall from the sky, littering Corbin's onyx feathers with dusts of white. He moves to my shoulder and nudges my cheek. I kiss his beak before he darts upward.

We'll be waiting for you.

With the bird gone and the snow growing thicker, there's no other choice but to head back to the hut and meet Elora.

The warmth of the small fire inside melts the snow from my lashes and cheeks. Elora and Cade are already here. She hardly looks at me when I walk in, still angry that I've not agreed to her Ceremony.

Yet.

I glance at her bare arms and feet. "You're going to want to dress warmer than that for the Ceremony tonight."

She nearly spills her tea as she turns to me abruptly. Her eyes narrow, as if she doesn't believe me. "You're doing it?"

I suppose it'd be difficult to believe me after our argument today. She was so insistent it had to be on her birthday.

Had to be tonight.

My stomach churns as I take a seat at our small table.

"Here you go, Lady Elwyn." Cade passes me a cup of tea. "Something to warm you up."

"Thank you." I take a long sip, savoring the notes of cinnamon and something spicy I can't quite place. "Finish up your tea and get dressed, a storm is coming and if we're to do this, we're to do it quickly."

Elora hops to her feet and sprints to our small room but as she passes by, she kisses the top of my head. "Thanks, Mum," she whispers. Then, she's off.

The snow squalls make it difficult to see up the mountain. Even more worrisome, an odd feeling has settled over my body. My hands, typically tingling with magick, have calmed. My head and vision cloudy. I rub my temples and attempt to whisper to Corbin through our bond, but there's no answer.

Elora and Cade chatter while the other Enchantresses set up for the Ceremony. There are only a handful of us left, but we make every body count up here. Everyone has a job. A purpose.

"Are you ready, *susi*?" I ask Elora, and her smile widens. "Let's begin."

The Ceremony lasts only a few moments. It's a risk, using this magick, and one I don't take lightly. Rumors of hunters trained to seek Enchantresses have been filtering around, but with Elora's determination and the weak ward I've placed, all I can hope is that it's enough. Elora holds the Stones in her hands, her brows pinched together. When the Ceremony is complete she glances at me, then back to the Stones.

She frowns deeper. "I don't feel anything."

"Sometimes it takes a while," I lie. Knowing very well that until her spirit guides find her, she won't understand her Dyrsjel magick.

And it hits me.

Right then.

That I have made a grave mistake.

All these years I have guarded her from knowing her lineage. From anyone else knowing her lineage for fear they'd use her to get to the Awakening Stones. Use her to take what was never meant to be theirs but now I see my error.

All these years instead of shutting her out to keep her safe, I should have been teaching her.

Training her.

Panic rises in my chest, my lungs burn against the strain I've put on them. "Elora there's something—"

Shouting sounds from just outside the wards.

Cade steps forward. "Hunters?" He looks nervous, his hand trembling as it wraps around the hilt of his blade.

"What can you See, Mum?" Elora asks, standing to join Cade and I.

I close my eyes, calling on my magick, hoping it will somehow respond and show me what I need to See.

But it's not there.

Just as I open my eyes, it hits me. A swatch of navy blue against the pure white snow.

My stomach drops and my fists clench, because what I'm seeing now, I am certain I've seen before.

White and blue and crimson.

The same vision I had the day Elora was born.

This is it.

Save the girl! Corbin's voice is muffled in my mind. I trace the skies, but through the thickness of the snow, I can't find him.

"Go, *susi!*" I yell, pushing Elora forward. "We have this handled!"

Her eyes look curious for a moment before more men in Valebridge uniforms swarm out of the trees just below Nevek Peak.

They'll be here any minute.

"I won't leave you! I can fight!" She reaches for me, but Cade steps before me and pulls her into his chest. He mumbles something I can't hear, but it seems to relax her because when he moves out of the way, her golden eyes are lined with tears but her face has softened. She kisses him quickly, giving me a nod before she's running.

The men have crested the hill and the Enchantresses around me ready themselves. Elaine is next to me, a Stormwielder. She raises her hands and a thick layer of static bounds through the air. I glance at Elora, meeting her eyes. She screams and I dare to glance behind me to see Cade on his knees. Elaine flicks her wrists up and a bolt of lightning splits the earth, but the men are quick.

Their iron shackles and poison arrows hit the women around me like sitting ducks.

And there are so many of them. So, so many. I snap my gaze

to Elora again and just as she begins to step forward, I know what I have to do. I know what the Fates were trying to show me all along.

Protect the Stones.

Protect the girl.

I can't let them capture me.

If they take me, they'll have control over the Stones. They'll use me just as they'll use her.

The men move closer, their presence pushing down on my decisions, forcing me to do what I've Seen.

Every moment of her life was leading to this. Every moment of *my* life was leading to this. Keeping her safe, guarded, making sure she was *here,* on the mountain, and not in Valebridge after all.

You'll find a way, susi.

You'll find him.

You'll make this right.

I mouth the words "I love you," but I fear she can't see me through the thick flurries of snow so I smile at her just to be sure.

My daughter.

My heart.

My soul.

My little wolf.

I love you.

I love you.

I love you.

Screams erupt around me. I don't have much time.

The blade isn't as heavy as I remember, but I don't think twice as I bring it to my throat and fulfill my part of the prophecy.

Thirty-Three

The walk back to mine and Jarek's room seems to stretch for miles. Jarek's been resting most of the day thanks to Sorin, though I can't say I blame him for his anger. When Galen and his parents moved to Loxley, the two were instantly inseparable. Even when Galen left for Ramshire to study, they found ways to get into mischief.

But, Galen was my friend, too. A thought I've refused to settle on for too long. The betrayal is still too deep. Too unreal.

My gut twists as I round another corner of the ever-winding Jade Guild. The spirits I pass as I walk through the hallways mostly keep to themselves. A few rush me, grappling at my hair and shoulders, their lips moving, their eyes wide. I don't open the portal to hear them, not with having already used my magick today.

My head pounds and hands still tremble from seeing my father and Elora's mother as I stand at the door of our room. I'm eager to tell Jarek of my magick, but as I place my hand on the knob, the image of Jarek boarding a ship for Scandavi rushes forth. The back of his head as he disappears into the horizon makes my eyes mist. I slide my hand from the doorknob.

How can I continue to share his bed knowing soon I won't have him at all?

What if I wished to come with you?

A question I'd asked out of panic. Desperation. And he denied me. My throat narrows and just when I decide to head back to the main room, the door swings open.

"Oh," Jarek says. His tall frame takes up most of the space. His hair in a knot atop his head, a few blonde pieces hanging around his face. He adjusts his ivory tunic, which is much too small, showing off his sculpted arms. The bruising on his face has gone down with Tallulah's help, but his lips are still split and purple. "What are you doing out here?"

I lean against the wall, crossing my arms. "Truth?"

"Truth." Jarek mimicks my pose in the doorway.

"I was debating whether or not to come in." Shrugging, I glance to the ground. The words are acidic as they leave my tongue. Blunt and to the point, but he asked for the truth and it's about time I give it. He will go back to Scandavi to care for his people, and I will remain here to care for mine. Continuing to pretend our future doesn't end in heartbreak is more painful than anything.

I glance at Jarek again just as his face crumples. He hardly looked shaken up after Sorin beat the shite out of him, but now, he looks as though I've shot him straight in the heart. My stomach sinks and before I can stop him, he takes a step forward and wraps his hands around my shoulders. "I told you we'd find a way, Sam. Me leaving doesn't mean the end of my love for you."

"I know that." I pull out of his grip. "But loving me and being with me are two different things. We can love each other an ocean away but that doesn't mean we'll have a future, Jarek. What is that saying? If you love something let it go? You're asking me to let you go, so please just let me." It's painful to swallow, but I force myself to as Jarek takes a step backward, giving just enough space between us for the air to run cold.

"If getting Sorin on the throne and Roman off of it does anything to help appease Mother Gaia and end the blight, the seas will be more calm. I can visit—"

"I don't want to talk about this," I say. Deflection and denial are more familiar to me than breathing, but when Jarek sighs and runs a hand down his face, my stomach swirls with guilt.

"I'm trying my best to live with my heart in two different places, Sam." He bites his bottom lip then winces, likely remembering how bruised it still is. "Tell me the truth."

"I already have."

"No," he says, shaking his head. "Tell me the truth, would you board a ship with me and leave the people of Loxley to fend for themselves? Leave Sorin to sit on a throne he may not be welcomed onto? Leave your mother?"

My stomach sinks again and I'm not sure my legs are strong enough to keep me upright. "No." I clear my throat. "I would not board a ship. Not yet."

He nods. "That's my point, my queen. I'm not asking you to let me go, I'm asking you to seek your truth and accept it. No matter how difficult of a truth it is. You act as though I don't have fears." Jarek's cheeks flush as he crosses his arms. "You expect me to live here as though my life there never was."

I recoil back, the sharpness of his truth landing its blow. "I don't expect that at all—"

"I have thought of my sisters and Ma every day since the moment I was forced on that ship," he says. "Have imagined every terrible thing that could possibly be happening to Scandavi, and in every moment of joy, I've chastised myself for it because I am living my life here without any knowledge of what's happening to my country."

"You speak of Scandavi as if it's your personal responsibility." I reach for his arm but he moves just slightly away.

A muscle feathers in his jaw, his brows pinched together. "Everything I love is my responsibility," he says. "That includes

Scandavi." He steps closer, cupping my face in his hands. "That includes you."

"I'm sorry," I whisper into his chest. "I've been cold to you but it's only because I'm scared."

"I know." His cheek rests on the top of my head.

"I just don't know who I am without you anymore." The admission churns my stomach. The very core of the truth I've been avoiding. The truth Jarek so desperately wants me to face. Because with him gone and Sorin in Valebridge, who will I be? I've spent my life looking after my adoptive brother. Making sure he stayed safe. Following his lead in Loxley and the trades. Then, I met Jarek and dove headfirst into his intoxicating love. I have never had a moment to just be Samaria. And the thought of being alone. Being just *me* is debilitating.

"When the seas settle"—Jarek pulls me back—"when things have calmed in Valebridge and the people of Loxley have rebuilt, come be with me, my queen. Mother knows I'll be waiting."

I try to hide the tears by turning my head, but I'm not quick enough before his thumb drags gently across my cheeks.

"Jarek, Sam." We both glance down the hall. Evren stands with his auburn hair tossed in a low bun, his dark trousers and shirt perfectly polished. "Thomas has someone in his custody. Found him at the southern end of the forest lurking around."

"A hunter?" Jarek asks, taking my hand in his.

"Not sure." Evren shrugs. Jarek and I meet him at the end of the hallway. "We have him held in the greenhouse, he doesn't have a uniform, but after some questioning, he's admitted to being a former guard."

After a few twists and turns, we arrive at the greenhouse. Sorin and Elora are already there, looking in, their hands clasped together.

"Who is he?" Jarek asks.

Sorin turns but Elora doesn't. His face is like stone, his brown eyes full of fire.

"That," Elora says, her back still facing me, "is Cade."

It takes a moment before I fully understand who she's talking about. Then it hits me square in the chest. My breathing falters as I step forward and take her arm. "Cade?"

She looks at me, and while I expected sorrow or confusion, I'm met with only rage. Her gold eyes flare so brightly, as if they're made from the sun, and I know there's more to this story than I've been told.

"What do you want to do, Elora?" Sorin wraps his arm around her. His tense shoulders and pinched brows tell me exactly what he wants to do. I glance at his bruised knuckles before looking back at the man in the greenhouse.

He can't be more than a year older than Elora. His blonde hair is much too long and his face much too thin. Tallulah is perched before him, her arms crossed. Cade begins to speak and with one swish of her wrist, Tallulah sends a strand of ivy over his mouth.

Not just a Florecas, I see.

"Should she be using magick?" I ask Evren who is just to my right.

"I wouldn't think to tell her otherwise," he says, a smile twitching at the corners of his lips.

"Let the hunters come," Elora says.

The hair on my arms raises, the magick I'm slowly growing familiar with sends a rush of energy to my fingertips.

"Let them come and let them see what happens when they do." Elora takes a steadying breath as she turns to Sorin. "I want to speak to him."

THIRTY-FOUR
ELORA

SORIN'S HAND BURNS AGAINST MINE AS WE CLOSE THE greenhouse door behind us.

Cade glances up from where he's tied with the ivy. My heart falters but only for a moment.

Tallulah turns to me, a look in her blue eyes I haven't seen before. Something darker swirls in them, and I realize that she, too, must have her own demons. Magick is thick in the air and my heart races knowing the risk she's taken to use it, and yet I can't find it in myself to feel any fear. I meant what I told Sam. If hunters come, they'll see firsthand the magick they've been hired to hunt.

I almost welcome it.

"If you need anything," Tallulah whispers as she passes by, "we'll be right on the other side of the door."

I nod, but I don't take my eyes off of Cade. His skin is pale, a sheen of sweat coating his upper lip and brows. His eyes dart between me and Sorin, their hazel color the only thing about him that's familiar.

I used to love those eyes.

We stare at each other for a moment longer before he opens his mouth—

"Why are you here, officer?" Sorin speaks first, drawing Cade's attention.

"Was sent here to find you, mate." Cade straightens his shoulders to the best of his ability, the ivy pressing tighter around his chest as he moves. I glance over my shoulder. They're all there, waiting to help if needed. Tallulah hasn't lowered her wrists, her blue eyes like ice through the window.

"And are you here alone?" Sorin's hand tightens around mine, so I return my gaze to the two of them.

Cade's lips turn up in a cruel smile, igniting the fury slowly rising in my chest.

"Just going to stand there, Elora?" Cade eyes me from top to bottom, and I fight to shrink away from him.

Don't be afraid, Alaric whispers through our bond.

I need one of you to check the wards.

The wolves don't answer but I feel in my body as Hati and Alaric leave the keep.

"You're awfully confident for someone tied to a chair." I release Sorin's hand and take a step closer.

Cade smirks but I know him well enough to know he's embarrassed to be here. He never did like to lose.

"How many more chances will they give you, Cade? How many chances until your time runs out?" I kneel before him so we're eye level.

He turns his head to avoid my gaze.

"You betrayed me," I whisper. "My mother, who was nothing but wonderful to you—"

"Do you still not get it?" Cade whips his head and we're so close our noses nearly brush. But I don't back away. "Your mother kept her lineage, *your* lineage, a secret—"

"To protect me!"

"To protect herself." Cade shakes his head, a smile dancing on his lips. "She only wanted to prolong her life, Elora. Not yours. If she told you about your Dyrsjel magick, you could have protected yourself that night. Could have saved her. But she didn't. So, who is to blame? Me or her?"

My knuckles tighten and I reach for my daggers.

Only to remember they aren't there. Taken from me the night Cade took me to Valebridge.

Cade takes notice right away and laughs. Sorin steps forward and reaches for my arm but I swat him away.

No more running.

"So, what?" Cade says through a laugh. "Are you going to kill me, unarmed and tied up like an animal?"

He continues to laugh, and all of the rage I've let fester the past few weeks comes rushing to the surface. The scars around my wrists begin to burn. Images of the Enchantresses in their cells, their bodies weak and violated. I bite my tongue, calming the sea of rage storming inside of me. Steadying it. Reassuring it.

Won't be long now, susi.
Show him what it means to betray a Dyrsjel.
Show him what it means to betray a Leigh.

Sorin's lips brush against my ear, silencing the voices in my head. He crouches behind me, his warmth encompasses me and my knuckles relax slightly. "As far as I'm concerned, your word is law, love," he says against the shell of my ear. "So, say it and consider it done."

A shiver runs down my spine not just at his words, but what he's offering. To take Cade's life so I don't have to. I turn to him and say nothing but for whatever reason he knows what I need to do. He nods before stepping away.

"I guess I shouldn't be surprised," Cade says, gritting his teeth. The door creaks faintly beneath his words. "You're practically an animal yourself these days."

My fist collides with his jaw with a sickening crunch. I shake my hand at my side, ignoring the pain in my knuckles. He spits out a pool of blood onto the floor and the sight of it has my stomach churning. He opens his mouth so I lunge for him again.

No more talking.

My nails dig into the flesh of his chin, and when he tries to pull away, it only encourages me to dig them further. "I have thought of little else since the moment I was locked in that cell." Blood begins to trickle down his chin.

You have teeth, little susi, use them.

"I have gone over this moment a million times and then a million more. All the ways I could make you suffer. All the ways I could make you bleed." Cade squirms beneath my grip. "Or burn." The air in his lungs flutters, in and out. In and out. All the weeks lying dormant, my magick is eager now and doesn't hesitate as I command the air to turn to fire.

"So do it," he screams. His face reddens, his eyes bulging. He tries to wriggle again but everytime he moves, the ivy around him tightens. "Kill me and get it over with." His hazel eyes find mine, and despite the pain he must be in, he steadies himself.

Always something to prove.

The flames snuff out as my magick retreats, leaving Cade gasping before me. Low growls fill the space raising the hairs on the back of my neck. Leaning closer, I brush a piece of fallen hair from his forehead. I smile when he flinches, a disturbing satisfaction to see a man who has hurt me fall before me.

"I'm not going to kill you, Cade."

His eyes widen as four shadows encompass the both of us.

"But *they* are." Smiling, I tilt my head as the wolves' flank my sides. I drop his chin and spin on my heels to head straight for the door.

Leave nothing behind. Ruse dips her head and bares her teeth as I walk by. Then Rook, then Grey and Skoll. All of their attention now focused on Cade and only Cade.

"Elora!" Cade shouts but I grab Sorin's hand and pull him

into the hallway. "Elora!" My name is the last plea on his lips before the wolves rip into him. I don't look.

I don't need to.

Because as Sorin and I continue down the hallway, each and every shadowed corner is filled to the brim with Cade's screams. I focus on the warmth of Sorin's fingers laced around mine as the tear of flesh and crack of bone sounds behind us.

ALARIC AND RUSE settle at my sides as Sam, Tallulah, and I recline in the chairs near the hearth in the kitchen. I wasn't sure how long it would take them to end Cade's life, and it turns out, they didn't need much time at all. The pups have put themselves to bed, leaving the main room much too quiet.

Cade's screams pulse in my ears, but I focus on the warmth of the fire. Hati and Alaric found no other guards lingering around the Jade Guild, and despite the gnawing feeling in my gut, I have to trust that we're safe at least for tonight.

"You sure I can't get you something for those?" Tallulah asks for a second time. I shake my head, glancing at the red and purple bruises skirting along my hands.

"No," I say. "I want them as a reminder." She smiles, her face softening as if she understands why I might want that. I run my finger over the knuckles of my right hand. They sting and ache but it brings a smile to my face anyway.

"You know I killed a man once." Tallulah meets my gaze, her tawny skin dusted with pink. "Two, actually." She sighs, refocusing her gaze on the fire. "For so long after, their faces visited me every night. A reminder of the terrible thing I did, but it's that moment, I think, that haunts my husband the most."

The fire crackles, small embers shooting onto the tile floor.

"How do you mean?" I ask, tracing the edge of my cup with my finger.

"I don't think it was the act of me killing them that haunts him," she continues. "But that he wasn't able to take that burden from me. Wasn't able to protect me in the ways he thought best." She sighs, delicately running a finger over the lace of her gown. "We all do terrible things, but it doesn't mean they're undeserved."

"I'm not sorry for Cade." I take a small sip of my wine, though my stomach sloshes when I do. "If isolation came with a lesson, it would be that we're all monsters in the dark. And I think I'm okay being one in the light too."

"Here, here." Sam raises her glass, casting me a wink.

"Are we monsters?" Tallulah asks. Her brows worry together. "Or are we just women fighting back against a world that's been taught to hate us. Or maybe it's easier to label ourselves as something frightening rather than sit in our contentment with blood on our hands."

I take a sip of my wine, mulling over her words.

"Elora is *definitely* a monster." Sam tosses a grape at me, her voice laced in humor.

"Well she's certainly braver than me," Tallulah says before downing the rest of her tea.

"Monster I can accept." I cup my wine glass tighter. "But brave..." I shake my head. "I've made a lot of mistakes. Ran away one too many times to be considered brave." My eyes fixate on a single log in the fire. Burning brighter than the others. Orange and red and a deep set blue. "It wasn't bravery that got me out of Valebridge. It was the realization that I have more to run to than from these days." I nudge Sam's elbow, making her smile before taking a long sip of the huckleberry wine.

"Well said, little wolf." Sam smiles at me over her cup.

Tallulah sighs. "Today's been trying," she says. "I think I'm off to bed. Sleep well, you two." She brushes a gentle hand across my shoulder as she leaves the kitchen. "And for the record, I still think you're brave."

I tip my wine glass close to my lips before I smile into it.

"I'm calling it a night as well." Sam stretches her arms dramatically overhead. "I just came to see if you're all right."

"Perfectly fine." And the sickening truth of it is I *am* fine. Maybe that's the problem. Where there should be sorrow or guilt for what I did to Cade, I only feel relief.

"Okay," Sam says, "I've got a burly man with a sore head to tend to."

My laugh is muffled behind my glass, but Sam catches it anyway.

"I miss laughing." She sighs. "When this is all over, I'm making a point to laugh at least once a day."

She ruffles my hair, and in a moment's time, it's just me and the wolves and the crackling of the fire.

Ruse yawns a few moments later, showing off her teeth, still stained with a tint of red.

"Want a refill?" Sorin saunters to my side, dangling a bottle in the air.

"I better not." My mind drifts to the last time I drank too much wine and I wince.

Loxley.

Sorin must read my thoughts because he puts the bottle aside and runs his fingers over my sore knuckles. Their soreness is replaced by an electric thrum as his skin connects with mine. His finger glides over each knuckle in a barely-there touch, but it's enough to make me shiver. It's only when Ruse yawns again that he removes his hand to pet her instead.

Join the pups, Ruse. She growls so I reach down our bond again and again until, reluctantly, she gets up and heads for the stairs. Alaric stays by my side, his heavy head now placed in my lap.

You should go to bed, too.

He snorts out a loud huff of air and settles further into my lap. Sorin reclines in the seat next to me, and for a moment, I let myself pretend this is our life.

Me and Sorin and the wolves. A blazing fire and a belly full of fresh bread and wine. His fingers laced with mine. Sam laughing and Jarek...not being bruised at the hand of Sorin. I'm lost in the daydream when Calix joins us.

"I don't mean to intrude." He gestures to mine and Sorin's clasped hands. His hair is a mess, as if he suddenly woke from his sleep. Alaric perks up, his ears standing straight. "I wondered if I could have a word with you two." His gaze passes between Sorin and I.

"By all means, Lord," Sorin says. "Pull up a chair."

Calix smiles but there's something uneasy about it. Like it's painful to do so. But he pulls over a wooden chair anyway, fingers twiddling in his lap.

"Something on your mind?" Sorin takes a timid sip of his wine, watching Calix over his cup.

The Lord of the Onyx Guild tenses, the worry in his eye causing my stomach to swirl.

He's regretting his decision to help us.

We're just another burden.

More mouths to feed.

"Yes," Calix says. "There's something I've been meaning to talk to you about and seeing as how we will be traveling to the Onyx Guild tomorrow, it seems as though I've run out of time." He glances at his hands again before back at me. "Tell me, Elora, do you remember anything from when you lived in Valebridge?"

My brows pinch together, wondering why this is the conversion he wishes to have.

And why now?

"Bits and pieces," I admit. "After I lost my mother, most of my memories are a bit hazy. Memories of my childhood seem to come and go."

Sorin rests his hand on my knee.

"I see." Calix nods. He feeds a log to the fire, the bright sparks sizzling and snapping.

You're safe with him, Alaric says.

Shush.

"I moved here from Scandavi when I was just a boy, nearly thirteen," Calix says.

I nod, now understanding how he and Jarek have gotten along so well. Some sort of countryman camaraderie, I suppose.

"My Ma and Da had connections with the first ruler of the Onyx Guild, Lady Birna. She was my Ma's great, great aunt, and when she passed, the Onyx Guild was left to my Ma's cousin. But she never married. Never had children and so, eventually, it was left to me." He smiles, the lines around his eyes crinkling as he does.

"When I became Lord of the Onyx Guild, a new law had been passed. A law that would allow Enchantresses to produce heirs, to keep magick alive in Valebridge."

"Arrangers," I say. "We know of this law, my mother had one of her own."

"Right," he says before clearing his throat. "I, myself, was selected to be an arranger. I was young, unmarried. It made perfect sense to contribute an heir to continue to bless our country and king with magick." He pauses and my stomach starts to sink. Dread and nerves war with each other and I fight the urge to leave.

Run.

Alaric must sense my shift in mood because his wet nose nudges my arm. I run my fingers through his coat to not only relax him but myself as well.

"The role was supposed to be simple. Be assigned an Enchantress, produce an heir, and that was it. I was happy to do it, to help Teravie." Calix sighs, eyes bouncing between us and the fire. "I had no idea that by doing so, my entire life would change."

"What are you trying to say?" Sorin asks, placing his empty wine glass on the table to his left.

"I never intended to fall in love with the Enchantress I was arranged to. It was never supposed to be more than the arrangement, but—" Calix runs a hand down his bearded chin. "But you knew your mother better than anyone, Elora. So, you know how impossible it was not to fall in love with her."

Air fights its way out of my lungs, but it's trapped. My throat squeezes tighter and black crowds my vision.

"What did you just say?" Sorin's tone is stern and low, asking the question for me.

My head spins and thoughts race. Alaric's nose nudges my arm again, reminding me to breathe.

"Elwyn Leigh was the Enchantress I was arranged to." Calix's voice shakes, but I can't bring myself to look at him. "It was so much more than that. She was so much more..." My eyes snap to Calix. He meets my gaze, his hands clenched in his lap. "I loved your mother, Elora." His face blurs as tears well in my eyes.

I can't hear this.

This can't be happening.

Alaric grumbles but he doesn't bare his teeth. He stays planted at my side. His magick runs next to mine, easing the panic filtering into me.

"You left her there." A tear spills from my cheek, landing on my lips, leaving a salty taste on my tongue. I don't bother wiping it away.

You left me.

Calix's face breaks. He crumples forward, bracing himself with his elbows on his knees. "I wanted you both to come with me. I swear, I tried to get her to leave but she wouldn't. She was so set that you needed to stay safe. So set on staying—"

"Don't make this her fault." My jaw clenches, that white hot anger I've known so well these last few years ready to boil over the surface.

"I'm not." Calix shakes his head. "I would never." He runs a hand over his jaw. "The laws of Valebridge have always been clear. Enchantresses are to live with the king so he may access their magick as needed, and if Elwyn was anything, it was loyal."

He hangs his head for a moment, and I feel as though I may combust. My body can't decide if I'm angry or glad that a piece of my mother lives on through this stranger's memories.

"She served King Silas with unwavering dedication."

Alaric rumbles in his throat again but my head is spinning, thoughts bouncing between having a father and having a father that left my mother. Sorin's grip tightens around my knee, reminding me where I am.

I have you.

"I insisted your mother come with me to the Onyx Guild despite the law, but she refused. She Saw something the day you were born, and it frightened her. She never told me what it was, but a part of me already knew. The sacrifices she would have to make for you." He gestures between Sorin and I.

I glance at Sorin who looks just as perplexed as I do.

"Sacrifice?"

Calix dismisses Sorin's question, poking the fire again. "Elwyn did what she thought was best by keeping you in the only place she knew to be safe, Elora. So, cowardly, I moved on. I obeyed her wishes and left. But I should have fought harder." He places the stoker down, seemingly content with the now raging flames. "I love my wife, but I have regretted leaving your mother's side every day. Mostly, I have regretted leaving you."

Our eyes meet but it's all too overwhelming. This other part of myself I never thought existed. A piece of the puzzle I thought I was fine to be missing, and yet now that I know the truth, I can't help but wonder how I'd feel when that piece is in place.

"Does your wife know of me?"

"No," Calix admits, and I'm not sure if I'm relieved or heartbroken.

"The Onyx Guild is within the Kirsgard Mountains," Sorin says. His hand has found mine again, and between him and Alaric, my anger settles a bit. "Is that why she fled there after King Silas was slain?"

I glance at Calix in time to see him nod. "It was as close as she was willing to get to me after I married. But as stubborn as she could be, your mother was also smart. She knew I'd keep her safe, for as long as I possibly could." His brows pinch and he busies himself again with the fire that doesn't need tending.

I watch him closely. His hair, flecked with gray, still houses strands of golden blonde so similar to mine I can't believe I hadn't noticed before. The curve of his nose matches that of my own as well. I look away. Too afraid to find anymore of myself in him. As if it will take away the parts of me that are my mothers. The parts that are myself.

"When we got to the mountain that night, we were too late." Calix faces me again.

My heart races and I ignore the voices rising in my head. They nip and bite at my ears, demanding attention, but I keep my eyes locked on Calix. Forcing myself to look at him. To see him. His face is soft for a lord, not lined in arrogance like Thaddeus. I glance at his hands as they tap against the top of his legs. A nervous habit, perhaps. One that's much too similar to my own. I bite my inner cheek, distracting myself with the sting and sharp pain.

"The guards had left and the blood..." Calix shudders and my momentary distraction is ripped away. "I have beheld many horrible things in my life, but the memory of your mother fallen upon the snow is an image that haunts me every night."

So, we have something in common, I want to say.

"I had my men bring her back to the Onyx Guild. Where she was properly laid to rest."

I close my eyes to fight off tears. The thought of her not buried in the snow, a relief and somehow my heart squeezes thinking of her broken body being carried, buried or burned.

"Then, we searched for you," Calix says. His hand reaches forward, but I don't reciprocate so he tucks it back into his lap. "I followed a trail of blood and I both hoped and prayed it wasn't yours."

My fingers trace absently over the scar lining my neck.

"You came for me?"

Calix frowns, his mouth turned down. "Of course," he says as if it is the most obvious thing in the world. "Of course, I came for you and when I didn't find you, I thought all was lost. Thought you perished in the woods or were taken by the guard."

He scratches at his jaw again, his fingers trembling as he does. "Then, I heard Thaddeus had locked up his Guild so I did as well. Thinking there was nothing left for me on the other side and that's where I've stayed the last few years. But a few weeks ago, Sorin arrived in Jade."

He glances at Sorin whose body is rigid beneath his dark shirt. "Word flew to the Onyx Guild of a man who claimed to be the true heir, searching for justice against the new king. And I knew." Calix smiles, something soft and broken.

I twist in my chair, my throat closing in on me with every word.

"I knew it was you he searched for, Elora." A loose strand of hair falls in my eye as I shake my head, but Calix continues on anyway, his voice growing distant as I succumb to the voices in my head. "Somehow, I just knew my daughter was alive."

THIRTY-FIVE

SORIN

"Tell me you're okay." I graze Elora's back with my fingers but she curls tighter onto her side. Her hands are pressed firmly against her ears.

"Elora, look at me." She doesn't so I slide closer to her. "We don't need to talk," I whisper, "but I need you to remember that I'm here." I peel her hand from her ear, leaving my fingers tangled in hers.

She pulls my hand tighter to her chest. "It's all too much." Her voice breaks at the end and there's nothing I can say to ease her pain, so I don't try. "The entire time I kept wondering to myself, what kind of person could leave my mother? She deserved so much more. And yet—" She buries her face into her pillow, muffling her words. "And yet I am selfish because all I can think about now is what a gift it is that he is *here*."

I keep my arms wrapped around her and give a kiss to the back of her head. "You can wish for two things at once. You can wish your mother had better while also wishing to know your father. It doesn't make either wrong and it certainly doesn't make you selfish."

Her breathing stutters, her fingers clawing at my arms so I

settle in, committing to this spot for the rest of the night if I need to.

"You don't have to stay," she says but I shush her.

"I'd like to see you make me leave." This earns the faintest of laughs and before long, we both drift off to sleep.

"WE SHOULD HAVE A PARTY." Letty and Eviey's voices marry together as I join the others in the main room of the keep several hours later. It must be the middle of the night, given how dark the inside of the keep is, but by the sounds of Letty and Eviey, they have no plans to rest anytime soon.

Elora is still sound asleep, and while I plan to head right back to my spot by her side, the dryness of my throat forced me to wake.

The large, stone fireplace crackles at the center of the room, a few chairs scattered about it. I spot the kettle and pour myself a cup of tea.

"No parties," Sam says, shaking her head. Jarek smiles widely, the bruising on his face a slight yellow now.

While the Loxlians and most members of the Jade Guild have been transported to Onyx, the few of us that remain fill a hole in my heart.

Agnes and Letty and Eviey. Sam and Jarek. Elora. If I squint my eyes hard enough, it almost feels like home.

"It's the least we can do, Sam." Jarek kisses her and it's small, but she flinches. "You have your magick!"

Shite.

With so much going on and now the revelation about Calix and Elora, I haven't even congratulated my sister. Her eyes find mine from across the room and I brace myself for the harsh look. But she surprises me, smiling instead.

"Dancing!" Letty shouts. She pulls Sam and Eviey to the

center of the large, open room, spinning them in a circle. Eviey laughs as they spin, and for a moment, I'm transported back to the night of the full moon celebration.

Loxley.

Home.

My throat burns at the image, so I look at the flames.

"Something interesting in there?" Sam steps beside me, bumping me with her shoulder.

Shaking my head, I glance at her. She looks less tired. Her eyes are as bright as the fire before us and her skin glows under its warm light. "You broke away from your dance so soon?"

She rolls her eyes. "The twins want to have a party before we leave tomorrow evening. As if the brink of war is the time for celebration."

"Of course it isn't." I close my eyes, listening to the twins and Jarek sing behind me. "But you are worth celebrating."

She's waited too long for this.

Much, much too long.

And as much as I'm dying to tell her everything Calix told me, I bite my tongue instead. She deserves this moment. She deserves everything.

"Very true." She smiles at the flames. "Plus, once *that* one starts singing, you know he won't stop." Her finger is directed at Jarek, and as if hearing her, he begins singing louder than before.

"We steal from the rich, even more from the richer. You better watch out, or Sam's arrow will get ya!"

My sister and I share a laugh and I didn't realize just how much I needed that. How much I need her. "Tell me of your magick."

She glances at me quickly, something warring in her eyes. "It's late," she says. "We can talk about it tomorrow."

"I want to know now." I cross my arms and shoot her a grin.

She sighs, looking down at the fire. "According to mum," she says, "I'm a Spirtiwalker." She turns to face me again. "I saw

Father. I spoke with him." My mouth drops open which makes Sam smile. "That's exactly how I felt." She laughs, but it's quiet. Nervous.

"Let's have the party," I say, my mind still in disbelief. "Tomorrow, a proper celebration before we leave." I wrap my arm around her shoulder and despite the tension between us the last few weeks, she hugs me back.

"Can you see it, love?" I ask, pulling her back tighter to my chest. "Right there." I point just past her shoulder.

A tiny yellow bird is perched on a low branch of a nearby pine.

She glances at me over her shoulder, a smile stretching across her face. "What is it?"

The bird sings, high chirps drifting through the woods. Its bright yellow and dark feathers are prominent in the otherwise gray and green surroundings.

"It's beautiful." She takes a step closer but raindrops hit heavily on the branch, causing the bird to fly away.

"A goldfinch." I step forward and wrap my arms around her middle. "They're meant to bring good fortune." I kiss the side of her neck, savoring the jasmine scent of her hair.

"You believe that superstition?" she asks over her shoulder.

"Of course," I say.

Her smile widens, a spark of light catching in her amber eyes. I'm not sure I really do believe in superstitions as such, but seeing the bright look on her face, I'll go along with it. If it makes her look like that, I'll be the most devout believer in Teravie.

The rain increases, soaking our hair and clothes. Laughing, I grab her hand as we sprint through the forest.

"Some good fortune!" she yells over the rising storm.

"I never said good weather!" My laughs are muddled

through the rain and thunder. Dark clouds roll in, blocking any light from beyond the pines. A gall of wind splits between us, breaking our hands apart.

"Where are you!" she screams.

I stumble, tripping over an exposed root, losing sight of her. I try to straighten myself but I'm pulled down by another root. They encompass me, holding me tightly to the ground

"My love—" A vine snakes its way around my mouth, muffling my voice.

"Help me!" she screams again and again and no matter how hard I try, I can't reach her.

The dream startles me awake, a cold sheen of sweat coating my forehead. Rolling onto my side, I watch Elora's back rise and fall, the steady sound of her breathing relaxing the tension in my shoulders. I run a hand through my hair, gripping it at the roots. The dream, while not necessarily a nightmare, felt so real that I need something tangible to hold on to. It also isn't the first time I've had it.

Me, Elora, and a rising storm. It always ends the same as well. Her needing me. Me unable to reach her.

Elora stretches next to me, so I roll closer to her. "Good morning," I whisper against her hair.

The sun is still tucked away, only fragments of moonlight slipping through the small, round window.

"Is it morning?" She rolls over, wrapping her arms around my neck.

"I have no idea."

"Have you slept?" she asks, threading her fingers through my hair.

I shrug, pushing her hair from her face. I don't tell her that no, I've barely slept. Too many racing thoughts. Too many scenarios playing in my head for me to relax. Too many dreams that feel like memories.

"How about you? Did you sleep well?" She does the same, shrugging at my question instead of answering, but there's a hopeful glint in her eye that settles my stomach. "Do you want to talk about Calix?"

"I don't know what there is to say." She looks away from me, chewing her bottom lip. "I suppose it doesn't change much, does it?"

"Maybe it will," I say.

She slides her hands from the back of my neck and places them on my chest instead.

"You get to decide what kind of relationship you want, and if you choose none, then that's all it will be."

She frowns, but nods.

"The twins want to have a party today."

This makes her smile, which steadies the erratic rhythm of my heart. "For what exactly?"

"Sam," I say. "But knowing them, they'd throw a party just to celebrate waking up." I laugh, leaning forward to kiss her. The soft moan she lets out shoots through me, so I roll on top of her, bracing my elbows on either side of her face. "I don't think I'll ever get used to that sound." I kiss her again, cupping her chin and holding her close to me.

Her teeth graze my bottom lip as she pulls away, but I pull her right back and kiss her deeper.

Then, the vision hits me again.

Elora and myself in the thick of a storm.

Three old women, their skin wrinkled and worn. Their eyes, glossy and white.

Elora breaks our kiss away, gasping as she does. Her eyes are blown wide, and when she parts from me, the memories stop.

"Kiss me again." I grip her chin and she does as I say. She kisses me harder than before. tangling her fingers in my hair, raking her nails against my scalp and neck.

And just as I suspected, the dream comes rushing back.

Slicing our hands, our blood dripping into the mossy earth. Thunder claps loudly around us, and even though my grip is strong, Elora slips away from me until she is gone. Gone. Gone.

Our kissing grows frenzied, her hands are pulling at my hair, teeth grazing my bare shoulder and neck.

"Open your eyes," I say, desperate to see her.

Elora's eyes snap to mine.

"Please tell me I'm not the only one having these–"

"Visions? Dreams?" she says, still a bit breathless from our kiss.

"Yes."

"I've been having them too," she says. Her cheeks are flushed, her hair wild and untamed around her face. "In Valebridge, I had dreams of you that were so vivid, so real I thought it was my mind playing tricks on me." She smiles, brushing a piece of hair from my forehead. "Which isn't unusual, so I didn't think anything of them."

I roll off of her, giving her space to move onto her side to face me. "Tell me more about them."

"It always starts the same—"

"With a storm," we say at the same time.

"Yes," I say again, relief unclenching my shoulders. "You and me in the forest. The storm."

"Don't forget the bird," Elora says through a smile.

"A goldfinch."

"It's almost as if we're being shown pieces of our future. Moments not yet lived. Maybe it's the fates giving us something to look forward to." She curls into my chest, her body warm against mine.

My heart sinks when I realize our dreams must not share the same outcomes. I don't tell her more details. How my dreams always end with us separating in one way or another. How she screams for me and I'm unable to reach her.

"It still feels foreign to say," she says against my chest, "but I love you."

I tilt her chin up so she's looking at me. "I love you, too."

Her lips are soft against mine, that little noise she makes heats up my entire body. I've hardly had time to think of the fates and how they've entangled mine and Elora's lives together. After the memory I had in the Wicked Wood, our connection has only grown stronger. Deeper.

Elora sits up, propping herself on an elbow. "I need to say something."

"Okay."

She takes a large breath, closing her eyes for a moment. "When my mother died, I thought the only way to stay protected was to build a wall around myself. Strong enough to keep any and everything out. I thought I was content with that. Thought it was exactly what I deserved."

"Elora..." I take her hand, but she shakes her head.

"Let me say this." She tightens her fingers around mine. "I need to. I have learned, albeit the hard way, that there's no point in keeping yourself so guarded. Even if life hurts, there's so much to be celebrated. And all of these middle moments, small or large, I don't want to take any of them for granted."

"Am I part of your middle?" I smile, tucking her hair behind her ear.

"No," she says. "You are the beginning, middle, and if I had my way, the very end. I know it hasn't been long—"

"You don't have to do that." I kiss her knuckles. "What we feel for each other doesn't have to be based on a construct such as time. You and I love each other, and we don't have to prove it to anyone."

She lays back down, her head on my chest. Her fingers dance along my stomach, each line they make is followed by a familiar electric charge.

"I hate what happened to you," I say. "I hate that it was someone I trusted that hurt you."

Her fingers pause, her head tilting again so she can see my face.

"I'm sorry."

"I know," she says.

"In every moment of your absence, one thought pressed

forth more than all the rest." She tilts her head to the side, and I have to take a large breath to settle the swirling nerves in my stomach. "When I'm king, I'll need a queen."

Pink flushes across her cheeks, her freckled nose crinkling slightly with her smile. "Are you asking me something, thief?"

I sit up, bringing her with me so she's straddling my lap. "Begging, love."

She parts her lips, making our kiss effortless and smooth.

"Marry me," I say between kisses. Her lips turn up, smiling against my mouth. "The thought of you by my side, as my queen..." A shudder runs through me as another vision teeters on the edge of my mind.

She nuzzles her face into the side of my neck.

"There's no other ending for me."

"You want me to be your queen. Your wife?"

Heat blooms throughout my chest. All of the small moments we've spent together building to something greater. Every lightning filled touch. Every hurdle and heart ache. The memories of our mothers. The visions of our future. There's nothing I'm surer of than this.

"I want you to be my wife," I say. "But more than anything, I just want to be *your* husband."

She pulls back, a wide grin splitting across her face. "Of course I'll marry you."

Thirty-Six

Samaria

Gasping, I sit up with a start, clawing at the panic in my chest.

"Sam?" Jarek reaches for me but I push him away. "What is it?"

"Nothing," I say a bit breathlessly. "Just a nightmare." One I can't remember but I'm sure involved flames and Loxley and Jarek. The same repeated images for the last several days.

"Lie down, Sam." Jarek reaches for me again and this time I don't push him away. He wraps me in his arms, placing my head against his chest. "Are you finally going to tell me what's been going on?"

His fingers run down my arms. I close my eyes, honing my focus on the movements of his chest. I want to memorize his heartbeat. The way his lungs expand. The scent of him and his taste.

"Yes," I whisper.

And so, in the darkness of our room, I do.

I tell Jarek of the pain I feel every time I think of Loxley. I tell him of the brokenness inside of me every time I think of him leaving. I tell him of all the envious feelings I have toward my brother and the ridiculous resentment I feel toward my mother.

I tell him of my magick and seeing my father. Of seeing Elora's mother. With every admission, little by little, the heaviness in my shoulders begins to lessen.

He strokes my shoulder with his thumb as we lie curled into each other. "I wish you would have told me sooner."

"So you could pity me?" I smile, attempting some lightness after so many weeks floating in the dark.

He takes my chin and directs my face toward his. "No," he says. "So I can help you." His lips meet mine briefly, and my stomach erupts as a swarm of butterflies works their way through me.

"I've decided something by the way," I say.

"Have you?"

I prop myself on my elbow to get a better look at him. His blue eyes are the color of the sea. Not the water closest to the shore but the deepest parts of the ocean. Filled with secrets and life. "I've decided that you're right."

He throws his hands up dramatically and gasps.

Arse.

"About what?" he asks through a laugh as I pinch him under the blanket.

"That even an ocean isn't grand enough to keep me from loving you."

Jarek stops laughing, his face growing more serious.

"When the blight is over, and the seas have calmed." I climb on top of him. "When the people of Loxley are settled, I'll come for you."

He closes his eyes as I take his face in my hands.

"I'll board a ship." I kiss his cheek. "I'll sail across the ocean." I kiss his other cheek. "And I'll find you."

Jarek pulls me into him, his kiss bruising and claiming and that's all it takes until I'm lost in him. He peels off my camisole and tosses it aside, then my undergarments.

"On your back." His lips graze the shell of my ear before nipping the bottom. His hands wrap around the back of my legs, tugging me toward him.

"Jarek." I moan as he trails kisses across the inside of my thigh, then the other.

"Let me see you, Sam," he says.

My legs fall open and he takes his time, kissing me, looking at me, driving me mad with his tongue. When I've had enough, I pull him up so his body encases mine.

"Needy." He chuckles before kissing my neck.

"For you?" I say, wrapping my legs around him. "Always."

This earns me whispers of praise, and my body ignites as the last gap between us closes. His body works against mine as my fingers pull through his hair. My legs clench around him, and when he angles me just the way he knows I like it, stars erupt behind my eyes.

"Good girl," he mumbles against my neck. "But you can give me another."

And so, I do.

"You're still flushed," Jarek whispers as we head to breakfast.

Or perhaps now it's closer to lunch.

"I am not." I push him lightly, but he grabs my arm and wraps me into his side.

As we reach the kitchen, the smells hit me first. Freshly baked bread, sugar-coated blackberries with mint, and... I stop just outside the doorway and take a large inhale.

"Coffee!" I scream, abandoning Jarek in the hall.

My mother, Letty, and Eviey all chuckle as I help myself to a cup of the freshly brewed liquid. It's spicy, rich aroma calms me instantly, and I savor the first sip even though it scalds my tongue.

"Morning," Elora says through a laugh.

"Where did you get this?" I ask Agnes as she slices the bread.

"Lord Thaddeus," she says. "Since we're leaving tonight, we figured we'd make the entire day a celebration. Although he and Calix plan to leave shortly. The other Guild members are arriving this week and they want to get a headstart."

My stomach drops thinking of the other Guilds. Of all we have left to do.

Agnes turns to place the basket of bread on the counter and winces before nearly dropping it.

"Agnes?" Elora says, dropping her knife onto her plate.

"You okay, Mum?" I rush to her side, setting my coffee down on my way.

She brushes me off and glances at the twins. "I'm fine, Sam."

Letty hands her a small satchel.

"Just tired, I'm an old lady after all and the last few weeks have been trying." She smiles as she dumps the contents of the satchel into a cup of hot water. "Tallulah gathered me some tea to help with the pain, I just need to sit down for a while."

I'm reluctant to let go of her arm, but when she insists a second time, I finally do. I drink my coffee in weighted silence with Jarek and Elora at my sides.

"Well, we're off." Thaddeus and Calix join us in the kitchen. Thaddeus pauses at the counter before plopping a blackberry into his mouth. "Make sure to leave by nightfall, don't want to get caught in the Trinity Forest after dark."

"Why not?" Elora asks. "Oh right, vicious wolves."

Was that a *joke*?

"I've heard they're feral, beasts." I decide to lean into it. "They'll rip your throat—" I wince, remembering just how feral the wolves truly were yesterday on Cade. "Too soon?"

"Too soon." Elora throws a blackberry at me, and I'm mad when I don't catch it in my mouth.

"I wanted to thank you," Calix says, stepping to join Elora and I at the table. "I know you didn't have to hear me out, but I'm thankful you did."

All humor and playfulness washes from Elora's face. She smiles, tight and closed, and Calix must take it for what it is because he only nods before he turns.

"Calix," she says, standing from the table.

He turns to her, his eyes wide. Hopeful? I missed something, clearly.

"I'll see you at the Onyx Guild," Elora says. His face lights up, like she has just tossed him a line in a raging sea.

He and Thaddeus pack a few provisions, say a few more goodbyes, but as they leave, a wave of unease hits my gut. I stand and follow them, keeping light on my toes. Thaddeus is already in the caravan by the time I make it outside, but Calix has stopped, bracing himself against a pillar, his hand hanging loosely at his side. My heart constricts, the wave that I felt earlier intensifies and it is still an unnatural feeling that I forget the wave is my magick calling to me. Taking a deep breath, I accept its presence and that's when I see her.

Elwyn.

She manifests with a glowing aura filling the space next to Calix. She reaches for him and when she does, his hand flexes before he shudders and moves forward. Just out of her reach. Her eyes trail him and it isn't until he's in the caravan that she vanishes. Gone. Like she was never here.

I stumble back into the kitchen in a haze.

"You're up late by the way," Elora says between bites of jellied bread. She smiles but her eyes bounce between me and Agnes. A similar weariness in them that I'm sure is mirrored in my own.

I retake my seat and bury my face in my coffee cup.

"Oh, we've been up," Jarek mutters next to me.

I cut him a glare but it quickly melts when I'm met with a smile.

Elora pours herself a cup of coffee, bringing it to her nose and taking a long inhale just as I had done. Agnes pats her arm lightly, a smile tugging at her lips.

"Did something happen with Calix?" I ask over my mug.

Elora sighs, dropping the last bits of her bread on her plate. "Yes, actually. Turns out, he knew my mother."

"Oh?" I take another sip of coffee, savoring the bold yet nutty flavor.

"Yes," she says. "He *knew* her."

"Knew her…" I place my mug down.

"Apparently they *knew* each other very well."

I throw my hands over my mouth. "Elora!" I move to sit beside her. "Calix is your father?"

"It would appear so." She shrugs, but I don't miss the smile on her lips before she takes another bite.

"This is what I get for going to bed early." I sigh. "I want all the details on our way to the Onyx Guild." I pick my mug back up and cradle it between my palms. "Where is my brother, by the way?"

"I'm not sure," Elora says. "He was gone when I woke—"

"Miss me that much already?" Sorin enters the room as he does every room, like he owns it. He kisses Elora's cheek before pouring himself a cup of the delightfully sinful liquid.

"Where were you?" Elora asks.

"A walk." He shrugs before taking a large gulp of coffee and setting his cup down. "Was feeling restless. Now!" he shouts, clapping his hands together. "Today is our last day at the beautiful Jade Guild, and since we've agreed to wait until nightfall to travel with the wolves, I heard talk of a party?" His voice is boisterous but something about him is off. His shoulders are tense and darkness lines under his eyes. Then, I notice how he twists our father's ring on his finger.

He's nervous about something.

But what?

Letty and Eviey lay out a small plate of mixed cheeses and cured meats, along with the sugared blackberries I smelt earlier. Tallulah and Evren join us, filling their cups with tea and plates with breakfast.

Lunch?

I still have no idea what time it is.

"We must celebrate our Samaria." The twins rush my sides, pinching my cheeks just as they did when I was a child.

I groan into my cup. "It's not just about me. Surely there's something else we can celebrate too." I look to Sorin for help, anything to keep the focus from me for a moment. I'm typically the first to jump on the opportunity for attention, but after seeing my father yesterday I'm still shaken up.

Sorin's face cuts into a wicked grin. One I know too well but have seen so little the last few weeks. "There's one thing we can celebrate."

"Sorin," Elora says, holding up a hand before he can elaborate. They share a look and despite my brother's odd demeanor it's difficult not to laugh at just how opposite they are. Her brows are furrowed, and Sorin's grin is wide. He props his elbows on the table and bats his thick, dark lashes at her.

"Perhaps a wedding?"

MOST OF THE afternoon is spent packing the remainder of the Jade Guild's belongings; the rest of the larder items, some cots and blankets, and boxes upon boxes of plants Tallulah insists we bring. But after most things are secured, we shift our focus to the celebration. When Sorin told Elora about a wedding, of course she insisted on doing nothing of the sort. But with a little convincing from the twins and a grotesque amount of talking from my brother, she conceded and now here we are.

Just outside the keep is a small garden that Tallulah happily explained she grew from scratch.

"Not an ounce of magick was used to grow these beauties," she says, pointing to the beautiful dahlia's and orange pumpkins.

The twins took the last of the candles and lined them down a small path between two pine trees. The sight brings me back to Loxley. My eyes sting but I continue to set a few chairs out, although I'm not quite sure how this works. I've never attended a wedding before but somewhere to sit seems like a good idea.

I smooth the wrinkles from my deep, emerald dress. It's too tight for my curves, but Tallulah was generous enough to loan Elora and I each something to wear, so it felt wrong to decline.

"Sam." Agnes peeks out the doorway. "Elora needs you and Tallulah to come help her." Tallulah and I share a smile as we head in.

Tallulah walks ahead of me, reminding me the way to Sorin and Elora's room. Her dark hair is braided in a crown, ivy woven throughout. Her skin is luminous against the pale pink dress she wears.

When we enter the room, my breath catches. Elora's hair is swept back but loose, a few golden waves framing her face. The dress, one of Tallulah's, is a beautiful sage with delicate yellow flowers across the bodice and down the tight sleeves. The neckline is high, but when she turns around, doing a spin for us, the back is swooped low, showing off her ivory skin.

"Well?" she asks, her cheeks turning as pink as Tallulah's dress.

"Beautiful!" Tallulah says, clasping her hands together. "I knew it would fit."

"Beautiful," I whisper.

"May I?" Tallulah steps forward, gesturing to Elora's hair. She shrugs. and as Tallulah raises her wrists. my stomach drops.

"Wait." I step forward. "Hunters?"

Elora and Tallulah share a glance, smiles splitting across

their faces, and before they say anything, I already know. They're not worried about hunters anymore.

Because they're not afraid.

Perhaps it was easy for us to be frightened alone in all of this, but we're not alone anymore. I square my shoulders and take a deep breath. If they're not scared, then neither am I. I'm a Mother-blessed Enchantress, for fuck's sake. My palms tingle, magick flowing through them with ease. My skin prickles as a spirit enters the room, raising the hairs on my arms.

Elwyn steps to my side, her glowing skin flickering, as if she may fade away any moment. She holds her hands to her chest, and although she can't cry—at least I don't think she can—her face twists as if she is. An ache forms beneath my breast for her.

Tallulah flicks her wrists, drawing my attention, and Elora and I both gape as beautiful white flowers begin to blossom in the palm of her hands. She places them in Elora's hair so they cascade down her loose waves. She flicks her wrist again, and this time a slightly larger, white flower grows. She tucks it behind Elora's ear and grins.

"Now you're ready." She spins her to the small mirror and the smile on her face is almost enough to bring a tear to my eye.

"I told your brother this could wait," she says to me through the mirror. "But he wants to ensure we're married before he meets with the council. Besides, you know how stubborn he can be."

I choke on a laugh. Of course I know, because he gets it from me.

Elwyn's spirit draws closer, so I raise my wrists slightly, making sure the movement is subtle enough that Elora doesn't see. I don't wish to upset her, especially on this day. But I open the window between the spirit and myself, giving her just enough time to pass along a message.

"She is radiant."

THIRTY-SEVEN

ELORA

"Nervous?" Jarek asks as I grab his arm. I bite my tongue and nod. "If it eases your nerves, remember it's just Sorin at the end of the aisle." He laughs which makes me smile. It feels so good to do so.

Jarek walks me outside. I shiver against the damp air, but he tightens his grip on my arm, grounding me from the fleeing feeling I have gnawing in my gut.

Agnes waits at the end of the aisle of candles and flower petals. Evren and Tallulah stand, their hands clasped together. Then, I look at Sam and her smile gives me the last bit of confidence I need. She's beaming in a long, silk emerald gown. She gestures for Jarek to sit and for me to step forward.

I wait until I'm directly in front of him to finally look up at Sorin. He's in black pants and a long-sleeved, black shirt buttoned all the way up to the collar. His tanned forearms peek out from his rolled sleeves. His eyes widen as I step closer, his smile stretched across his face. I clasp my hand around his, mostly to stop the fidgeting he's doing with his father's ring, and when our hands connect, all of the nerves in my stomach disappear.

"You are..." He bends and places a kiss to the back of my hand. "Wow."

My stomach erupts again. A new sense of nervousness weakens my knees. I grip his hands tighter to steady myself.

"Sorin Rudhek and Elora Leigh," Agnes says, "I apologize I'm a bit rusty, but I'll try my best."

The breeze picks up, sending a flurry of pine needles and crisp, fallen leaves around us. Alaric and Ruse join my side and a soft brush of warmth runs down my spine, my magick alerting me that the puppies are here too.

"The heart of your heart and the soul of your soul, the two of you shall join together as one. Not only in this life, but all of those hereafter." Agnes folds her hands in front of her. "Do you take each other as partners in this life? Vow to protect each other. Love each other. In the face of every hardship?"

"Without question." Sorin squeezes my hand tighter.

"Without question," I repeat back.

He grins widely, his full lips begging to be kissed, and lucky for me, Agnes says the word not a moment too soon. Sorin wraps one hand around the small of my back, his other weaving through my hair and then his lips are on mine. Soft and sweet and the most overwhelming sense of home washes over me.

"Sorin Rudhek and Elora Leigh," Agnes says through a laugh, "your souls are now one. Bonded, for life."

As everyone claps and cheers, my stomach somersaults again. But before I can panic at all the eyes on me, Sorin pulls me down the aisle.

"Where are we going?" I ask, but he doesn't respond as he leads me back to the keep.

Singing and dancing sounds from behind me, but I whisper down my bond to the wolves to keep an eye out on the perimeter as Sorin and I slip inside a small closet.

He spins me so my back hits the wall as he kicks the door shut. There's no window, the faintest light from the afternoon sun trickles under the door.

"Did you think you could wear something like *that*, and I wouldn't whisk you away?" He kisses my neck, nipping at my earlobe.

"In a broom closet?" I ask.

He laughs against my skin, but before I can make more of an argument, his lips are on mine. I tilt my head back, so he kisses my neck, dragging his teeth along my skin, his hands pushing my dress farther up my thighs.

"Okay," I say, my breaths giving away my need, "a broom closet it is."

He laughs again before scooping me up and pinning me against the wall.

His fingers dig into my skin, his hips setting a bruising pace. There's nothing soft about our bodies connecting this time. Sorin kisses and pushes into me at the same time, like we have no time to waste. It's quick and desperate. My hands can't grip him hard enough. His lips can't kiss me fast enough.

My legs shake as they wrap around his waist. His fingers dig into the backs of my thighs, and every time I think I may fall, he pins me harder to the wall. Each slide of his tongue and nip from his teeth drives me closer to the edge and all the while, there in the very back of my mind, is the images from our dreams.

The storm and the forest and the yellow goldfinch. Sorin's hand in mine.

Sorin stifles each of my moans with his lips, letting out a few of his own against my mouth, before we both find our release for the first time, together.

Panting, he places me back on my feet, kissing the tip of my nose. His arms bracket either side of my body and he cages me there against the wall for a moment. Our chests collide, still working tirelessly to catch up. He touches his forehead to mine in the briefest of moments before he steps back and straightens my dress.

"I rather like your hair down," he says as he runs his fingers through my hair to smooth it. "Your hand?" He holds his hand out for me to grab. "I owe you a dance, wife."

IT'S NEARING MIDDAY and dark clouds begin to litter the sky. Soon we'll pile in the caravans and leave for the Onyx Guild. A small twinge of sadness crosses over me as I watch the trees dance in the wind. When Sorin is king, and I am queen, we'll live in Valebridge. We'll rule Teravie. We will not spend our days running through the forest, that part of our lives will close and the thought has my heart squeezing.

"I won't ask where you've been," Evren says, interrupting my thoughts, "but only that we're happy to have you here." He hands Sorin and I each a glass, and when I take a sip, I'm relieved it's only water. "To Sorin and Elora."

"To Sorin and Elora!" everyone shouts at the same time. Heat rises to my cheeks but Sorin's hand at the small of my back grounds me.

We set our empty glasses down, and Sorin pulls me close for a dance under the pine trees. His face tucks into my shoulder, his mouth resting on my neck. We sway back and forth, no music between us other than the creaking pines and faint sound of thunder, and all I can think of is how perfect this is. How complete this moment feels, and for the first time in a long time, I allow myself to be happy. Without any guilt. Without any worry for the future.

Just happy.

"Mum!" Sam shouts from behind us. Sorin and I turn before he dashes forward, meeting Sam and Agnes on the ground just as the wolves let out a low growl.

What is it? I ask Ruse, but she doesn't respond. She scurries to the pups, nudging them toward the keep.

As I join everyone surrounding Agnes, my stomach drops.

Milky white replaces the honey tones of her eyes as they roll back.

"*They come in threes*," Agnes mutters from Sorin's clutches. "*Follow the path as the crow flies, there you'll find—*" Agnes' eyes snap back to her honey color, her hands clawing at her chest. She gasps as her hands continue to claw at her chest, unable to catch her breath.

"Mum!" Sorin shouts, holding her head in his lap. "She can't breathe," he says, his eyes finding mine. Sam steps forward, hands trembling as Agnes gasps again.

Tallulah and the twins rush forward. Tallulah drops to her knees and begins digging in the small bag dangling from her hip. "Damnit!" she says, "I don't have any Hawthorn-root. I'll have to conjure it."

"What's it used for?" Sam asks, clutching onto Agnes' hands.

Tallulah sits, stunned for a moment, just as I am frozen in place.

"I think it's her heart," Tallulah finally says.

Sorin leans to Agnes' ear and whispers something I can't make out. My chest tightens, my breathing shallow. Agnes' hands fall to her sides, her body going slack. I force myself to move to Sorin's side. Kneeling next to him, I wrap my arm around his shoulder.

"We've got you, Mum," he whispers.

The wind rushes again, this time with a dampness that promises rain. Agnes grabs Sorin's hand and then Sam's and then, as quickly as it all happened, time slows.

"Here!" Tallulah shouts from behind us. The plant sits perched on her palm. "Hawthorn-root." Her dark hair sticks to her face. She catches my eye for a moment, but doesn't wait before shoving the herb into Agnes' mouth, forcing her jaw to work in chewing motions.

A few moments of tense silence settle over us, all eyes fixed on Agnes.

"Come on," Tallulah whispers, her hands clasped to her chest. As if she herself is responsible for Agnes' life.

A heartbeat later, Agnes gasps again, eyes wide and alight.

"Mum." Sam strokes her cheek. "You're okay?"

Agnes remains silent, but her face softens, her hand drawing soft circles over her chest. Sorin's shoulders remain tense, his face focused on his mother, but a shift in the air has my attention drawing to the wolves.

All six of them have their haunches raised, low growls pulsing from their throats.

Another clap of thunder booms in the distance.

"We need to go." I squeeze Sorin's shoulders but he doesn't move. "We can't delay our trip to the Onyx Guild any longer."

No one moves.

"Sorin..." I squeeze his shoulders again.

"Elora is right," Evren says to Sam and Tallulah. "We'll help Agnes inside to wait while you ready the caravans."

Sorin stands on shaky legs, and Sam does as well. She joins Letty and Eviey to make the final preparations for our departure.

"What is it that they sense?" Evren nods to the wolves. He lifts Agnes slowly, Jarek holding onto her arms. Sorin reaches for her, but she swats him away.

"I'm fine," she whispers, but the color in her face drops, and I don't miss the wince as she takes a slow step forward.

I glance back to the wolves and reach out to them again, but none of them respond, their gazes fixed on the woods that line the Jade Guild.

"I'm not sure what they sense," I admit. "But whatever it is, we need to prepare ourselves."

"This morning on my walk I felt like I was being watched," Sorin says.

I spin to face him.

"And you didn't think to tell anyone?" Evren asks, a bite in his tone that doesn't go unnoticed. Sorin and Evren face each other, deep lines forming between their brows.

"It could be anyone," Tallulah says. "It could also be no one. Storms have a tendency to bring new life to the forest, perhaps the wolves only sense that change?"

A swift breeze rustles the flowers in my hair, sending a chill over my exposed back. "We'll discuss this inside." I turn for the Jade Guild, not bothering to check if anyone's followed.

I know what I have to do.

DESPITE ALL OF us being huddled in the meeting room, it's quiet. Not a pin drop, not a gust of wind through the cracks. Unusually, painfully quiet as if the storm has melted away. My stomach churns as I reach out to the wolves.

What do you see?

There is someone approaching, Alaric says.

How many?

Can't tell.

Keep yourselves hidden for now.

"The wolves sense someone approaching the keep," I tell the group.

Their eyes all land on me at once, sending a fit of doubt straight to my stomach. I clench my fists at my sides and try to remember that I am among friends.

Galen was your friend.

"The caravan is ready," I say, cutting off the voices in my head. "You must hurry, we can no longer wait for nightfall."

"If it's Galen," Sorin says, "I should be the one to go."

"No." I shake my head. "I'll go."

"Absolutely not," Sorin grabs my arm and it's only then I remember I'm in a gown.

"Well of course I'll change first." My attempt at humor goes unnoticed, Sorin's gaze bouncing between me and Agnes. She's curled up in a chair with a blanket across her legs. "The Stones are already packed. They must travel with Agnes. She can't let them out of her—"

"Elora." Sorin's voice is stern. Deep. "You're not going alone. Don't even suggest such a thing."

"You have all spent the last few years protecting everyone around you. And we have"—I gesture to Sam and Tallulah—"have spent it hiding and silencing magick under the guise that it wasn't our own to use."

Sorin's grip loosens around my arm.

I lean in close so only he can hear me. "I'm tired of running, Sorin. Tired of being afraid. Tired of being told what I can and cannot do."

He flinches, moving his arm from me entirely.

"Get your mother and sister to safety. Get the Stones as far away from here as possible." I slide my hand into his. "Let me do this."

His brows pinch together, but I turn and slip out of the room without looking back.

AFTER CHANGING INTO MY BREECHES, tunic, and cloak I'm teeming with anticipation to meet the wolves.

So far, we only see one.

Keep an eye on him.

Alaric responds with a huff of approval.

"Just wait." Sorin grabs my arm as I turn for the bedroom door. "Please."

The unease in his tone makes my stomach knot but there isn't time to overthink what we do next. "I'm sorry about cutting the wedding short." I lean into his touch. "Perhaps there will be time later—"

"Come with us," he says. "Let Thomas and Henry go in your stead. If the wolves join them, they can tell you what they see."

My chest aches. The last thing I want to do right now is leave him. Especially with Agnes and her health.

"I have no doubt Thomas and Henry are wonderful swordsmen," I say. "But they aren't me." They don't possess a magick that's far more destructive than any blade.

"And what is your plan should you run head first into Galen and his men?" His face twists a bit as I pull away, so I grab his hand. I bite my tongue so as not to tell him that is my exact hope.

"He put me through unimaginable things, Sorin." I relax my shoulders. His dark eyes scour my face, but I try my best to feign as much confidence as I can to not worry him further.

"He hurt you," I say, "but he destroyed me. In so many ways."

Sorin stiffens under my touch.

"You wish to kill him." He sighs before pressing the heel of his palms to his eyes. How many nights did he also lay awake, wondering if we'd see each other again? I may have been the one in a dungeon, but there are plenty of other ways to be caged.

"And what if I say yes?" My voice trembles. "What if that is exactly what I wish to do?"

His grip around my arm tightens so I shift closer, pressing my free hand to the side of his cheek. He kisses my forehead. "Then I'll only be sad to miss it."

"It isn't like last time," I whisper, knowing he'll know exactly what I mean. Not like the time I traversed down a ditch to save Ruse.

"I'll go with her," Jarek says from the doorway, his boots creaking the floorboards beneath him. Sorin's eyes are still on me when I turn to Jarek and nod.

"It should be me going." Sorin kisses my knuckles.

"You need to get everyone ready to leave," I say. "Sam needs you. Agnes needs you." I bite my lip. "You all need each other. If what the wolves saw is true, if someone is coming, we'll need to be quick. Jarek and I will go. You and Samaria get everyone to safety. The Guild members are waiting for you at Onyx. You don't have time to stall, and we absolutely can't risk you being hurt."

He clenches his fists. "I feel useless."

I step onto my toes and kiss his cheek. "You are so much more important than you realize," I whisper. "Everything hinges on this meeting, Sorin. *Everything.*"

He attempts a smile, but it comes out forced and broken.

"Sam and Tallulah will be able to help you, if needed. Plus, Ruse and the pups will go with you, that way I can be in communication with them."

I cradle his face with my hands. "I'll be fine, don't be such a worry," I say as playfully as I can muster. Playfully enough that perhaps I can trick even myself into believing the words. I kiss him deeply, ignoring the fact that Jarek is still in the room. His mouth presses into mine, his body relaxing within my touch.

When we finally pull away, my cheeks heat as Jarek clears his throat. "So…" I turn to him just as he's piling his hair into a knot on the top of his head. "We ready, susi?"

"Ready." I give Sorin's hand a final squeeze.

"The moment you scope out the hunters—"

"I know." I cut Sorin off with another quick kiss.

"And if anything feels out of place—"

"Sorin," I say again, following Jarek out the door. "We'll be right behind you."

He closes the distance between us again, his mouth meeting mine with an intensity that has me doubting my decision to part from him. Something cold and smooth slips onto my finger, so I break apart our kiss. Raising my hand, I place it against his chest to admire how his father's ring looks on me.

"I can't take this." I begin to pull it off when his hand wraps around mine, stopping me.

"You can and you will." He kisses my knuckles. "I love you."

"I love you, too." I give him one more quick kiss, right on his dimple, then I'm out the door.

Dread snakes down my spine as the door clicks shut behind me. Nerves and anxiousness battle with each other but there's something else happening within me that I can't explain. I don't let the feeling linger as I reach out to Alaric through our bond and follow Jarek outside the keep.

Jarek, Alaric, and I tread lightly through the forest to the outermost part of the ward where the wolves sensed someone earlier. Though, we've been walking for over an hour with no intruders in sight. I rub my hands over my arms, the dampness starting to chill my bones.

It's quiet, Alaric says.

My head cocks to the side, and when I realize he's right, I stop and close my eyes. No birdsong. No creaking tree limbs or owls. No wind. Just as it was quiet inside the keep, it's somehow more so outside. I lived in the forest long enough to know that when the trees and animals quit stirring, it is never a good thing.

"Jarek," I whisper.

He turns, unfastening his ax as he does.

I bring my finger to my lips, indicating not to make a sound. Not a breeze through the trees or the crunch of branches. The rain has even ceased, leaving the forest a blanket of gray.

He glances around us, at the otherworldly stillness of it all. His ax molds to his hand, eyes set on an invisible target. Magick itches at my palms but I push forward with Jarek and Alaric in my tow.

My breath hitches as we breach over a mossy hill and there—

My eyes blow wide as I grip Jarek's arm and turn him. He

must see the same thing I do, because in an instant, his body tenses under my touch. Alaric growls, low and deep as dozens of hunters turn in our direction.

"Why aren't they making any noise?" Jarek asks as we both crouch behind a fallen tree.

Shaking my head, I ignore how my hands slightly tremble as I run them down my face. "I don't know."

"We have to run," Jarek says. While I don't disagree, I also don't want to lead them directly to the Jade Guild.

Have you left yet? I ask Ruse.

Soon.

"We can't let them go to the Jade Guild," I say, keeping my voice as low as possible though with the eerie quiet still plaguing the forest it sounds as if I'm shouting. "Sorin and the others haven't left."

"Fuck," Jarek grumbles. "Your husband is stubborn."

"And Sam isn't?"

He grumbles something in Scandavi, but it sounds like agreement.

I peek over the fallen log. The men remain deathly silent as they approach, their black boots stomping over dried leaves and twigs but not a sound to be heard. It's as if they're under some sort of protection. Some sort of spell.

Galen.

My stomach dips.

"So, we fight, then." Jarek bumps my shoulder as I crouch back down and glance at him. His eyes are uncertain but there's a small flicker of heat in them, like chips of ice so cold they burn. He, like me, is tired of running.

Hiding.

Get everyone to leave now, Ruse. In any way you can.

Her concern is thick and heady through our bond, her magick swimming with mine like pools of midnight. Ready to catch me. To guide me should I need it.

I turn to Jarek with a fresh shard of confidence. "We fight."

We give ourselves another minute before I take a steadying breath and move from behind the tree. A man catches my eye from the army line and like a cork being popped, all the sounds of the forest come rushing forward. The shrill of dozens of men screaming and shouting. Metal clinking and arrows flying. My eyes go wide, my fingers freezing at my sides.

"Come on, susi," Jarek says. "Give them fucking hell."

Several arrows blow past us, whizzing and whipping through the air as we run forward, stopping every few paces to duck behind a large pine. Jarek dodges them with ease, his eyes set on the archers at the front line. My eyes dart past the line of soldiers and guards, straight to the line of horses poised in the back. Officers or generals. Or perhaps, *traitors*.

"Stay behind me," I shout at Jarek over my shoulder, but either he doesn't listen or doesn't hear as his body brushes my side.

The men are still several yards away, but I don't wait a moment longer to flick my wrists, pulling up the dirt at their feet, creating a massive hill of earth and rocks and moss. Most of the men tumble, shouting and toppling on top of each other.

Then, I'm running.

But this time, I'm not running from the fight.

I'm running straight toward it.

Alaric is at my side, his magick intertwining with mine, wrapping itself around my soul like a tether between this world and the next.

Jarek grunts as an arrow brushes between us, but we don't slow. We keep pushing forward. Using my magick, I swipe at the ground like second nature, clearing roots and rocks from our path. The men are close enough now that their shouts become clear. All it does is fuel the simmering rage on my fingertips.

"Remember not to kill her," one shouts.

"The boss needs her alive!"

"Contain her hands!" The panicked undertone of their voices snap something inside of me and I am finally not afraid.

Not afraid of these men. Not afraid of my magick or using it. Not afraid of being the last Dyrsjel. My chest puffs out as I swipe a large branch out of our path.

Stay out of the line of arrows, I say to Alaric as we reach the final few feet between us and the men.

Alaric ignores me and goes for the first archer's calf, bringing him to his knees and eventually his death.

Jarek's blade collides with another archer's throat. His bloody scream is quickly drowned out by gagging as I strip the air from the lungs of another two others. They drop to their knees, bodies flailing like a fish from water. Another two rush me, this time their short swords drawn but they're not quick enough. Raising my hands, I do the same as I did before. I reach into their lungs, stealing their air and gifting it back to Mother Gaia. Back to the soil and the trees and the wind.

See me, Mother.

Metal clashes behind me and Jarek shouts. Turning, I see he's been hit in the leg with an arrow. Alaric beats me to his side, his teeth around the throat of Jarek's assaulter. The blood on Jarek's leg ignites a fire in me, but at first glance, it looks like it isn't a fatal hit. My palms heat as I spin and face what's left of the men.

Alaric's magick pushes mine forward, giving it the extra strength it needs to do what must be done. My chest heaves as more bodies topple over the hill I've created, and the longer I look, the more my stomach sinks.

The next line of archers raises their arrows, and this time they're tipped in fire. Just as those that burnt Loxley. As the first blazing arrow glides through the air, every single person I love flashes through my mind.

My mother.

Agnes.

The twins.

Jarek.

Samaria.

The wolves.

Sorin.

My hands are steady as I raise them before me.

The first flame-tipped arrow dips down as though it will drop right before my feet. I don't give it a chance before I flick my wrists up, catching the fire with my magick, suspending it in the air like an orb. Using my opposite hand, I let the wind flow through my fingers. I open my mouth, and I fill my lungs with it. Then, my stomach. As much as I can possibly fill myself with, then I push it all forward until it hits the flames.

Heat and light explode around us, singeing the hair on my arms as I use all my energy to push the fire away from Jarek, Alaric, and I and toward the line of men. My hands shake and sweat beads across my forehead and upper lip and then everything explodes.

Screams are engulfed by the flames, ripping and roaring through the forest until my knees give out and I drop to the ground. Trees groan and crack under the heat of the fire, smoke plumes from each direction.

Faintly, I can hear Jarek calling for me, but the buzzing in my head is louder than his voice.

My chest hollows out as another tree falls, embers sizzling the pines and marring the bark.

As the heat dwindles and the screams fade, the smoke settles around the scorched forest. I swallow my tears. The men that once stood are now reduced to nothing but soot and ash and right in the center of destruction lands a tiny yellow bird.

A goldfinch.

My hands are blazing as I cover my eyes, unable to stomach the destruction I've caused. The people I've...

I killed them all.

You did what you had to do, Alaric says.

But the forest.

It will regrow, susi.

A noise amidst the eerie crackling of trees burning draws my attention.

"Jarek?" I call out, but through the black smoke I can't see him.

"Elora." The name settles over me, freezing my scorching hot skin. My eyes snap open as I suck in a sharp breath. It's not Jarek's voice, and he isn't the figure that steps through the smoke.

Galen.

I'm on my feet in an instant, my hands ready to burn him as well when a wave of nausea roils through me, bending me at my middle.

"I'll admit, it took longer than I anticipated to find you." Galen steps closer, that coil of sickness pushing up my throat. He dusts a bit of fallen ash off of his shoulder, the movement opening his shirt just enough for me to get a glimpse at a purple stone that hangs from his neck.

"Elora!" Jarek's voice steadies me. I can't see him through the smoke, but he sounds close.

Alaric is even closer, the pulse of his magick bolsters my spine. Galen's boots crunch over fallen branches as he takes a step closer. My hands go up again, but all he does is smile.

"Go ahead," he says. "Use it just like I taught you."

My hands tremble as I call my magick, it burns through my veins seeking justice of its own.

I drop my hands to my sides. "No."

I rush him, my movements quick against the pillowy soot that now coats the forest floor. I close my hand around his neck, pushing his back against a tree. He has the audacity to smile so I clench my fist tighter until he gasps. "I'd rather feel it with my hands when you take your last breath."

He wriggles beneath my grip, his blue eyes turning red. My nails dig deeper, my face pressed close to his.

"What a waste," he whispers, strained and broken.

I push harder, and use my other hand to use my magick. It

spools up my arms, ready to finish the job when Galen's head collides with my nose.

I recoil away, instinctively clutching my nose where blood begins to pour. My eyes snap to his again, my wrists up. Before I have the chance to do anything, he slips his fingers around the purple stone and vanishes.

"Galen!" I shout, my throat hoarse and dry. Blood runs down my chin. "Gale—"

"There you are." Jarek and Alaric rush my sides. "What happened?" He tilts my head back to inspect my nose.

"Galen was here." I wipe the blood from my face using the back of my arm.

Jarek curses, placing his ax back in its holster. "Let's go."

I follow him through the burnt forest. My stomach reeling, thoughts spiraling. Galen was right there, and I let him slip away.

A sharp pain spreads throughout my chest as Jarek and I begin to crest the hill. Clutching my heart, I wait for the familiar darkness to seep in.

Just a panic attack.

But as I rub circles over my chest, the pain doesn't ease. Instead, it travels to my side. Then my head and before I know it, I'm on my back.

"Elora!" Jarek joins my side and cups my head, angling me onto his lap.

Words swim on my tongue, but the pain is too blinding to form any of them. My knuckles whiten around Jarek's forearms. The sting on the back of my neck, pulsing, growing sharper by the second.

It's almost time.

Thirty-Eight

The last of the supplies as well as my mother, the twins, Evren and Tallulah are loaded into the caravans ready to be on their way to the Onyx Guild.

I tighten the reins on Amis and give her a quick kiss on her velvety nose. I've made sure to pack Elora and Jarek everything they'll need for travels, though they will have to share the horse. The thought makes me smile, remembering how appalled Elora had been to share a horse with me the first time we met. Amis whinnies as Ruse joins my side, her large frame towering next to me.

"Hi, girl." I reach out my hand to pet her, but Hati and Rook come bounding out of the keep, bumping into me as they do. The pups are now nearly as tall as my waist, but their energy reminds me they're still so young. I smile at their rowdiness then turn to head inside the keep, just to ensure we haven't forgotten anything.

Just to stall a little longer.

I hate that Elora and Jarek left, and I hate it more that I didn't go with her.

But damn if she wasn't right. The meeting with the Lords and Ladies of the Guilds can't be postponed. I drag a hand through my hair, my boots on the threshold of the keep when I'm tugged backward by my cloak. Glancing over my shoulder, I expect one of the pups but it's Ruse who has a mouthful of fabric in her mouth. "What is it?"

She nods toward the woods, to where Elora and Jarek have headed off to. Something stirs in my chest, like panic fighting its way through my skin.

My stomach skins. We should have left this morning. Should have risked being seen traveling across the Trinity Forest in the daylight. A wave of dread settles over me like an ink pot spilled to paper. It seeps through each of my pores, staining down to my marrow.

The wind hisses, sending flurries of leaves through the air.

"Sorin!" Sam calls from inside. "Are you almost ready? There's a storm coming in, we'll want to get a move on."

"Be right there," I say over my shoulder, but Ruse doesn't let my cloak go and that feeling of dread only intensifies.

She tugs again, making me take a clumsy step toward the woods. Then again, and again.

"Okay, girl." I pet her snout and when she doesn't balk away at my touch that feeling of dread is confirmed.

Something's wrong.

"I'll check it out if you take care of those rascals first." I point to the puppies, and she finally drops my cloak, barking softly at the four pups wrestling. They straighten themselves and follow their mother. When they're safely inside the keep, I pick up my bow and quiver and head straight for the woods.

Sam's voice fades behind me. My name traveling on the wind, spiraling through the trees. But I follow my gut and trudge forward.

At first, there's nothing out of the ordinary about the woods. Droplets of water hang from the pine branches. Muddied puddles that more so resemble tiny lakes force me to weave my way through the forest. I trace the horizon, waiting for any sign of movement. But there's none. No birds. No sway of the wind despite having just felt it moments ago.

The eerie quiet of the forest raises the hair on my arms and back of my neck, but when I spot two sets of boot prints in the mud, my shoulders unclench. My fingers tighten around my bow while I pick up my pace.

Deep in the woods now, I follow what I believe to be Jarek and Elora's steps. They twist and turn, carving a path along the mud-soaked forest. When their tracks disappear, I perch against a tree to catch my breath. Wishing I had Elora's ability to speak with the wolves. If I could reach out to Alaric then—

I stop at the sudden burst of noise. Screaming and shouting, all coming from over the hill a few miles away. I don't think twice before I bolt in that direction, somehow knowing Elora and Jarek must be there, too.

I should get Sam and Tallulah.

The thought comes and goes quickly. I trudge on and up a small hill, running blindly through the thick forest until I slam directly into something hard. I stumble backward and catch my balance.

"Sorin?" Roman stands before me, his eyes blown wide as he watches me regain composure from my sprint.

"What are you doing here?" I ask through short, strained breaths.

He takes a step backward but I follow him until his back is pinned to a nearby tree.

"Why are you here?" I grit through my teeth, my nocked arrow aimed directly at his chest.

His eyes dart between me and my bow.

"Is Galen with you?"

"No," he says. "I came to warn you to leave."

I lower my bow and he takes a thick swallow.

"You're a little late for that." I clench my fingers tighter around my bow. "Tell me where Galen is."

Roman half smiles, straightening himself from the tree.

"Why, so you can kill him?" As he asks the question his smile fades and his green eyes drift to the ground. Rain drips from the trees, coating his dark hair and thick lashes.

"Do you want me to kill him?"

His eyes snap to mine but he doesn't say anything as he pushes off the tree and starts toward the hill.

"Galen will end, Roman. Either by my hand, or yours."

"You have some nerve," he says over his shoulder. He takes two more steps when the silence of the forest snaps and an erupt of sound sends both of us jolting backward. Screaming and metal fill the air.

My heart races. I place the unused arrow back in my quiver and push past Roman, determined to follow the sound and find Elora until I'm forcefully tugged backward.

"You're going to take them all down with a single bow and a few arrows?" Roman chuckles from behind me. His hand slides from my arm when I turn to look at him. A purple stone hangs from his neck, sparkling in the tiny bits of daylight that have managed to break through the storm clouds and trees. Roman must notice my gaze because he reaches up and clutches the stone, tucking it beneath his shirt.

"Is that the magick you've stolen?"

His hand tightens around his shirt where the stone lays beneath.

"The magick you've hurt people for?" I take a step toward him, and he takes one step away. "Hunted for?" Another step forward. "Killed for." My anger seeps through my gritted teeth, the sounds of shouting and fighting almost drowned by the pulsing of blood in my ears. We continue this back and forth dance until he's backed against a tree. His hand remains clutched on the stone, but his face drops.

"All of that is true," he says. The stone begins to glow, a beautiful purple light, transfixing me in place and then, Roman pushes me out of the way, knocking me backward.

"Roman!" A flock of crows shoots from a nearby tree just as branch snaps to my right as I stand.

"You should run," Roman says, not several feet away from me. "Get your girl and go. It won't be long before he's here. I just wanted to warn you."

I take a step toward him, but when I do, he disappears again behind the trees.

"Roman!" I slide a new arrow between my fingers, holding it taught against my bowstring. A shiver runs over me as the air turns frigid. Thick, white blankets of fog roll in and despite my initial intuition to trust Roman, the feeling of being cornered like prey has my other instincts kicking in.

The one to survive.

I hold my breath and close my eyes. Screaming and shouting still sound from beyond the hill, but I tune it out and focus on what's directly before me. The branches sway as the wind changes course, but through the rustling of leaves, I hear him.

Another branch snaps. I smile as I spin and launch an arrow through the fog-ridden trees. A scream sounds and the fog begins to dissipate, turning again to wind and rain.

Not very light on your feet, little brother.

Roman stumbles into view, clutching his arm. It's brief, but our eyes meet before I hear a distant cry. It could be my name that's being screamed, I can't be certain, but the sound slices right through me.

Help me!

Elora's voice from my dreams echoes in my mind but when Roman groans, I notice then the arrow has only brushed his arm. He cradles the wound, blood seeping through his fingers.

"Roman, we must stop this," I beg. "I've already been deemed the rightful heir, the Guilds will affirm me and the council will have no choice but to follow suit. Galen will be stopped one way or another, but *you* can end this now."

He tips his head back, dark curls falling from his face as he screams low and feral. "You have no idea what you're talking about," he says. "I never wanted this. And if you think I have the power to—" Tears line his green eyes silver, but he swallows hard. "I never wanted any of it," he says again, this time no louder than a whisper. "I only wanted him." His head hangs heavily, one hand clutches his shoulder where the arrow sliced him open.

"I see that now." I drop to my knees, the wet moss soaking through my breeches.

The shouting from below us has died down considerably and my feet twitch, ready to run toward Elora.

Roman moans, drawing my attention. He reaches for the stone around his neck but hesitates.

"I'm sorry for that," I admit, pointing to his arm. "Despite everything, I think you and I could have—"

"Please," he says, his green eyes snapping to mine. "Please don't say what I think you're going to say." They glisten with tears again and my heart aches. Still playing the role of Corrupt King even when there is no audience. I suppose it's a difficult habit to break. The mask you wear to prove yourself to others doesn't easily slip off.

"Don't tell me what we could have been," he says. "It's no use because we weren't. I was born for the sole purpose of being king and you got to live your life just as you wanted. Travel as you wanted. *Love* as you wanted." There is venom laced in that one word, but more so, there is envy.

"And now," he continues, "you will take the one thing I have ever had. The one thing I risked everything for. My crown. Without it, I'm nothing." He runs his fingers through his hair, gripping and pulling. The battle in his heart is worn across his face making him look much older than he is. "Perhaps it's for the best, after what I've done."

"You are not nothing, Roman," I say. "You are good, I see it in you. You wouldn't be right here with me if you weren't."

His hand slides from his hair, back to his arm where the bleeding has slowed. He watches me but says nothing.

"In every small moment we've shared, in every mercy you've shown Elora. Crown or not, you are *not* nothing. We all drift away from ourselves sometimes." I let out a long breath. "Let me help you find your way again."

My legs shake as I stand, nerves getting the better of me. "Let me help you. Let me be your brother for a few minutes. At the very least, let me help where I've hurt." I nod to his arm, then place a hand over my heart, where the silver arrow is stitched. An oath of sorts, a promise. If I can somehow get him to Tallulah, she could help with his arm.

His face pales, his head rolling to the side.

"I owe you that much," I say.

"Don't believe him."

My chest tightens, the voice behind me, one I know all too well.

Roman's eyes widen as he glances just past me, he grapples to take hold of my cloak, but I turn so quickly that he loses balance and falls.

Galen stands before us, his blonde hair grown out slightly from when I saw him last, his blue eyes lined with red. "Sorin, don't believe a word he says."

He takes a step forward, flinching when Roman shuffles behind me. As if he's *scared* of him.

"Come with me, Sorin." Galen holds out his hand and my stomach twists. "Please. Help me end this mess that he's started." His voice wavers and everything I thought I knew morphs into doubt.

Maybe this wasn't his doing, after all. Maybe it's Roman I cannot trust. If he saw Elora, perhaps she let him live for that very reason.

"Galen," Roman cries from behind me.

I glance to where he's at on the ground. My instinct is to turn to him. Help him and then find Elora, but I'm rooted in place. Caught between a person who I've known and loved my entire life and a brother who I barely recognize, yet feel such a strong responsibility for.

"Sorin," Galen says, drawing my attention back. "I promise you, this isn't what you think. *None* of this is what you think."

His hand is still raised between us, a promise, a beacon. But the longer it's held there, the longer I stand with my hands at my sides. Something contorts on his face, his composure chipping away.

"You would believe him over me? Your oldest friend?" He drops his hand, eyes falling to Roman who is still behind me.

Roman mutters something, but my body is still stuck. Paralyzed between two worlds.

"If this is about her," Galen snaps, "whatever Elora told you is a *lie.*"

The words slither through the air between us, wiping away the doubt I felt earlier. It's all I needed to hear to know the truth.

The truth lies in the scars around her wrists. In her painful recounts of all the ways *Galen* hurt her.

"This ends right now, Galen." My voice shakes, but I'm not embarrassed by it. Something pungent filters through the air, filling my nose. Glancing beyond Galen, down the hill, I see smoke has engulfed the forest.

Elora.

"You hurt her." I reach behind me for an arrow. "You hurt Loxley."

Galen stiffens, his eyes watching my hands as I nock an arrow.

"You've always been so naive," he says. "Believing whatever is told. Never questioning or finding answers for yourself." He takes a step forward, and I pull the arrow taut. "Think for yourself for the first time in your life. Make your own conclusions."

My fingers betray me as they tremble against my bow. Before I have a chance to decide, Galen lunges at me. He grapples for my bow, his fingers bruising against mine. I manage to shove him off of me as my bow falls to the ground. I don't have a moment to right myself before he's back, his fist connecting with my jaw. I grunt, shoving him off of me again. Blood seeps from my nose where he got the first hit.

"This is it, then." I wipe the blood on the back of my hand. I don't wait a moment longer before I spring forward and tackle him to the ground. He groans as our bodies collide with the earth. His fingers claw at my arms as I wrap my hand around his throat.

"Sorin," he says through labored breaths. His eyes meet mine, wide with panic. All our memories push down around me. Our childhood. Our friendship. The many years we trusted each other. Loved each other.

"Sorin," he says again, this time much more breathless. A plea and the sound of his panic weakens my grip. He claws at my hand before his eyes shut and his body goes slack.

My chest heaves, nausea roiling in my stomach. I bring myself to my feet before grabbing my bow. I turn to help Roman from the ground where he cradles his arm, his eyes bouncing between me and Galen. I try not to think of him lying lifeless on the ground. Try not to focus on the sound of his voice as I stripped him of his last breaths. I wipe my hands on my pants, before reaching out my hand to Roman.

"It's over," I say. "If Tallulah is still at the keep, she can help heal you. She can—"

Roman scrambles to his feet, his eyes going wide. "Wait! Don't—"

A sharp pain pierces through my back and chest, snuffing the air inside my lungs. Glancing down, I drop down to my knees.

Roman's hands slide from my cloak as he buries his face behind them, a broken cry leaving his lips.

My head tilts as a sharp pain blooms throughout my body. I cannot tell what caused the injury. It could be a blade. It could be magick. But the one thing I know for certain is that there's blood.

A lot of blood.

Too much of it all at once.

"I'm sorry," Galen says, his voice hoarse.

I force myself to turn, sucking in a sharp breath at the unimaginable pain.

Galen's eyes are glazed and red, his hands trembling before he steps closer. "I'm sorry," he says again as he tucks a purple amulet into his shirt.

I gasp, the pain blinding my vision for a moment before I'm tumbling backward.

Galen catches me before I hit the dirt, cradling my head in his lap. "I've never used Arma magick before," he says, almost to himself. Something cold slides against my skin, and I realize the blade Galen used is being manipulated without his hands, through magick kept locked inside that stone; I would guess. My chest tightens further. "Roman must be king," Galen whispers. "He *must* be king, Sorin."

Words fail me as I watch Galen's face. His eyes are silver lined, his lips downturned.

"Leave, Galen," Roman growls, now by my side.

The pain has moved from my chest, down to my sides.

Roman glances at me, then yanks off the necklace from around his neck. "Just take this and go." Roman's voice shakes but Galen doesn't move, doesn't reach for the amulet. He stays, his hands upon my face, his eyes locked on mine. My friend. My brother.

"I trusted you," I manage to say through a cough.

He flinches, and it's the first moment I see a flicker of emotion in his eyes. He opens his mouth, then swiftly closes it. He looks to Roman, a muscle in his jaw feathering. "I'll go when I'm certain you will remain on the throne." There's a sharp edge to Galen's tone, so at odds with the softness he's holding me with.

Blood pools at the sides of my mouth, causing me to cough.

"Galen," Roman says again, long and drawn out. As if saying his name alone is a cause of pain.

"This was always the plan," Galen says. "Now there is no threat to your crown."

Of course.

"You were my friend." My chest heaves, each word spewed from laborious breaths. My lungs, desperate to fill the hole in my chest. The effort has me groaning, the pain searing through my body.

Galen closes his eyes briefly, and when he opens them again, my heart cracks.

"You were never supposed to be here, Sorin," he whispers. His fingers draw through my hair. "You were supposed to stay in Loxley. You had forgotten about the throne until she—"

I cough again, cutting him off. Blood drips down my nose and despite the fight brewing in my chest, my eyes close.

"Why couldn't you just let this be!" Roman shouts, it sounds like he's crying more openly now, and despite the pain, despite the blood, my heart aches for him. He deserved a better chance than this. Deserved a better love than this. It never needed to go this far.

Without another word, Galen slips from under me, laying my head gently in the dirt. Blood seeps through my shirt, coating my entire abdomen. My head is dizzy, and when I crack my eyes open, the two of them are a blur of color before me.

"I have only ever wanted *you*, Galen. I don't need this magick, this power," Roman shouts. He pulls at his hair again, making it stick out in every direction.

Galen's eyes leave mine as he turns to Roman. "After everything, how can you still be this naïve? This magick is for *you*. Everything I have done is for *you*," Galen says much too calmly. "For us. Can't you see that? We will rule not only Teravie, but every country and continent..." He licks his lips. He looks like hell, his throat red and angry from my hand, but then again, I've just been stabbed by an enchanted blade. I'm sure I look like hell too.

"I didn't want Sorin to get involved," he says, "I didn't want it to come to this, but I did what was necessary to keep your place as king. I will sacrifice every damn person left in Teravie if it ensures you never have to be treated the way your father treated you again. To ensure no harm will come to another person at the hand of an Enchantress." Galen pinches the bridge of his nose. It's the smallest gesture, and for a moment, I forget what he's done. For a moment, I only see Galen, my friend. My closest ally. The brooding scholar with a passion for knowledge and life.

"I have guaranteed that you will go down as the most powerful king in history," he continues. "For the first time in our lives, we are the ones they fear, not the other way around. Is that not enough for you Roman? Is all this sacrifice not proof enough of my love?"

Roman straightens himself, wiping a hand down his face. He winces, gripping his arm but the bleeding has slowed and a sweep of ease washes over me.

He'll be okay.

"What good is love when it ends in blood?" Roman says. "What good is power when there is nothing left of the world? What good is magick when all it does is burn and destroy?"

They stare at each other but say nothing else. Galen has warped his own mind into believing that what's done to the Enchantresses is for Roman's own good and not for himself. For his desire to be the best. To avenge his sister. I fight to keep my eyes open.

Just a little longer. Stay awake a little longer.

"Sorin!" Sam's voice lights a flicker of hope in my chest. She'll be here any moment. She will be here, and all will be okay. Tallulah will help heal me and Elora will—

Come on, Sam. Please hurry.

I reach my hand for Roman, for one last chance to keep him here with me, but I'm too late.

Galen drags him by his weak arm toward the trees. Roman doesn't fight him, and I'm not surprised. They have burned the world hand in hand in the name of love, even if it's one that is virulent and hopeless.

My head is heavy as I roll onto my side. Galen turns, meeting my eyes. His steps falter for a moment before he's slipping through the trees with a shattered Roman in tow.

My eyes are heavy, fighting to stay open, and when they finally close, a small swatch of yellow is the last thing I see before my vision goes dark and the world around me quiets.

Mother be damned, I really do hate silence.

THIRTY-NINE

SAMARIA

RUSE HAS BEEN AT MY HEELS SINCE THE MOMENT Sorin left. Biting gently, pulling my cloak, and when I finally conceded, she sprinted from the Jade Guild barking at the puppies behind us.

She now leads the way up a small hill, the four wolves running beside me. It's only been a few miles but with the rain and the mud, the terrain has been torturous. I stop for a moment to catch my breath.

The puppies stop as well, but Ruse does not. She disappears over the edge of a small hill just as a wave of fog begins to settle over us.

"Sorin!" I shout breathlessly, weaving around fallen branches and knotted roots, the fog limiting my visibility.

Hati, Skoll, and Grey lead the way, Rook stays at my side, keeping pace with me. I curse myself for not training the last few weeks as I make the final descent down the hill, the burning in my lungs a momentary distraction from the erratic beat of my heart.

My mind drifts to Agnes as Rook and I stumble over another knotted branch. I right myself, dusting off my breeches. Letting my mother leave without me had been one of the most difficult decisions, but with Tallulah, Evren, and the twins joining her to the Onyx Guild, I suppose she's more protected than ever.

Smoke fills the air below us, scorched trees and burnt earth come into view but there's something else tugging at my middle.

Ruse howls, the sound breaking the eerie silence of the forest as I slide down the rest of the hill. Wiping my hands clean of mud, I rush toward the wolves. They stand in a half circle, bouncing lightly on their feet. But what stops my breath is the sight of a spirit in their mix.

Her red hair is faint, her skin glowing much like Elwyn's, and when I approach, she doesn't turn to me. Flicking my wrists up, I open the portal between us, giving her the option to speak but as I do, she dissipates so quickly I don't have the chance to pass a message.

As I join the rest of the wolves, I drop to my knees. "Sorin!"

Blood covers the ground beneath him, his eyes have gone glassy and his lips dry and pale, and when I glance to his chest, it is frozen. Still. Unbeating and unmoving.

"No, no, no" I whisper, placing his head in my lap.

"No." I press my hand to his chest, hopeful to find a beat there and when it is vacant I choke on a sob. All the resentment I've felt for him the last few weeks mocks me. How silly it all seems now.

Acid burns my throat as I crumple forward, encasing his body with mine. "I'm sorry," I whisper, the words sticking to my tongue as if I don't deserve to say them aloud.

Leaves tumble past us but not as cold as one would expect from this time of year. Warm. Comfortable. Tearing my eyes from Sorin, the forest transforms before me. The sun peeks through a somber sky and with it, the clouds disperse, leaving nothing but milky gray. The wind whips again, this time creating a tunnel of leaves and branches around the two of us.

The wolves howl, but it sounds so far away. As if they've been transported somehow. Or we have.

My head dizzies from the spinning leaves. From the lack of movement in my brother's chest. From the devastation I know this will bring my mother. I grip him tighter, holding onto his body as if I can somehow change this.

There's a certain silence that only happens right after death. Thick and tense, as if the world around us has paused, but the leaves continue spinning, trapping us inside. Reminding me that while my brother is dead, the world continues.

And how unfair is it? That the forest dares to breathe and live while he can no longer.

Magick itches at my palms, and I wonder what would happen if I used it. How he would look. If his spirit would be here.

My body trembles as tears spill down my cheeks. A pitiful cry leaves me as I clutch him tighter.

He's gone.

The pain in my chest sharpens, but as I readjust Sorin in my lap, my breath hitches. His eyes have rolled closed but that isn't what's drawn my attention. It's barely there, but as I squint, I swear I see it.

Movement.

I press my hand into his chest, just as the leaves around us begin to move faster. The twigs and branches whiz in circles around us, buzzing with life despite their dried and dead appearance. My hand shakes against his chest, but I close my eyes and wait.

FORTY

ELORA

"HANG ON, ELORA," JAREK SAYS. "WHATEVER'S happening, someone must be able to help. You just have to hold on a little longer." His voice is muffled, and pain slices through my temples when I attempt to shake my head. Jarek must read my expression because he sets me back down, settling me in his lap.

My heart races and I try to sit up, but when I do, blood erupts from my nose and mouth.

"Sorin—" My words are cut short by a gurgled cough. Blood spews from either side of my mouth, staining my tunic.

"I'm sure he's okay," Jarek says.

I attempt to shake my head again, but the pain only increases.

Go help, Sorin! I want to scream but the words don't come.

Jarek and Alaric watch me with widened eyes. They don't understand what I'm trying to tell them. That whatever is happening to me, is because it's also happening to Sorin. Because when I took his debt from Grawgeth, I didn't wager the same terms. I did not give her the last ten years of my life, as Sorin had.

Instead, I traded my life for his.

Reckless, Sorin called me and now I'm beginning to believe him.

A soul for a soul.

One death for the other.

I clutch at the imaginary wound on my chest, pressing into it as if it will do anything to stop his fate.

Or mine.

Alaric lays at my side, his cold nose brushing against the back of my hand. His whimpers are broken and soft. I try to comfort him through our bond, but the sharpness in my chest is too distracting. All consuming.

Where are you, my love?

I focus on my surroundings. Clinging to the image of Jarek at my side. To the feel of Alaric licking my cheeks where my tears have fallen. Any and every tangible thing I can grasp onto but then, they start to slip away.

Jarek's face becomes blurry. Alaric's warmth begins to fade. My chest tightens, and as it does, more blood rushes out from a wound that isn't there, leaving me in a deeper panic.

Thunder slams around us, thick clouds polluting the sky. The rain begins, sending relentless sheets of freezing water from the sky. Jarek hovers over me, trying his best to keep me dry but it's no use.

The storm is vicious. Galls of wind whip around us, rattling the branches on the trees and whipping the fallen leaves into the air, but through all of the gray and muted tones of the forest, a tiny fleck of yellow whizzes past me.

"Sorin!" I cry out, but Jarek just runs a hand down my cheek. His face, just as bewildered as mine.

He doesn't understand.

Somewhere, something has happened to Sorin and now my bargain with Grawgeth will be repaid.

But he will live, a voice chimes in my mind.

Yes, he will live, susi.

He'll rectify all the hurt that's been done to the Enchantresses.

He'll prove our loyalty to Mother Gaia.

He'll end the blight.

He'll *live*.

Jarek's hands roam over my body with tenderness. Searching for a wound he won't find. The blood continues out of my mouth. My head spins as the treetops turn in on themselves.

Is this what he felt? The panic and the fear and the agonizing pain. My heart lurches thinking of Sorin lying somewhere. Of his life slipping away. Tears spill out of the corner of my eyes, pooling in my ears and stinging my cheeks. I should have been smarter with my terms. I should have found a different way to break the bargain.

I should have...

I should have...

That's what the end is filled with. All the should haves. All the things you wanted to say but didn't. All the things you wanted to do, but never made time for. The mind floods you with the faces of all the people you love and the moments with them that have been too short.

Too late.

"Tell him—" Another cough cuts off my words, more tears slide down my cheeks.

"I'll tell him," Jarek says. His voice waivers, but his hands are steady as he pushes my hair from my face. The rain has soaked his hair as well and tiny droplets fall from his chin and nose. "I'll tell him how you love him, even if he is a stubborn arse," he says through a laugh, but I can tell he's crying by the choke that comes after.

I wish I could laugh too, because that's exactly what I would tell Sorin if I had the chance. That I love him, undoubtedly. That he is stubborn and loud and absolute perfection in human form. My eyes find Jarek's, the pinch between his brows settles.

"I'll tell him how much you love him and how you can't wait to love him again in the next life." He continues to stroke my hair, reminding me so much of when my mother would do the same.

Lost in his words, I don't realize the pain from my body slipping away. The overworking of my heart and lungs now replaced with a light tingling, starting in my legs and traveling up my torso and arms.

"This isn't the end, susi," Jarek whispers. "Not for you and Sorin, not for any of it." A tear slips from his eye as mine slowly roll closed.

I curse at myself. Shout inwardly to keep them open. Keep them on Jarek. Focus on Alaric but they don't listen. They won't open.

Why doesn't it hurt?

Jarek's hand finds mine, gripping it firmly. But through all the haze, I realize he has something cradled between our palms. Gently, he folds my hand open and with the last bit of strength I have, I manage to crack my eyes. The card is crumpled and stained but the image is clear.

The Queen of Spades.

"To take with you, wherever it is you're going," Jarek whispers against my ear.

I try to squeeze tighter to his hand, but I'm so weak that the card lays limply in my palm. Just as my eyes begin to close, there it is again. That small spot of yellow in a dark forest and I realize just before my eyes close, it's a bird.

A goldfinch.

The one from my dreams.

Darkness overcomes me as my eyes close again. But I've never been afraid of the dark, so my body settles into the familiarity of it. Then, music, faint and light accompanied by a howl I know so well.

Ruse.

She isn't far.

Alaric sends a howl back, telling her to hurry. She may be here any moment.

But it will be a moment too late.

Nothing will stop the bargain I made.

Nothing but Grawgeth.

Alaric's fear wraps around my own, constricting me like a snake. Paralyzing. His head lands upon my stomach, his warmth a temporary comfort.

My heart wants to race but it's already worked so hard, so it slows instead. Jarek's other hand slides around the back of my head to cradle me.

All I see is darkness.

Until it shifts and there he is. His voice, like a soft melody in my ears. I forget where I am. Forget what has happened. Forget what comes next.

"Sorin," I whisper, my body twitching. The inky, dark mist lifts as he strides forward, extending his hand to me. My momentary reprieve lapses as I glance beyond him. To the leafless birch trees and carved trunks that bleed black.

"It's okay, love. Come with me."

Fear forces itself up my throat, closing off my airways, but I focus on my Sorin and not the fate of my bargain. My body relaxes in Jarek's arms. Alaric howls, long and slow.

Then, my demons go silent and it's quiet. So, so quiet.

The line between my brows smooths. I'm no longer afraid. No longer in pain. I'm simply gone.

FORTY-ONE

SORIN

"It's okay, love. Come with me." I hold my hand out to Elora, ignoring that I can't feel anything around me.

Not the wind or the rain. Not the chill that should be deep in my bones.

My eyes settle on the blood around her mouth, the soaked tunic and fear lined in her eyes. "Take my hand."

She reaches out as her eyes roll closed, our fingers brushing against each other. And despite the hollow vat in my chest, when our fingers touch, a spark ignites in me.

Like a fog slowly rising, her spirit lifts from her body, free of the blood and the pain. She glances over her shoulder before facing me again.

"You're here?" Her fingers trace a line down my cheek, and I feel it in every part of my body. Deep in the marrow of my soul, I feel her.

"I'm here." Wrapping her in my arms, that spark burns through me, heating me from my core to my fingertips and with it comes a slight movement in my chest.

A beat.

"Elora," I whisper against her hair as the wind picks up, cages us in a tunnel of leaves.

"Elora," I say again, but she doesn't answer. I pull her back to see her face, but it's no longer her.

Her face has changed, from the freckles across her nose to the usual pink on her cheeks. Black is inked into her veins, her cheeks sunken and hollow, and then she's slipping from my grip. Her soul disappearing right before my eyes.

The wind and rain lashes around us, thunderous claps reverberate the trees and she's fading away.

"Wait!" I scream after her soul, clawing my way across the forest floor, endlessly reaching to no avail. The beating in my chest grows stronger and as I take a lungful of air, she's gone.

I snap my eyes open. Sam is cradling me in her arms.

"Sorin," she says, shaking my shoulders. "Thank the Mother!" She's crying, her tears painting lines down her face.

I take a large breath. And another and another but choke on the cold sting of air.

"It's okay," Sam says as I sit up. "You're okay."

My breathing mellows, falling into a steady rhythm.

Sam checks my back for wounds, her hands frantically searching, pulling up my tunic but there's no wound.

No evidence of Galen's betrayal.

Ruse yips next to us as she paces back and forth.

"We need to go," I say, my voice hoarse. Ruse meets my eye again before she tips her nose to the sky and howls.

"Give yourself a minute," Sam says, hugging me tightly. "It's a miracle you're alive."

"No," I say, my voice gruff like I've just woken from sleep. "It's a curse."

"Slow down!" Sam shouts, but it's no use. I'm running through the trees as if I wasn't just dead on the forest floor.

Wasn't just watching my sister grieve me. As if I didn't just speak to Elora from the other side.

I shake off the memory, not willing to lose my focus on getting to her as fast as possible.

Maybe there's still time.

Maybe I can save her.

"I can't," I shout over my shoulder. "We need to find Elora, now!" My legs nearly give out, but I continue on. The wolves have darted ahead, their connection to Elora leading our way.

"What's the hurry?" Sam is breathless behind me. "She and Jarek are together, it isn't as though—"

I stop so abruptly, Sam barrels directly into my back. I turn toward her, and the expression on my face must scare her because she backs away, tears still stained on her cheeks.

"What is going on?"

"She took my bargain from Grawgeth," I admit, my chest heaving from the pace we've been keeping.

Sam sighs, bracing her hands on the tops of her thighs. "What?"

I cradle my head in my hands. "And she didn't just take the same debt. She didn't trade the last years of her life." I look at her again, my stomach dipping with unease. "She traded her life for mine, she must have." I nod to just beyond the hill, where we just came. "I saw her when I died, she was there and—" I bite my tongue, the pressure mounting in my chest near painful. "She traded her *life* for mine. And I died back there, Samaria. You know I *died* and then I was brought back."

A tear slips from my eye, the reality of my words bringing me to my knees. The soil is damp beneath them. A pain pushes through my chest but it's faint, like it's long been healed.

"No," Sam whispers, crouching to the ground next to me.

A breeze fills the spaces between us, stinging against my cheeks and ears.

My head tips up, looking at the sky. "I died and then, before I could argue my way out of it, I was alive again. Don't you see what that means?" My voice cracks on the last word as I stand, Samaria pulling me to my feet.

"She's gone..." she whispers, flicking her wrists up. "I don't feel her spirit." Her eyes light up as she glances behind her, as if she's checking to see if someone is there. "Perhaps she isn't gone?"

I turn, marching up and over the hill where the wolves wait. "We need to hurry."

We rush down the hill, the increasing rain making it that much more difficult to traverse. I spot Alaric first, then Ruse, then the pups.

"Jarek!" Sam shouts and sprints in his direction. But I don't follow. My feet remain planted in the soil. Her body lies crumpled in Jarek's lap.

She's gone.

The proof not only right before me, but inside of me.

When Sam reaches Jarek's side, she looks to Elora and covers her eyes. It takes everything in me to go to them. But step by step, I do.

Ruse and Alaric whimper as I drop to my knees beside Elora in the dirt, the puppies sitting uncharacteristically still.

I scoop her up and place her head in my lap.

"There was nothing I could do, Sor." Jarek's voice is broken, but I don't look at him.

I stroke Elora's hair, pushing it from her face. I clean the edges of her mouth with my cloak, freeing it from the blood that's begun to dry there.

"We should have come with you," Sam says through her tears. "Maybe we could have stopped this."

"Nothing could have stopped this," I whisper. I run my finger between Elora's brows, smoothing the crease before finding her hand and grasping it in mine.

"But if we had helped you—" Sam sobs.

The wind shifts, rustling the leaves that litter the forest floor. The rain slices lines down my face and arms.

Before long, the leaves create a tunnel, much like the one I was encased in when my heart stopped beating. They swirl around Elora and I. I hold her tightly, hoping it's enough to keep her here with me. My father's ring is on her finger, the black metal coated in mud. My fingers twitch to reach for it, but I leave it instead.

The leaves and wind are ferocious and as the skies open up further, Elora begins to fade.

"No!" I shout but it doesn't do any good. Little by little, her body dissipates into the wind. From her boots to her hair, she floats away from me like stardust.

I clutch the soil beneath me, digging my fingers into the leaves and dirt. Grasping for any lingering piece of her that may still remain. That piece inside of my chest that belongs only to her cracks open wide, and I scream and curse and clutch the ground until my throat is hoarse and my knuckles white.

Memories flash so quickly behind my eyes that I can't be certain if what I'm seeing is from this life or the past.

Each memory is filled with golden hair and a freckled nose.

A hard-earned laugh and an easy scowl.

A passionate kiss and connection that comes all too naturally.

A crown and a storm and a bargain made.

Then, she's slipping from my grasp. Fading away into a world of black nothing. No matter how hard I try to find her hand, she's just out of reach.

"Can you sense her, Sam?" Jarek's voice pulls me from the depths of my memories.

My head rolls forward, hanging limply from my shoulders.

Sam doesn't answer him right away. She watches me rise, dirt and blood caked on my hands and clothes. Her face breaks and I know her answer. I push my hair from my face with trembling hands and look away from my sister.

I can't bear for her to see me like this.

So broken.

"I can't sense her," Sam says.

"Because her spirit isn't here," I say. "It's now bound to the Wicked Wood."

As soon as I see Amis back at the Jade Guild, a small piece of hope ignites in my chest. I don't wait to explain my plan before I place myself in the saddle.

"Sorin!" Sam shouts as she catches up to me. "Where are you going?" She's panting as she reaches the horse. She grips the reins tightly, as if that will do anything to stop me from going.

"I am going to get my wife." I yank the reins from her hands. "You and Jarek will join the others at the Onyx Guild immediately."

She shakes her head, her lip quivering. Her eyes move past me for a moment and then to her right and then quickly to her left.

"Samaria, look at me." The sharpness in my tone has her snapping her attention from the spirits I'm sure are flooding her and focusing on me. "I know it couldn't have been easy—"

"Seeing you die?" She frowns, biting her bottom lip.

My chest deflates, and again I find myself torn between two worlds. The one where my family is here and alive and the one where Elora is dead and may never breathe again.

But I have to try.

I know that I'll never be able to live with myself if I do not try to get her back. If there is magick in the world strong enough to trade our deaths, surely there is magick strong enough to bring her back to me.

My stomach swirls at the thought, drifting to Galen. To his sister, long dead and burned and yet he still fights for her. A sick and twisted thought turns over in my mind, making my already empty stomach churn.

Grief will drive you to depths you weren't sure existed. And he has lived with his far longer than I have. Long enough to drive him to madness.

Sliding down from Amis, I cup my sister's face, forcing her to look at me. "You will go to Onyx. You will convince the members of the Guilds to wait for my arrival. You will see to it that no harm comes to our people when I am gone—"

"Sorin, I can't."

"You can," I whisper.

Her fiery eyes flicker, a beacon of warmth in the otherwise dreary forest.

"You can and you will because there is no one more capable than you."

She doesn't smile as she wraps me tightly in a hug.

"I'm sorry for what you had to see," I say, and her body tenses. "But let me try and make this right. I have to."

She takes a step backward, nods, and by the time Jarek steps forward to grab her, Agnes joins us.

"Mum? You should have left hours ago," Sam says, gesturing her forward. "Elora—"

"I know, Sam," Agnes says. Her gaze slides to me, and the memory of her on the ground, struggling to breathe makes my throat tighten. "That's why I stayed."

I'm abandoning them when they're hurting the most.

"Follow the path as the crow flies," Agnes says and at my puzzled look she raises her hand. "In order to get her back, follow the path as the crow flies. There you'll find that of which you seek."

"I know how to get to the Wicked Wood," I say through a sigh, exhaustion seeping into my bones.

"Yes," Sam says, cutting me a scowl. "He's been there two too many times."

Agnes steps forward, placing herself between Sam and myself. Her hands tremble as I wrap them in my own. "Follow the path as the crow flies, there you'll find what you seek. The crones always come in threes, it's only with them the bargain can truly be broken."

"The crones?" Jarek steps forward and wraps his arm around Samaria.

Agnes nods, her honey eyes blazing against the dimming light. "The Fates, Sorin. You must find the Fates. If there's any chance at saving Elora from the Wicked Wood, any chance of you ending the blight, they'll give you the answers you need."

Shaking my head, I run a hand through my hair. The Fates have not been seen since the founding king and queen died. They are more myth than anything. "What makes you so certain they'll show themselves to me?"

"Because, son." Agnes smiles, her eyes crinkling. "They've met you before."

My gaze snaps to Sam and then to Jarek, their wide-eyed stares match my own.

"What do you—"

"Be safe," Agnes says, reaching out her hand. I take it I look at Sam again.

"Be swift," Sam says. "Be bold." She wraps me in a hug. "I know you are a Rudhek by blood," she says quietly, "but you were raised a Trednik. So act like one and let that unrelenting stubbornness guide you until she's back."

When she pulls away, it feels as though miles are stretched between us. Her sobs as she held me on the ground echo in my mind, but the wolves step next to me, distracting me from my racing thoughts.

"You're all coming?" I glance at Alaric. His amber eyes are glazed over, his heart, I'm sure, just as shattered as mine. But when I look at Ruse, there's nothing but anger and spite lined in those emerald eyes. She bares her canines and I don't question her again.

A caw breaks the momentary silence between us and my gaze darts upward. Sure enough, as Agnes Saw in her vision, a crow flies overhead as if leading the way.

"Straight to the Onyx Guild." I point to Sam but she's busy snuggling Hati, giving her a scratch behind the ears and ruffling her head. Hati whines but as I heel Amis in the sides, she follows Ruse and the others.

I run Amis almost all night, pushing her as far as she can go, following the distinct caw of the crow. I don't stop for water, relying on the small canteen attached to my saddle. Don't stop to eat, and only when the puppies have exhausted themselves, do we rest. This continues for three nights. For three nights we weave our way through the rain-sodden pine trees. Through the bogs and swamps. The wolves keep their pace, occasionally howling and barking at the pups to press on. The caws overhead, the only indication we're still going the correct way.

On the fourth day, the sun is barely rising when the crow stops and perches on a low branch.

Amis whinnies, her hooves stomping in the dirt. I run my hand down her mane. "Easy girl."

The crow tilts its head to the side, its silver eyes boring into me, making me advert my gaze. Around us are naked birch trees much like those of the Wicked Wood. The ones filled with black sap and tangled branches. The ones that have haunted my nightmares for many years. But my eyes catch on a particularly disfigured grove, their branches bent and trunks impossibly crooked.

"Didn't think it could get much worse than the Wicked Wood," I mumble as Amis prances unsteadily.

My ears ring as the crow caws again before taking flight directly to the grove. "Of course, that's where the crones would be." I guide an unsure Amis toward the trees, the wolves at her sides. "Why couldn't they live somewhere like a meadow?"

My breaths get trapped in my throat, and as we approach the grove of birches, I realize that the center is actually a pool of inky, dark water.

I tie Amis off, giving her a much-deserved rest. All six of the wolves join my side. Alaric nudges my hand, so I run it slowly along his coat. Reassuring him as best I can. Ruse's stony demeanor hasn't changed for a moment. The wolf pups whine behind us, and when I turn around, I realize they're sitting in a line, watching.

"Not coming?"

Ruse breaks her gaze from the trees only to snarl at my question.

"Fair enough." They are her children, after all.

I tuck my hands in my pockets before taking a long, tiresome breath. Something cold and foreign brushes against my fingertips. I pull my hand from my pocket and suck in a sharp breath.

Roman's necklace.

I don't know when he gave it to me, but it stings as I slide it around my neck, the weight of it like an anchor. Steadying myself, I take my first step into the grove.

Forty-Two

Roman

"You're hurting my arm." I attempt to pull free from Galen's grip, but it only causes him to tighten his fingers further.

"I don't care," he grumbles.

We trudge up another hill, and by the time we make it to the top, I collapse with exhaustion.

Galen halts, standing above me. "Get up."

"No." I roll onto my side, cradling my arm where Sorin shot me with a Mother-damned arrow. "I'm not going with you."

Instinctually, I reach for my necklace only to remember it isn't there. A smile creeps over my lips. I knelt beside Sorin as he took his last few breaths. Had mourned momentarily for this brother I didn't know but somehow felt connected to. I slipped the amulet into his pocket as quickly as I could, hoping that by some miracle, he would be able to use the Healing magick stored inside to help himself or someone would find him in time to help him.

"Then where will you go?" Galen sits, his back pressed against a nearby tree. "If not Valebridge, where Roman?" He scoffs, wiping dirt from his boot. "Heal yourself and we'll continue until nightfall. Once we're back in Wickersham I'll secure some horses before heading back to Valebridge."

I sit up, the pain in my arm excruciating, burning, but luckily no longer bleeding. "Why did you say those things?"

Galen watches me as I cradle my arm. His gaze slides to my neck and when he finds it empty of the necklace his cheeks turn red.

"You told Sorin I was lying."

He clicks his tongue and shakes his head. "You cannot be that dull." He rolls his eyes. "I was trying to get him away from you, Roman."

"He wasn't hurting me."

"Wasn't he?" He gestures to my arm. "Why is it that I am constantly needing to prove myself to you?" He slides his necklace off as he settles next to me. "It wasn't enough that you left me in Wickersham, but now this?" He tsks, running a finger down my cheek. "I went through a great deal of trouble looking for you, the least you could do is be thankful."

I turn my head, doing my best to remove myself from his touch. "Where are the guards?"

"The Dyrjsjel you freed killed them all." He grips the amulet until it begins to glow.

"How did you manage to get away?"

He laughs, making me flinch. "The same way you should have." He gestures to the necklace but my eyes land on the claw marks around his throat.

"You could have saved the men."

He sighs, throwing his head back. "I didn't have time to think of it." He bites his lower lip. "Unfortunately my mind was elsewhere." He cups my face in his hands. "I only needed to find you. The men can be replaced, but you—" He kisses my knuckles.

I slide my hand away. "Did you hurt her?" My stomach churns, distracting me for a moment from the pain in my arm. I flick the amulet in his fingers. "With this?"

"No." He pushes my sweaty hair away from my face. His fingers lingering on my skin. "I could have, but she's too valuable." He cocks his head to the side, studying me. "How many more times must I tell you, Ro, that for you, I will let the world burn so long as you're safe. The men knew the risks of coming here, and there are plenty more of them in Valebridge eager to have their shot at finding her."

His lips press against my forehead again and the urge to lie down makes my head spin. "I needed to find you. When you left me in Wickersham, you broke my heart." He pulls away, wrapping his fingers around the wound on my arm.

"I—"

My chest tightens and suddenly my arm doesn't feel so bad. He wraps his fingers tighter around my wound, and a moment later, Healer magick emerges stitching my arm back together.

Good as new.

"Now let's go, I want to make it to Wickersham as soon as possible, there is still work to be done." He pulls me to my feet and keeps his hand clasped in mine as we make our way down the hill. His thumb rubs against my skin, heat blooming where our skin connects.

Only this time, that heat is not passion. Not lust.

But anger.

Hot and heady. As I follow Galen back to Wickersham, my brother's words ring true in my ears.

"Galen will end either by your hand, or by mine."

FORTY-THREE

SAMARIA

SURPRISINGLY, THE RIDE TO THE ONYX GUILD MOVES swiftly and with ease. As we pull into the Onyx Keep, the horses slow, their hooves crunching under the ice and snow. I wrap my arms around myself to keep warm. The black stone walls of the keep are stark against the snowy backdrop of the Kirsgard Mountains. A drawbridge lowers, granting us access and moving the horses forward.

Jarek sits across from me, his eyes fixated out the window. In the days it took to arrive, we've hardly spoken of what happened to Sorin and Elora.

Have hardly spoken at all.

I run my fingers over the Awakening Stones in my lap before securely placing them in a bag on my hip.

The door to the caravan swings open and to my surprise, Ulric stands on the other side. He holds up a hand and I take it before stepping out into the frigid mountain air. "You made it," Ulric says. "I'm so relieved!"

His eyes dart past Jarek and I, so I recline out of the way, and when he sees Agnes, he lets out a long breath.

Jarek steps out next, and while I'm shivering against the harsh wind, he looks comfortable among the cold. His eyes roam the mountains in the distance before landing back on me. There's a moment of silence between the four of us before Jarek slams the caravan doors shut and the driver leads the horses away. Ulric grabs my arm, then my mothers.

"Everyone's waiting for you, Sam." He smiles, Agnes nestling into his side, stealing some of his warmth.

After changing and scarfing down a quick meal of boiled eggs and fruit, Jarek and I find our way to the meeting room.

I freeze, dropping Jarek's hand, when out of the corner of my eye I catch a glimpse of a spirit.

"My queen?" He reaches for me again, but I'm already moving toward the apparition.

The spirit smiles, mouthing my name over and over again, though with the portal closed I cannot hear her. I reach out for her, flicking my wrists up but as soon as the portal opens, she's gone.

"Are you okay, Sam?" Jarek's voice draws my attention.

"Yes." I sigh and take his hand, following him into the meeting room.

Enchantresses, both living and in the spirit realm, all watch as we take a seat around the black, marbled table. Their eyes are hopeful. Angry. Thirsty for a revenge I'm not sure I can promise.

"I..." I bite my tongue. Where do I start?

Hello, I'm Samaria. Another person who sat by and did nothing to help you—

"You have nothing to fear here, Enchantress," a woman says, seated across from me. She's older, her fiery hair pulled tightly in a bun, accentuating the sharpness of her cheekbones.

"How did you—"

"She's an Empath," another woman says. Her glowing, glacial eyes give her away as an Enchantress immediately. She glances at Jarek for a moment, her eyes widening. "Sailor?"

Jarek laughs and extends his hand across the table to meet

hers. "Sera," he says. "I can't believe it." She smiles, her hand still locked with Jareks.

"I'm missing something," I whisper. "You know each other?" Finally, they drop hands and Sera pours me a glass of water and slides it across the table.

"Many years ago," Jarek says, "Sera saved my life."

I glance at her again, her dark hair is cut blunt to her chin, her eyes beaming over her glass.

"Where are Calix and my mother?" I change the subject.

"Here," Calix says as he enters the room. He glances around before his eyes land on me. "Elora? Is she here?"

My heart races, my chest much too tight. He doesn't know she's gone. How will I tell him this daughter he has barely just met has died. "She—"

"There's been a slight delay," Jarek says, taking my hand. "We will continue on without them for now." Calix nods before taking his seat at the end of the table.

I glance over my shoulder, relaxing a bit as Evren, Tallulah, and Thaddeus join us next.

Clutching my glass of water, I scan the room that's filled to the brim with Loxlians, people of the Jade Guild, and the Onyx Guild. There are two empty spots at the head of the table and the sight of them sends a whirl of doubt through me.

Sorin should be here.

A heavy silence settles over the space, not even Calix offers any words until the doors swing open and the final two guests arrive.

The first woman is dressed in head-to-toe sapphire. Her blonde hair is swept over her shoulder, her eyes wide and gleeful. Tiny seashell earrings dangle and sway as she takes her seat next to Calix at the table. She crosses her hands and whispers something in his ear. Rings of every shade of blue adorn her fingers made of shells and sea glass and pearls.

Must be Lady Oletta of the Cerulean Guild. I glance again

to the seashells on her ears, wondering if she fished them from the Holden Sea herself.

A throat clears behind me as Lady Mordona of the Bloodstone Guild passes by. The spirits tense around the room. Each of them narrowing their gaze as she sits on Calix's opposite side, with Thaddeus on her other. Her dark skin is radiant against her deep, crimson gown. Thick, teardrop bloodstones hang from her ears and when she catches my eye she gives me a sly grin.

"Now that we're all here," Thaddeus says, "let's get started."

"Wait a moment, please." Lady Mordona holds up an elegant hand, even her nails are painted the color of blood. "Correct me if I'm wrong, Calix, but I don't see the guest of honor." She turns so her gaze is only on me. Her eyes narrow, and as I begin to shrink against her scrutiny a cold, a featherlight hand dusts my shoulder.

Then the other.

Under the table, I raise my hands, opening the line of communication with the spirits. Elwyn whispers in my ear, *"Don't be afraid of her, Samaria."* I have become accustomed to her voice; she has hardly left my side since Elora...

I struggle to swallow as another spirit whispers in my ear.

"Samaria."

I glance to my left. The same spirit I swore I saw when Sorin died. The same one I saw just now in the hallway.

Her body ebbs and flows like a breeze. Her dark, red hair is long and loose. Her skin glowing much like Elwyn's. Her rich eyes flare as I meet her, and for a moment, I forget she's dead.

Elwyn smiles and nods, extending her hand to the spirit Enchantress. They clasp hands, their faces beaming.

"Celia," Elwyn says and my stomach drops.

Sorin's mother.

"So, Samaria," Lady Mordona says, interrupting the rising panic in my chest, "where is your brother?"

Every single pair of eyes in the room lands on me. My legs

tremble as I stand, but I stand anyway, dropping my hands to my sides.

Be strong.

"He has gone to find the Fates."

Just as I thought, the room erupts in gasps and hushed whispers. Lady Mordona scoffs, throwing her hands in the air. I watch closely as Lady Oletta leans into her, whispering something I'll never know.

"You have wasted our time, again," Mordona snaps, looing at Calix and Thaddeus. She stands to leave, not bothering to right her chair as it topples backward and the thrumming in my chest intensifies.

I have to convince them Sorin is the heir. Have to convince them to back him in front of the council.

Without Sorin being here.

Have to prove that he is the king, otherwise...

"Wait!" I block her path before she can reach the door.

"Move, girl." She pushes past me, but I dart in front of her again.

"He may not be here," I say, "but I have this." I slide Sorin's decree of birth from my pocket, thankful that despite his urgency to leave, he remembered to pass it to me.

Lady Mordona's eyes don't leave mine, even as I hold the parchment into the air. "I have seen this," she snarls. "It isn't enough. The four families of the Guilds have been entrusted by Valebridge for centuries to help oversee all of Teravie. It's just as much our duty to look after this country as it is the kings. We will not so readily appoint a new ruler without solid proof that he is the rightful heir. We are all enraged at the outcome of King Roman, but this is not enough."

She shoulders past me, and this time I let her go.

What would Sorin do? What would he—

A cold drift breezes across my neck so I flip my hands up. *"What would you do, Sam?"* Celia's spirit whispers in my ear. The hair on my arms and neck raise.

What would I do?

I've never been as eloquent as Sorin. Never been as diplomatic or level headed. Always the first to lose my temper or spoil a surprise.

"Be strong," my mother would say.

Right, be strong.

Don't cry.

Chin up.

Smile. Wider.

Your brother is looking up to you.

Set the example.

Be the example.

Be strong. Be strong. Be strong.

Keep his secrets.

Better yet, keep quiet.

But always, *always* be strong.

I take a large breath and turn to face the door, that bubbling rage straightening my spine.

"Show me your rage then," I say, "because I do not see it. Show me, and I'll challenge it with mine. The rage of a first born daughter."

Her heels scuff against the stone floor as she stops in the doorway.

"I assure you, it would not be a fair match." She glances briefly over her shoulder. "If you leave now, Lady Mordona, you are writing off the deaths of hundreds of Enchantresses merely because you don't see this piece of paper as proof enough for change." I hold the paper out again, even though her back is turned to me. "Are their lives not worth a second glance?"

Please.

Please look at it.

When she doesn't turn, I spin on my heels.

"And what of you, Lady Oletta?" My voice has risen and all the chatter around me ceases. Sorin has always been the one to spin a tale as smooth as butter but perhaps that isn't what is needed today.

Perhaps something sharper is needed today.

"Are you as enraged as Mordona claims you to be?" She stiffens, her eyes drifting over my shoulder, I'm sure to where Mordona still stands. "Are you willing to let Roman continue to kill and imprison women like them"—I point to the Enchantresses at the table—"like me, because of a piece of paper?"

Lady Oletta's eyes may be warmer than Mordona's, but there's something off putting about the way she watches me. Like I'm an all too easy catch and she's been hungry for far too long.

No one says a word so I continue on, buying as much time as I can until Sorin makes it here.

If he makes it here.

"I'll be the first to admit that I have regretted my choices the last five years." I ignore the eyes burning into me and instead power all of my focus on Lady Oletta. Mordona shifts behind me, her gown scratching against the marble floors, but I don't turn to her.

The presence of Elwyn and Celia's spirits crowd me, but this time I don't feel suppressed by them, I feel empowered. "My family and I lived in a place called Loxley."

Jarek slides his hand to the back of my arm, giving it a squeeze.

Keep going.

"It was a village of outcasts some would call it." A few of the Loxlians in the room chuckle. I find Ulric in the crowd, but his face is stoic, watching me through tearful eyes. "We paved our own way, living outside the jurisdiction of Valebridge long before Roman was on the throne, and when we heard of his injustices, we…" I run the back of my hand across my forehead. Beads of sweat trickle down my temples. Elwyn and Celia wrap their arms around my shoulders.

I keep my arms low, but raise my hands to open the portal.

"Go on, Sam," Elwyn whispers at my side. *"Keep going."*

Right.

Keep going.

"We turned a blind eye." I look at the Enchantress seated around the table. The one Jarek called Sera watches me over her glass, her lips turned up in a smirk.

"We chose to keep our own safe instead of fighting for those who needed us most. And for that I can confidently speak for every Loxlian when I say, we're sorry. Truly, sorry."

It's quick, but I don't miss Sera's lip trembling before she covers it with her water glass. Tallulah is in the chair to my right, her fingers find mine and I *finally* exhale.

"My brother is the rightful heir to Valebridge."

Lady Mordona bumps me as she passes by. She retakes her seat next to Lady Oletta.

"It has been proven by this verified decree of birth as well as from the Fates."

"A bold claim," Oletta says. "The Fates have not been seen in Teravie since King Bastian and Queen Soleil called upon them hundreds of years ago."

"Yes." I drop Tallulah's hand to cross my arms. "That is exactly my point, Lady Oletta. The Fates have somehow driven my brother and Elora together. He has seen it multiple times in visions and through the nymph Grawgeth." The women stiffen but Thaddeus shoots me a quick grin. "Five years ago Roman made a choice to banish our magick. Harvest it from us as if it were free to take. And when did the blight start, Lady Mordona?"

She purses her lips and looks to her lap.

"Lady Oletta? Surely you have seen affects from the constant storms in the ocean considering your Guild resides nearest the coast. Have you not noticed?"

She chews her bottom lip but slowly, she nods.

"And you think there is no correlation? That when the

Enchantresses have been mistreated, Mother Gaia has mistreated us in turn?"

"We hear you, Samaria," Lady Mordona says, a sharp tone lacing her voice. "So, what are you suggesting? The four of us alone cannot coronate Sorin, we need the backing of the council."

"So, then I will get it," I snap. Lady Mordona laughs but I cut her short. "And you will help me." Her eyebrows raise but I don't give her a chance to speak. "I am tired of sitting by and watching. I am tired of hiding. Tired of running." I turn from the Guild members and address the room of people before me who have fallen eerily quiet. "I am tired of those who live in Valebridge telling me what I can and cannot do. Where I can and cannot live. What rations I can and cannot have."

A few voices chime in.

"Here, here," one says.

"About time someone says it," whispers another.

I turn back to the head of the table, the fear and uncertainty that nearly crippled me earlier has washed away and underneath it all, a new voice flows from my lips.

One of confidence and courage. Of anger and spite. Vengeful and compassionate all in one.

"I will not wait for you to decide the fate of our country."

The ladies share a glance, their lips pressed tightly together.

"Aye." Jarek stands, taking my hand. "Neither will I. I'm with you, Samaria Trednik."

"Me too." I scan the room to find the voice. Thomas sits perched on a small chair in the back of the room. His golden skin and auburn hair, easy to identify. "I'm with you."

My heart swells and I clench onto Jarek's hand.

"We're with you, Sam," Tallulah says.

Evren nods, his green eyes holding a hint of mischief. "We're with you, Sam," he says.

Tears sting in my eyes and I don't bother holding them back

as I watch each person save for Lady Oletta and Lady Mordona rise from their chairs.

The same three words echoed over and over again.

"We're with you."

"We're with you."

"We're with you."

When the last person rises, my hand is shaking in Jarek's. I glance behind me, hoping Celia or Elwyn's spirit are still there but they're gone.

"Well look at you," Lady Mordona says. "Seems as though you're quite the talker, just like that brother of yours."

Sour words build on my tongue, but before I can spew them, Oletta stands abruptly, startling both Calix and Thaddeus. "What is your plan, Samaria? To waltz into Valebridge and demand Sorin take the throne?"

No, I want to say.

Of course that isn't my plan. Because this—I look to my right, at every person still standing watching me—is bigger than the throne.

This is justice for an entire country.

Not just Enchantresses, but every single one of us.

"No, Lady Oletta." I drop Jarek's hand and brace myself against the table. "My plan is to go to war."

FORTY-FOUR

SORIN

THE GROUND BENEATH MY BOOTS IS SOGGY, AND when I take a step closer to the small lake, I hold my breath. Not because of the pungent smells, but because of what lies beneath. Just below the surface, barely visible in the inky dark water are two faces.

Two women, not three.

Shite.

Their dark hair spools around them in spider-like tendrils. Their ivory skin is smooth and their cheeks are rosy. I lean closer over the water's edge. Their lips are pouty and berry-stained red.

Let us out!

I stumble backward at the sudden voices, tripping over a half-buried rock in the moss. Alaric and Ruse are at my sides, but for the first time since I've known them, they cower. Whimpering away.

"Not a good fucking sign." Shaking my hands to regain some feeling in them, I stand up and glance into the pool again. My heart slams against my ribs, doubt tightening around my spine when another caw from the crow, I'm certain it's the same one, sounds again.

Just as it does, the women in the water snap open their eyes.

Two sets of large, doe-like eyes the color of the very moss on which I'm standing stare back at me. Their lips curl into a smile and a tether pulls taut in my stomach.

I yank my hand back, demanding control over my own body, but that tether pulls tighter and tighter until my hand dips into the water.

As soon as my hand submerges, they don't hesitate. Their pointed nails claw at my skin and when I try to break free, they dig in farther, piercing my skin.

"Ruse! Alaric!"

Growls sound behind me but before the wolves can approach, the women begin crawling out of the pool, limbs contouring in unnatural angles. The crack of their bones is sharp against the eerie quiet of the forest.

As the first emerges, my heart races as her long black hair shifts, turning white and silver. The second woman climbs out, her porcelain skin withering, creases and lines etching into her as she takes a full breath. Gone are the beauties under the water, and before me are the crones.

The Fates.

"Hmmm," the first says, taking a step forward.

Ruse growls next to me, her haunches raised and teeth barred.

"I remember you." The crone giggles, her voice and laugh sounding much too young and sweet to match her ancient, sunken face. "Don't you remember, sister?"

The other cocks her head to the side, her face splitting into a wicked grin. "How could I forget," she says. "But where is your little wife?"

The crones erupt into laughter, the sound of it clawing at my ears. I hardly have time to contemplate when and where Elora and I have met these women before they scurry toward me, their jagged nails reaching for my skin.

I take a step backward, putting as much distance between

myself and them as I can. "I think you already know where she is." Alaric brushes against my fingertips.

"It would appear you already know as well, Bastian." My stomach rolls at the name.

"My name is not Bastian," I say, a bit defeated. Shadows stretch across the forest as another day turns to night. "My name is Sorin Rudhek, I am—"

"The king does not remember." The fates laugh again, the high shrill piercing my ears. "So why are you here?" The crones take a step forward, their long, silvery hair covering their naked bodies.

"I need…"

They continue to approach, and when my back presses into a tree, my stomach drops. Alaric tries to angle himself between us but even he scampers away as the crones close in on me.

Inches from my face, they stop. Their cloudy eyes scan my face while their fingers prick at my cheeks. Inspecting every inch of me.

"I need to know how to break the bargain. How to bring Elora back to me."

The first crone throws her head back and laughs and it takes everything in me not to cover my ears or run away.

"What makes you so sure such a bargain can be broken, King?" The second crone joins her sister in laughter and the doubt I felt earlier intensifies.

There is no saving her.

There is no bringing her back.

"She is lost, lost, lost," the two chant in unison. There's something melodic about their tone. Something familiar and frightening and yet the longer they sing, the more I can't take my eyes off of them.

Ruse's bark snaps me from my stupor, the puppies whining behind me. I glance over my shoulder. Rook and Skoll have hidden behind a tree, but Grey and Hati stand tall, their eyes darting between Ruse, Alaric, and the crones.

"Lost, lost, lost! Just as she was before!" The crones continue to chant when a tiny, yellow bird perches on a branch. The bird opens its beak, and despite the noise from the crones, its soft song drifts through the wind and the rain and all at once, I'm overcome with memories.

Elora and myself.

The shared dreams and visions.

The storm and a crown, a bargain, and a *goldfinch*.

"You called me Bastian before," I say, squaring my shoulders and projecting my voice over their relentless chants and the rising rain. "What did you mean by it?"

The crones grow silent, their heads again whipping in my direction with unnatural speed.

"Let us show you, King," the first crone says. Dread fills my veins as she reaches for my hand. "It will only take a moment." Her nails dig into my forearm but I rip it away, leaving lines of red across my flesh.

"Nothing is ever free," I say. "Name your price for helping me first."

The crones curse under their breath, whispering nonsense to each other. The goldfinch behind them sings again, bringing forth another muted vision in my mind of Elora and I, hands clasped tight. A jolt of pain shoots through my palm. I glance down at my hands, both unmarred.

"How far are you willing to go, to find what's been lost?"

I wipe my hands on my breeches, attempting to erase the phantom sting. "As far as it takes and then some."

The crones glance at each other again.

"We will help you find Soleil, if you can help us find something in return."

Sighing, I run my hand down my face. "Her name is Elora, not Soleil. You must be mistaken, Soleil was the founding queen, I'm not sure—"

"We know of what we speak, King *Bastian*." The crones smile, their pointed black teeth making my hands shake. "But it seems as though you don't." They begin to chant again, swaying together, voices shrill and carrying through the forest.

"Take our hands, Bastian." They reach out to me, still swaying and chanting under thick, black clouds that have rolled in.

Alaric barks, his teeth sinking into my tunic. Begging me to stay.

"I have to get her back." I pet his nose and with a labored breath, I grab the crone's hands.

The world goes dark around me, the wind biting my ears and cheeks, but through the mirth and fog, a forest comes into view and I'm slipping away. Out of this body and into another.

I stand with Elora by my side, our hands clasped tightly together, the sting of our freshly cut wounds a distraction from the gale howling around us. I stare at her profile. At her strong nose and golden hair whipping wildly around her. She is so much the same and yet, there is something so different about her.

"Elor—" I open my mouth to speak but the words are muffled and faint.

"The deal is done." One of the old crones steps forward. A wicked smile split across her weathered face. Though they look the same, there are three of them now. Their black fingernails and teeth are sharp and glinting under the moonlight.

Elora flinches at my side as leaves and debris swirl around them, creating a tunnel of earth and wind, obscuring my vision.

"Enchantresses shall bear a piece of Mother Gaia, their magick will preserve what you've built in Teravie. They will help bridge the gap between magick and non-magick, just as you've asked."

What we've built?

A branch breaks from a tree, spiraling between us, breaking our hands apart.

"And in return?" Elora shouts, though her voice is nothing more than a whisper against the storm.

The three crones chuckle; their laughs amplified by a sudden gust. A strand of Elora's hair pulls loose from her golden crown, blocking her eyes. She pushes the hair back, now soaked from the rain, and her eyes widen as the Fates begin to speak together.

"Your souls are bonded." Their voices begin to fade as the wind increases. "You are bound to each other; you are bound to Teravie. And when Mother Gaia calls for aid, you will answer. You will follow. In any lifetime. For however long. Your souls belong to Her now."

We both jump as a crack of lightning splits across the sky. Through the torrent of the storm, her hand finds mine. A flurry of yellow flashes between us.

A goldfinch.

She steadies herself before returning her attention to the Fates.

"The truth will reveal itself in time," the crones mutter, their tattered black robes blowing in the wind.

I open my mouth to question them, but another forceful gust blows us both backward. We tumble to the muddy forest, separating as we do. The rain bites my skin and stings my eyes. I grapple for Elora's hand but come up empty.

"Soleil!" I hear myself yell against the groaning trees and downpour, not entirely sure why that was the name that left my mouth and not Elora.

She screams back but it sounds so far away. I reach for her again but am too late before the light of the moon snuffs out behind a sheet of black clouds, sealing us in total darkness.

She screams my name over and over again as I did hers and when the wind finally dies and the stars begin to shine my throat is hoarse and dry.

Scrambling to my feet, I find her a few feet next to me.

She lies on a bed of earth, around her broken branches and leaves. Moss sticks to her hair and when she sits up, she stifles a cry.

She reaches under herself and gasps, using her free hand to cover her mouth as she brings forth from the ground four glowing stones.

I'm pulled from the memory like a fish from water. Gasping, I clutch my chest. My lungs, burning and begging for relief.

"Do you see now, King?" The crones circle around me. "You and Soleil have been brought back. She, Mother Gaia, has brought you back, to save Teravie. She has called in her bargain and you have one chance to make this right."

My lungs burn. "It's not possible."

"Isn't it?" They step closer, stealing the oxygen around me. "Tell us, King, have you no memory of your past life? Have no intuition of all the love you had before?" The crones sniff the air, their heads tilted back. "Deep down, Bastian. You already believe it."

My breathing is shallow as I take in their words. As I recall each and every moment with Elora before this.

Have we met before? Some of my first words to her on the bank of the Galdosa River. I was sure even then; she was no stranger to me. Her lightning touch, the way her body molds to mine. The instant connection and familiarity. The acute sense of home when she's wrapped in my arms.

I fall to my knees. Visions of storms and forests and a goldfinch playing in my mind. Visions I thought of our future, now I realize, were actually our past.

"In order to save your wife," the crones say, interrupting my racing thoughts, "she must remember who she *really* is. She must remember."

I scramble backward before standing, straightening my shirt. "And what do you seek in return?"

"Like we said," they say together, "we are also looking for something that has been lost."

As I watch them, I notice more and more about them. The shape of their pointed teeth. The sallow color of their skin and hair long enough to reach their waists. I can see the beautiful women still lurking beneath, just as they lurked beneath the water.

There are only two of them and there must be three.

The cloud in my mind clears and everything makes so much sense. Why the Fates have been quiet, why there is one missing. Confidence squares my shoulders as I take a step toward the women.

"Grawgeth." I spit the name out of my mouth like poison.

The crones freeze, their limbs tangled together, their clouded eyes blown wide.

"Grawgeth is..." I step forward again and the crones dart back. "Is your sister? The third Fate?"

Their eyes narrow, dark brows cinched together above milky white irises.

"Perhaps she is," one of the crones says. "She has forgotten, like you." Their eyes narrow as they turn to each other. "Like your wife." They link their arms together. "Find our sister, return her to us by destroying the Wicked Wood, and your debt will be considered even."

They turn to head back to the pool, their silver hair like wisps of a spider's web swaying in the wind. All the confidence I had moments ago fades as my chest tightens and breathing falters.

"How will I find her?"

They turn, and before I can blink, they're inches from my face. I hold my breath, hoping the stench of decay is from the pool behind us and not from their mouths.

"It has been a long time since we have been united," the first crone says. "That wicked wood she created has been a poisonous vat to the forest. And all out of spite." The second nods, her mouth tilting upward. "Free your wife, destroy the wood, and Grawgeth will never be tied there again."

"Tell me how to destroy the wood and I'll do it."

The crones smile, their pointed teeth dripping black. "You must give it something. Something to take with it."

I open my mouth to beg for more clarity, but the crones hold up their hands. "Destroy the wood so our sister may never find her way back there."

I nod, my lungs burning from the pent-up breath. "To break your queen from the curse of the Wicked Wood, Soleil must remember who she was."

My fingers run through my hair, pulling slightly on the ends, frustrated at the time I've wasted here. "So that's it? Just... tell her who she is?"

The crones laugh, but this time it's not shrill like before. It's low, rumbling like an oncoming storm.

"That isn't what we said, King." They shake their heads, their voices mulling together. "She must *remember* who she was, and she shall be set free, but the wood must be destroyed. Otherwise, it will pull her back, Bastian. It will pull and pull and take and take and your wife, and our sister, will never truly be free." They turn for the pool again, their hands clasped together. "Destroy it." They say over their shoulders.

"Grawgeth will return," one whispers. "We'll finally be whole."

"I'll never make it in time!" I shout to their backs.

They cackle again, loud enough to startle a murder of crows in a nearby tree. "Use the magick, Bastian." Without a glance backward, they plunge into the pool and out of sight.

Sinking back to my knees, the bitter air fills my chest as I welcome it into my lungs.

Ruse and Alaric nudge my sides, the puppies running forth as well.

"We need to go." I stand on unsteady legs, leaning on Alaric for support. "Back to the Wicked Wood, I'm afraid."

Alaric whines and it's enough to make me smile.

"The feeling is mutual."

I lock eyes with Ruse, she dips her head and soon the puppies fall in line behind us.

As we make our way toward Amis, a faint burning hits my chest. Reaching inside my shirt, my fingers lock around the smooth amulet. The purple stone shines in the fading light and as I'm about to tuck it back into my shirt I'm hit with a thought.

Use the magick.

I stop, letting the wolves proceed ahead without me. Taking a long breath, I glance to the wolves and to Amis. To the forest and the trees and the moon fighting its way through the dark sheet of clouds.

"Get to the Onyx Guild." Alaric and Ruse look at me, and as I bring the stone to my lips, Ruse rushes forward. "Don't stop until you're there."

I close my eyes and picture everything I can remember about the Wicked Wood, reaching out for the magick I know is trapped inside. Something in here must be able to help me. Get me to the Wicked Wood—

On the next breath, I'm somersaulting through the air. Darkness encompasses me, my head spins so fast I think I might throw up. Or at the very least scream, but there isn't any time before I'm crashing to the ground.

Sitting up, I rub at my eyes then the stiffness in my joints. The sky has darkened, but it's not much later given the moon's position. My arm jolts forward as something nudges me.

Not something.

Someone.

Ruse.

"What are you doing here!" I scurry to my feet as the massive wolf snarls. "So, you come all this way and you still give me that face?"

Shaking my head, I touch the amulet again. The burning has stopped, but the power trapped inside makes my entire body buzz. I tuck it in my shirt. "Let's get on with it, then."

I roll my eyes, and Ruse follows. She must have jumped with me at the last minute. After a few tense steps, my stomach drops.

The Wicked Wood are exactly as they were the last time I saw them. Dark and terrifying. Empty yet overflowing. Full of lost souls trapped in the trees. Full of broken dreams and hope long lost. Ruse keeps close to my sides as we take a step in.

Then another.

And another.

"Just like last time," I whisper to myself. Perhaps to Ruse. "We'll get out, just like we did before. Right, Ruse?"

Her gaze is fixated on the trees before us. The darkness shifts, gray and purples swim together and at the end of the tunnel a figure forms.

Grawgeth.

No.

Elora.

She moves closer, the moss at her feet parting with her every step. Her face contorts as she comes fully into view.

Do you see me, love?

Her skin is patched with moss and bark across her breasts and down her abdomen. She cocks her head to the side, the glow of her golden eyes now flat and dull.

Please, see me, love.

On a deep breath, I take a step forward. Vines and leaves and thorns stretch before me. Crawling, wrapping themselves around my ankles and up my legs, pinning me in place. The thorny vines draw droplets of blood from my legs and arms.

Elora closes the distance between us, her vacant eyes scour my face. Sharp nails run down my jaw, leaving burning scratches. "Why have you come to my Wood," she hisses and her voice is not her own. It's not one, but many. Just as Grawgeth's had been. An orchestra of all the souls trapped here.

"I've come for you, love."

She grips my jaw tighter, her nails digging into my skin.

"If you seek passage, my price is not cheap." My jaw stings but I ignore it, looking into her eyes, searching for some piece of her left.

She must remember who she is.

"I don't seek passage," I say. "I've come for you, Elora."

She flinches, scurrying backward. "I do not know that name." She raises her chin, moss and vines curl at her feet. Slithering like serpents up and around her legs and arms.

I step forward, and as I do Ruse growls, low and deep. Elora's gaze snaps to the wolf. Her eyes widen before they narrow.

She recognizes her.

"Again, Ruse." I take another step and Ruse growls.

The forest revolts with every step I take. Roots erupt from the earth, blocking my path to her. More thorny vines sprout, catching on my pants and arms. Ruse begins to howl, long and slow and Elora bares her teeth.

"Elora, your name is Elora."

"Stop it!" Her teeth are still barred and it only makes Ruse howl louder. "Stop it!"

With her distracted by the howling, I've managed to weave around the forest floor and am inches from her. Her arms hang at her sides, her fists clenched, but there on her left hand, my father's ring.

I reach for her hand, but as I do, vines and roots crawl up my arms again, tightening around my muscles, making my hand stiffen.

"I require payment for passage through." Her gray eyes are narrow under her dark brows but I swear I see a glimmer of gold in them. Ruse continues to howl, and Elora shakes her head. "Payment or I end your life, now!"

She releases my hand, an ache already forming from the pressure around my wrists. When I make no other movement, she throws her hands together in a thunderous clap. Sharp branches burst from her shoulders, across her chest and down her arms. Vines and roots and thorns crawl over her legs, and when she holds her hand out to me, the threat is clear.

Payment or death.

Payment...payment. I pat my pockets and the weight of the amulet presses against my leg. Quickly I pull it out and dangle it between us. Her eyes flare as she watches it spin lightly from the gold chain it's attached to. Ruse stops howling and the creaking and moaning of the trees takes its place.

"Where did you get..." She steps forward. The spikes and thorns melt away, the moss and vines at her feet retreat back into the ground and soon she is bare before me save for the bark around her chest. She doesn't break her gaze from the amulet, its purple light pulsing in the darkness.

"Enchantress magick, Soleil." She hisses at the name, recoiling back from me. I shiver against the dropping temperatures as I inch closer but I focus on her eyes. On the faint flicker of gold I see in them. She reaches for the amulet, completely transfixed by it, and when she presses it to her fingers, I use her distraction to test my theory.

I press my mouth to hers, hard. She leaps backward, but I wrap my arms around her to hold her in place. She wiggles and growls before biting down on my lip so hard blood pools in my mouth. Her nails slice against my skin as I break away, leaving enough distance between us for the roots to erupt from the ground and encase her, protecting her.

I want to reach for her again. Want to brave the claws and the thorns and vines just to have one more taste of her lips.

But I don't.

Instead, I close my eyes and focus on every memory I have of her. Not just of this life, but our life before.

Please remember me.

Remember, you.

FORTY-FIVE

ELORA

THE MAN BEFORE ME CLOSES HIS EYES, WHISPERING things under his breath. There's a flutter in my otherwise vacant chest, faint and delicate, and yet it holds more power than that of all the Wood.

I don't know why, but I take a step forward, allowing the thorns and vines to drop around me, and press my lips against his again. His body jumps before it relaxes against mine.

Images flash through my mind as quick and bright as lightning. Strobing in and out, in and out leaving me little time to linger on any of them for very long.

We're there, this man and I, standing on a balcony, overlooking a sea of people.

Then the memory flips, and we're stuck in a storm, his hand desperately searching for mine. He never finds it.

My body relaxes and as it does, the man kisses me again, placing his hands along my back.

The images don't stop, if anything they grow more and more intense the deeper he kisses me.

We're together again, but now our hair has grown white and our skin has become wrinkled. I watch myself as I kiss him then, softly on his weathered cheek. He smiles at me and that fluttering in my chest happens again.

The memory persists, but now we are curled around each other as we take our last breaths.

Gasping, I pull away from him, but the man holds me tight.

"Elora," he says, his lips red from where my teeth scraped against them. His brows are pinched together, and I get the faint feeling that it's unusual for him to look so distressed.

I let the roots and vines around him fall, and he takes full advantage, wrapping his arms tighter around me and kissing me again.

As his lips connect with mine, I see him in this life.

Across from me on a riverbank. Dark brown eyes meet mine, and even if I didn't know it then, something snaps in me now. Something about the way he's looking at me. Something about the line of his jaw and the bridge of his nose. Like I've studied him before. Have taken the time to memorize each and every part of his face, down to the very dimple on his cheek.

I kiss him deeper, tangling my fingers through his hair. A soft moan leaves his lips and so I don't pull away. Bringing his bottom lip through my teeth.

And he kisses me too.

His hands roam my body, snagging on patches of bark and a few rogue vines. But it doesn't stop his determination. I'm lost in his passion, barely noticing as something cold slips around my neck. A frozen sting jolts me and my eyes flash open just as a burst of light explodes around us, the trees creaking and snapping.

I jump but the man holds me tightly. He kisses me again and again until my skin begins to heat and the fluttering in my chest grows steady.

Beat.

Beat.

Beat.

He groans as I bite his bottom lip, and when we finally break away, I open my eyes and realize he's already watching me.

I should know you.

I run my fingers along my lower lip, savoring the lingering heat of his touch, watching his face as I do. His dark eyes never leave mine. His lips are moving, his eyes wide and frantic. He's saying something, a name.

"Soleil," he says. "Your name was Soleil. And now it's Elora."

Elora.

The name turns something to my chest, and when I back away, he grabs me again. Glancing down, his arms are bloodied from where I've scratched him. His lips swollen and bruised from my sharpened teeth. But he raises his arm anyway and shakily places a hand upon my chest.

The forest around me groans, the trees swaying but there is no breeze. He lets out a long sigh, his shoulders slumping forward, his hand still on my chest, pushing against the steady beat now happening from inside of me.

My eyes gloss over.

I should remember you.

I'm lost in the confusion of it all. How did I get here and how did this man find me? For a moment, I question the memories. Surely a trick of the wood. But when the man tucks a piece of hair behind my ear, the beating in my chest intensifies.

I remember *something*. I just don't know what.

"Come on, love." He holds out his hand. Thorny brambles shoot up from the ground to create a barrier between us. He sighs, dropping his hand to his side. "Your name was Soleil Arden, I was Bastian Arden."

That fluttering in my chest has turned from delicate to frantic. Over and over there's a slamming against my ribs, a bruising pace.

"You're now Elora Leigh, the first and last Dyrsjel and my

—" He glances at the wolf. She nudges his hand, as if she understands him. "You're my wife."

"I…"

He reaches out his hand again, finding a break in the wall of thorns between us. His fingertips brush mine. We stand that way for a moment, his skin lighting a fire against my own.

"I don't know you." I rip my hand away. "Pay the price or—"

He drops his head, cradling it in his hands. "I don't need you to know me." He glances at me again, worry forming between his brows. "I just need you to remember who *you* are. Think of our kiss, Elora. Think of the memories. They are not what's coming, but what's already been. Please—" He tries to step forward, but I raise my hand and move another wall of thorns in his path.

"I am the keeper of the Wicked Wood." My voice amplifies and the trees shudder. "Pay my price, thief, or lose your life."

His eyes light up and he grips the woven barrier of thorns between us, not minding the sharp edges against his palms. "What did you just call me?" There's a hopeful desperation in his voice. "Say it again. Call me a thief again."

Images flash behind my eyes again. This man and the river. His lips on mine in a room that's unfamiliar. Me, cradled in his arms in these very woods.

So lost in the memories, my grip on the thorns between us falls, and he makes his way to me again. His fingers entwine with mine, heat blooming against my frozen skin. "I'll spend the rest of my life reminding you why you fell in love with me," he says, "but right now I just need you to remember yourself."

He kisses my forehead and it's the final threshold on my memories. Like a dam breaking, they wash over me. Consume me. They make me forget and remember all at the same time. I forget the pain and the fear of dying and remember what it was to live.

With him.

I drop to my knees, clawing at my chest, at the erratic beating and sharp pain.

"I have you," he says, joining me on the ground.

"I am Elora Leigh." My voice wavers, but he wraps me in his arms, a small flutter stirs, this time in my stomach. "And you are Sorin Rudhek."

His body shudders against mine so I clutch him tighter.

The wolf howls again and my confusion turns to excitement because I remember. "Ruse."

Sorin nods, his hands stroking my bare back. A gale of wind whips around us sending branches flying, dirt and rocks littering the air. We have been here before.

We *have* been here.

A crack of lightning illuminates the sky, bringing a memory with it.

I sit up, tears streaming down my cheeks. Mud and twigs entwine in my golden hair but that isn't what catches my breath. I hold my hands before my face and in them are the Stones. As I bring them to my mouth, and kiss each one gently, my eyes turn from amber to gold.

My eyes snap open as I suck in in a sharp breath. I bring my hands to my mouth, now swollen and pink from our kissing. "I was..."

Sorin nods, reaching for me again. "You were the first Enchantress, love." He hangs his head, letting out a long breath. "Our souls—"

"Have been reborn," I finish for him. There goes that fluttering in my chest again. "It's you." I trace my fingers over his face. Around his full lips, down his nose. "I remember you."

His face breaks, leaning forward so his forehead presses against mine. "I love you."

Beat.

Beat.

Beat.

His fingers entwine with mine again. "I knew you, even

when I didn't," he says. "My soul craved its other half and now that I've found it, I refuse to let go."

My body shudders.

"I meant it when I said I'd spend the rest of this life reminding you why you love me," he says. "I don't ever intend for you to forget again. I want all of you, this life and in the last."

Beat.

Beat.

Beat.

"But I need you to do something now, Elora," Sorin says against my hair. Screams erupt from the trees, piercing my ears. "I need you to destroy the woods."

My head spins and chest aches, like a block of ice slowly thawing under the sun. I was dead and now I'm not. There are so many questions but no time for answers.

"We have to destroy the Wicked Wood, Elora," Sorin demands again. "It's the only way to ensure you'll never be trapped here again."

My mind races. Images from our lives past and this one blurring together. "I can't..." I rub at my temples. "How am I to destroy it? Grawgeth said it would just grow back." My chest tightens, pain blooming beneath my breast.

"Maybe this will help." Sorin gestures to the necklace he's placed around my neck. "Maybe there's something in here that can destroy it?"

I wrap the stone in my hand and my magick stirs, drawing to life after days of death. "I..." I bring it to my lips, pushing the cold stone against my mouth, and all at once, I'm filled with magick.

Healer and Seer magick swims together. Memoria and Arma and Stormweilder magick light a fire beneath my veins. It burns and hisses, but I hold the stone close to my lips, searching until the one magick I need comes to the surface.

I suck in a sharp breath as I spin, turning toward the woods.

"Elora?" Sorin steps to my side.

Plague magick pushes forth, silencing all the others. I glance down at my arms, veins turning black.

"Elora," Sorin says again, but I sprint forward, heading directly back to the Wicked Wood. Sorin screams my name again, following close behind, but I don't stop until I'm right in the center of the wood. Right in the very place he just kissed me.

"Stand back," I say over my shoulder. I have no idea if this will work. No idea if Plague magick is powerful enough to destroy the sentient wood but it's the only option I have. The only option to ensure the Wicked Wood can never draw myself or Grawgeth back here. Without a second thought, I slam my hand down to the ground, letting the magick run through my fingertips and bury itself deep beneath the soil, into the roots of the trees.

The forest erupts. Trees hiss and sway, branches break free, and when I glance up, my heart skips a beat. The deformed, skeletal birch trees of the Wicked Wood have turned black.

"Don't let go of me," I say in a panic, not entirely sure what I'm doing. I grab Sorin's arm. "Ruse, come." She does in an instant and the three of us hold each other as I grasp the necklace and pull us out of the wood just before the trees come crumbling down.

We tumble to the ground in a heap, Sorin's body under mine, Ruse just to my left. More and more screaming sounds from behind us, grating against my ears. I push myself off Sorin and spin toward the wood.

The bark on the trees peels back, roots seeped in black. They crash to the ground, groaning and hissing. The amulet pulses around my neck in time with my thoughts so I bring my fingers to it, giving it a gentle stroke.

"Elora?"

Glancing over my shoulder, Sorin has stood, dusting dirt and broken bits of tree limbs from his clothes and hair.

"Are you all right?" He reaches a tentative hand forward then drops it.

Ruse joins my side, her nose nuzzling my shoulder and a sense of ease washes over me. "Yes I'm all right."

"And you remember—"

"I do," I say, and his dark eyes light up, his face perhaps hopeful. "I remember everything."

His arms wrap around me with lightning speed, his lips on my neck, my forehead.

I reluctantly pull away, so many things in my mind still mixed together. "But we're not done."

"No," he says through a sigh, "we're not."

A splintering crack sounds as a large birch tree tumbles down.

"The Fates said we must leave the Wicked Wood something, to somehow ensure they don't grow back. To make sure Grawgeth doesn't find herself back here. To ensure you..." He doesn't finish the sentence but we both tense anyway.

I shiver.

"Here." He wraps me in his cloak then takes my hand. His fingers tighten as if he needs to touch me as much as possible to remind himself I'm real. "Any ideas what the wood would want? Aside from a soul." He smiles and it sparks something in me. The movement in my chest has taken on its regular rhythm, but his face makes it falter a beat.

"I have an idea." Sorin follows my lead as I walk to the edge of the Wicked Wood. "I need a blade." I glance at his back. "Or an arrow."

He pulls his quiver, handing me an arrow without question. Ruse nuzzles my side as I slice the arrow along my palm.

I'm okay, girl.

She doesn't believe me but doesn't argue as I cut the line just a little longer. Gritting my teeth, I let my blood pool in my hand. "Here." I wipe the arrow on the grass before handing it to Sorin. "You need to do the same."

His face pales, but he does as I say, slicing a long line down his palm until it's also full of blood.

"So do we just drop it in?" Sorin looks as though he might faint and I almost laugh.

"We bury it, give it back to Mother Gaia. Back to the earth." There's one spot in the forest that has yet to crumble so Sorin and I settle at a birch, dig a small hole at the base of the tree before dropping our blood in and covering it with dirt.

The tree groans, swaying from side to side. Its branches, long and spidery, thrash against the oncoming Plague magick, but for the first time since being near these woods, I don't feel afraid. Our hands clasp together, stinging where they've been freshly cut. The memory of our past lives floating in my mind.

A storm, a crown, and a bargain made.

"We need to go, love."

My toes dig into the soil, eyes transfixed on the darkness spreading through the woods. Sorin tugs my hand. With a final glance at the woods over my shoulder, my breath catches as three figures emerge, hand in hand, heads thrown back in laughter, before they disappear into the wind.

USING the amulet has become much too easy, and I start to understand how this type of power could become intoxicating.

We arrive back at the Jade Guild just as the rain begins again. Alaric and the pups were there, waiting. As if they knew we'd be back.

After changing into fresh clothes, Sorin packs a small bag with the last of the larder items. I stand in the doorway, watching as he assembles, disassembles, and reassembles the bag again. He scratches his brow and closes his eyes for a moment.

"Need some help?" He jumps at my voice then quickly relaxes as I wrap my arms around his middle from behind him.

"No," he says, dropping the bag onto the table, "but sleep would probably do me good."

"Dying is exhausting."

He spins me so my face is in his chest, his chin resting atop my head. "I don't think I've ever been that scared before." His lips brush against my hair before he tilts my chin with my thumb.

"I was scared too. Thought for certain I'd never see this dimple again." I press up onto my toes and kiss it which makes him smile more. "Will you tell me what happened? One day, when this is all over."

He closes his eyes and I regret asking until lips meet mine for a gentle kiss. "I'll tell you. I promise." He strokes my hair, warming my chest. "I can't believe you were my wife before," he whispers against my ear. "I've never felt so relieved."

"Relieved?"

He smiles before kissing the tip of my nose. "When we met on the river, I told you a piece of me snapped into place. And the longer we were together, my love for you became overwhelming. All-consuming. But it was mad, wasn't it? To love someone so fiercely in such a short time."

I dig my fingers into his back, letting my head rest against his chest. Finding comfort in the movement of his heart. In the movement of mine.

"But now it all makes so much sense," he says. "My soul belongs to you, yours to me, and I have never felt so whole."

A tear runs down my cheek, but Sorin dries it up with the tip of his finger. "There is still so much to be done." My chest tightens thinking of all that's left to do. To right the wrongs that have been done to Teravie. To ensure our bargain with Mother Gaia is paid.

"The Mother entrusted us to keep Teravie safe," he says. "If She believes in us enough to rebirth our souls, I believe in us too."

After finally organizing the bag enough for his liking, we meet Ruse outside.

"Are you sure it will transport us again?" Sorin asks, earning him a scowl. He laughs and begins to say something about how much he missed that face but I cut him off.

"I have no idea what this is capable of," I remind him, holding the amulet in my fingers. "But what other choice do we have?" We're running out of time.

Sorin nods and takes my hand. "Get closer," I tell wolves and they do, huddling as close to me as they can. "Now, to the Onyx Guild?"

Sorin scratches his chin, his stubble more pronounced these days."I imagine by now that Samaria has either frightened the Guild members off or she has convinced them to help." His eyes meet mine. "Which would mean she won't be at the Onyx Guild."

At my puzzled look, Sorin takes my hand, lacing our fingers. "We have to go to Valebridge."

FORTY-SIX

ROMAN

VALEBRIDGE IS COVERED IN AN UNFALTERING MASK OF gray when we arrive. The white pumpkins that lined the drawbridge have been cleared, the last of the Autumn Moon swept away. The council stood in my absence, making sure everything has run the same as before. A small part of me wonders if I've ever been needed at all.

"Happy to see you, Your Majesty." Councilman Horrice nods as I take my place at the head of the table. "We trust your trip went well, considering your early arrival? We weren't expecting you for several more days."

I open my mouth to speak but, of course, Galen does so for me.

"Weather was turning on us." He slides into the chair next to me. "We made the choice to end the Dyrsjel hunt a bit early."

A few of the older council members scoff and whisper. Likely debating how much truth lies within Galen's explanation. I suppose it's all true. Minus the very large detail about the dozens of guards and hunters who are now dead from Elora's hands. I stiffen as his hand lands on my leg under the table. Through gritted teeth, I brush it off and focus on the council.

"Let's make this brief," Galen says. "The Dyrsjel is still out there and she's dangerous. Without her magick, we won't be able to pull from Mother Gaia directly. We need her ability to wield the Stones to continue harvesting magick—"

"And what do you propose?" Councilwoman Maeve sits forward, the gold rings on her dark fingers reflect in the low light of the councilroom. "We have spared dozens of guards, not to mention the man-power it's taken to train and disperse hunters throughout Teravie. Our resources and expenses aren't expendable, Sir Galen. There is only so much we, and the people of Valebridge, are willing to give to continue this cat and mouse chase." Her brows pinch together and my spine stiffens. She smooths the lapels on her navy robes. Her dark hair is cropped short, and when she catches me staring, she smirks. "Perhaps it's time we take this issue to another vote."

Galen laughs as he shrugs but his hands twitch in his lap. "We already did vote after Silas' passing five years ago. We voted that controlling the Stones ourselves would put an end to reckless use of magick. It would give us the power—"

Maeve holds out her hand, and Galen snaps his mouth shut. "You are a brilliant young man, Galen. But I wasn't asking for your permission for a vote." She glances at me, resting her hands in her lap. "Ultimately, the decision is yours, Your Majesty. But I propose a new vote as to whether or not this pursuit of the Awakening Stones is worth all we have already sacrificed."

Six sets of eyes land on me, including Galen's.

His fury rolls off of him like fog but only if that fog was poisonous and deadly. I can feel it in his stare. In the way his body has stiffened next to mine.

For so many years we have made decisions together. Have destroyed the trust of the kingdom for a pursuit of something that was never destined to belong to us. And for what? A false hope that with the power of the Stones we would be feared. Protected.

"A vote?" I make sure to glance at each member of the

council to see if they also share Maeve's thoughts. When five heads nod back, I let out a long breath.

"All in favor—"

"No," Galen snaps. He grabs my arm and turns me so our faces are close enough for him to whisper. "Stick to our plan, little bird." There's panic laced in his tone. "We need the Stones, Roman. We'll have access to magick we haven't even dreamed of." His hands tremble as they grip mine but his touch does nothing to soothe me.

Instead, it ignites me.

"You do not decide for me, Galen." I rip my hand from his and face the council.

"All in favor of ceasing the hunt for the Dyrsjel, say aye."

Without a second's hesitation, five aye's sound around the table.

Galen's face reddens as I turn to him. His eyes meet mine with a glacial rage and as I tip my lips up his brows furrow deeper as I whisper only to him, "Aye."

Back in my chambers, the air is suffocating as Galen paces silently across the floor. I take a seat on the bed, a new sense of purpose and power running through me.

For the first time in five years, I made the decisions today and that alone holds more power than a stone ever could.

Galen's boots snag on the corner of the large, navy area rug, and when he nearly trips, he curses and pulls his fingers through his typically manicured hair.

"Why, Roman?"

I flinch at his tone but remind myself who's in charge here. *You are the king, Roman, act like it.*

"We've given it all we've got, Galen." I wave him over before patting the bed next to me.

He hesitates a moment before relenting and joining my side.

"Sorin's likely dead by now and without him, there isn't a threat to the throne." My stomach curls at the thought of Sorin not living. Another skeleton looming over my head. "Elora may still have the Stones, but what need do we really have for them?"

He bristles before letting out a long sigh.

"For once," I say, "let's just be you and me." The thought curdles my stomach, but after years of abuse from my father, I know when to use honey rather than vinegar.

"I suppose a break wouldn't hurt." He grabs my hand and kisses my knuckles. "I'll give the remaining hunters a week to recover their losses, visit their families. Then we're back on the hunt."

His nails scratch against my skin as I pull my hand abruptly away. "That isn't what we voted on."

Galen laughs, showing off his perfectly pointed canines.

"I don't care what the council says." He rolls his shoulders, as if he's just rid himself of the burden of their respect. "You shouldn't either. You're the king, Roman. You don't need their vote, not really." He leans into me. His fingers comb through my dark hair and I'm reminded why it's been so easy to follow his lead all these years. He pushes our foreheads together, mint and pine waft off of him and it's the same as it's always been.

Him and me and this spiral of intoxicating infatuation.

Except now I see him for who he has always been.

The cat does not give his motives away so quickly. He stalks, waits, and is patient with his prey. Gives the bird time to adjust, to relax. And when the bird is comfortable, no longer sees a threat to the always dormant cat, that's when the cat leaps.

"Little bird," he whispers. "All I've ever wanted was for you to trust that what I'm doing is for the greater good. Do you not trust me, Ro? After all of these years keeping you safe." His fingers dance along my arms.

He'll never stop.

Never see the pain we've caused for the sake of power and revenge for a sister he lost.

He grips the back of my neck, and because his forehead is still pressed to mine, I have nowhere else to look but down.

Down at him, at his chest.

And there, just under his loose, black shirt lies the answer to the riddle going round and round inside of my head.

"I trust you," I say, sweet like honey. I delicately run my fingers down his chest; he sighs at my touch. His face moves to the junction between my jaw and neck where he kisses me softly. I bite my bottom lip to refrain from flinching, keeping my fingers light until they reach his shirt.

I push it back and kiss his bare chest.

"*Roman.*"

I slide my tongue across his chest and kiss his collarbone before pulling him back so I can see him. He cradles either side of my face, watching me, before I lean forward and kiss him deeply.

He moans against my lips and my heart cracks in two. One half rejoices while the other mourns.

I open my mouth and his tongue slides over mine. I grip his shoulders tightly with one hand so he can't pull away. He mimics my movements. Holding my back tightly, pressing me against his chest. Putting the least amount of distance between us as possible.

But as the Plague magick from the amulet begins to pool from my mouth to his, he struggles. The black shadows curl around us as he wiggles and tries to move away from me.

"Ro," he pleas against my lips.

I hold him through his panic. Gripping him tighter to me. His nails claw at my back. His head whips around, breathless pleas escaping from his lips. A tear slides down my cheek, but still I hold strong.

Once I'm sure he's had enough, I break apart our kiss and lie his paralyzed body onto the bed. He twitches under my touch, his eyes wide and glinting with tears. His mouth is stuck open, black seeping from each corner. I trace his bottom lip with my thumb before gently pressing his mouth closed.

"I'm sorry, my darling." I kiss his forehead, then his lips. His body is stiff from the poison, but he manages to blink a few times, letting a few tears fall loose. "I was never afraid to fly," I whisper as I lift his head and place it in my lap. "I was only afraid to fall."

His eyes meet mine a final time. I stroke his hair and cheeks until after several excruciating minutes, his chest slows. My tears drop onto his chest, leaving tiny wet marks on his otherwise pristine shirt.

"But now, I'm not afraid at all." My heart twists and stomach sinks.

His brows pinch together, so I run my thumb between them to smooth his worry. He opens his mouth in a gasp before his chest falls a final time.

Everything in that moment stands still.

Time.

Breathing.

My mind is the only thing moving. Racing through images of the two of us the last few years. Moments of happiness and joy and pain and anger. Of passion and lust and a hopelessness that I confused to be love.

Because that's what we were. Two hopeless people who found strength in each other. That is what we were, until we weren't.

Until the idea of power became stronger than the contentment of love.

I clutch onto Galen's body, savoring the final few minutes of its warmth before he turns cold.

There's a commotion out my window. Voices rising, chanting something I can't make out, but I refuse to let go. Refuse to move. I push Galen's hair from his forehead, the veins in his face and eyelids stained black.

I grip his shoulders and I'm not sure who the tears are for now.

For me or for him.

Everyone I have loved has hurt me and I let them blindly. I took their affection and stored it away to remember when their soft hands turned violent.

The chanting outside the window grows louder. The clang of metal sounds through the rain but I don't get up. Instead I lie down and place my head next to Galen's.

I close my eyes.

I breathe him in, one last time.

I'm sorry.

I'm sorry.

I'm sorry.

FORTY-SEVEN

SAMARIA

"Down with the king! Down with the king!" There's a buzzing in my ears from the relentless yelling around me. Rain falls in buckets, soaking the ground and our clothes.

Men and women from not just Loxley, but the Jade and Onyx Guilds, even those from Wickersham have come together just outside of Valebridge to demand justice. The iron gate juts toward the sky, towering above us, wrapping around the entirety of the courtyard.

Tallulah and Evren flank my sides, as well as the other escaped Enchantresses, including Sera. Our arms link together as we watch a crowd form just inside the walls.

"Down with the king!"

Jarek's body presses in from behind me, his voice booming over all the others. "How long, my queen, do we wait before we take justice into our own hands?"

I look at the weary-eyed men and women on the other side of the gate. Watching us not with fear or hate, like I'd expected, but with curiosity. One woman comes forth, wrapping her hands around the iron gate. Her eyes are soft, her skin pale and wrinkled.

"Enchantresses," she shouts above the rising storm. I nod.

"May the Mother bless you." A tear slips from her eye, and before I can speak, a thunderous stomping of boots in the courtyard opposite us has the Valebridge crowd clearing.

Royal Guards.

"We can't just sit here, Sam," Evren says from behind me.

I focus on the guards heading toward us. Counting them, comparing our numbers. I'm grateful that my hands are occupied, otherwise I know I'd be picking my nails down to the cuticle right now. "How many, Sera?"

Sera holds her wrists up and closes her eyes. "Too many." Silver wells in her eyes but she brushes them away.

Shite.

"Give Roman a chance."

Spinning around, my knees go slack as Sorin weaves through the crowd. He's here and—

"Elora." I unloop my arm and cup my hands over my mouth. "How did you... Are you okay?" I fumble over my words as I wrap her in a hug.

"I'm okay," she says, "I think."

"It's a long story," Sorin says. Elora backs into his chest, her eyes not quite the vibrant gold I'm used to but she's warm and she's here and—

"Roman gave me this." Sorin pulls a necklace out from Elora's tunic. An amethyst stone glitters from a delicate chain. "His harvested Enchantress magick."

Tallulah gasps, taking a step forward. She traces the stone delicately with her fingers. "And you used it?" she asks.

"It's how we're here. If not for this, if not for Roman..." Sorin bites his bottom lip before tucking the amulet back under Elora's shirt. "Give him a chance to make this right."

I turn to Tallulah and Elora, who tries to smile but quickly turns to a frown.

"Please," Sorin whispers and it's the softness in his tone that has my mind made.

"One chance," I agree. The women at my sides nod and just as they do, a guard approaches the gate.

"You!" he yells, pointing a spindly finger at Sera. "You are under arrest for the use of magick—" The man drops to the ground, thick, vines of ivy wrapped around his ankles and wrists. My eyes bulge as I look at Tallulah.

She shrugs, holding her palms steady, the ivy sprawling from them tightening a little. "I didn't care for what he had to say."

She smiles and I know that it's now or never. Glancing at the courtyard, I see the silhouettes of the guards come into view through the dizzying rain. Beady and black; they swarm together like ants.

"We have to find Roman," I say to Sorin. "At least to convince him to call off his guard.".

Sorin sighs, clutching onto Elora's shoulders. Her hair is twisted in a braid, water dripping from the ends of it. She remains quiet, but her eyes flick to mine, a spark of curiosity brewing in them.

Jarek laughs from behind me so I glance over my shoulder and when I do, my chest tightens. "She's all right, pups." He kneels in the mud. Hati, Rook, Skoll, and Gray fight for closeness to Elora and just behind them are Alaric and Ruse.

We're all here.

Together.

Emotion swells in my breast, but before I let myself feel anything too deeply, I shove it down. There's work to be done.

Jarek stands, pulling himself reluctantly away from the puppies who are now grown nearly to his hip. Our eyes connect, and when I open my mouth, he shakes his head. "Go, we're right behind you."

Gooseflesh erupts over my skin as he kisses me. I have the sense to not let go but correct myself when the crowd around us continues to chant, their voices growing louder with the rising wind and rain. I pull away from Jarek and turn to the gate.

"Wait," I say, facing Sorin again, "you should go instead. He knows you. Try and convince him to stop this. Find Gal—" I choke on his name, but Jarek's hand on my shoulder settles the fire in my chest. "Find Galen and stop this."

Sorin glances at Jarek, their unspoken promises written all over their faces. Jarek claps him on the back, and Sorin winces but smiles. Turning to face the crowd, I find the kind woman from before. I whistle and snap my fingers to grab her attention but it doesn't work.

"You! Excuse me, miss!" After what feels like an eternity, she comes back to the gate, stepping lightly around the guard still pinned to the ground with ivy.

"What is it?" She keeps her voice low, and I have to push myself against the iron bars so I can hear her over the thunder. The iron burns against my skin, but I press myself tighter to ensure she can hear me.

"We need you to open the gate," I say. "We need to get inside before the guards come. Quickly!" Her body stiffens as the sounds of the guards move closer. I glance to Sera, her eyes locked on the castle, likely determining how many guards are where.

"Please," Tallulah begs the woman. Evren's at her side, his sword already drawn.

The woman is silent for a moment, her thin fingers running through the soft gray curls of her hair. Her eyes drift past me, and I follow her gaze until I see what has her so focused.

She's staring at Sorin.

"Mother above," she gasps, cupping her hands over her mouth. "The rumors are true? The king lives?"

How similar do he and Silas look?

"No." Elora joins us at the gate, the wolves following in her wake. My stomach swirls at the sound of her voice, it's hers but somehow it isn't. There's a coldness lining it, something distant. Ancient. Her fingers brush mine as she grips the bars, and my chest collapses when her skin is warm, not cold.

She's alive, Samaria. Just relax.

"Silas has passed, but this," she says, turning to Sorin, "is Sorin Rudhek, first born son of Silas Rudhek, the rightful heir of Valebridge and Teravie."

The woman on the other side of the gate mutters something like a prayer. "No," she says, shaking her head. "King *Bastian*. King Bastian and you—" She closes her eyes and brings her hands to her chest.

The hairs on my body stand on end, and when I look at Elora and Sorin, their faces have blanched. The woman mutters something again and just when I'm about to have Jarek break the damn gate down himself, the woman disappears.

"Shite," I mutter. "Elora, should we try the tunnels? Do you remember where they are?" A larger part of me is dying to ask her to use her magick, or the magick in the amulet for that matter but she's been through so much, I don't want to push her.

She frowns and opens her mouth, but before she can speak, grinding metal drowns out the chants behind me as the gate opens.

"Thank the Mother," I say through a sigh. "Jarek, Evren, Tallulah, and I will stay here and get ready for a fight." The three of them turn to me, their eyes as wide as I'm sure my own are. " Sorin—" I grab his arm and pull him forward. "Go find Roman."

"I'll go too," Sera says, wiping the black strands of her hair from her face.

Sorin nods and turns to Elora. He bends down to her ear and whatever he whispers makes her smile. She slides the necklace around him.

"Be safe." Sorin squeezes her shoulders before kissing her. When he turns to me, our eyes meet but there isn't any time for chatter before he's sprinting through the gate, following Sera into the castle. Every step he takes away from me, panic claws at my skin.

I have already seen him die once, I can't bear it again.

My chest heaves, mind racing with an endless amount of possibilities of what could go wrong. I'm about to sprint after Sorin myself when Jarek takes a timid step toward Elora. He grips her shoulders, the wolves tucked closely to their sides. My attention on them doesn't last long before the woman from before reappears, her face slick with rain or perhaps tears.

"Thank you for opening the gate." I step forward and join her side. "You and your friends should probably go, it may get a bit ugly down here."

The guards are in view now, their militant stance and glinting swords bright even in the gray afternoon light. I place my hand on her shoulder and she jumps, as if she hadn't realized I was there. Hadn't heard a word I said.

Out of the corner of my eye, my breath falters for a moment when Sera and Sorin head straight toward the guards but then in an instant, the two of them vanish. As if carried away in the wind. My mouth drops open, eyes scanning the area for any sight of them. I don't have time to contemplate when Jarek steps forward, his axes drawn. The guards shout, their voices mixing together.

"Queen Soleil," the old woman whispers, drawing my attention for a moment. I slide my hand from her shoulder to ready my bow.

"I'm not sure what you mean?"

The woman's face splits into a grin, emphasizing the deep lines in her face. She points, and I follow her finger to Elora who's still behind me. "She lives."

Confusion contorts my face as I nock my first arrow. A chill washes over me and soon Elwyn and Celia's spirits are at my side.

"Please." I push the woman forward as gently as I can. My fingers tremble against my bow, what used to be an extension of myself now feels so foreign. "You and the others must go." The woman smiles again before hobbling out of sight.

Most of the civilians have left, leaving an open space between us and the guards. Arrows soon litter the air.

I spin, moving and ducking under a guard before he can strike, trying to find a better vantage point. Something cold brushes against my cheek and when I turn, it's Elwyn.

I flick my wrist up.

"Look, Sam."

I turn, following her gaze, and in the courtyard are hundreds of Enchantress spirits.

"Why are they all still here?" My mind races but as the arrows whiz past me and steel clangs together I'm snapped out of the haze. I keep one wrist up, eyes scanning the courtyard.

"They're stuck here," Celia says. *"Just like we are."*

Evren shouts next to me, drawing my attention. His blade is already coated in crimson.

"Use your magick, Sam."

I duck, dodging an arrow as it flies overhead. "I don't think speaking to a hundred spirits is going to help us win a fight!" I realize too late that I've yelled the words aloud. I draw another arrow from my quiver, letting it soar before it sinks into a guard a few paces away. I flick my wrists back up.

"You're a Spiritwalker, Sam." Elwyn's cool fingers brush against my cheek. *"So, walk with them."* She cups my face and shivers rake over my body. *"Fight with them."* She steps aside just in time for me to stop another guard with an arrow to the chest.

"Fight with them," I repeat, breathless from another kill. I toss my bow to the ground.

"Samaria!" Jarek is sprinting toward me in my peripherals.

Fight.

"Sam!" Jarek shouts again.

Fight.

Jarek's voice carries over the carnage and the rain, but he doesn't make it before I flick my wrists up and open myself up to the spirits before me.

My eyes roll back for a split second before they right themselves. And when they do, gone are the screams and fighting sounds of the courtyard. Instead, my ears pop, voices and sounds muffled around me.

Jarek is at my side, his mouth moving but his words are stifled. He grips my shoulders and shakes me, but I'm unmoving.

I take a step forward, holding my hands up to my face to examine the ghost-like mist I've become. I glance over my shoulder to where my body still stands. Jarek is fighting around me. His axes swinging, his blue eyes wide.

Tallulah and Evren are there as well, engaged in battles of their own. And Elora— I scan the area until I see her, handling a guard of her own.

"Come," Elwyn says, waving me forward. Before I'm halfway through the courtyard, walking clear through guards as if I'm nothing more than the wind, more Enchantresses than I can see have gathered around me.

"Spiritwalker," they whisper. Over and over again.

"Spiritwalker."

"Spiritwalker."

"Mother blessed."

"Open yourself up, Sam." Elwyn grips my shoulders.

I don't know how I understand what she means, I just do. A deep, primal part of my being snaps open and as it does the power of my magick unleashes.

Like a bolt of lightning, my magick spears through the courtyard, touching each and every spirit in its path. As it lands on them, color flushes their cheeks. Their eyes ignite, and they all look so *alive*. Then one by one, their wrists begin to swish and an endless amount of magick, kinds I could have never imagined, begins to circle in the air.

A woman with steel eyes flicks her wrists to the skies as if she's speaking to the storm, bringing forth heavy hail that she directs toward the guards. Their screams are muffled through the portal but as they begin to fall, my lips spread into a smile.

"Hold onto your magick tightly, Samaria," Celia says. Her eyes are alight, her red hair gleaming. "Don't let it slip, the spirits need you in order to use their magick."

My words are lost but I nod quickly before another Enchantress steps forth. Her silver hair is bound in a thick braid, her dark skin weathered like a decades old map. She smiles at me before facing the guards and raising her wrists.

Dark tendrils roll from her hands, seeping through the cracks in the stone ground beneath us before wrapping around the ankles of a dozen guards and bringing them to their feet. Their heads hit the ground with a wicked crunch, and the Enchantress tips her head back and laughs before she regains her composure and does it again and again.

My magick continues to pulse through my palms, threading out into the courtyard, giving energy and life to each spirit before me. And they accept it like an offering. I push my magick further, my anger fueling me for each Enchantress stuck here. Taken advantage of. Used and abused and tortured and—

My rage becomes palpable, my teeth clenched so tightly my jaw aches, but the sting in my palms intensifies, more and more magick pushing its way through me.

"Sam!" his voice is broken, but I'd know it anywhere. Jarek calls my name again, and as I glance over my shoulder to where my body remains, my grip on my magick waivers.

Jarek's tangled in a fight, his ax straining against a steel sword, two men flanking his sides. Elora is running toward me, her hands raised, staving off several guards, setting them aflame.

But what panics me, what sends an icy thrill through my veins, is the guard before *my* body, holding a knife to my throat.

FORTY-EIGHT

SORIN

After using the amulet to avoid the guards, Sera guides me through the castle. A part of me wonders just how long she was a prisoner here as she weaves in and out of various halls and passageways with ease.

"It's this way," she calls over her shoulder.

As we move through the winding hallways, the sounds from outside draw my attention. Chanting rises from the crowd as I peer out a window. It's only with the noise from outside that I realize how quiet the castle itself is.

"Sera, wait."

She stops several feet ahead of me, tilting her head.

"Where are all of Roman's guards?"

Her face twists, and she glances down the hall behind her, then back to me. More shouting comes from outside.

"Down with the king!"

My stomach sours as I glance out the window.

The guards meet the gate where the crowd is rushing through. I spot Sam in the distance, her arrows flying with precision, hitting target after target. Frantic, my heart races as I look for Elora. The wolves flank her and Jarek's sides, their teeth bared but there are so many people. So many guards that my eyes can't work fast enough.

Sera joins me near the window. "There are two men in the room just around the corner."

"We need to get back out there," I say. "If they plan to take down an army, I can be of assistance." I reach for my bow, but Sera stops me, her nails digging slightly into my forearm.

"You must find Roman." Her blue eyes pulse in the gray light, flicking between me and the window. Her hand is trembling, eyes darting around me. "Put an end to this, Your Majesty." She slips her hand from my wrist and my knees threaten to give way. "Second door on the left, just around the hall. That's where you'll find them. I'll go find the council, they've got to be hiding around here."

"You have no weapons." I pull a dagger from my boot, but when I offer it to her, she brushes me aside.

"I don't need weapons, I can be very persuasive." Her smile lights up her otherwise cold face, and before I can say anything else, she takes off in a sprint back the way we came.

Peeling myself away from the window, away from the sounds of Elora and Sam and Jarek in battle, I take each step with a leaded foot toward the room Sera told me.

Second door on the left.

I nock an arrow, and as I do, the amulet around my neck burns. As if it's reminding me there are far greater weapons at my disposal than my bow. My fingers draw toward it, a moth to a flickering flame, the desire to test each and every magick stored inside becoming distracting.

But it's a magick that isn't mine.

That was never meant for anyone but them.

The Enchantresses.

Mother Gaia.

Pausing, I rip the chain from my neck and drop the amulet into my pants pocket, nulling the desire to use it. With another steadying breath, I approach the door.

It's already open, just a sliver, giving me a glimpse inside. Sera said there were two men inside, but the room is unnaturally still. I push on the door, testing for any creaks, but when it slides open with ease, I nudge into the room, arrow first. The only sounds that fill the space are from outside, screaming and clanging. My heart lurches.

I should be down there.

There's another window just across from me, and that's where I find him.

Roman.

"You," he says without turning from the window. "So you're alive after all?"

With shaking fingers, I aim my arrow straight at his back.

He turns, his face is pale, his eyes red. "If you've come to kill me, just do it." There's no emotion in his voice, but when his eyes dart to the bed, his face crumples.

I follow his line of sight and struggle not to fall to my knees.

Galen's body is on the bed, not an ounce of life left in his face. My chest tightens, and when my grip on my bow loosens, I don't scramble to grab it.

"I've done many unthinkable things," Roman whispers. His boots are heavy as he passes by me to sit on the end of the bed. "But this may be the worst yet."

My throat burns, and when I look at Roman again, he is sitting with one hand on Galen's chest.

I can't breathe.

The voices outside grow louder, their shouts incoherent. The amulet pulses in my pocket, begging to be used, but I drop my bow and draw my hand to the blade tucked into my boot. My fingers tremble as they wrap around the hilt. This is my last chance to make him see. My last chance to let him make one right choice.

I spring to my feet, the dagger poised between my fingers. It takes me two steps to reach him and a half a breath before the dagger is tucked under his chin. His eyes meet mine but he doesn't flinch. Doesn't fight back as I dig the blade a little deeper.

"Make his death mean something, Roman."

He closes his eyes, his face aged since I saw him only a few days ago.

"Make it count. Call off your guards."

He leans into my blade, letting it dig further into his flesh as he laughs. "If you think they'll listen to me, you haven't been paying attention," he says. "They will follow Galen's allegiance, even in his death."

He grabs my hand and pulls the dagger toward him, aiming right for his heart. "If you're not going to do it, I will."

He pushes the blade deeper but I rip my hand away and shove him backward. The blade falls to the floor and I scramble to reach it, but Roman is quicker.

He knocks me out of the way, fisting the blade. He stands before I can and turns, pressing his boot to my chest. He opens his mouth, perhaps some final words lingering on his lips. The blade is pressed tightly to his throat, his boot pressed tightly to my chest, and I'm paralyzed by it all.

Elora.

Galen and Loxley and the Wicked Wood.

The Fates and my life before this one.

And Elora.

Because it always starts and ends with her.

She is the moon in my sky and I will not leave here without a kingdom to present at her feet.

My head is swimming, my heart pounding, and just when Roman moves, I charge him, tackling him to the floor. I sigh in relief as the metal clink of a blade hits the floor just out of reach.

FORTY-NINE

ELORA

BETWEEN THE ARROWS FLYING AND THE STEEL clanging, I can't keep up with the movement around me. So different from the quiet of the wood. So angry and violent and dreadfully loud.

"Elora, move!" Tallulah calls, unleashing her ivy to stop a guard inches from my face.

I hadn't even noticed he was there. I back up a step, placing my hands over my ears.

The ivy wraps around the man's throat, and within minutes, he's given up his fight with death. My eyes go wide as I watch the snake-like plant slither back into Tallulah's palms, as if it were never there at all.

"Are you all right?" She grasps my hand, dragging me toward the crowd when all I want to do is run away from it. Evren grunts from behind Tallulah; I peer around her just as he pulls his blade from a guard. His own face and arms bloodied but there's no telling who the blood belongs to.

I push past Tallulah, weaving through men and women fighting, swords clanging, bones breaking. My eyes land on Samaria, her hands raised as a dozen more guards head our way.

"Sam!" She doesn't move, her body rigid, her bow tossed to the ground. "Sa—"

Something heavy collides with my back, bringing me to my knees.

A rough hand yanks me up, his breath hot next to my ear. I wriggle my wrists, trying to free myself from his grip, but a sickening crunch has the man dropping his hold on me and toppling to the ground.

Scrambling, I scurry backward, just as the wolf pups begin to attack him.

"Elora!" Jarek calls my name, but I can't find him. There are so many people, everyone screaming and running.

"Elora!" he says again and this time, his hand wraps around my arm, pulling me up. "Stay with me."

His hands tremble, his blue eyes lined with uncertainty. I nod, attempting to regain my composure. Jarek pulls me through the crowd until we're near Samaria again. Her fiery eyes are glossed over and white, her face blanched and her body unmoving.

"What is this?" I ask, the words all running together. "What's happening to her?"

Tallulah and Evren join us, their chests heaving and faces gaunt. Another line of guards rushes from the castle. Tallulah raises her hands, but they tremble and she winces as she attempts to move her wrists.

"She must have opened herself up," Tallulah says through a grunt, a long strand of ivy wrapping itself around another guard. "She's using herself as a portal for the spirits."

My eyes drift past Sam, into the courtyard where guard after guard drops to the ground. Some slam into it, as if being yanked by some invisible rope. Others cower, hail from a few perfectly placed clouds pelting their faces and hands.

"You've exhausted yourself." Evren clasps Tallulah's hands in his, shaking his head. I can't decide if there are more freckles on his face or blood splatters. His sword hangs from his hip, dripping red. "We've all exhausted ourselves," he says, turning to Jarek and I.

"You need to—" I'm cut off by a guard to my right, his blade nicking my shoulder. I dodge just as he swings it again, this time it barely misses the top of my head.

Jarek groans and when I brave a glance, he is going toe-to-toe with another guard. His ax straining, the red in his face spreading to his neck.

"Tallulah!" Evren shouts as he swings his blade, stopping a man just before he reaches her.

The light stone ground is painted red. Another gush of air hits me as the guard tries again with his sword, but he misses and that's when I call my magick, whispering to the rain falling from the sky, coercing it to turn to flame. As the man before me burns, a satisfied smile spreads across my face.

But all too soon, it slips away when I glance back at Sam and a guard is there, a blade to her skin.

"No!" I lunge myself forward just as he swipes it, a line of red beading across the delicate skin of her throat. She drops to the ground, her eyes rolling in the back of her head. The man raises his blade again, but all in a breaths time, Jarek is there, with his ax embedded in the man's stomach.

"Sam," Jarek drops his bloodied ax to the ground.

Sam coughs, her eyes resuming their natural color. "I'm okay," she says, her voice hoarse. "He didn't cut me deep." She sits up, her breaths short.

"We can't continue on like this," Evren says, holding Tallulah up. Her face has gone pale while her palms are angry and red.

"We're not alone." Sam nods to the courtyard where all I see is guard after guard swarming toward us. She holds a hand to her throat, pressing against a wound I fear is much worse than she's letting on. "Enchantress spirits." She glances at me and then to Tallulah. "I just need to open myself up again—"

"No." Jarek's voice is firm but Sam brushes him off, holding her hands in the air. "You'll run your magick dry. Not to mention the risk—"

"I'm not afraid, Jarek," she says and then her eyes meet mine and I know what we must do.

Together.

"Neither am I," I say. Squaring my shoulders, I clench and unclench my fists, looking between Jarek and Evren. "You need to get as many people as you can outside of the gate. Take the pups, Alaric and Ruse will stay with me."

Ruse barks, her teeth barred.

She's just as ready as I am.

"I want to fight," Tallulah says, but as she steps out of Evren's grip her knees go slack. Her face crumples, something broken and defeated passing over it.

"You've done more than enough, Tallulah," I say. "The others will need you, please. Go with them."

She glances up at me through her dark lashes and nods.

"It's too dangerous," Jarek says, grasping my shoulder. I place my hand on his, but only for a moment, before Sam fires an arrow and Evren is swinging his blade.

"There is no more time, Jarek! Get as many people out as you can."

His attention directs to Sam, to the red trickling from her neck. He nods and then he's ushering herds of people outside of the gates, leaving Sam and I to fend off the rest of the guards.

I quickly assess the remaining guards before my eyes drift to the people fleeing to the forest.

For so long, I feared my existence would be nothing more than a hollow shell moving across the shadows of the earth. Death, teetering at the edges of my mind, a sweet promise never quite fulfilled. But now I've seen death. Seen all it threatens to take from me. And while I do not fear it, I no longer welcome it.

Sam steps next to me, her final arrow trembling in her fingertips.

My fingertips burn, my palms heating. I glance at Sam again, her bow hanging at her sides, her face bloodied.

"This is it, Sam," I shout against the rising storm of guards now charging from the castle. Most everyone else has left the courtyard and it's just me and Sam and our magick.

Her eyes slide to her left, then to her right, as if she's seeking approval from someone who isn't there. My stomach drops as I watch her face, speckled with crimson.

"I'm ready." She closes her eyes briefly before they snap open again, milky and white.

Ruse and Alaric don't wait for my orders before they're charging toward the guards. A few turn and run, not realizing just how much the wolves love the chase.

As the last wave of guards approach, I take a steadying breath and raise my hands.

The two guards before me fall to their knees, grasping at their chests as their lungs fill with dirt. Sam brushes my arm, her eyes are glazed, her wrists still raised.

"Sam!" I shake her, but she doesn't budge.

My heart races as two more guards approach her side, but I don't have time to stop them before another reaches me on my left. His blade nicks my arm, warmth spreading through my tunic. But my magick and I have grown comfortable these last few weeks and now it's almost as natural as breathing. I move my wrist, calling to the rain to turn to ice and impale the guard's neck.

I turn as he drops and my eyes go wide as Sam remains in the same position, unmoving, with a dozen dead guards at her feet.

Guard after guard filters toward us, some dropping before they make it a few steps, others managing to weave through the invisible soldiers Sam somehow has control over and make it close enough for me to steal the air from their lungs or better yet turn it to fire.

The wolves haven't stopped either, their coats matted and teeth red.

The courtyard soon falls quiet. The wolves have disappeared beyond where I can see but pride and rage and joy all war in my chest and I exhale.

We've *won*.

Sam falls, bumping my side with a yelp. Her cheek hits the ground and her eyes snap open, vibrant as flames.

"Sam." I drop down and grasp her arm. "You have to get up!"

She cradles her head and moans.

A boot slams into my back, shoving my face into the cobblestone next to Sam. She winces as she attempts to stand and is met with the heel of a boot to the side of her face.

"Filthy," a man snarls.

I squirm, attempting to get free, but the iron burns as my wrists are locked together once again.

FIFTY

SAMARIA

"GET OFF OF HER!" MY THROAT STINGS AS I SCREAM, the wound from the guard, festering. I kick my legs, biting any hand that dares come close to my face, but the guards don't stop until they've drug both Elora and I to our feet.

Her cheeks are fiery, hair plastered to her face, and her wrists... My stomach knots as metal grates in my ears.

"Put your hands out." A guard steps forward, so I spit in his face. He turns but it's too late. He wipes his face before his fist connects with my jaw and I'm seeing stars.

"Sam!" Elora growls, kicking her feet out.

The wolves howl next to us, and I manage to crack my eyes open just enough to see that they've been tied down.

Elwyn and Celia are at my sides, their hands clean and hair neatly combed despite how hard they fought only moments ago.

Who knew being a Spiritwalker meant also channeling the dead. My magick has depleted since using it. But I wouldn't change it. They saved our arses more times than I can count.

A tear runs down my cheek, stinging the bruised areas.

"Hey," I say over my shoulder to Elora, just as darkness begins to encompass my vision.

Thick clouds blanket the sky, dark and ominous. Thunder cracks in the distance, a low rumbling of promise that the worst has yet to come. Elora looks up, her golden eyes wide, feral.

"At least we're together." My voice cracks on the last word and her face falls.

The final clasp of iron around my wrist is like a death sentence. Inevitable yet terrifying all the same. We're dragged forward and just when my vision wanes, I hear it.

My knees buckle as the sound of horns come from the harbor. The guard holding me doesn't catch my fall, and my knees smack to the ground.

"What was that?" he asks his companion. They both shrug just as the horn sounds again, this time much closer. My head is spinning and I know Elora can't be in better shape, but there must be something we can do with the guards distracted. Must be some way...

Another blast of the horn, and the guard drops my arms completely to cover his ears. I'm a bit envious I can't do the same as the horn blares over and over again, but I use the noise to my advantage. Rising to my feet, I keep light on my toes, raising my arms over the guards head and then quickly slamming them down so his throat is pressed against my locked wrists.

Then, I squeeze.

The guard holding Elora drops her, coming to his friend's aid, but he doesn't make it far before Elora attacks, her teeth digging into the flesh of his calf. From the amount of blood pooling on the ground, I suspect she's more wolf than she thinks.

When my guard has stopped squirming, I release him and he drops to the ground.

"You'll pay—" The guard holding Elora stops, his body crumpling forward onto the stone ground, an arrow protruding from his back.

Elora and I glance to the castle, to the many windows lining the front, but it's too far to make anyone out.

Elora sways as I pull her to her feet.

"Are you all right?"

She nods, but doesn't speak, her chin still stained red. When I'm sure she won't fall, I leave her side and swipe the keys from the guard's belt. When we're both unchained, I grab her and hold her as close to me as possible. I lost her once already, but twice would have been the end of who I am as a person. There would be no coming back from that. No—

"Samaria!"

Elora and I break apart, her eyes lighting up.

"Jarek!" I shout, running toward him and the wolves. He must have freed Alaric and Ruse on his way to us, but they follow at a safe distance, keeping the puppies in a tight herd between themselves and Jarek.

"We must hurry." Jarek's eyes go wide as he grabs my hand and trudges forward. We move past the bodies of the guards, past the wreckage from Elora's magick and from mine.

I flick my wrists up, opening the communication between this realm and the next. Pain lances through my palms, but when I see the spirits are still there, it eases. All the women who fought beside me, some young, some ancient crowd around me. The magick in their souls swims with mine, lighting a path of gold light before me.

"You saved us," I tell them.

Too many voices sound at once. I can't understand what they say until Celia steps forward. Her eyes, the same dark brown as Sorin's, her face much too young.

"You saved yourself, Sam." She reaches to brush the curls from my face but her hand drifts through me, my energy much too low to keep the bridge between us strong. *"Go."*

She gestures for me to follow Jarek and Elora and as I do, the other spirits form a line on either side of me. Whispering words of encouragement, of praise, of love. Not just for their families that remain on the other side, but for *me.*

Another horn sounds, this time much closer and Jarek doesn't slow, his feet carry him swiftly through the woods just outside the castle grounds. He glances at me over his shoulder, and while I expect sadness or fury, instead he grins. I tilt my head, still stumbling behind him, when Elora catches my hand.

"Okay?"

I nod. "Okay."

Elora tugs my hand, forcing me to stop. "I need to go find Sorin." She glances back at the castle and as much as my heart hates it, I let her hand go. "I'll see you—"

"When I see you."

Smiling, she turns and sprints just as Jarek grabs my arm. We weave our way out of the last of the brambles and that's when I realize we're heading for the cliffs on the east side of the castle.

"Jarek!"

He doesn't stop, doesn't slow, until we've reached the cliff edge where the harbor waits below.

Bending, I brace myself on my knees, my chest heaving and lungs burning. But before I can scold Jarek for this waste of time, a final horn sounds. This time loud enough that I jump back and cover my ears.

Jarek cheers, screaming something in Scandavi I don't understand. He waves his arms through the air and I follow his stare.

Down to the harbor to where a fleet of ships waits.

All bearing the white and yellow Scandavi flag.

We rush forward, glancing over the edge of the wall that separates the castle from the cliffside. The horns from earlier blasts again and climbing up the wall are dozens and dozens of men and women. They're dressed in leathers and furs, their hair all braided, or shaved on the sides. Ink marks any exposed skin, and when they reach the ledge and topple over, their weapons shine as they begin to slice through the few remaining guards.

My breaths hitch.

They look exactly like Jarek.

A woman with blonde hair woven in several different braids climbs over the ledge several feet down from us, her hands bloody, but her face is bright.

Jarek sprints in her direction, and when the woman sees him, she drops her weapon and meets him halfway. My throat tightens as they embrace each other, her fingers clawing at his arms, as if she can't possibly get him close enough.

My stomach knots as I walk toward them, fingers lacing together in front of me.

"Sam," Jarek says through a laugh, "this is Cora. My younger sister."

My stomach flips, my expression clearly confused because Cora and Jarek both laugh. "Oh. I'm so happy to meet—"

"Yeah, yeah," she says. The dark paint under her eyes only enhances their blue color, the color of seaglass, just like Jarek. Her Teravian isn't terrible, but I strain my ear to make sure I'm hearing her correctly. "I'm just glad we made it in time to help your sorry arse." She punches Jarek in the arm, and he grabs her to ruffle her hair. "The guards on the coast were not happy with our arrival, but we took care of them." She smooths her braids, casting Jarek and I a wink.

"How is that you're here?" The question is out before I mean to ask it.

"Ah," Cora says, slipping free from Jarek's grip. "We got word a few weeks ago that Jarek was still alive, so we sailed the next morning. Would have come a hell of a lot sooner if it hadn't been for the Mother-damned sea. It's been raging for years, we've barely made it off the island before now and even so, we hardly made it this time."

"But it was calm?" I ask, hope lining my voice. "The sea, I mean. It was calm?"

She tilts her head, the long, loose braids she wears slipping over her shoulder.

If the sea has calmed, I could join Jarek so much sooner... Or he could visit me and—

"Not really." She shrugs, dousing my hope. "Lost an entire ship, but still calmer than it's been since I watched this big lug sail away without me four years ago." She pinches his arm. "Figured it was worth the risk to see if the word was true."

Jarek smiles before grabbing his sister again.

"I could kill you for disobeying me and leaving," he says, playfulness lining his voice. "But damn if I'm not happy to see you."

Cora smirks, squaring her shoulders.

"Who sent you word?" I bite my tongue, promising myself it's my last question.

Cora fixes her gaze on Jarek, then on me. Maybe he thinks I miss the shake of his head, but I don't and now even more questions begin to arise. Cora picks at her nails. "Calix something. I can't remember."

Calix Winterborne, Lord of the Onyx.

I recall him and Jarek meeting for the first time. Their odd interaction, the way Calix had clasped his hands together as if in prayer.

"Enough chatter," Cora says. "Nasty wound you got there." She points to my neck. "Let's get you cleaned up along with the rest of this shithole."

FIFTY-ONE

SORIN

ROMAN STRUGGLES AGAINST ME AS I HOLD HIS BACK to my chest. The blade's on the ground, just out of reach.

I squeeze him tighter. "Would you stop it?"

"No." He bites my hand.

I drop my hold, pushing him off me. "Did you just bite me?"

"You wouldn't let me go."

Sighing, I run a hand down my face and push past him, making a conscious effort not to look at the bed while I head for the door.

I'm two steps away, when I hesitate. Turning, I locate my blade on the ground but don't bother trying for it. If Roman really wished to hurt himself, he'd find a way. "Call off your guard."

He licks his lips, before glancing at the window. "And what makes you think they'll listen to me?"

I step toward him again, my peripherals catching on a lock of blonde to my left, making my stomach twist. "You are the King of Teravie," I say, "so fucking act like it."

He flinches before something passes over his face. As if he has forgotten who he is the whole time. Forgotten what power comes from such a title. What privilege. Forgotten that, despite what he's done, he has the control to reshape the future.

He smooths his dark hair back, straightens his shirt. "I'll go now."

A horn sounds from outside, loud enough to have Roman and I both flinching.

What the fuck was that?

We both dart to the window, and when I see Elora and Sam in shackles, my heart stops.

"Fuck," I mutter, pulling an arrow from my quiver.

"You'll never—"

My arrow slices through the air. Soaring impossible lengths, until it lands in the back of a guard, dropping him to his knees.

"Call them off now, Roman." My heart races as I head for the door but it's kicked open before I reach it. A guard is there at the threshold.

"Your Majesty," he says, peering around me. "We—" He pauses when his eyes snag on Galen on the bed.

"You were just who I was coming to find, Stefan," Roman says. "Call off the rest of the men. This is over."

"You killed him," Stefan says, dismissing Roman's orders. "Or was it you?" He turns his attention to me, and before I can grab an arrow, he pulls his sword and lunges. I jump back but fumble, falling to the ground.

"Drop your weapon!" Roman steps forward. "That was a direct—"

Stefan turns his attention from me, swinging toward Roman.

"You really think I'll listen to you," Stefan says, lunging again. Roman dodges, his eyes wide. "You would be nothing if not for him and this is how you repay him." He swings his sword, nicking Roman's arm.

Jumping to my feet, I forgo my bow and instead reach for the dagger. Stefan has Roman cornered. His sword is angled for

Roman's heart, and as he pushes it down, I reach him, slicing through his uniform, right between his ribs.

Gasping, he spins toward me, eyes aflame but face blanched.

I yank my blade out of his side and am ready to end his life when he tackles me, sending me backward. My dagger falls to the ground, and I scramble to reach it but Stefan pulls me back. He screams, clutching his side but he somehow finds his sword, the cool metal pressing against my neck.

I reach for my knife again, but Stefan's blade pushes against my sternum.

"Enough of this!" Roman shouts.

Stefan raises his sword, aiming for my heart, but when he lunges to plunge it into me, Roman jumps between us, taking the brunt of the hit.

His body falls on mine, the blade protruding from his chest. "No."

I'm trapped under him as Stefan pulls the blade free. Blood pools from Roman's chest as I roll him off of me.

The guard laughs, clutching his side. "You'd swear *fealty* to that?" He snarls in Roman's direction, whose face is pale, his body crumpled on the floor. "Always been spineless, even with Galen by his side."

He raises his sword again, but I don't give him another moment to speak before I sling my dagger forward, landing it directly in his eye. He screams, dropping his sword, grappling for the dagger. His movements are too stunned, and I finish him off with a swift puncture to his throat.

I scramble back to Roman's side. His entire abdomen is soaked in blood, his eyes fighting to stay open. "Let me help you." I reach for the amulet in my pocket. "I can fix this."

His hand wraps around mine. "Don't," he says. His breaths are labored, his green eyes hardly open. "Let me do one good thing. Amidst all of the terrible—" He closes his eyes, a tear slipping down his cheek. "Let me do one good thing."

He pats my hand, so I remove it from my pocket, leaving the amulet inside.

"No more taking what isn't mine." He shakes his head, more tears streaming down his face. I cup the back of his head, trying to angle him better so he can breathe.

"I'm sorry I didn't know you," I say and for whatever reason I mean it.

The wolves howl from outside and my body goes rigid. *Elora.*

"I was never great company anyway." Roman smiles again, but this time it's weak and broken. "Go."

"I won't leave you here." I shake my head. "Not like this."

He pushes my hand away, more blood rushing from the wound in his stomach.

If only he'd let me use the amulet to heal him... I glance to where the other necklace lies across the room.

"This is where I belong, Sorin." His eyes close, his chest slowing. He takes another slow and labored breath. "I'm not a good person. I'm not like you."

"You could be," I say. "I see it—"

"No." He shakes his head, a small wince escaping his lips. "Do you know what most people would do when faced with evil?"

The blaring horn sounds again from outside. I swallow against the thickness in my throat as his eyes meet mine.

"They'd turn and run for their lives. And do you know what I did?"

I shake my head, ignoring the blood soaking through to the floor.

"I leaned in and kissed evil goodnight."

He laughs but it's quiet and broken. "You and I are not the same, and I'm glad for it." He closes his eyes again, his face somehow paler than before. "Besides, I'm not afraid of death."

My chest cracks as his breathing falters. "No?" I ask and a faint smile curls up the sides of his lips.

"No," he whispers, "because in death, I'll finally be free."

I wait several more moments by Roman's side. Wait for his breathing to increase and his eyes to open.

They never do.

When his chest falls for the final time, I pull two coins from the bedside table and place them over his eyes.

I scoop up the other amulet and shove it in my pocket, not willing to risk it being left for anyone to find.

With a final look at Galen and then at Roman, I slip from the room with a new determination in my steps.

I need to find my wife.

BY THE TIME I make it to the courtyard, it's empty aside from the bodies of bloodied and mutilated guards. My stomach churns, hands trembling as I nock an arrow.

"Elora!" My voice echoes back to me, and as my knees begin to give out, a familiar voice drifts through the courtyard.

"Sorin."

I spin toward the east.

There she is. Running toward me, blood staining her face and clothes, hair unbound, flowing behind her.

Six wolves in tow.

My queen.

My heart.

The other half to my soul.

She collides into me, her arms wrapping around my neck. My fingers tangle in her hair as I breathe her in. "You're okay, love?"

She nods, still pressed firmly against me. "You?"

"I'm okay." I run my fingers through her hair, down her back, and up again before she finally lets me go. Despite the constant rain, blood still coats her face and under her nails. "Sam and Jarek? The others?"

"Everyone is safe, at least I think." She brushes my hair from my forehead. "Roman?"

I bite my tongue. "He's gone."

Her brows pinch, a wash of worry sweeping across her face.

"Galen is dead. Roman got to him before I did and Roman he—"

Elora's body stiffens, her hands gripping tighter across my back.

"He saved my life."

She leans away just far enough so I can see her face. "I'm sorry."

Shaking my head, I twist my finger around her loose hair. "Do you think we've done it? Have we stopped the blight?"

Her brow furrows. "Not yet," she says and I don't question how she knows. "You and I together were sent back here to heal Teravie. To protect it. To ensure that no harm comes to Enchantresses."

I nod, unable to speak for the first time perhaps in my entire life.

"If Roman killed Galen, would that mean we failed?" she asks.

"No." Sera joins us. Her arms are crossed, a smile tugging at her lips. "Glad you made it, heir." She pats my shoulder, giving Elora a quick nod.

"And how would you know of ending the blight?" Elora asks.

"When you've been imprisoned long enough, there's not much else to do other than learn. Read. *Listen* to others." She steps closer, grabbing my hand, then Elora's. "I sensed you out here, I just left the council room." She glances between Elora and myself. "You two are the very soul of Teravie, not just Bastian and Soleil. But the soul of our country."

She clasps our hands together and a sting shoots up my palm from where we sliced our flesh open in the Wicked Wood.

"You made a vow to protect us, so do it." She gestures to our hands. "And when you're finished, the council is waiting for you. The Lords of Jade and Onyx got to them before I did. Found them hiding in the cellars." She saunters back to the castle, holding her hands out to the pouring rain.

After she's gone, it's just Elora and I in the courtyard. A breeze blows past us, bringing saltwater and brine from the nearby coast. "What do we need to do, love?"

"Blood and bone," she whispers. "We gave our blood to the Wicked Wood to close it, maybe that's what we need to do here." Her eyes are frantic, glancing past me. "There."

She points over my shoulder so I turn. And there, in the middle of the courtyard is a well, carved deep into the stone ground. She pulls me toward it and unease washes over me.

I've been here before.

As we stand before the well, she grabs the blade from my hip, reopening the wound on her hand. She winces, before holding it out for me. "Your turn." I hesitate but she grabs my hand before I can argue. She slices along the barely healed wound from earlier. "Blood."

"What about bone?" Blood trickles from my hand, pooling into my palm.

"The magick," she says. "We give it back."

I pull the amulets from my pockets and set one of them in her palm.

I wrap Roman's amulet in my hand, the buzzing of magick thrumming against my skin.

"Take my hand, husband." Elora smiles as I slide my free hand in hers. The blood of her body, the bone of the many Enchantresses killed, and the blood of my own.

Angling our hands over the well, a few droplets land, stirring the black water below. Elora whispers something, a prayer, a plea, I can't be certain before she opens her hand, letting the amulet fall to the bottom.

I do the same.

The gold chain flashes briefly before it splashes into the water, disappearing into the murky pool. The breeze from before stops, the sudden stillness clawing at my skin and all at once, the rain ceases.

Mine and Elora's breathing is the only noise between us until a bubbling sounds from the bottom of the pool. Peering over the ledge, I see our blood staining the stone as the water below hisses and spits. I almost tell Elora it's time to run when a figure rises from the water.

Holding my breath, I glance at Elora whose eyes are wide, but her lips are turned up.

A woman rises from the pool, her long, flowing hair the color of moss. Her jade eyes vibrant against her dark skin. When she smiles, thousands of tiny, purple flowers erupt over her body, covering her from breast to foot.

"You called to me, daughter," the woman says, her voice like birdsong and honeybees.

"Mother Gaia." Elora gasps, dropping to her knee. I do the same, my head spinning. "Forgive us," she whispers. "See our sacrifice and—"

"You came back," Gaia says, her long limbs reaching for Elora. She tucks her finger under Elora's chin, tilting her head up. "When I needed you most, you came back." The Mother smiles. Butterflies land on her shoulders, fluttering into her hair. "You have freed me. Freed them."

She sweeps her hand across the courtyard where hundreds of gold flecks of light spiral into the sky.

"Spirits. Enchantresses," Gaia says, turning her attention back to Elora. "Never forget who you are."

She brushes her finger along Elora's cheekbone, a tiny sprig sprouting from the back of her hand. When she pulls away, a new stone has been placed around Elora's neck.

Gaia sweeps her arms again and she, too, disappears into the wind.

The bleak sky breaks with the promise of sun, the birds chirp, and as I take my wife's hand, that piece of myself that belongs only to her sings.

INSIDE THE COUNCIL ROOM, my stomach sloshes and my hands can't decide where to rest.

My pockets?

Too casual for a king.

My hips?

Ridiculous.

Elora must notice my fidgeting because she takes one and my shoulders relax. Our bandages wrapped around our freshly sliced wounds are still tinted pink with blood.

This. This is the perfect place for my hand.

A council woman with dark hair cropped close to her scalp gestures for us to sit. When I do, I realize it's not just the council. Thaddeus, Calix, Oletta, and Mordona sit on the opposite end.

"When did you—"

Thaddeus raises interrupts, raising an ancient hand. "A story for another time."

"Sorin Rudhek," the councilwoman from before says, "the Guilds have provided us with your official decree of birth." She pulls a pair of tiny spectacles from her pocket, slips them on, before taking out the piece of parchment I've memorized since I was fifteen. "On this day, the twelfth day of Summer, Celia Aisling has given birth to a son to be named after his father's great, great grandfather; Sorin Rudhek III."

She glances at me over the paper, my hands slick with sweat but Elora doesn't drop them.

"By the country of Teravie, King Silas Rudhek and Celia Aisling claim this child as their own." She sets the parchment down, placing her spectacles on top before folding her hands. "And you are Sorin Rudhek IV?"

It's difficult to swallow, even more difficult to speak but somehow I find a way. "Yes."

Murmurs and whispers sound from the other council members but the woman's gaze remains on me.

"And are the rumors true?" She drops her voice low and the murmurs around the table begin to quiet. "Are you who they say? King Bastian and Queen Soleil?"

Elora's grip tightens around mine as she clears her throat. "Yes," she says, more surety in that one word than I've heard in her voice ever before. I don't know why but it fills me with pride. "Their souls live on. In us." She glances at me and heat rises to my cheeks.

"Gentleman," the councilwoman says, demanding the attention of each of the other members. They give her a nod, as if their decision has been made long before I arrived. "From this moment forth, Sorin Rudhek IV, shall take his place as the rightful heir to Teravie."

My chest deflates, the pent up air finally spilling from them, and for a moment, I wonder if I'm dreaming. If I somehow made this entire moment up. Surely this can't be real? After everything we've gone through—

Elora squeezes my hand, bringing me to the present.

"Thank you, councilwoman," I manage to say. She nods, reclining in her chair. "Thank you, all."

The other members seem less impressed but I catch Mordona and Oletta's eye, their promise for payment for their aid ringing in my mind. The council members stand, raising their glasses before them.

"To Sorin Rudhek," they say. "Long live the king!"

FIFTY-TWO

ELORA

MY EYES CROSS AS I SIGN YET ANOTHER PIECE OF parchment. It's been two weeks since we fought for our lives in the courtyard of Valebridge. Two weeks since Roman died. Two weeks since Mother Gaia has been freed, and in those two weeks, the paperwork hasn't stopped for a moment. The Stones have been placed in a secret trove that only myself and Sorin knows about. There's some relief in that, I suppose.

But between coronation preparation and rebuilding what's been damaged, there is always something to do.

Growling, I toss my quill down and rub my eyes. "Who knew becoming a queen meant filling out so much bloody paperwork."

Sam laughs, flipping through the pages of a book much too quickly to actually be reading. "Your mother says you were a terrible student." She clamps her mouth shut and my stomach clenches. She glances at me, then just over my shoulder.

"Is she..." I follow her gaze, looking over my shoulder. Nothing but a bookcase greets me back. "Is she here right now?"

"Yes," Sam says, drawing out the word. She sets the book down and places her hands in her lap.

"And does she still have that message for me?"

Sam nods, her dark curls bouncing. "Yes." She leans forward in her chair. "But only if you're ready, of course." She bites her bottom lip, eyes drifting again over my shoulder.

Several weeks ago, I couldn't imagine hearing a message from my mother. Couldn't imagine the wounds it would re-open or the pain it would bring. But after everything we've gone through, after the realization of mine and Sorin's connection, I've never felt more ready to face something. Have never felt stronger or more alive.

No more running.

"I'm ready." I take a deep breath, my body keenly aware of the cold spot over my shoulder. My stomach somersaults, fear snaking its way around my heart, but this time, I push back. Not letting it control like I so often have.

"Okay." Sam exhales through her nose, shaking her hands slightly before flicking her wrists up. "She wants you to know that she loves you."

I smile. "Of course. I know that."

"She also wants you to know..." She sets her hands down, cutting the connection.

"Sam?"

"Sorry." Sam attempts and fails to laugh. A tear wells in her eye but she blinks it away. "She wants you to know that you were never alone out there. Not for a single moment."

My mind flashes to the nights in the woods just after she died. The shivering cold and terrible noises that come from the forest after dark.

"She was with you, every step of the way."

Tears sting my eyes, the cold in the corner drifting closer.

Sam's hands raise again. "She also wants you to know..." She cocks her head to the side, confusion pinching her brows. "She wants you to know that whenever you need her, whenever you miss her, just listen to the wind." She shrugs, placing her hands in her lap again. "Whatever that means."

But I know exactly what it means. My chest cracks and the dam that's been holding my emotions breaks with it.

The wind has whispered to me before, in the darkest moments of solitude when my blade was heavy and my mind was weak.

Not yet, little susi, it said to me. And I listened to it, in the darkness of my cabin. I let its whispering tendrils wrap around me like a hug. I let it be the thing that saved me from myself even when I did not know it.

"Thank you, Sam."

"Knock, knock." Calix pops the door open. "I came to say goodbye."

I wave him in and Evren and Tallulah come in behind him.

Standing from my desk, I quickly smooth my tunic and comb my wild hair. "I'm sorry I wasn't expecting—"

"Don't," Tallulah says, "you're lovely. And besides, you're the queen now, you can do whatever you want." She smiles and then there's another knock at the door.

Jarek and Sorin, the last to enter. Sorin's wearing his usual black attire, our country's new crest pinned to his left lapel.

A wolf surrounded by four stones.

The five of them settle around the settee near the fire, leaving Calix and I to speak. "I—"

"Will you—"

We both laugh when we speak over each other and that's when I really study him. I let myself see all the parts of him I pushed away before. The slight bend to his nose, the golden flecks of his hair. The way he enters most rooms with a crease between his brow but quickly softens depending on who's there. So many parts of myself live in him and vice-versa.

"The Onyx Guild is a quick few days away," he says, sticking his hands in his pockets. "Will you visit? I mean of course, after you've settled here." He runs his hands through his hair. "What am I saying, you're the queen. How silly of me to request—"

I place my hand on his arm and his breath hitches. "I would love to visit."

His smile brightens his entire face, and when he goes to hug me, I let him. And it doesn't feel forced or foreign. It feels like a hug of trust and a bit of sorrow, lined with a future full of dinners and laughter and memories if he's willing to share them.

"I don't have much authority to say this," he whispers, still grasping me tight, "but I'm so proud of you and there's no doubt your mother would be too. Getting to know you will be my greatest honor."

My throat burns as I swallow and when he finally lets me go, I wish he wouldn't.

Sorin joins us, his hand finding the small of my back.

"Your Majesty." Calix dips his head, then winks before slipping out the door, leaving a smile plastered across my face.

"When do you leave?" Sam asks, hugging Tallulah and then a reluctant Evren.

"In a few days," Tallulah says. "I want to ensure anyone who was injured has their plan in place for care." Evren grabs her hand and she swings into his side.

We lost so many during the fight, a truth I haven't had the time to face.

Evren turns to me. "I wanted to thank you—"

"You don't have to." I hold my hands in the air.

Evren studies me for a moment, chewing his bottom lip. "But we do. We owe you so much." He dips his head, then so does Tallulah and I feel as though I may faint. Tallulah offers me a quick hug, and when I get to Evren, he takes my hand in his, bending to place a kiss on the back of it. "Long live the queen."

With Evren and Tallulah gone to find Thaddeus, it's just Sam, Jarek, Sorin, and I in the room. We take a seat by the fire, going over again and again all the things we must do in the days to come.

But as the chatter brews next to me, I glance to the window

and catch sight of the most marvelous thing I've ever seen and the voice around me fade.

A single crow sits perched outside my window, silver eyes looking in.

THE ROOM IS SUFFOCATING as I sit atop a tufted, patterned throne. Gold filigree lines the arms and back. I trace the seam, finding comfort in the consistent pattern that runs along the edge of the throne.

My hair is braided around my head, adorned with a crown of thorns and flowers. The gown that was chosen for me is made of deep, green silk and it does nothing to help the hotness I feel creeping over my skin.

I run my fingers down the buttery fabric, and despite how uncomfortable it is, I can't deny its beauty. After Sorin and I were sworn in, one of the first demands after freeing Enchantresses and rectifying the use of magick was changing the colors. So, instead of the navy that's haunted my dreams, Sorin and I wear matching green.

Like the forest.

The guard shoves the hunter forward again, and as Sorin and I rise, everyone in the room takes a knee.

Except for him.

I hold my chin high as the hunter's dark eyes meet mine. Sorin, who has been at my side, steps forward. His suit fits snug across his broad shoulders and chest and atop his head a small crown of golden thorns.

"You will bow before your queen until she says otherwise." Sorin's tone sends a shiver down my spine.

My staggered breathing is all I can hear as the rest of the room falls silent. Keeping my eyes on the hunter, he drops down to his knees. Sorin opens his mouth again, but I place a hand on his forearm, and he snaps his mouth shut.

As I step forward, the wolves join me. "State your name, hunter."

Sorin's hand flexes in my peripherals. The hunter remains silent at first, his face contorting into disgust.

"Your queen asked you a question." Sorin takes another step forward, the guards at the bottom of the dais stiffening.

"She is not my queen," he says. "Just as you are not my king—"

The guard behind the hunter tightens his grip, yanking his hair back and whispering things I cannot hear.

I clench my jaw, fingers clamped tightly together as I make my way off the dias until I'm only a few feet from the prisoner. "You were a sworn hunter to King Roman, is that correct?"

The man grunts, his eyes narrowed.

"Do you deny the crimes you committed, hunter?"

"No." He shakes his head as the guard grips the back of his neck, whispering something in his ear again. "No, *Your Majesty*."

The wolves at my sides lower their heads, but as I run a finger down the Ruse's back, they settle. "The punishment for your crimes is death. Are you aware of this?"

"Yes, Your Majesty."

My throat tightens, but I force myself to keep my chin held high.

He deserves this, susi.

A few beats of silence pulse through the throne room.

"However," I say. "Lady Mordona of the Bloodstone Guild has happily agreed to take one more prisoner to aid in the mining of the Montrok Caves."

The room murmurs, faint whispers echoing against the stone walls. The last of the guards and hunters around Teravie have all been tried and either killed or sent to the caves of the

Bloodstone Guild for mining, as Sorin suggested for repayment for her help.

The Montrock Caves are the farthest point South in Teravie. I'm not sure the sentence is much of a kindness considering how cruel Lady Mordona is known to be. Not to mention the legends of the magickal beings that reside in the caves. Known to keep to the dark, hoarding the precious gems for themselves.

"I'll ask you again to state your name," I say, bending down so only he can hear me.

"Frederick Bellthorn," he says with a thick swallow.

"Frederick Bellthorn," I repeat. "You have hurt countless Enchantress, have aided in one of the most brutal slaughters our country has ever seen. Have devastated an entire nation."

He has the audacity to smile, and my magick pushes against my skin at the sight.

"I regret none of it, Your Majesty," he snarls. "You and that bastard will see. When the Enchantresses overtake you, you'll see how wrong you were to give them their freedom back."

My magick snakes through my palms, settling around the oxygen flowing through his lungs. "Speak ill of my husband again," I say, pressing my magick tighter and tighter, "and it will be the last thing you do."

His eyes bulge, the lack of air turning his face blue.

I drop my hands and take a step backward. "Lady Mordona is waiting for you," I say over my shoulder before glancing at my guards. "Take him away."

FIFTY-THREE

SAMARIA

IN THE LAST SEVERAL WEEKS, ELORA AND SORIN HAVE been so wrapped up with meetings that I've hardly seen them, save for rare visits to Elora's office. Jarek and Cora have also been inseparable, getting ready for their departure and catching up on years of missed conversations.

We made a trip to Loxley; Agnes, Ulric, Sorin, Elora, and myself. I thought seeing the destruction first hand would somehow close the gap in my heart. Would allow the grief that's been swallowing me up to heal, but all it did was remind me of how much we've lost. How much we'll never get back.

Today, I'm making myself busy in the infirmary. Helping Tallulah the best I can as she mixes salves and remedies for the ill and injured. One of her hands is bandaged, open sores where she overused her magick still on the mend, yet she refuses to stop her work.

"Hand me that yarrow, will you?" She points to a bundle of dried white flowers and like one of the spirits that so often visit, I drift to it and hand it to her without thought. "Thank you."

She begins crushing the flowers and I watch her mindlessly, the methodic pounding of her mortar and pestle soothing me.

But then the pounding stops. "What is going on with you, Samaria?"

Snapping out of my daze, Tallulah has her arms crossed, ivy curling around her forearms like serpents. Since Roman died and Sorin and Elora were sworn in, the use of Enchantress magick has been restored and the thought is both exhilarating and terrifying.

Dozens of Enchantresses have come forth, some having found refuge in the forests much like Tallulah and Elora. Others, finding sanctuary high in the north, surviving in the cruelty of the tallest mountains. All, however, seemed to make it back to see the king and queen be crowned. To see magick restored.

To see *hope* restored.

"I don't know," I admit, leaning against one of the metal tables in the infirmary of the castle. "There's been so much change the last few weeks... few days, even. My mind is having a hard time comprehending everything." I offer a small smile but Tallulah doesn't seem to believe it and gives me a hug.

"You don't need to be okay, you know that right? No one expects you to be strong all the time, Sam." She pulls away, tucking a piece of hair behind her ear.

"Thank you."

Her face brightens as she turns and resumes her work.

"What will happen with you and Evren? Back to the Jade Guild?"

She begins mashing the dried yarrow into bits of dust. "Yes, back to the Jade Guild. It's home." She shrugs. "For a long time I think Evren dreamt of something larger, something different. But we've grown happy there. Content."

She smiles, her eyes gazing out the small window of the room. "It took Evren longer than me to realize what we had right in front of us was more than enough. Life doesn't need to be overflowing with adventure to be purposeful. To have meaning. To be exquisite and worth remembering." She flicks her wrists to conjure a few more dried herbs to add to her mortar. "Although," she adds, "I have been offered a job." She smiles at me, crossing her arms. "From the Queen."

"Tallulah," I say with a smile. "That's incredible. And what will you do?"

"She's in need of a Head Enchantress," she says, continuing her work. "I'll help educate Enchantresses as well as aid those who have been in hiding for so long." She says it casually, her hands busy making whatever concoction she's created.

"There isn't anyone better suited for the job," I say. She turns to me, another smile swept across her face. "I'll leave you to it." I gesture to the herbs. "I need to go find my mother." I pause at the threshold of the door. "I'm really happy to know you, Tallulah."

Wiping her hands on her apron, she crosses her arms, leaning against the workbench, ivy swirling over her arms.

"Likewise, Samaria. Don't be a stranger, wherever life takes you."

It doesn't take long to find Agnes. She and Ulric arrived just before the coronation and they've been just as busy with meetings as Elora and Sorin have. Figuring out where Loxlians will go, if they will rebuild or start anew in Valebridge. My mother's face has relaxed these past few weeks, the stiffness in her walk eased, and a part of me has to wonder if it was the blight itself causing her so many ailments.

"Don't linger, Samaria," my mother says, noticing me in the doorway.

Elwyn and Celia join me, their spirits never far from my side. I keep my hands clasped together, not opening the bridge of communication.

"I just came to check on you, see how things are going." I slide into a chair across from her as Ulric hands me a cup of tea.

"Things are moving along," she says, smiling at Ulric as he sits next to her. "We lost quite a few during the battle." She frowns before shaking off whatever dark thought may have crossed her. "But there are still so many people to relocate."

"Relocate?" I set my tea on the side table. "Will they not rebuild?"

Agnes and Ulric share a glance before she lets out a long sigh.

"Loxley was our safe-haven," Agnes says. "That feeling of safety has been robbed from us." She shakes her head, but when Ulric slides his hand into hers, she relaxes. My throat bobs. "Sorin and Elora have taken the throne, with them everything changes. There's no reason for us to hide, Sam. We've all agreed our home will be here. In Valebridge, or perhaps for some, in Wickersham."

"Wait." I hold up my hands, clenching my teeth. "When was this decided? Why was I not involved?"

"Sam," Ulric says. I snap my gaze to him but my stern demeanor melts as soon as I meet his gray eyes. "You needn't worry about us, if that's what's holding you back."

"Holding me back? What are you—"

Agnes leans forward and grasps my hand in hers. "You think I don't know you, Sam," she says. "And while it's true my focus has been on Sorin, I've always known you. Maybe better than you think."

My hand trembles in hers. After the battle of Valebridge I learned so much about my brother's past. About him and Elora and the souls that live within them. I learned of Elwyn and Celia's part to ensure Sorin and Elora lived. I learned of my mother's role to keep Sorin safe until fate decided it was time for him and Elora to be reunited.

"Go live your life, Sam," she says. "Go see all the things you have not yet seen. Feel the things you haven't let yourself feel. This is always your home, you will always have a place here, but my daughter, you were born for so much more. Can't you see that?"

My eyes sting as she lets my hand go, and the reality of it

crashes into my chest. If I leave, there's no saying when I'll be back. "But I'll miss you."

She smiles, tears lining her eyes. "And I you. But he is your heart, Sam. You go where your heart goes." She glances at Ulric, his hand finding hers again.

A tear slips down my cheek as we stand, the three of us joining for a hug.

"We love you, Sam."

My throat burns, but I swallow down my emotion as I pull away. "I love you too."

"Now, go." She winks and waves me toward the door.

Just as I slip out, I glance behind me and catch Ulric kissing her cheek.

The race through the castle is dizzying, and I try my best to remember the way to the meeting room but end up getting lost, twice. It isn't until I find Sera and she guides me that I make it to Sorin and Elora's chambers.

For the first time in days, I find them not buried behind a mountain of paperwork, but instead toppled on top of each other on the settee near the fire.

"Do you *ever* knock?" Sorin scoffs, smoothing his hair and shirt. Elora sits up next, buttoning her shirt quickly but missing a few.

I cringe.

Gross.

"I'm sorry, it's urgent."

You go where your heart goes.

"Tell me leaving with Jarek is a terrible idea." My mind has played out every possible way leaving *is* a terrible idea, and surprisingly, it also showed me all the good it could bring. So I need them to confirm it. I need them to tell me what I should do.

They share a glance with each other. Their silence makes my fingers twitch as I pace through the room. "Loxley is gone, and with mother and Ulric aging surely it would be reckless for me to—"

"Sam." Sorin's hand lands on my arm and I stop.

"What? Why are you looking at me like that?"

Why are you looking at me like you're about to say goodbye?

"As much as I will miss my sister who loves nothing more than challenging me," he says, his grip firm around my arm, "I think you already know what you must do." His face softens, his hand slipping from me. "You are Samaria Trednik of Loxley. You don't need anyone's approval to make a decision about your future. Your country loves you, your people love you." He bends closer, so his words stuck between him and me. "I love you."

Elora joins us, her arm wrapping around Sorin's middle. "If you're looking for someone to tell you to stay, it isn't us."

They both smile and yet my stomach sinks.

"But—"

"Write as often as you can," Elora says. Her wrists are still scarred, but the pain must be less because she grasps me tightly.

"I'll miss you," she whispers against my ear.

When I pull away, I soak in the beauty of my queen. Golden hair to match her golden eyes, battle scars and a permanent crease between her brows. The most beautiful queen, Enchantress, sister, I've had the honor of knowing.

Sorin sighs dramatically, running a hand down his face. "You and Jarek have been annoyingly inseparable from the start, anyway. It only makes sense."

"You know," I say, crossing my arms. "You and I used to be annoyingly inseparable too, little brother."

A flicker of emotion passes his face, and I quickly look away.

"My point, exactly." He takes the two steps between us and wraps me tightly in his arms again, and I can't help the memory of him lifeless on the floor. I push away, and he frowns.

"I don't think I can do this."

"You can," he says. "You will. Now go before I exile you."

Rolling my eyes, I turn to Elora.

"Scandavi is only a few weeks away." She takes my hand. "The seas have calmed, there will be many opportunities to visit." She smiles, placing her fingers under my chin. "I'll see you when I see you?"

"See you when we see you." My stomach drops as I leave the room, closing the door behind me on not just my brother but an entire life. But something different presses into my mind.

Not something, but *someone*.

Outside, I squint against the bright sunlight, a rarity for this late in the rainy season, until I find Jarek on the docks. He and Cora's crew have been prepping the ships for days. Cupping my hands around my mouth, I shout across the docks. "Hey sailor!"

"I'm not a sailor—" He stops when he turns and sees me. "Sam?" Putting a crate down, he meets me halfway. "What are you doing out here?"

"Was wondering if you had room aboard for one more?"

Jarek's eyes light up, his mouth dropping open.

"Though, I suppose I should ask the real person in charge." I peek around him. "Where's Cora?"

He scoops me up, making me squeal. "You're coming?"

I lace my arms around the back of his neck.

"Are you sure? There will be time later, if you're not ready."

I press our foreheads together, savoring the scent of the salty sea mixed with pine. There's no one in the world that knows me better than Jarek, and when I told him I had to stay, he was willing to let me because he knew it's what I needed at the time.

I tangle my fingers in his long hair. He would have let me stay because he loves me that much. Enough to let me go. But also enough to let me choose.

And he is all the choices I've ever made manifested into one perfect person. "Yes, I'm coming," I say. "I go where my heart goes."

THE SHIP GROANS and sways as we pull into a small port several weeks later. I rub the sleep from my eyes, drinking in the misty covered cottages and jagged mountain landscape before me.

"Scandavi," Jarek whispers, wrapping his arms around my middle. I recline my head, letting it rest against his chest. "We're home, Sam."

I bite my bottom lip, something stirring in my gut.

"You two—" Jarek and I turn to Cora, her blonde hair done in several small braids, her blue eyes as piercing as Jarek's–"Save the lovey shite for later. Jarek, help us toss the lines."

Jarek kisses my cheek then quickly gets to work.

My gaze drifts back to the sleepy seaside village before me and the smile tugging at my lips spreads.

Home.

Thomas takes Jareks place next to me, a few other Loxlian's behind us as well. Together we behold our new surroundings. The stone chimneys and the vibrant green grass. My chest tightens, glancing at the mossy roofs and small puffs of gray. So reminiscent of Loxley that I have to pinch myself to keep from daydreaming.

"Our new home," I say to Thomas. His hand finds mine and he lets out a long, strenuous breath.

Once off the ship, my legs wobble as Jarek guides me through rocky sand and up to a small, stone house.

"Jarek?" a small woman with dark, braided hair emerges from the home. Jarek drops my hand and sprints toward her. The woman sobs into the crook of his neck as he picks her up. "You're here!"

"Aye," he says, placing her down. She cups his face, tears lining her round cheeks. They whisper to each other, quiet enough I can't hear what they say but from the way the woman's face beams, I imagine it's only good things. Jarek places a hand on her swollen belly before he wraps her in another hug.

"There's someone you need to meet." Jarek pulls the woman toward me so I quickly wipe my hands on my breeches. "Helen," he says, "this is Samaria."

"Hello." I extend my hand, but the woman pushes it away and instead grasps me in a firm hug, her stomach taking up any extra space between us.

"So lovely to meet you," she whispers. "It seems as though my baby brother has a lot to fill us in on." She smiles as she steps back, just as Cora joins us.

"So sentimental, you two." Cora rolls her eyes, but her smile tells me just how happy she is to be reunited with her siblings as well. "Come on." Cora pushes past us and waves a hand through the air. "You know mum already has the kettle on, and I've got a lass to get home to."

She winks over her shoulder and waves us forward. To my surprise, she trudges right past the small house on the shore and instead heads up a grassy hill. Helen follows after her, folding her hands across her belly.

Jarek wraps me in his arms again, my back against his chest.

"Is this not your home?" I ask, pointing to the small cottage where Helen was.

Jarek chuckles, running a finger down the side of my neck. "It could be if you prefer it."

I glance at him over my shoulder. "Prefer it to what?"

He tightens his grip around me, squeezing so tight my lungs fight against my ribs. "That's my actual home." He points to the top of the hill and as I follow his finger my mouth drops open. "This is just the beach house where we stay from time to time. But if you prefer something smaller..."

He shrugs behind me, but I can't take my eyes off of the large, stone castle perched atop the grassy hillside, overlooking the ocean and mountains.

"Why does your home look like a castle?" He lets me go and moves past me, but I pull his arm backward so he's forced to stop. "You have some explaining to do."

He laughs again, closing the distance between us, kissing me.

"I do," he says. "I never thought I'd be back here so I let this part of me die along with my hope. It was a constant reminder of who I'd never be again, so I swallowed it down along with many other things." He squeezes me tighter, the sea-mist spraying lightly against my cheeks. People filter past us, carrying crates and ropes and what little belongings they had to pack. "But now that we're here, now that we're safe, I want you to know everything Sam."

"Know what?" I pull away, so I can better see his face.

His eyes crinkle at the sides, his lips twitching at the corners. He bites the tip of his thumb, giving me his most innocent face, and I shake my head and laugh, glancing again at the stone castle atop the hill.

"It seems you already have an idea," he says through a laugh.

"You are…"

"Some would call me a prince." He shrugs then laughs when my mouth drops open. He sweeps his hand across the air; to the vast grassy hillsides and a sky wide open and blue. "This will be mine to rule one day, and yours if you'd like. There's no one else I want by my side, Samaria."

"You should have told me." I cover my mouth with my hands, my head dizzying at his words and this proposal to lead alongside him.

Jarek steps closer and wraps me in his arms again before kissing me slowly. "I know." He shakes his head. "For that I'm sorry."

I run my tongue over the tips of my teeth, peering at the massive stone structure perched atop the hill. "You'll have to show me just how sorry you are later," I say.

A smile stretches across his face. "I think I can manage that," he says before kissing me. "Jeg ser deg, Sam."

I see you.

I freeze, the smile wiping from my face.

"I see how strong you are for everybody else. I see the love you're overflowing with for your people, for me." His eyes glaze but to my surprise he doesn't hide it. "I see the mask you wear and I see when it begins to fall how quickly you pull it up. I often wear the same one."

I grab his hand and bring it to my lips, kissing the ink lining his knuckles.

"But you don't have to wear that mask anymore, because I see you. I've always seen you." He cups my face, kissing me again. "Besides, I never thanked you for saving my life, so consider a country my way of doing so."

I slap his chest. "I've never saved you."

"You did." He brushes my dark curls from my face. The mist from the sea now mixed with a few tears of my own. "That day in Copenspire when we met, you saved me in so many ways, I just didn't know it yet."

He kisses me again, this time quickly before he spins me toward the hill. "Now, come. At long last, my queen," he says, taking my hand and leading me up the hill, "let me show you to your throne."

FIFTY-FOUR
ELORA

"AND THE CROPS IN WICKERSHAM AND COPENSPIRE have been more than fruitful, Your Majesty. We've had to extend the fields twice over to accommodate." Councilwoman Maeve sits across from me, her dark hair only slightly longer than it was when we met three years ago.

After the coronation, Sorin and I let the rest of the council go, replacing it with those we seemed more fit.

Agnes and Ulric were the first obvious choices as well as Evren and Tallulah.

But there was something about Maeve, something that told me I could trust her. And luckily, three years later, I still do.

My heart swells hearing that the crops we replanted several years ago are not just surviving, but thriving. It's been a straining few years repairing the damage from the blight, but finally, it feels as though we've made it through to the other side.

"And the rations?" I ask, swirling my finger along the rim of my teacup. "Have they continued to increase?"

"Yes, Your Majesty, just as you asked." She smiles, her long, jade earrings catching in the light. "But with the towns growing their own food again, there hasn't been much need for them."

"Make sure they're sent anyway."

Maeve nods as she jots a few notes down.

"There is one more thing," she starts, "about the Wicked Wood."

My body tenses, nails digging into my palms. "What about it?" A shiver runs down my spine, remembering the last time I was there. Remembering how close I was to not returning.

Maeve eyes me over her notebook before setting it down. "There's been no new growth." She shrugs. "It seems whatever you did that day, was enough to—"

"They're here!" Sorin bursts into our room, startling Hati and Skoll who are dozing by the fire.

Maeve and I both turn, and neither of us has to ask to know who he's talking about.

"They're here?" I stand from behind my desk. He grins, nodding and gesturing me forward. "Maeve we'll—"

"Of course, Your Majesty," she says. "We'll pick this up another time."

I weave around her, making sure the wolves know to stay behind this time.

We race through the castle halls, my stomach swirling and fingers tingling. Once we reach the large oak doors, Sorin doesn't wait to knock before he swings them wide open.

Sam and Jarek both glance our way, matching grins on their faces. I hardly have time to take in the scene before me when a cry pierces the air. I jump slightly at the sound and Sorin laughs.

"Can run with a pack of wolves, cannot handle a baby crying. Noted." He pinches my sides, and I scowl at his back as we join Samaria and Jarek at the table.

"Aunt Elora and Uncle Sorin," she says through a smile, "meet Satori, Princess of Scandavi and your new niece."

I glance down at the now quiet babe and my breath catches. Her skin matches Sam, but her hair is Jarek's, blonde and curly. Her full cheeks puff out as she wiggles in Sam's arms.

"She's beautiful," I whisper, stroking a finger down her velvety cheek.

"Looks just like her mother," Jarek says. He straightens his shoulders, his eyes glued to Samaria.

"My sister, a mother," Sorin says, a joke lingering in his tone. He cocks his head to the side and grins when I frown at him. "I'm proud of you."

My brows raise and when I glance at Sam and Jarek, their faces are morphed into surprise just as mine is.

"That's it?" Sam laughs. "No jokes? Nothing about how I can hardly—"

"No," Sorin says. He kisses the babe's forehead, then Sam's.

"Is Calix joining us?" Jarek asks, brushing Satori's hair from her forehead.

"Not tonight," I say. "He'll arrive in two days, however. I'm sure he'll be excited to see you." I pinch Jarek's arm. Calix and I have not only maintained our relationship the past few years, but it's blossomed just as well as the crops. He's become one of my most trusted allies and even someone I can confidently say I love.

"Before I forget," Sorin says, "I have a gift for Satori." He leaves the room for a moment, and when he comes back I bite my tongue to keep from laughing.

"A bow?" Sam says, her eyes going wide. "You got my three month old daughter a bow?"

"And arrows." Sorin's smile widens as he sets the ivory bow and quiver on the table between us. "Never too early to learn," he says. "And besides, she may be a princess but deep in her blood she's a thieving Trednik."

Sam's face softens. She leans forward, running a finger along the curved lines of the tiny bowstring. "It's beautiful. And you're right, she is my daughter. Which means she'll be shooting better than you in no time."

"Must we have this argument again." Sorin sighs, dropping back into the chair next to me. "I could out shoot you—"

"You two never stop, do you?" I cut Sorin short and Sam laughs, startling Satori in her arms.

"Siblings," Jarek grumbles, but there's humor in his tone.

"Speaking of," Sorin says, "is Cora here?"

"Of course." Jarek runs a hand through his beard. "Can't keep that woman from the sea if I tried."

After Cora came to our aid in Valebridge, Scandavi and Teravie have mended the wound caused by Roman and Galen. Having Cora here in our home feels as natural as the tides.

Satori stirs, soft cries filling the space. "That's my cue," Sam says. "I'll see you for dinner?" We nod as she leaves, her hips swaying, soft coos whispered in the air.

"I should go with them," Jarek says. He extends his hand, but Sorin stands and brushes it to the side. He grasps him in a hug and then they turn to me and gesture me forward. The three of us hug and laugh, and when we break apart, I pull Jarek's arm back around my shoulders.

"What is it, susi?"

"Sorin had a gift for Satori, but I have a gift for you." I smile and wait for him to do as I say. Sorin's brows pinch together but he remains silent, to my surprise. "Hold out your hand."

Jarek holds out his hand, and I place the crumbled card face up in his palm.

"All this time, Elora?" Sorin shouts. "You've had it all this time?" He's laughing now and I join him, but Jarek doesn't. His eyes stay fixated on the Queen of Spades, perhaps remembering the last time he gave it to me.

He squeezes my shoulders and plants a kiss to the top of my head. "Thank you, little wolf."

The walk to our room is mostly silent, save for the scuff and tap of our boots upon the stone floor.

"Do you ever think of having one of those?" Sorin slides his hand in mine.

"A child?" I ask. My hand tightens around his out of instinct and he laughs.

"Yes, a child."

I replay Satori's chubby cheeks and sleepy yawns in my head. How easy Sam moved with her and knew exactly what she needed.

A natural.

I slide my hand from Sorin's and wrap it around my necklace. The gift from Mother Gaia I never take off. We round the last corner to our chambers. "Would you think me less of a woman if I say no?"

My arm yanks backward as Sorin comes to a stop. He pulls me closer and grips my chin. "Never." He kisses me softly on the lips and there's something so tender about this moment, my stomach dips in response. The necklace pulses lightly, the Dyrsjel magick within it ready to be gifted when I deem fit.

I've never told anyone of the gift from the Mother.

Not even Sorin.

It's like She knew something about me that I had yet to discover. And when I am ready, my lineage will be passed along, and with it, the ability to control the Awakening Stones.

"What about you?" We resume our walk, the buttery light of afternoon seeping through the windows. "Do you want to start a family?"

Scoffing, he pulls me into his arms again before backing me against the wall. "I already have a family." He kisses me again, this time on my pulse.

Opening the door to our room, he scoops me up and takes me straight to our bed.

Wicked man.

"You're my family." He places me gently on my back and brackets his arms above either side of my head. There's mischief in his dark eyes but before he can make good on it, several growls fill the space.

Stifling a laugh, I bite my bottom lip.

"Yes." Sorin rolls his eyes before glancing at the wolves. "You're my family too. Though"—he leans in closer so his lips brush mine—"I wouldn't mind if they could busy themselves elsewhere for a while."

"We're supposed to be changing for dinner."

"Then we'll need to take our clothes off first."

"By the Mother, do you ever stop talking."

"If you'd like, I can find something better to do with my ton—"

I clamp my hand over his mouth. "You're infuriating," I say through a smile, moving my hand away.

"Yet, you love me." Sorin smiles.

I take the opportunity to kiss him. "That I do."

His lips are on my throat, my jaw. Laughing, I kiss him again before turning to the pups. Though, pups isn't really appropriate now seeing as how they're just as large as Ruse and Alaric.

You heard him.

Reluctantly, the six wolves stretch and peel themselves away from the fire before exiting through the large door that leads to the veranda.

"It's the law to bear an heir," I say between kisses.

Sorin scoffs before pulling back so I can see his face. "So we'll change the law." His next kiss takes my breath away while his hands find all the places he knows I need them most. "It's not like we haven't done that before." His smile melts the last of the tension between my shoulders.

Having a child isn't something I've ever considered though the thought of needing an heir had crossed my mind a time or two.

For so long, I thought not wanting a child was because I'm too broken, but maybe it's because I'm already whole.

Just as I am.

Just as we are.

And with the gift from Mother Gaia, I won't need a direct bloodline to continue the Dyrsjel magick.

Sorin's teeth grate against my throat, and my back arches in response.

It's euphoric, this feeling. Loving someone unconditionally, and having them love you back.

His lips are on my neck, and I bring my legs around his waist.

I have nothing but love for Sam and Jarek and their beautiful Satori. I couldn't name two better people to raise a child.

But Sorin and I have our own family. Our own way of doing things.

Sorin fists my hair and kisses me deeper than before. He moans against my mouth as I push my hips forward. He pulls away to discard his clothes.

His eyes connect with mine and every single moment leading up to this flashes through my mind.

Valebridge and the mountain. My mother and the cabin in the woods. Sorin in the river and our tumultuous journey that brought us to this very moment. He watches me for a moment, unmoving, as if he's also recalling the same thing. Our life before this one. The deal made with the Fates. A promise to Mother Gaia to always protect Teravie. Every single moment, choice, mistake has led to this and I would do it again. Over and over, I'd relive it if it meant finding him. And perhaps one day I will, should Mother Gaia ever need our souls again.

He drops to his knees and pulls off my pants. He kisses my ankles, then my calves, and continues upward until his teeth are around my undergarments and then, they're off as well.

I close my eyes, and let the memories from earlier fade away. My fingers clench around the sheets.

I arch into Sorin's touch but he pins me down with his free hand, continuing his movements with his mouth. I wish I could go back in time just to show that girl on the mountain just what life had in store for her. I'd tell her that through all the turmoil, life finds a way of showing you the beauty in it. And despite what she thinks, despite what her mind tells her, she is worth living to see that beauty.

On a shaky breath, I whisper a goodbye to that lost girl on the mountain. I wish her well on her way. I'll miss her, that broken version of myself.

Because without her, I wouldn't be here.

Sorin's body frames mine again, and before he has a chance to go anywhere, I pull him into me for a long, slow kiss.

I sigh against his mouth, and my body relaxes under his touch.

He's the home I sought for so long.

The family I craved.

The family I didn't think I *deserved*.

And what a family it turned out to be.

Just me and Sorin, and a pack of wolves.

EPILOGUE
ELWYN

THE VEIL BETWEEN THE LIVING REALM AND THE beyond wanes in the silvery moonlight. Behind me, a light glows. It beckons me, drawing me toward it, but my eyes drift back to the room before me.

Candles flicker on the tabletop where a feast is laid out. Sorin and Elora sit at opposite ends of the large, wooden table. Jarek and Sam are there as well, chatting amongst each other. Agnes holds Satori, rocking her back and forth in a slow, even tempo.

Finally, my eyes settle on Calix. His hair is more gray than the last time I saw him, but his face is full and happy. He's raising a glass, speaking proud words and praise for our daughter. His wife is by his side, her auburn hair cascading over her shoulder, gray lining her temples. She places her hand on Calix's and leans forward to whisper something to Elora that makes her smile.

My eyes bounce between them, all three of them, and though it isn't there to beat, a flutter stirs in my chest.

How many years did I dream of this? Of Calix and Elora together. Knowing each other. Loving each other. My eyes sting as my gaze drifts back to Elora.

I don't miss her blush as she takes a sip of wine.

Don't miss her smile as everyone claps at the table for the work she's done as their queen.

Sorin rises, raising his glass to Elora, and an eruption of laughter sounds around the table.

Celia joins my side, resting her head on my shoulder. "They're perfect," she says and I nod my agreement.

They truly are.

Each and every one of them.

"We should go," I say to her. The light that's behind us grows dimmer each moment we delay and the portal grows smaller.

Celia puffs out an exacerbated breath. "Can't we haunt them a little longer?"

I chuckle and kiss the top of her head. "I'm afraid our part is done."

My eyes linger on Elora. Her hair is unbound, cut shorter now, falling around her shoulders. Her eyes bounce between her guests as she takes bites of her food.

I have committed her face to memory and yet I fear the moment I turn, all will be lost.

"We may be dead," Celia says, "but damn if this doesn't hurt."

I squeeze her hand.

I thought I knew pain the day my life ended on the mountain. Thought death was the most terrible thing that could happen to someone.

I had no idea that instead, it's actually what comes after that hurts the most. Being stuck on this side while everything changes just out of your reach.

But I suppose it hasn't all been terrible.

My eyes flick to Sam, and she glances at us over the candles. Her fiery eyes soften, and when she raises her wrists, I shake my head.

We've overstayed as long as we can and she has already done

so much. If we don't leave now, we risk vanishing completely. No hope for a life in the after. Sam smiles, tucking her hands back in her lap.

The light behind us flickers and Celia and I both turn.

"All right, then," she says through a sigh. "Let's go, El." She takes a step forward and gestures to a darkened corner. " You too. You're one of us now, whether you like it or not."

The young man steps forth from the shadows, his green eyes catching mine before he follows Celia toward the light.

"Cheer up, sweetheart." She pats his cheeks, and though he tries to hide it, a small smile turns up his lips.

He hasn't spoken in all the years he's been by our side, but his eyes say enough. That of all the words in the world, none would ever be enough to express the brokenness and heartbreak of his life. We share this, the three of us. And maybe it's why the Mother brought us together after all.

"We've got you, dear." Celia holds out her hand, and he slips his fingers in hers. "I suppose this is it."

"This is it," I repeat.

The light dims as the two of them pass through, but I stop to take one last look around the table. One last look at my daughter and the family she has created for herself.

I wasn't lying when I gave the message to Sam that day. When I told her to tell Elora I was always with her. And truthfully, I always will be. Corbin will watch her. And the family she has created for herself will catch her should she need it.

And I'd like to believe a small part of me will live on in her and despite the pain and anguish, seeing her here makes it all worth it.

She was always worth it.

The light behind me pulses again, and so, with my daughter's face fresh in my mind, I turn and take the final step through, joining Celia and Roman on the other side.

Acknowledgments

I cannot wrap my head around the fact that we're here. In the acknowledgments of my third book and the conclusion of Sorin and Elora's story. This story has come a long way from where it began and I couldn't have done it without so many of you.

To my husband. Always. My partner and biggest supporter. And my son for being the driving force behind all that I do.

To my editor, Brit, for all of your guidance. For being the calm in my storm of chaos. For pushing me and teaching me and growing with me.

To my alpha and beta team; Jaclyn, Jenna, Katie, Krystal, Kaitlyn, Leah, and Sarah. This book wouldn't be the same without each and every one of you. I'm so grateful to have you on my side, cheering in my corner.

To my family. Your unwavering support has always been something I can rely on. A comfort, knowing that even if I fall, you'll be there to catch me.

To Stephanie, for loving all of the versions of me. From twelve years old to now and forever.

To my friends, both old and new, that match my weird and make me feel seen and heard.

And last but not least, to my readers. Books would be nothing without you. Thank you for giving me a chance. For giving Elora a chance. Thank you for reading a story of grief and depression and finding the glimmers of light within it. For showing me through all of your messages, reviews, DM, and comments that I'm not alone. Your excitement and love for these characters is what drove me forward in the murk of drafting this book. It's what motivated me to push myself and this story. Thank you.

About Kristen

Kristen is a Pacific Northwest native who thrives on coffee, nature, and reading. She spends her days running after her son and managing a business with her husband. She loves writing stories that stretch the imagination, tug at the heartstrings, and make you swoon all at the same time. The Enchantress Awakens Duology is her debut series with many more to come. Be sure to follow along for the most updates on her Instagram.

instagram.com/authorkristenmoore

MORE FROM KRISTEN

Enchantress Awakens

Through the Wicked Wood

As the Moon Falls

Through A Somber Sky